Someone To Watch Over Me

Sky Sommers

Published by Sommersby OÜ

ISBN: 9789949811199

Printed and bound in Estonia by AS Pakett
Laki 17, Tallinn, Estonia www.pakett.ee

For Henri

ACKNOWLEDGEMENTS

Thank you to Estel and Grace, my two guardian angels who always offer kind and sometimes funny words of encouragement. That...and a roof over my head.

Thank you also to my editor, Shreeya Nanda for edits at the expense of sleep. I would also like to thank Konsta for the consult on explosives, which probably landed us both on Facebook watchlist. Any mistakes remaining are my own.

A huge thank you to Emmi, my now-17-year-old illustrator who drew what you see in here at age 14. You're awesome!

Thanks to Lana Maklakova optimists and pessimists each get their own ending.

May there always be anonymous guardians to save us from the Victors gone bad.

Also, for those who like the frog – don't worry.

Table of Contents

Prologue

Of Princes Charming

Victor locked the ladies' room door behind him and rested both of his palms against the mirror, on either side of Grace's face. At six feet four inches he towered over her, ignoring the shock in her lovely grey eyes that were darting around, trying to find a way out.

'Why did you have to flirt with all the men at the bar? You're MY woman. My woman doesn't flirt with anyone but me!'

'They are my mates from the university.' *The one she never finished on account of family circumstances.* 'We're celebrating. It's a reunion,' she whispered.

Her imploring tone enraged him even more, so he grabbed the strap of her dress, 'You're wearing the dress I gave you...'

As a birthday present.

'You're living in our apartment...'

That she had inherited from her parents, where he had only ever been a live-in-guest.

Her unresponsiveness was making him even more agitated, 'You. Are mine! Always have been. Always will be. And don't you dare forget it!' Victor squeezed her shoulder, making Grace wince at the pain and the closeness of his scotch-infested breath.

She had learnt not to antagonise him. She didn't need another trip to the emergency room. Ignoring the pitter patter of her heart, she kept her face as motionless as she could.

The more still she became, the more angry he got.

Mistaking her stillness for dismissive arrogance, Victor reached behind his back and extracted a gun.

The hummingbird in Grace's throat missed a beat as did the world. Life faded away. Nothing existed but this shiny black object that Grace saw up close and very personal.

Victor traced the outline of her cheekbone with the barrel of his gun. Tenderly.

Grace felt the tiny hole in the cold muzzle dimple her skin.

Stupidly, it reminded her of the sand cakes she used to make at the beach when she was a kid. Victor's insanity had clearly deteriorated. He had no gun when they had split up a year ago.

He directed the thing away from her and she dared to exhale.

In slow motion, Grace saw him say something. The air around them had turned to molasses. All she could see was the gun swimming towards her.

When she didn't reply, the gun was back at her temple.

All thought stopped. Grace froze as did the hummingbird hiding in her throat.

Victor stroked her hair, her shoulders, her face.

His eyes turned soft. Victor smiled and for a moment it seemed like it was the good old times. She almost reached out to touch him and didn't. Lowering his forehead to hers, he moved the gun to his own temple and his mouth continued moving.

The silence was deafening.

She saw the gun move back and forth between them through the molasses air.

Grace saw Victor step away. His left hand travelled to the back of his head to ruffle his hair, a gesture of confusion she knew well. The space between her and the door was wide open, tantalising her with a promise of a miraculous escape.

Time and sound woke up with a pop.

'...don't you see?'

Only interested in seeing her freedom, Grace turned and ran.

She didn't know how exactly she got back to her group or how she managed to burrow herself into their midst.

All she saw as she sat down, white as chalk was Victor, stalking the perimeter of her cage made out of the warm bodies of her friends.

'What's the matter, doll? Is he bothering you?' one of the guys asked her.

Grace looked at him. Really looked at him. She had no clue what his name was. They had not moved in the same circles at university. But at the moment she trusted him more than she had ever trusted that psycho she had lived with for two years whose tall lanky form was drawing admiring looks from the ladies at the bar. Grace understood the admiration. Victor's effortless Prince Charming upper-class manners and knee-weakening good looks had lured many before her. Until she found out the hard way there was no fixing the dark and tortured moodiness that sometimes slipped through his polished smile.

'I need to go. Very quickly. Very quietly,' she whispered, 'so that he' her eyes darted towards Victor, 'doesn't see me leave.'

The guy just nodded.

'Can you help me?'

He nodded again, extending his arm to touch hers in what was doubtlessly intended as a reassuring gesture.

Grace stopped him with her eyes. She couldn't risk a bar fight that would undoubtedly follow and endanger the one man who could transport her out of here.

An eternally long ten minutes later, while another of her university friends was purposefully accosting Victor for cigarettes, Grace slipped out of the bar and into the car of her anonymous do-gooder.

Victor came after them with tyres screeching.

After they took the less obvious turn, after they watched him tear past their hideout at 100 miles per hour, after she realised she had finally escaped him - that was when Grace exhaled next.

When Grace saw Victor's car disappear around the bend she sobbed into the warm shoulder of her saviour just as Pink lamented on the radio that 'who knew'[1].

***

Victor got up from the ground that had unwillingly met him.

The bend had been too steep.

He could see his car wrapped around an injured pine. Some unrecognisable red mush was seeping from the broken window on the driver's side.

'Fancy atoning yourself, kind Sir?'

A tall figure materialised out of light and folded up its white wings with a neat whoosh.

Victor squinted his eyes to see better.

Nope, when the silvery light faded, it was just a man. A tall bloke with shoulder-length curly blond hair like a girl who had appeared out of nowhere, by the looks of it, but just a man nevertheless.

Victor thought he saw the bloke holster a sword between his shoulder blades like it belonged there on any normal day.

He blinked.

Nope, just a man adjusting the collar of his white shirt, no sword hilt anywhere to be seen.

Victor felt slightly woozy, but he was positive he couldn't be seeing things that he didn't believe in.

'At least you can be thankful that you didn't kill her. If you had killed the girl in the lavatory of that bar, maybe I wouldn't be standing here, making this generous proposition,' the preppy-looking bloke leaned into the nearest pine and crossed his arms.

'What proposition?' Victor asked on autopilot, trying to figure out whether he had seen the guy at the bar or not.

The man's stern expression signalled he wasn't liking what he was about to say, 'I've been tasked with offering you the position of a guardian angel.'

Victor concluded he was hearing things. Nope, he was seeing things as well. The wings were back.

Taking Victor's silence for a question, the guy continued, spreading his plumage, 'To serve any being that needs a guardian in this or any of the other 63 known dimensions. For instance when they need to be protected against the likes of you,' the bloke pointed and Victor was suddenly glad he had put the sword away first, 'well, against the likes of who you used to be.'

'Used to be?'

The angel stared at him.

Victor turned to his car and the unrecognisable red mush that was still seeping from the broken window on the driver's side.

Oh.

'As I was saying, I'm offering you to serve as a guardian to protect against control-freak stalker bullies like yourself.'

'Hey,' Victor did not feel like being called names, especially after he had just found out he was dead.

'Do you really feel that I was out of line?' A pair of forget-me-not eyes looked at Victor reproachfully.

Victor thought about it. His entire life with Grace passed before him. How he made Grace call him at exactly 4.10pm after her university lectures had finished at 4pm. How every time she hadn't, he had been on the M5 going West at 100 miles per hour at exactly 4.11pm. How he used to refuse to meet with her friends and how, eventually, she stopped talking to them. How he had been jealous of every guy that even looked her way in the street and about all the fights they had. He had done that to countless women before and after her and none of them stayed too long because of it. Grace had been the only one to stick by him for two years straight. He thought it was something special until she too, proved him wrong and walked away. Not wanting to admit she was worth changing for, he convinced himself it was easy come, easy go like with all the others and had seduced himself into the bed of another accommodating fan that same night. Victor had always blamed the women for leaving just like he blamed his floozy of a mother for walking out on him and dad when Victor was five.

The angel had not been out of line. Victor knew he had been a controlling jealous bastard. Funny how he was able to see that now, as if assessing someone else's life without a shred of anger. Without any emotions at all. He felt light as a feather and like he could do anything at the same time. Out loud Victor said, 'I guess you might have a point.'

'So, how about it, fancy making up for your atrocious behaviour by serving as a guardian angel?' the recruiter asked.

Victor thought he detected a hint of a French accent. At Eaton he had known plenty of posh French boys speak English just so. He had already made up his mind, but figured clarification wouldn't hurt, 'What is it exactly that you propose I do?'

The angel smiled, 'Very good. You accept then.' He offered Victor his hand, 'My name is Gabriel. Allow me to brief you on your job description when we get to the Agency.'

When Victor took the proffered hand, a cocoon of silvery light enveloped them.

***

If anybody had looked behind the opal glass of the face of Big Ben in the Elizabeth Tower, they would have seen a dark man with salt and pepper hair leaning over an image of a girl sobbing into someone's shoulder in a battered blue Mini Cooper.

The man with grey peppered hair made a swiping motion at the glass surface of his desk and saw the live feed of Victor and Gabriel having a conversation. He shook his head and tsk-tsk-ed.

He had sent Gabriel to recruit them an angel and an angel Gabriel did recruit.

A pixie wafted in through the revolving magic mirror, folded her purple wings and landed on the edge of the mahogany desk. She looked at the man whom she saw as a Hindu Goddess clad in a pink, gold-trimmed sari. Not her favourite, but she couldn't very well dictate her boss what not to wear. 'Not that I question your wisdom, oh Supreme Goddess, but don't you think sending an archangel to protect this girl was a bit of a waste of everyone's time?' the pixie asked.

'Feet off the glass surface, Loretta! I've told you Watchers countless times, leaving you paw prints all over the visuals distorts my view of what's important,' said the Indian-looking man, swiping her off and ignoring the Goddess comment. All guardians saw him as they wanted to see him. Amongst other things, he was frequently addressed as Zeus, Chieftain, Pirate King, Mer-King, the First Secretary, Leader of the pack and Toymaster. Goddess was just a gender-denominative.

'My, aren't we in a foul mood today...' Loretta said. Seeing no give, she picked up her combat boots and extended her wings. Mid-flight, the pixie finally admitted, 'Well, Daisy and I like seeing things from your perspective, which unfortunately involves trampling on your desk.' She pointed at herself, 'Tiny, see.'

The man sat back into the leather chair, 'Yes, yes, fine. Just don't bring any troll gunk from Dialysis X here on the bottom of your shoes or if you do, clean it up! Then you can stand on my desk anytime you like. Deal?'

The pixie nodded.

The man laughed, 'You know me better than that. To trust a pixie's promise, I need you to say it out loud.'

'Deal!' the pixie said sourly, thinking how much time getting the radiation-contaminated goo off her Doc Martens was actually going to take.

'Why do you think sending Gabriel was a waste of time? He managed to recruit us a new guardian. So, by my measure, it's not a waste of the Agency's resources that a rescue turned into recruitment,' the Boss said.

Loretta closed her purple eye, 'I guess if you put it that way... then yes, some good came out of it. Although, we don't actually know whether this bad boy,' she pointed at the screen where Victor was standing in the lobby of the Agency next to Gabriel, drinking it all in, 'can actually let go of his old ways and help girls he used to bully. Why you sent Gabriel to save a girl who could clearly handle herself is beyond my wits. She had no need for a guardian, she didn't even request one!' The pixie scratched her ears, hoping to keep them after directly challenging her Boss.

The Boss rose and went to look out from behind the dials at the square below, 'I wasn't that clear about who he should... recruit...or save for that matter.' It was interesting that Gabriel made a call and recruited the bad guy and not the girl.

'I would have saved the girl as well, not the brute,' the pixie said, sensing her ears were out of harm's way.

'Even though there isn't an ounce of magic in her?' the Boss asked.

'When Victor was holding her by her throat, she was afraid, petrified even. Yet, without the ability to rely on any magic powers whatsoever and without calling for any help, she managed to extract herself from a very sticky situation,' Loretta said. 'She's not a regular damsel in distress, is she?' Loretta asked.

'No, not a damsel. Someone...significant enough for the tally to falter and for one of the Watchers' screens to start recording her otherwise very ordinary life,' the Boss pointed behind Loretta at the revolving mirror.

The pixie squinted at the tally, closing her green eye. The black column of Evil next to the mirror was now significantly lower than the white column of Good. 'The tally sensed she was in danger?' she asked, 'That's why one of the screens started recording her life? She's important? Why?'

The Boss shrugged, 'Your guess is as good as mine.'

'Courage, quick thinking, extracting herself from a bad situation,' the pixie summed up, 'A resourceful future guardian angel?'

'What you said could also be the mark of a hero,' the Boss smiled and reminded the pixie to file the recording.

1. The bend had been too steep

1. Take a Bow
Gabriel

Gabriel opened his eyes to the Aurora Borealis. He liked sleeping in the cold, amongst the blocks of ice that tentatively offered him four walls of shelter miles from any settlement. The Boss had tried to persuade him to stay in the confines of the Agency where the laws of Time did not quite apply. Gabriel had joked that he would be equally well preserved in the icy Mystic North dimension. Having extracted a promise that Gabriel would daily spend time at the Agency to keep his angelic balance, the Boss had settled for his archangel living off premises.

Inhaling the frost, Gabriel cast aside the deer skin and sat up. The feel of snow thawing between his toes was invigorating. With a couple of thunks Gabriel broke the ice in the basin, brushed his teeth and looked around for a door to see what job the Watchers had fathomed for him today. He finally found the door in the wall under the basin. It must be Loretta at the Watchers' station today. Had it been Daisy's turn to watch over everyone, he would be looking at a delicate ice-carved cupboard at an appropriate height where his pick of the most necessary items of clothing would be neatly laid out. Fairy magic was more considerate even if pixie magic was sometimes more quick.

Each rescue had to be approached individually, just like every new recruit. The charges didn't always know that a guardian angel had stepped in to save them. If guardian angels went around introducing themselves, no one would ever get rescued. Most people could sense something, though. Hence, the stories and beliefs about good Samaritans or someone watching over them to avert danger. So, no flaming bushes, displays of world-altering magnitude or Jericho volume voice-overs. At least not in this day and age.

Recruitment was fun as well. Only the experienced angels recruited, in addition to rescuing. Some recent recruits, like Victor, would only be awed and persuaded by a winged being of light. Others believed Gabriel was an angel immediately after they discovered they were dead even when he was in his jeans and a T-shirt. In all of his years of service, Gabriel had noticed that those who needed to atone for their past deeds needed more flashy proof of his credentials than those who had led good, decent lives.

Neatly folded jeans and a white T-shirt lay in his tiny cupboard.

A casual start to the day. He wasn't immediately called to some tricky rescue requiring special gear.

Lovely.

He would rather be comfortable when rescuing whoever needed to be rescued. No one had ever complained about what he was or wasn't wearing when they ended up keeping their life or limbs. Still, to infiltrate or blend into the surroundings, special attire was sometimes necessary and provided during transportation. Pinstriped suits and other formal wear were just slightly better than chain mail. He didn't miss chain mail. He didn't miss it at all.

Gabriel geared up, slightly grazing the nooks of his wings, making them itch for a second. If he was being sent to a human dimension, he might have to get rid of the wings completely. He sighed and decided to fold them inward just in case. The nooks disappeared and the T-shirt evened out on his back.

Out of habit, he fastened the scabbard and his sword that was showing no signs of wear even after 856 years after his recruitment. The scabbard and the sword would have to be cloaked as well, if it was a daytime rescue in any human dimension where magic still equalled miracles. Gabriel hoped it would be an Earth rescue. He hadn't taken one in a while. Even with the folded wings and shielded sword, in human form, he blended in.

For him, Earth had not changed that much compared to the Crusades. It was cleaner and thanks to the Agency's trading efforts also a lot technologically smarter, but earthlings didn't make much of a fuss about magical beings walking around amongst them. The magic on Earth was gradually fading, thanks to a silly bet Olden Earth Goddesses had made a few millennia ago.[2] Still, even when he had used up most of his energy on a save, which caused hi wings or sword to uncloak, the present-day humans usually never fussed, thinking he was going around in fancy dress.

Moments later, Gabriel walked into the light. All of the known 63 dimensions and probably a few unknown ones connected directly to the Agency. Its location changed frequently, going back and forth between mostly Earthen cities that the Boss fancied taking up residence in. The Agency's pan-dimensional office would mould itself for hours, days, years, decades or even centuries into any convenient place as if it had always been there. Gabriel hadn't known the Agency to stay put anywhere for millennia in Agency time. For the past 150 Earth years or 300 Agency ones they had resided in merry old London.

Taking a few stairs at a time up the white marble staircase, Gabriel gave the oak door a gentle push.

The old man dressed in his usual regal attire from Earth's Arthurian era looked tense and grim, not his usual self. He did not motion for Gabriel to sit down, which was also unusual. Gabriel preferred to stand anyway, but every morning they went through the rigmarole of his liege offering him a seat and Gabriel politely declining. Just like he had never sat in front of Guy de Lusignan, his king, he would never sit in front of this Boss either.

'You wouldn't have the time,' the Boss motioned at the mirror behind Gabriel that had stopped revolving and transformed into a live video feed. In slow motion, a tiny girl with shoulder length jet black hair walked into an alley to throw away some garbage. Gabriel recognised the girl Victor had taunted years ago.

The greying man adjusted his crown and cut the pleasantries short, 'One of our screens has just started recording this girl's quite ordinary life. She hasn't asked for help but the fact that her life is being recorded at this very moment means two things. She is somehow significant enough to change the face of her dimension or perhaps even this Agency and someone has already formulated an intent to harm her. As per our experience, she has anywhere between five and 15 minutes to live. We don't know how someone intends her harm, but since I'm not seeing anyone lurking to enter this dead-end alley, I'd guess it might be a shooting, maybe a drive-by. She has no time left and doesn't even know it. The tally confirms it,' the man nodded at the white and black columns by his revolving mirror.

The black tally on the left side of the magic mirror was considerably and alarmingly higher than the white tally on the right. Gabriel hadn't seen that happen before. Ever. The tallies were mostly even, on any given day.

'Evil is up, Good is dangerously down. The Watchers alerted me four minutes ago. If you don't jump in now, in less than a minute the girl might be dead. Go fix it. You know the rules - she's your charge until she's safe. You have five seconds left.'

Without thinking, Gabriel leapt through the mirror into the girl's dimension, transforming himself into a kitten that cowered behind the dumpster a few feet from her.

He mewed loudly.

The girl bowed down to pet him.

The bullet flew past where her head had just been and hit the brick wall. Fragments of red stone and terracotta dust scattered all over Gabriel the kitten.

The girl looked up at the clouds wafting across the narrow chimney of the alley. 'Someone must be walking up on the roof again,' she mused, dusting off bits of brick from her hair.

The girl turned her attention back to the red fur ball, ''Here, kitty, kitty, kitty... Are you hungry? You must be hungry, come on, let's go get you some milk...'

***

The dark-skinned man in loose white robes watched the tally even out as the girl picked up Gabriel the kitten and headed out of the alley. He knew Gabriel could do it, that he would save her. Still, she wasn't out of the woods just yet.

2. 'Here, kitty, kitty, kitty...'

2. A Damsel in Distress
Charlotte

Staring down the prongs of a pitchfork, Charlotte was feeling slightly faint.

'Easy does it, Andy. Andy? Andy...don'tcha want a cookie?'

She had unwittingly roused her cousin from his post-breakfast slumber when she was making hay in the barn. Gripping the lethal appliance, her cousin blinked at the unwanted sun, looked right through her, his bloodshot pig-eyes telegraphing annoyance. He was upset. Not as upset as Charlotte sometimes got for having to do all the work around the farm, but his upset could actually have consequences.

Judging by the sickly-sweet scent, Andy must have had a bit of a pot session and wasn't thinking quite clearly, hence the pitchfork. She was counting on him having the munchies, hence the offer of a cookie.

Charlotte was sending up a little prayer for help. *Any help?*

She'd been a good girl, done her chores, helped her neighbours, gone to church, kept herself out of trouble. She didn't deserve death by pitchfork. *Please, pretty please.*

Far far away, a tinkling bell rang and a fairy pushed a button. On her split screen of 16 frames, a new frame moved to the central position, flashing 'ANY HELP', dimension and map coordinates blinking in huge red letters across the screen.

The fairy made a swiping motion with her wing, sending the screen to an available guardian angel. A split second later she was speaking into her headset without any preliminaries, 'Victor, any help is required in an assault by pitchfork situation in a barn in Tempest, Texas, Earth dimension. Yes, the girl is about to be forked to death. In a barn. Check your watch, I've sent the coordinates to you already. The request is for any help, so you have some discretion. Yes, it's a damsel in distress again, and no grumbling, you're still on probation. Yes, I do know it's been two Earth years of it, now get to it!' she hung up.

Daisy adjusted her golden locks and sighed, which made her blue wings flutter. She wished all the calls were as easy as this.

She went back to sorting out the remaining cries for help. There was always someone needing to be rescued.

Luckily, that's what the Agency was for. Guardian angels assigned on demand, any hour of night or day in any of the known 63 dimensions.

Do you require the services of a Guardian Angel?

With or without wings?

Or a Prince Charming?

A Knight in Shining Armour, perhaps?

Well, then, all you have to do is ask and one will be provided for you, free of charge!

Having nightmares and wish to be rescued from them?

No problem, we will send someone to sort you out.

No job was too small at low tide, but when they were short-staffed, which was what they usually were, they had to prioritise their rescues.

Daisy pushed the 'Reality freeze' button, which didn't stop time - there was no stopping Him - but instead made Time pass slower in the 16 priority dimensions. Even insomniac fairies that fielded the rescues needed breaks. The calls were coming in 48 hours round the clock. Time privileges of the Agency - stretching the time-space continuum, and in case of resurrecting angels, asking Time to turn a blind eye altogether - was the only way to ensure the angels got to most places when they were needed.

Her shift was going to be over in 10 Agency hours. Then Loretta was going to take over. The call centre was terribly understaffed, which is why Daisy loved the reality-freezing button.

Sadly, sometimes even this function did not help the most fickle of clients, usually damsels in distress, who had a tendency to be too pernickety about the specifications as to who exactly they wanted to charge to their rescue. At the very beginning when the Agency had just been founded, sometimes, a guardian angel didn't get there in time because they didn't know whom to send who would fit the specification. So now the Watchers had a silent agreement that if the situation was looking like a picky damsel in distress, they would send whoever was available.

The damsels, after they were saved from almost certain rape, mugging or death, usually mostly never complained their high standards were perhaps met only half-way.

Daisy blew on her lavender-rosemary tea and unfroze time.

Reality regained consciousness.

3. A Prayer for the Dying[3]
Lanie

Lanie was hovering over her dead body, slumped in a foetal position behind a dumpster in a dark alley under the Strand. This had seemed like such a good shortcut just a few minutes or a lifetime ago, depending on how you looked at it.

She had just wanted to help the poor homeless man who had asked her for money to buy bread. Before she could even open her wallet to give him a few coins, in desperation he had grabbed for her entire purse. He must have been hungry for too long. In his rush to get away with the loot, he had pushed at her. A second later, her temple had connected with the corner of the dumpster and now there she was.

Lanie felt herself get lighter. Floating upwards, with regret and troubles seeping away she sincerely hoped he would buy bread and not booze with the money he had taken.

As she was wafting over London Bridge she saw a double-decker bus impacting at full speed with a Mercedes, which flew over the railing and into the murky waters of the Thames.

Lanie's instincts were telling her to help the poor soul. If she could save one more life before she left, it would be that one.

With that thought she was sucked under water.

Twenty minutes later, Lanie was sitting in an ambulance that was charging for the nearest hospital. Next to her, the stretcher housed the man she had pulled from the car onto the steps of London Bridge. Lanie huddled into the blanket, smiling.

A few hours later, dressed in dry borrowed clothes, she was still smiling, sitting next to the comatose man she had saved who was now hooked up to all sorts of tubes. Unconscious, but alive.

'Visiting hours are over, luv, why don'tcha go home?' The kind nurse patted Lanie on the arm. 'He might'n't wake up anytime soon. You've been through buckets today yerself. Why don't you go home, lass?'

Because she could not remember where home was. Yet somehow, that didn't really matter. As she was leaving the hospital room, Lanie took one last look at the man through the glass. His chest was rising and falling rhythmically. The tubes were keeping him alive. Lanie started walking towards the exit to the ICU ward. As the nurse turned to go back to her night station, Lanie wished she could just stay there, in the room with the sleeping man she had rescued.

In an instant she was back in that room, on the other side of the plexi-glass.

There were no chairs, so Lanie did the only thing she could think of. She climbed into the cot, careful not to disturb any tubes sticking out of the man and carefully wrapped herself around his left side.

Peter. His name was Peter. That's what she had heard the nurse call him earlier.

With the morning shift came the paramedic who had resuscitated Peter in the ambulance.

Seeing a girl in a volunteer's stripy outfit sleeping next to the man she had zapped back to life in her ambulance yesterday almost made the paramedic call security. All they needed was a groupie helper suffocating patients in their sleep. Then she recognised the girl. She was the one who had dragged this man from the Thames.

The paramedic's mouth twitched and she entered the hospital room without knocking.

The girl's eyes flew open.

'You did a brave thing yesterday. But this is not allowed. You have to go,' the woman said.

The girl nodded and left the room without a word.

The paramedic was so focused on the guy she had brought back to life she didn't notice the girl was padding the floors barefoot.

The man had a pleasant face. She had already noticed that yesterday when she was trying to get his heart beating again. A kind face. A shock of floppy dark hair. Athletic build. Even in a coma, the man was gorgeous. He couldn't help it, so why should she? The woman sat on the side of the bed the volunteer had just vacated and watched the man sleep, lusting not just for his speedy recovery.

As Lanie padded the halls, she heard someone whisper for help from one of the rooms and she went to see what she could do. Over the next few hours she found out there was quite a lot she could do around here. Bringing them water, extra blankets, turning on televisions or just chatting to them to keep their spirits up. Helping the patients kept her occupied the whole day. When the ward quieted down and most of its populace was falling into a slumber, she remembered Peter and found herself at his side, on the cot. He looked much healthier. She sat there and told him about her day until the lights in the hall went off, one by one.

The next morning she was careful to sneak out before the nurse came to check on Peter. If that was all she got, she was happy to spend her time keeping watch over him.

4. There Would Be An Again
Gabriel

Grace knew she was going to be horribly late for work if she fed the cat. She chose the cat.

The fur ball did not seem to be very comfortable being held. When she put it down on the kitchen counter next to the milk, it froze, then sniffed and took a few tentative steps towards the saucer, eyeing her suspiciously.

'Oh, I'm sorry, you're probably not used to eating this high, let me make it better.' She took the milk and the cat and put them both down. 'We don't want you to have vertigo,' she patted the floor next to the saucer.

Grace thought she saw the cat smirk at the word 'vertigo'. She must be imagining things. *Ok, it was a stupid thing to say because she wasn't even sure cats could have vertigo, but it wasn't like the cat could understand human speak.*

Gabriel started to lap his milk with enthusiasm. He never ate breakfast simply because in the Mystic North, Valhalla and at the Agency nobody was ever hungry or needed food, to be precise. Suspended state dimensions were in-between-worlds where normal rules didn't apply. But in this dimension - *whatever it was and he would find out soon enough* - here he felt the need for sustenance. The milk tasted nice and fresh. He should stock up for when he needed to rescue her again.

There would be an again, he was sure of it.

That bullet had been meant for her. She seemed to attract guns, for some reason. About four Agency years, so two Earth years ago Victor had waved a gun in this girl's face. Vic had improved since but this girl was still plagued by firearms. The Boss didn't seem to know why or who the shooter was, which means the Watchers didn't know either. Yet anyway. It was all for Gabriel to figure out, now that he was on site.

He looked at the empty plate. How could he have finished all the milk?

'Good kitty. My, you were very hungry, weren't you? Well, why don't I pour you some more and leave you to it. I have to get to work now, if I want to keep my job.' Grace poured some more milk into a bigger bowl, watched the cat hesitate for a second before it started on the milk again.

The cat did not just judge whether this additional quantity would fit into it, did it?

Thinking she was imagining things, Grace shook her head and closed the front door behind her.

All the way to work Grace couldn't help but see red cats with white stripes on every corner. Exactly like the fur ball she had left behind at home.

Gabriel the cat was standing in front of a perky coffee shop that the girl had just entered.

Was this breakfast on the way to work or was this work?

He tried hard to peek in from the hood of a parked car and saw the girl put on an apron.

This was work.

Phew. He could turn back into a man. He was partial to cats, but that didn't mean everyone in this dimension was. On the way here, he had had a few serious encounters with local boys out for some fun and torture and only narrowly avoided a careless biker.

Stumbling into the coffee shop, Grace earned a concerned glance from Emma, the cook. 'Another critter rescue?'

Grace nodded happily and went to put on her apron.

The bell at the entrance chimed.

'Gracie, customer!' the man at the till half-barked, half-guffawed. 'I swear, if you were not kin and in need of a job and I in need of a waitress for minimal wages, I would fire you on the spot.' Mumbling, he assessed Gabriel to be a paying customer.

Grace motioned for Gabriel to follow her to an empty corner booth.

The radio coughed and switched to a guy persuading someone she's his true love, his whole heart and begging the girl not to throw that away.[4] When the ballad took a rockier turn, the cook in the kitchen switched the radio station.

Grace gave the new customer a menu and was startled to see him looking right at her. Oddly, in the sunlight, for a flash of a second, his eyes looked the same colour as the eyes of the kitten she had found this morning - amber. She had just adopted a critter and seeing him everywhere was very post-partum. For the umpteenth time, Grace regretted not becoming a vet - a promise she had made to her dad at the tender age of five.

Grace's blond customer smiled and said, 'Grace.'

She smiled back. It was hard not to. The man looked good-natured and trustworthy. Not to mention drop-dead gorgeous. 'Sorry, do I know you from somewhere?'

'Nope. I just heard the owner - your uncle, is he? - say your name. Well, truth be told, he used an affectionate version of it, so I'm only assuming it is Grace, not Gracie, right?' The man had eyes that could pierce concrete.

'My, what big ears you have,' Grace couldn't help it.

The man crooked a smile.

As trustworthy as he looked, he seemed to be angling for more than just coffee. She had a sixth sense about these things. Grace briefly mused whether all the axe-murderer conversations started this way - politely and all smiles - and decided to avoid pleasantries. She nodded and enquired, 'What'll it be, mister?'

'Gabriel,' said the man and tilted his head as if listening to something.

Grace's right brow crawled up her forehead.

'My name is Gabriel.'

Fine. She could be civil. 'What'll it be, Gabriel?'

'Eggs over easy and some coffee. Black, please.'

Grace jotted all of it down, 'Milk on the side or no milk at all?' She had learnt to ask that since 'black' with posh City types could mean 'milk on the side' and she hated it when they didn't tip her for something she 'should have just known' or 'could have just confirmed with them'. In jeans and a white shirt, he didn't look like a City boy, but she never could tell these days.

'No milk at all, just black is fine. I've already had my share of milk today, thanks to a good soul,' she heard him say as she walked away.

What a perfectly odd comment to make.

Grace looked back to get a better look at the man. For a

second she thought he looked bright and eager, reminding her of her stray kitten after it had finished its first saucer of milk.

Her mind was playing tricks on her again.

Kittens didn't turn into men and men, well, men were no kittens at all. Especially not the ones that tried to chat her up at work. She had learnt that the hard way.

Before university, she had been working in her uncle's coffee shop, part-time, to earn herself some pocket money. The inheritance from her parents, Gods rest their souls, had provided for her schooling and enough to pay the utilities and taxes. She didn't know then that her dabbling in waitressing for pocket money would end up being her vocation.

Victor had been a customer with all charm and smiles and look where that had almost led her and had definitely led him. After a year of wooing, two torturous years living together, a spectacular break-up involving the police, after the incident at her reunion Victor had been found dead in a ditch and she had been scarred off men for life. That was two years ago.

She returned with Gabriel's coffee and eggs, clinked them down, said her 'here-you-are-s' and walked away without smiling. It didn't matter if she didn't get a tip. She'd rather not be tipped than be afraid for her life.

5. The Devil in Tempest
Charlotte

Looking into Andy's stoned eyes Charlotte knew that today was the day she was going to die. She tried to edge as far away from the pitchfork as she could, but the beam came up hard and fast as it was bound to do. She felt the prongs dent her neck. She had begged and pleaded for any help for all of the thirty seconds that it took Andy to get a firm grip on one of the two pitchforks he was seeing. There was nowhere to go, nothing to be done and no way out. Despite her pleas, help was not on its way.

There was a thunderclap outside the barn.

'Anyone home?'

Yes, a very good question at this point, considering how much Andy's pupils were dilated.

An arm reached out from behind Andy and swiftly grabbed the pitchfork.

Charlotte felt the pressure on her neck ease and exhaled with relief. Too early, as it happened.

No longer deterred by the fork, Andy was free to advance right at her, arms outstretched.

Before his paws could clasp around her neck, the six-foot Andy was lifted up in the air like a sack of potatoes. An almost tender shove later, Andy flew ten feet, his bloodshot eyes as wide as saucers, connected with the barn door and slowly slid to the floor.

Charlotte made sure Andy was still breathing before she turned to inspect her unexpected saviour. The tall and impossibly handsome biker in black denim was looking down at her. Against the morning sun, with his dark curly hair and the pitchfork still poised in his hand, he looked like the Devil with a halo.

'Are you alright?' The devil asked Charlotte.

'Fine...now...thank you.' Instinctively Charlotte massaged her neck. Her fingers went sticky and wet. She looked down and saw red. Lots of red. Strands of hay laying on the floor advanced in slow motion. Before the darkness came someone warm and big caught her. Then it was lights out.

Charlotte came to the sound of her aunt Flo's keening. She opened her eyes and observed the scene. Aunt Flo was wailing over Andy's unconscious body while her uncle Ted looked like he had half a mind to go call the cops on the stranger who was still there. The stranger stretched his hand out to her uncle, 'Victor.' *The devil was called Victor.* Charlotte noticed uncle Ted didn't reciprocate Victor's gesture. *How rude.*

Victor just smiled, 'You should keep your boy in check. He almost killed the girl.'

Annoyed that he saw her just as a 'girl', Charlotte was nevertheless prepared to give a full account of the situation when the keening sound stopped all of a sudden, 'How dare you? My Andy wouldn't hurt a fly. He would never ever accost Charlotte!'

The biker walked up to Charlotte and silently helped her to her feet. Without saying a word, amid the comforting sounds of clucking hens and barking neighbourhood dogs, he walked her over to her outraged aunt Flo and Uncle Ted, who looked like he wanted to be anywhere but there. Still in silence, he lifted Charlotte's chin up and pointed at the bloody marks that Andy's pitchfork had left.

Since aunt Flo still looked puzzled, Victor pointed to the pitchfork. 'You're welcome to match the prongs to the cuts.'

Aunt Flo's jaw fell open while uncle Ted looked mighty uncomfortable.

'It might be a good idea if the kid,' Victor nodded at the heap that was Andy, 'laid off the pot. I understand this is not the first time he has endangered...Charlotte, was it?' he looked at her and she nodded.

'How dare you! My boy would never...,' aunt Flo huffed and puffed.

Victor bent down and retrieved a joint from Andy's breast pocket.

Charlotte wondered how he had known that this was where Andy kept them.

'You put it there while he was unconscious! This is

outrageous! My boy!!!' Aunt Flo was hovering over Andy, trying to protect him from any bodily harm that might be lurking in anyone's thoughts.

Charlotte braced herself for more wailing.

'Thank you,' uncle Ted said and shook Victor's hand.

The wailing never came. Neither did the keening. Charlotte blinked back her surprise. *Well that was something. Uncle Ted had come through for her after all. Apparently, water could be thicker than blood.*

Aunt Flo composed her jaw quickly, but refused to issue any gratitude. Instead she zeroed in on Charlotte, 'And what did you do to provoke Andy?' Leaving the question hanging, aunt Flo wiped her tears and savoured her familiar role of chief prosecutor in the family, 'I'm sure he had to be mightily provoked to be incensed to this....this....point.'

'I swear...' Charlotte said.

'Don't swear, dear, it's unladylike,' aunt Flo reproached.

'Aunt Flo, I promise I didn't do anything to make him mad.' *Except maybe live and breathe.* If they didn't believe her, she was going to suffer extra chores for a week.

By the look aunt Flo cast her, she seemed to have the same problem with Charlotte living and breathing as did Andy. Smiling unpleasantly, she enquired, 'Victor, was it? What were you doing in our barn with our Charlotte at this early hour in the first place?'

Charlotte blushed despite her best efforts. *Her aunt was making it sound like she and Victor had been doing something illicit in the barn this morning or possibly all night and Andy had just happened in on them! Gosh, her aunt would take this to mean exactly what she thought had happened although nothing did! Not that Charlotte wouldn't want it to happen, if it were to happen with this hunky guy, for instance.* Charlotte blushed deep crimson, chiding herself for inappropriate thoughts.

Victor pointed behind him at a Harley Davidson gleaming in the morning sun, as black as the getup of its owner. 'My bike ran out of gas, so I thought I'd pop by and ask to buy some as you seem to have machinery around when I witnessed your 'boy' nearly running the girl through with that pitchfork. He was so worked up it seemed safer - for him - to gently knock him out rather than scuffle with him. Trust me, considering the inebriated state he was in, scuffling would have led to more injuries than the bump on the head he has now.' Victor looked at Andy, as pudgy as Charlotte was toned. Victor suspected she probably did most of the work around here.

Charlotte looked at her rescuer's lean mean muscular form. *Andy wouldn't have stood a chance against this one, high or sober. Had Andy chosen to scuffle, he would have injured himself from just bumping into Victor. Badly.*

Aunt Flo bristled. Uncle Ted scratched his jaw. Charlotte was trying hard not to smile. She didn't know whether it was the truth finally dawning on them that their son was a pot-headed bully, or the fact that a biker, someone they figured for 'simple folk' had used a word like 'inebriated' that had caused both their jaws to drop. She was enjoying the show. She would probably pay for looking much too happy later and in full. Right now she was trying hard not to smile. To distract herself, she started humming Taylor Swift's 'I Knew You Were Trouble'. The song started as innocently as her morning - once upon a time, a few mistakes ago[5].

The kind stranger turned his dark eyes on her, making her shiver involuntarily at his deep gaze, 'Do you enjoy what you do here, Charlotte?'

'What?' escaped her in a squeak.

'Do you enjoy what you do here, Charlotte?' Victor repeated with patience.

'Yyyes...?' she said as her mind was screaming *No no no no no!!!*

Sensing her hesitation, Victor felt the need to explain the obvious to all of them. He turned to her uncle since he seemed to be the only adult who had any of Charlotte's interests at heart, 'If she stays here and he,' Victor pointed at the still unconscious Andy, 'doesn't get cleaned up, then this,' he waived the pitchfork around, 'will keep happening. Someday she might not be as lucky as she was today. Maybe she could move elsewhere and you could lend a hand without putting her in mortal danger?'

A place of her own? She had dreamt of this for as long as she had moved to Tempest!

Uncle Ted nodded. He didn't need another death by pitchfork in this family.

Victor made a mental note to explore the family history just in case it came in handy if persuading uncle Ted to do the right thing today went awry.

'I always regretted taking her in,' said aunt Flo suddenly.

Charlotte felt a pang of sadness. *She had always known it, though. That's why she had tried so hard and been so good. So her uncle's family would not have to regret taking her in after her own ma and pa had passed away. Still, with all the sour looks and unhappy stares auntie gave her especially around dinnertime - as if what little she ate could ever diminish Andy's chow - this was the first time her uncle's wife had admitted this out loud.*

There was something about the demeanour of this tall dark handsome stranger that prompted people to tell the truth.

'Let me help you with the gas,' uncle Ted offered, leaving his wife silently outraged that instead of helping her carry their son into the house he had offered to help the stranger who had hurt him.

Uncle Ted just figured the sooner the stranger gets his gasoline, the sooner he will leave, taking with him these bouts of honesty that had never plagued his family before. If only he could persuade Charlotte to leave with him. 'Girl, lend me a hand,' he huffed as he passed Charlotte.

Great, now she was 'girl' to everyone. Accepting her subservient destiny in this family, Charlotte followed her uncle without as much as even a sigh.

Ten minutes later, she was back with a tank of gas. Uncle Ted had found something more useful to do in the main house, leaving her to tend to the devil. Alone.

All was still, apart from the roosters who were congregating to serenade the late morning for a second time today. As she put the tank down, she wondered if she was allowed to be curious around strangers. Charlotte had always wanted to know what bikers did for a living, but she was too shy to start the conversation first.

Victor was contemplating his options. *The rescue wasn't over until it was over. He wasn't done until his charge was safe. Until he got her out of here. Failure was not an option. Decisions to relocate could take months and as much as he enjoyed the fresh scent of hay, he would prefer not having to rescue her every single morning. He couldn't constantly live on the premises or nearby either. Even one month in his old dimensions was enough to turn him back into a human and lose his immortality. He didn't have a month, he didn't want to be here for a month. Turning back into his old self was not a good option. He had to speed things up a little.* 'So, your dream is to move away?'

There was a sharp intake of breath from the girl. She wondered whether he could be a mind reader.

Victor smiled, 'No, I'm not a mind reader,' *a blatant lie and from an angel!* 'You're kind of transparent. The way your face lit up when I mentioned moving was a tell-all.'

Charlotte shuffled some dirt away from under the front tyre of the bike with the toe of her boot, 'I'd make a poor poker player, I guess.'

Poker? Atlantic City then, maybe? Out loud he asked, 'Have you ever played?'

She shook her head, smiling shyly, 'No, but I heard Andy talking about online tournaments and planning a gambling trip to either Vegas or Acapulco.' At the mention of the cities her face became dreamy.

Vegas? Acapulco? He would bet anything she just wanted to get out of here. This wasn't a bad idea. Not a bad idea at all. 'If you could pick any place in the world, where would you want to live?' he asked. *Hopefully far away. Too far for random visits by aunt, uncle and cousin dearest.*

'Italy,' Charlotte exhaled the word without having to think about it.

'Italy?' Victor raised an eyebrow. *That could be arranged.*

'Italy,' she nodded, 'I don't care where or what I would do when I'm there, I just want to be there.... Ever since I was a child, I've always dreamt that I would live in Italy someday...' She had seen every single movie featuring the country from 'L'uomo Delle Stelle' to 'Letters to Juliet'. Her travel guide was looking worse for wear and she occasionally managed to cook an Italian dish or two on the sly on the nights when it was her turn to feed the troops.

'You need to save up some money if you want to buy a one-way ticket to Italy,' the devil suggested.

One-way ticket? Charlotte thought about it for all of two seconds, 'That would be a dream...'

Seeing her light up, he asked, 'I don't suppose the next of kin pay you much for your work here.'

Try nothing. 'I get food and shelter,' Charlotte shrugged apologetically as she sat down.

'And they are saving money on not hiring a farmhand or two...since you seem to be doing the work for both, you and.... whatshisname.'

'Andy.'

'Andy. Who isn't that grateful, if you've noticed.' Victor leaned into the door jamb.

She had noticed. Charlotte felt a bit awkward in the presence of this stranger who seemed to be reading her like an open book. She didn't know where to put her hands, so she elected to sit on them instead. Doing nothing but sitting on the doorstep of the barn mid-morning felt good. The morning had been eventful. She had had to fend off Andy before but not like this. *Never like this.* All of a sudden, Charlotte felt tired. She hadn't realised how tired until she had sat down.

'Aren't you a bit tired of being taken for granted?'

Despite her moment of fatigue, her protective instincts over her last remaining family made her rebel, 'That's rather rude, don't you think? Judging me when we've just been acquainted the whole of ten minutes?'

Defensive. Poor kid. She probably didn't know any other way to be. Victor tried to look as sincere as he could so she wouldn't think he was mocking her, 'My apologies. I was actually criticising your folks, not you. They are the ones taking you for granted and they shouldn't be. They should show some appreciation.'

Damn right! Despite saying it only in her head, Charlotte clapped her hand over her mouth. *It must be the tired talking. Golly.*

'You thought something un-Christian like?' Victor crooked a smile, amused.

'Uh-uh.' Charlotte was putting on her most believable poker-face.

'You did!' His smile widened.

Her poker-face, bad as it was, was cracking, but she would still not give up, 'Nuh-uh.'

This innocent flower was so much fun. Victor gently poked Charlotte in the ribs with a finger, 'You thought of a cuss-word, didn'tya? Tell the truth!'

Charlotte burst out laughing, 'Tell the truth? What are we, five?'

'You did! You did think of a cuss-word!' He was so delighted his face dimpled.

Charlotte couldn't help but giggle. With dimples, he looked less like you-know-who.

He gave her a nudge and winked.

Noooo...the devil just winked at her! The thought seemed so ridiculous she could not help but giggle again. *The devil had come to Tempest and rescued her. What would they say in church?* Charlotte nearly doubled over with laughter. *Not only had he rescued her, he rode in on a black Harley and rescued her. And now he was making her want things. He made her want a new life and a new place to live. The devil sure was a smooth talker. He had made her talk of things even her kin knew nothing about. They just thought her pasta and Osso bucco dishes were her pretending to be on some reality TV show about chefs.*

Once she had stopped laughing, Victor decided it was as

good a time as any to ask, 'If you had some savings, would you go away? Right now?'

The devil was tempting her. 'Yes, but I don't have any savings. I need to earn honest money for a long time before I can go.' *But she was going to go. That's what she had decided and that's what she was going to do, come rain or shine.*

Victor looked at the dreamy damsel an thought *I will have to get her a job. Something that would cover a one-way plane ticket to Italy. Even better, a job in Italy? He'd have to think a while. Meanwhile, he could...*

'Charlotte,' uncle Ted's voice was stern. He shuffled at the door, loath to come into the barn.

'Yes, uncle?'

When Charlotte looked up at him, her baby blues so earnest, Ted thought she deserved a break. She deserved a good life and a chance of better people around her. Better than them anyway. She'd always have family. But no one said family, this family, was what she chose or deserved or wanted. This one was a dreamer. She could be so much more. And it was her time to fly the coop. Looking as uncomfortable as he felt, he quickly said what he had come here to say before he could change his mind, 'Maybe you could go live with my cousin Mae for a few days, in town? Until things settle down here...'

Charlotte thought quickly.

Ted's great aunt Mae was as old as the bog and lived in a tiny town house in downtown Tempest. She anticipated there would probably be chores to do around the house, cleaning and cooking and such, but there would be no farm work. She would have time to draw, she would have time to think, she would have time to sleep!!! 'Yes, that would be lovely. Thank you, uncle Ted,' Charlotte said in a rush before her uncle could take it back and sealed it with a hug.

Uncle Ted looked slightly mollified. He felt half-ashamed for sending her away. He knew he had said only for a few days, but that was for Flo's benefit. Once the girl was gone, he'd make sure she stayed gone. He also knew he could persuade his wife later with the argument that mattered most to her - that there would be one less mouth to feed. 'Good. Good. I'll go give her a ring right now. I'm sure she'll be delighted.' Having said his piece, Ted nodded at the biker and headed back to the main house.

Too true. Aunt Mae had been the only one that had praised her Osso bucco.

By Charlotte's smile Victor gathered it was a safe bet Mae was probably a fantastic old broad and would be amenable to the idea of taking Charlotte in. For once, his meddling wasn't really necessary.

Charlotte helped to put the canister away after Victor was done pouring.

'You're going to have to learn Italian when you're going to be living there, you know.'

'When?' *He had said when, not if.*

'When.' He nodded, sure of himself.

This guy, he didn't say much, but he sure gave her good ideas. Charlotte smiled, 'Honestly? I'd love to learn the language.'

'Maybe I can give you a hand?' Victor offered.

'You know Italian? No way!' *The devil was full of surprises.*

'Way. My momma was Italian. Half my cousins are Italian. Learning the language kind of came with the family.' Victor felt as surprised as Charlotte looked. He hadn't volunteered that much of personal information to any of his charges before. *Ever.*

'Ok, say something in Italian, otherwise I find it hard to believe you could ever teach it.' She didn't really. Tall dark and handsome, she could full well believe he was Italian. *Half-schmalf.*

'La dolce vita.' He winked at her.

Charlotte felt the giggles start again.

'Seriously? Everyone knows that one. Nope, no way are you Italian. No. Way.'

'Gelato.'

'You've got to be kidding me...' Still, she was laughing.

'Pizzeria...mascarpone...prosciutto con melone...'

Charlotte threw her head back and just laughed and laughed, 'Are you going to recite the menu to me? Very 'A Fish Called Wanda'.' *Without the bedroom scene.*

Victor realised he enjoyed making Charlotte laugh. She was so bubbly, so full of life. He had missed people, no, he had missed a girl, laughing at his stupid jokes. This one deserved to live, she deserved to go to Italy and start a new, good, nice life there. 'Tuoi occhi sono come le stelle scintillanti reflessi nel mare.⁶'

Wow. That was definitely not something off the menu. 'Now that sounded like some real Italian. What does it mean?'

'Charlotte?' Uncle Ted shuffled into view from the recesses of the main house. Not wanting to re-join them, he had opened the veranda door and was shouting from afar.

'Yes, uncle Ted?' she hollered back.

'Mae says she'll have you whenever you make it over.'

'How about now...' Charlotte mumbled under her breath.

'How about now?' yelled the devil at uncle Ted.

Shoot, he had heard her. Charlotte blushed.

Uncle Ted shrugged.

Victor thought how he could motivate her, 'If you go now, I could give you a ride. I can wait while you pack.'

Charlotte was getting itchy feet and it wasn't because of the hay all over her clothes and hair. *It would take her all of two minutes to pack. There was nothing to stop her from going now. Beside the farm work and the other chores. All she had to do was decide. It was awfully tempting.*

'Otherwise, how would you find out what I said to you in that beautiful language that you love,' the devil towered over her shielding her from the sun and she thought she saw him wink.

How did he know that she loved the sound of Italian? That the real reason she watched the Italian movies was just to hear them speak. The devil was tempting her. Charlotte decided the best way to avoid temptation was to give into it, 'Just wait here for two minutes, ok?' She dashed in and out of her bedroom like lightning, picking up the photo of her parents, her passport, stuffing the few clothes that she owned into a plastic bin bag. Her toiletries were soap and water, she could get that anywhere, certainly at auntie Mae's.

When the girl appeared almost exactly two minutes after she had sprinted off like someone was after her, Victor was amazed. *Well, apparently some women could pack in two minutes flat.* 'Hop on,' he said and started the chopper.

'Tell me what you said first.'

'That I will tell you only after I've deposited you at auntie Mae's and I have my lemonade as a thank you for the ride.'

Cocky. Well, what did she expect? Bikers that saved people had to be cocky. Humble and awkward wouldn't just cut it in the South. She jumped on and held tight, closing her eyes. It felt like she was running away. Without looking back, without regrets, only waving a quick goodbye to uncle Ted. Auntie Flo hadn't even bothered to come out to send her off and Andy was probably still passed out.

3. The Devil in Tempest

Victor could sense that she had crunched her eyes shut, she was holding on so tight. She might be scared, but she could still enjoy the scenery of her ride to freedom, 'You can open your eyes now,' he said as soon as they were on the move.

Charlotte opened her eyes and saw the chestnut alley she always thought was the closest thing to the real world that she would ever see. It was speeding past her on both sides now, quickly becoming a thing of the past. Her future was wide open.

With the girl holding on to him, Victor felt relief that he had almost completed his rescue. Well, save for finding her a job, which would be easy once they got to town.

Victor dropped Charlotte off at Mae's, looked at his watch, turned around and left with a brief, 'See you around, kid.'

Charlotte thought she had preferred 'girl' to 'kid'.

Aunt Mae came out onto the porch with her arms spread wide, 'Goodness, child, I thought I'd never persuade your uncle to give you up. Now I don't know what changed and I don't care, come hither.'

Charlotte disappeared into Aunt Mae's hug. She felt wanted and loved and at home.

Aunt Mae next zeroed in on the most important thing, 'The young man that dropped you off, is he someone special, child?'

Charlotte's ears went pink, 'Auntie, it's not what you think.'

Aunt Mae sat down next to her on the porch swing, 'It never is, child, it never is. So why don't you tell me?'

So Charlotte did. Mae patted the girl on the arm empathetically, while she finished her story of this morning's horrors, 'So, you see, auntie Mae, I don't actually know him at all, he just saved me from Andy and gave me a ride to your house. And he promised to teach me Italian, although I don't know how long he plans to stay in Tempest.'

Mae pursed her lips, nodded and pronounced her verdict, 'While his actions speak otherwise, he doesn't look like a reliable sort of fellow. So take care before you fall head over heels,' Charlotte coloured to her roots this time, 'Make sure he's going to stick around, child. And if he is any sort of a southern gentleman, he knows how to behave and how not to behave under my roof.'

'Yes, auntie.' *Charlotte wouldn't dream of having boys over while staying with Mae. She had been brought up proper and so far, had only had one boyfriend in high school who had broken up with her immediately after he discovered she wouldn't 'put out' as the jerk had put it. So, auntie need not have cautioned her about boys. Boys were not an issue. The devil, however, was.*

'Now, more importantly, let's tend to your wound,' Mae motioned for Charlotte to follow her, 'Into the kitchen, lass.' As much as Charlotte wanted to go and get comforted in the kitchen that always smelled like cinnamon and lavender, she couldn't help one last look at the street where Victor had disappeared a while ago.

Charlotte wasn't sure whether all damsels being rescued felt even a little bit the way she did. Grateful. But there was something else as well. For some strange reason as soon as she had seen him off, she had wished him to turn around at the end of the lane and come right back. She had a little bit of a crush on her saviour. All the damsels did. *Probably.*

At the end of the lane when no one was watching, Victor rode his bike through a wormhole straight into Gaian New York and materialised there as a frog.

6. Fight or Flight
Grace

'The blond cutie in the corner seems quite taken by you,' Emma said at lunch time, nodding at Gabriel in the corner booth. At Grace's angry inhale, Emma shrugged, 'Else it's the coffee.'

Grace looked at the ancient filter machine and shuddered, knowing exactly how seldom they cleaned it. 'No one could be fond of that coffee. Maybe it's your muffins?' she offered.

'He ain't staring at me, doll,' Emma smiled.

At 5PM, when Grace's shift was ending, the man was still there.

Gabriel.

After mounds of muffins, pasta for lunch and salad for dinner not to mention a river of coffee, the guy was still there. By then even the kind-hearted Emma grew suspicious, 'You know, I thought he was taken with you, seeing how his face lit up like a Christmas tree every time you did him the kindness of bringing him his food. But he hasn't even tried flirting with you! He's just sitting there.'

'Lord, no. Not another stalker. Am I to stalkers what honey is to flies? Do I have 'victim, feel free to haunt' tattooed on my forehead or something?' Grace quietly scandalised. 'I tried to give him the cold shoulder and no-smiles treatment throughout the day and yet, there he is.'

Both peeked at the object of discord from behind the till.

Engrossed in yet another phone conversation, Gabriel was standing outside, in the rain. His blond hair was flat and wet, but somehow, instead of looking greasy, his shoulder-length ringlets made him look like a hot angel. Hot enough for the female passers-by to turn back for another look and a drool. It could be that his solid, toned six feet four form and casual, non-builder glam had something to do with it.

Grace's mouth began to water. She had to admit, the man was a dish. A dish that had sat and stalked her for a day.

'Mind you, he did seem to be waiting for someone, slipping out every once in a while, talking on his phone,' Emma said.

'Maybe whoever he was waiting for never showed and I was just eye-candy for the day?' Grace said, handing in her apron and trying to figure out how to leave unseen. She doubted this was the case. Guys who made suspicious phone calls and were waiting for people or stuff could very well be detectives or drug pushers or worse. Grace didn't want to alert poor kind Emma to the possibility that their coffee shop had been potentially earmarked for a drug lair. Drug lairs meant drug busts sooner or later. Drug busts could mean ill repute, loss of customers and potentially going out of business. If she had a choice, she hoped he was waiting for a date or if a drug bust was on the cards she hoped he was at least an undercover police officer, not the offender.

'Aww, honey, it's progress, that is,' Emma hugged Grace so close her nose was instantly buried in her boobs. 'For the first time after he who shall not be named, you're finally warming up to the idea that not every guy is out to get you. Maybe this one is the good guy you've been waiting for after all? Maybe he's just shy.'

Grace shook her head. *Trust Ems to flip from suspicion to trust in less than a minute.* In her mind, that guy and Grace were already happily married with three kids. Ems should know better. She single-handedly nursed Grace out of the slump and over her relationship fears after she escaped from Victor's clutches two years ago. 'You're far too trusting, Ems.'

'And you are far too careful. Lightning never strikes twice,' Emma said, finally releasing Grace.

Grace opened her mouth to point out that she was still in recovery mode from being victimised and until full recovery, there was a high probability she might attract men like Victor, according to her shrink anyway. Deciding against it so as not to worry her closest friend with the true extent of her non-recovery, she said instead, 'No one that handsome is that shy. And don't think that just 'coz you coaxed me to date again and help me sort the good apples from the bad that I will stop trusting my instincts.'

'Well, why don't you ask him out, have your first coffee date here and we'll be able to find out more about him? Soon?'

Grace's horrified expression said it all. 'You're not usually egging me on, Em, what gives?'

Emma shrugged, 'He just seems reliable, that's all. You might even get to date number two with this one. I mean, look at him.'

They both peeked from behind the till. Again.

'Vic had looked like eye-candy as well. Dark and dangerous eye-candy. Nope. I'm staying off sweets this time.' Although Grace had to agree with Emma's assessment, this one did look good natured and reliable. The fear of being wrong yet again made the doubts pile up, 'I don't know. My instincts tell me to run,' she said.

Emma patted her on the back, handing Grace her purse, 'Honey, we both know that ever since he who shall not be named your instincts tell you to run from any man. Look at all the first dates you botched. I thought we talked about this. Heck, I thought you were making progress. I thought starting to date again was a break through,' Emma pouted.

With feeling, Grace puffed a stubborn curl out of her eye. No matter how straight she tried to pull her hair every morning, from the heat of the kitchen, at the end of the day, it ended up curling like fries. Mid-day she looked rather hip, with a few errant curls here and there but by the evening her frizz made the 80s Afro look tame.

Right. Fight or flight. Those were her two options. Freeze was not.

Neither was calling the police. Without any evidence of assault or improper behaviour, in other words without a few bruises or a dead body, they would just laugh at her. They had laughed at her before. Three years ago, to be precise, the first time Victor had slapped her across her face. Hard enough to make her eyes water but not hard enough to leave a bruise.

The guy they were talking about was back at his post and seemed to be looking out of the window. She could see his eyes were following her every move in the reflection. To prove the point she curled a finger at him, 'You.'

Obediently, he turned, smiling widely at her, happy as a clam, 'Yes? How may I be of service?'

Grace froze. That one sentence knocked all the feistiness out of her. That was what her dad always used to say when meeting people for the first time.

On the radio, a woman, like any hot-blooded woman would be, was flattered by someone's fascination with her but told the guy off for being uninvited.[7]

The guy looked sincere and helpful. *Maybe he wasn't a stalker after all?* Whether he was or he wasn't, she wasn't going to encourage him. Grace didn't want anything to do with him. *No sweets.*

Right, that was fight. Abandoned.

Now came flight. She was just going to run.

'You cannot, but thank you for offering,' she said and turned yet another cold shoulder.

Emma tsk-tsk-ed from the kitchen.

Grace waited until her penny-counting-uncle was blocking Gabriel's view before she put both hands on Emma's broad curvy shoulders, 'Ems, I love you dearly, but don't push me. I doubt he will be back tomorrow, if today he doesn't get a phone number.' *Or if he will, they will definitely know he's a stalker and they should alert the authorities.* Grace tried to smooth her hair before she bravely ventured into the night, 'Now go create a distraction so he won't follow me home, will ya?' she begged. Through the closing back door Grace saw the cook taking her turn in obscuring the blond cutie from view and hoped Emma as the blind spot worked in both directions.

Grace prayed to all the gods she knew that her exit would go unnoticed, especially if she legged it home now as fast as was humanly possible. She had a whole 12 hours with the cat to look forward to until her night shift tomorrow.

7. Princess Charming
Sally

Victor the frog could not feel his hind legs. He had been sitting in these bushes under the stairs for over an hour now.

Waiting.

Hopping out at the clickety-click sound of any stilettos to check if it was her.

Princess Charming.

He was the frog she was supposed to kiss so he would turn into a human as if by magic, making her regain her belief in happy endings, open her eyes and see her own happy ending that was supposedly staring her in the face.

Cradling his left hind leg, afraid to examine it for frost bite, he was hoping his would-be-Princess would come home soon. Victor sighed and checked the phone around his neck for time. *The girl was late. Very late.* So late that the novelty of the twin moons of Gaia, the Original Earth, as a backdrop to the twin towers of the World Trade centre was wearing off.

He heard stomping.

Buffaloes?

An angry mama?

Certainly someone with issues.

Victor hated Charges with issues.

He peeked.

Oh bother. That must be her.

He couldn't be sure. Daisy, a firm believer in future positive, had only sent him the Princess' would-be picture after she gets her happy ending. He only remembered a red dress on someone curvy and vaguely attractive. That was the future view. *If this was her, then it was a very future view.* Damn Daisy for never sending original pictures. Her explanation was idiotic – why leave a mark of how unhappy the Princesses used to be in the past – with that measure, everyone who was unhappy should burn all of their family albums.

He was silently praying he was wrong.

She would pass this house.

She would pass.

She would...

He saw sizable ankles attached to impossibly boring black Mary Janes on what looked like tree trunks carrying a huge pizza box stomp up the stairs above him.

...go home.

Well, hell's bells. This Cinderella was certainly going to be a challenge. Especially one that had issues on a perfectly normal Saturday night.

Victor didn't like working on two Charges at the same time, especially in different dimensions. While he still had to figure out what to do with Charlotte, he hoped this new Charge was a quick study, so he wouldn't have to be hopping between dimensions with vastly different time zones at the expense of sleep.

Guardian angels never got to choose their charges or the dimension of their choice, unless it was on their day off. Certain assignment profiles repeated as the Watchers learnt which assignments suited which angels best. Not everybody was good at everything.

This assignment was as ideal for him as a fish needing a bicycle. This was going to be a catastrophe. The Watchers should have known better. Victor sighed. *Either both Daisy and Loretta were being pixyish or they really had run out of all the good frogs if he was their only hope on a Princess Charming mission. Why else would they give him something so far out of his comfort zone?*

Victor stretched his hind legs. *Right. She was home. He could get started.*

The window next to the balustrade at the top of the stairs was cracked open.

The Princess-to-be lived on the ground floor. Lucky. Climbing to a third floor window as a frog would have been a bit of a hassle. He would have had to use the wand and someone might notice.

Victor ambled his way up the 14 steps, caught his breath and hopped onto the windowsill.

Inside, the lights were on but no one was home.

Victor spied a DVD of 'The Princess and a Frog' next to the TV. *If she was a grown-up who still loved and believed in fairy-*

tales, this was going to be as easy as pie.

The girl with a mop of unruly brown curls re-entered the living room. She was holding a box of pizza and a bottle of Sprite.

Behind the curtains Victor spied a movie night. By the looks of it, the fairy-tale movie was going to be the movie of choice this evening.

Easy as pie.

The girl put the pizza box down, loosened the waistband of her sweat pants, sauntered to the TV and picked up the DVD.

Here we go. Easy as pie.

The girl shrugged and threw the DVD into the bin next to the TV stand.

Erm...not as easy as pie?

Victor would have frowned if he hadn't been a frog.

The girl switched the TV on and picked one of the most violent films Victor had ever seen and he had seen plenty of torture and limb-jerking first hand, mostly off screen. In Dialysis X as well as in Xiaong Ra, where violence was a form of greeting.

Right. If a frog would simply appear before her and start talking, she would just squash it with something handy, and not give a second thought to whether she was going crazy or not.

It would take something drastic to get her attention. Or something really pitiful.

Victor tapped on the window with his hind leg.

No reaction.

Right. How could she hear above the ruckus? The movie was still in full blast.

Victor took a mini magic wand out from the sheath that hung from his neck, pointed it at the wires behind the TV and gently flicked.

The entire house went black.

Slight miscalculation.

Now he would have to wait for her to get some candles and call the power company.

Victor lifted his wrist and then remembered frogs don't have watches.

Hearing the silence settle in, he tapped the window forcefully enough for her to hear.

There was movement inside.

He rapped on the window again and said, in human speak and quite audibly, 'Please help me.'

He saw her approaching the window holding a baseball bat. *It didn't look like this was going to end well.*

He managed to hop away from under the window before it was crashed shut.

Two seconds later he was staring into two huge brown bespectacled eyes next to the candle she was holding.

Victor cleared his throat, 'Please help me. I need help.'

Nothing.

Victor tried a different tack, 'I know you can hear me.'

Nothing.

He rolled his eyes, 'Look, you're not going mad. Yes, you're seeing a talking frog at your window. But it doesn't mean you're mad. It means I'm in trouble and you should probably open the window and let me in. And then help me.'

The eyes goggled and disappeared.

Victor knew he was visible in the moonlight. He crossed his paws pleadingly.

Sally was looking at a frog on the street side of her windowsill. *A frigging talking frog.* She was quite sure it had spoken just now.

Maybe she was imagining things?

She looked at her Sprite. Nope, she had poured it herself and didn't remember spiking it. Also, no wine or beer en route home as Harry had cancelled on her half an hour before they were due to meet up. *Some best friend! So, unless the mushrooms in that pizza were psychedelic, in which case she was going to have a word with Vittorio at the pizzeria tomorrow, then there was actually a chance she was stone cold sober and still hearing frogs speak.*

The frog crossed his tiny paws, pleading as if it were human.

Had she fallen asleep during the movie with the DVD she had binned on her mind? Stinking cancelling Harry and his stinking birthday presents.

Sally pinched herself.

Nope, she wasn't dreaming.

She put the bat down. *It was just a frog. It might be slimy, but she was way bigger than him. Besides, as far as talking frogs went, they warranted some investigation.*

Sally approached the window and without opening it, asked, 'What do you want?'

The cold made Victor shiver. *If he told her what he needed from her she would never let him in. Some guile was due.* He shivered again. 'Please let me in, it's freezing out here.'

Sally weighed her options. *It was just a frog. Then again, a talking frog was not just a frog. What if she let it in and it turned into a monster and attacked her or something?*

The frog shivered visibly and coughed this time.

She couldn't be responsible for the death by freezing of a magical creature. Assuming he was magical. Talking frogs usually were. In fairy-tales. From what she could remember from childhood, anyway.

Sally lifted the window enough for the critter to crawl through. 'Pardon me,' the frog said and she nearly screamed when it leaped past her onto the low-rise living room table. The frog made itself instantly comfortable and started warming its front and hind legs near the candle flame like the hobos she occasionally passed when visiting the shadier parts of New York.

Sally tentatively sat on the edge of her couch. *Ok, there was a frog in her living room sunning himself. What if it requested food next? What did frogs even eat? Flies? It had said it needed help, right? Time to get some answers.*

'What kind of help do you need?' she asked.

Considerably warmer, Victor contemplated whether to tell her the truth now or wait a little until she came around to the idea that he was real and he was there and she had to deal with it.

'I saw you are not a fan of fairy-tales,' he pointed at the waste bin where the DVD had landed.

Sally was so shocked she forgot he hadn't answered her question, 'How long have you been loitering at my window, you stalker?'

He looked at her reproachfully. *Come to do her a favour and he gets to be called a stalker.* 'It's not like I crept into your bathroom and spied on you, you know.'

Sally didn't believe the conversation she was having. *Arguing with a stalker frog over what was and what wasn't appropriate stalker behaviour.*

'I had to get your attention somehow,' he offered, 'If it hadn't been for the power cut, you wouldn't have heard me at all.'

Wait. 'Did you cause the power cut?' Sally thought it was a perfectly normal question to ask, since the 'perfectly normal' factored in a magic talking frigging frog.

The frog shrugged.

'If you can do that, why can't you help yourself? Why does it have to be me?'

Good point. 'Personal gain,' he croaked, scratching his side against the candle, making sure he didn't rattle it. Sally guessed a hot lava rain of wax was probably a bit too much warmth for his liking.

'I don't get it. Personal gain of what?' She sat down and picked up a pizza slice. *No reason to go hungry even when in deep conversation with a magical creature.*

Victor exhaled in relief.

At least he had got a conversation started, soon she would get used to him, see his point, kiss him and be on her way of wooing her prince, 'I cannot do magic for my own benefit.' Otherwise he would have waved the wand at her and been gone half an hour ago. Victor the frog sighed and offered up the legend the Watchers had concocted for him, 'I cannot turn myself back into a human. Someone else has to help me do that.'

Now Sally knew she was losing it. *She had just heard a frog tell her he used to be human and wanted to turn back human again.* Just to be sure, she checked, 'Someone turned you into a frog and now you need help my help to turn back into a human being? What did you do?'

Victor narrowed his eyes at her.

'You were snooty at someone, weren't you?'

The frog rolled its eyes.

'You were, weren't you?'

'None of your business, is what it is,' Victor played along. *He'll have to think of a misdeed later since this Princess looked like a dog with a bone and not in a good way. Victor decided to c*hange the subject back. 'It would be much easier to explain how you can help if you liked fairy-tales.'

Oh, Sally liked fairy-tales all right. Well she had when she was seven and kids believe all sorts of crap. Like Santa and stuff. Believing in them actually happening was like believing she could win a lottery or marry the guy of her dreams. 'What does make believe have to do with me helping you?'

The frog shrugged, 'Well, for one, make believe is happening right here on your living-room table. And two,' the frog was actually trying to bend its paws counting but gave up, 'if you were a fan of fairy-tales, you would know what it is that girls do to un-enchant a frog and everything would be so much easier.'

Sally didn't have to think, 'To find a perfect guy you have to kiss a lot of frogs' was a saying she knew and lived rather well. She made a face, 'Hell, I have to kiss you? No way!'

Happy that their negotiations were proceedings so nicely, Victor nodded enthusiastically, 'Yup, that's exactly the help I need to turn back into a human.' *A blatant lie, since he could turn back any time he liked, but then she wouldn't turn into a Princess for her best friend to notice her.* Victor considered this to be one of the instances where lying was perfectly acceptable.

'I am not kissing a slimy frog! Yuck.'

Victor looked at himself and at the complete lack of slime and back at her, annoyed. *Trust this Princess to be squeamish. If he turned back into a human, she probably wouldn't mind. Kissing a hot looking biker was probably better than kissing a frog but ahe had to kiss a frog to turn him into a hot biker.*

Victor winced. All of a sudden, he saw the snag. What bothered him was that the Watchers hadn't seen it when they had sent him on this assignment. *He couldn't actually let her kiss him and turn into a hot biker. She would fall straight for the angelic biker who had no use for her and then bye-bye*

Harry, her best friend and true love. 'Fine, don't kiss me.'

'Fine!'

An uncomfortable silence followed.

Sally gave in first, 'So, if you don't want me to kiss you, how may I help you exit my living room?' She didn't sound particularly helpful.

Good question. The whole point of her kissing him would be to transform her into a Princess painlessly. Now that kissing was out, Victor guessed he would have to do it the old fashioned way.

Manually.

This would take time.

Since he knew shock-therapy sometimes worked, he demanded, 'Well, if you're not going to help me become human, I wish you would consider doing yourself this favour. I want you to change the way you dress.'

Sally looked at him with her mouth open like he was from another planet. *A frog from hell had come to tell her that her dress sense sucked? She got that from her mother often enough.* 'Buzz off.'

'I'm not a fly,' although since being magicked in this frog body was already making him irritable, he suspected it wasn't going to be long before he started getting cravings for flies, 'and I'm not buzzing off. You dress like you hate yourself, want to stash your body somewhere far, far away and even I could combine colours better than you do.'

Sally looked at her grey sweat pants and maroon T-shirt with a logo 'IF YOU DON'T LIKE WHAT YOU'RE SEEING, LOOK ELSEWHERE'. *She dressed the way she did because she did hate her body. Go figure. The frog was actually right, but she still felt like sulking.* 'Who do you think you are? Fashion police? Well, it's not like I can take you along shopping to give me advice, Mr Know-It-All.'

He hopped closer, looking all hopeful, 'Well, why not? You could put me in your pocket and I could ride along. Contrary to what you think, I'm not slimy,' he demonstrated he wasn't sticky by touching some papers on her table. 'All you have to do is hold open your pocket or a bag, I would hop into it and you don't need to touch me at all.'

Sally put her head between her legs.

Breathing exercises, really? He had stressed her out that much?

Sally kept breathing. *This was too much. Ten minutes ago, her life had been normal. Now there was a frog in her life, a goddamn frog that was giving her advice on how to dress! Give him another ten minutes and he would proceed to dating advice.* Sally had to ask herself why she was so willing to go crazy. *This wasn't real. Not at all. Not the tiniest little bit. Even if people did do-overs on those TV-shows, magic frogs did not pop into random apartments to give life-style consultations. All she had to do for all of this to go away was to close her eyes and count to ten.* She started counting, breathed in and out, in and out, and looked up. ·

The frog was still there. 'It's not like I'm asking you to hand over your money. Well, not to me, anyway. Paying a clerk at Barneys for some nice clothes would be progress,' the frog tap-tapped his hind paw. 'But since the shops are closed right now, we can start with a review of your closet.'

Sally put her head back between her legs only to come nose-to-nose with the frog. She screamed her lungs out.

'Better. I like seeing some enthusiasm,' the frog praised the reluctant Princess. 'Now, let's see your stuff...' the frog hopped towards her bedroom.

'Over my dead body will I let you paw at my clothes!' Victor had never seen anyone sprint from the brace-brace position. In her bedroom, with her back against her closet, Sally spread her arms wide to protect her collection of vintage wear.

'I admire your athleticism and speed,' Victor called after her mid-hop. *Athleticism could come useful.* 'Now quit looking like a martyr. Since you're already here, you can show me yourself. Which one is your favourite outfit?' the frog leaned back on the door-jamb and crossed his arms.

'If I show you my favourite outfit, will you leave me alone?'

Sally asked, relaxing. *Jesus-on-a-cross did look ridiculous from her full-length mirror.*

'Maybe,' the frog said, 'if it is a real stunner and if you can prove to me that this,' he pointed at her baggy trousers and T-shirt, 'is not the height of your fashion sense.'

From the back of the closet, Sally produced a woollen round-neck, sleeveless A-shaped magenta dress. A few white moths escaped its folds.

Aside from the moths, this looked half decent. If the trouble was that she hadn't worn her favourite dress in a long while, maybe there was hope yet that this could be a quick save.

Sally turned the dress around. It had virtually no back.

Lordy. Drag queens in London wore better ones.

Refraining from any comment out loud, Victor asked, 'Could you please lower it slightly so I can check the stitching? Stitching is important. Shows craftsmanship. Stitching is the real true mark of quality.'

The girl obliged.

Victor lifted his hind leg and peed on the hem.

'What the *!?^@!~*!' Sally screamed, swaying the dress out of harm's way.

Too late.

'Now look what you've done! You did that on purpose!' she yelled, propelling herself to the bathroom to find out whether she had something to remove the stain with.

He'd been prosecuted for urinating in public, doing it in front of a private audience of one was no problem at all. 'I'm sorry,' Victor said out loud, looking anything but. 'There's something about that colour that compels me to do this.'

When Sally emerged from her bathroom, carrying a tiny bottle and a clean rag, mumbling something about incontinent frogs and dry cleaning, she realised it was a big mistake to have left the dress in the same room as the frog that had tried to assassinate it.

Huge.

Within the space of thirty seconds that she had been gone, the sleeve was torn, the zipper missing, nasty gashes ran across the front and the colour... she didn't want to think what else he did to it to change the colour to THAT. 'You stupid thing, you have completely ruined it!' Sally was close to tears. *Never mind that she had worn it only once and it had somehow shrunk on her since.*

Thank gods for the magic wand. 'See, I told you - poor stitching,' the frog said, climbing over the dress towards her closet, 'What else do you have in there?'

'Noooo...' prima ballerinas would have envied Sally's leap across the room.

All that stood between her and her closet was the ruinous frog.

'You destroyed my favourite dress! I'm not going to let you even smell the rest of my clothes! Now, move!!' Sally demanded, thinking where best to shove the tiny bottle of detergent in her hand so it would bring about the maximum amount of pain.

Victor shrugged, 'Not that I can help it, I can smell your 'vintage' stuff from over here. When did you last have anything dry-cleaned? I thought girls were good at that kind of stuff? As about the dress, I did you a favour, you know. Hookers wear better dresses.'

'I can just squash you right there, you know,' Sally said, trying to remember whether her dry cleaner also removed stains from carpets.

'You can, but you won't,' Victor said with confidence. 'I'm about to give you some top-notch fashion advice and you'd better listen, if you ever want to look decent for yourself, if not for anyone else.'

'Why on earth would I listen to a frog for fashion advice?' Sally asked.

'Have you heard of Gok Wan?' Victor asked, hoping the name he had heard from girls discussing television shows too many times would ring a bell.

Sally nodded.

'I'm better,' Victor said. *He was. All of his girlfriends had said so.* 'I'm very particular about how a woman should dress to fit her body type, income and level of respect for herself. Right now you dress like you are a student who eats poorly, treats herself the same and has no clue that she has a perfect guitar shape hidden below all the ugly clothes. What you call vintage, I call cheap.'

Sally looked hurt but interested, 'I did get them for a bargain.'

'Whoever you got the clothes from probably collected someone's trash, to be honest,' the frog said.

'One man's trash is another man's treasure,' Sally parried.

'Tell me, when you eat leftovers, what does that make you?' Victor asked.

The frigging frog had just called her a pig! Sally looked around for something heavy.

'I didn't call you anything, I merely compared taking someone's old and ugly clothes to leftovers,' Victor said, 'You didn't even try to remodel them!'

'Ok, so I was lousy at home education, sue me,' Sally said.

'I'd rather give you invaluable advice, it's cheaper and quicker,' the frog parried.

'Come on, let's hear it!' Sally sat on her bed. Conversations with her mother had taught her that when you argue, fights stretch out of any reasonable proportion. She had learnt that shutting up and pretending to listen could make the hurricane pass by quicker. She could do it now as well. *If it got the goddamn frog out of her house quicker.*

'I didn't say it was going to be verbal advice. I'm more of a doer,' Victor surveyed her clothes' closet.

Mourning her ruined dress, Sally said, 'I'll say.'

'You did say you got them cheap, right?' he asked.

'Yes, yes I did,' Sally said, happy he was seeing the light.

'Then you won't feel like you binned a fortune, when all of this goes,' Victor concluded happily.

Pretending to listen would get her naked as in left with nothing to wear. Sally sighed, 'I have another proposition - why don't I take you by your hind leg and just throw you out unless you leave me the heck alone.'

'You won't.'

'Will too.'

'You won't.'

'Watch me.'

'You can't.'

?!?

The frog pointed at himself, 'Magical creature needing help. Do you know how the stories where someone who had refused to help a magical creature turn out?'

'The Beast...' Sally nodded.

'Right back at you,' the frog huffed, 'Try to do someone a kindness and all you get is name-calling.'

'No, I meant the Beast from Beauty and the Beast. The vain prince was turned into the Beast by a Sorceress when he refused to give her shelter when she had asked in the guise of a beggar-lady.'

Victor pointed to himself, 'In a guise,' then to Sally, 'refusing to help.' *Let's hope she won't notice that she's not refusing to help me but herself.* 'Do you care to find out the consequences of not fulfilling innocent requests from a magical *moi*?'

'How is raiding my closet going to help you transform back into a human?' Sally asked.

'Let's say if I help you, then I help myself,' Victor said.

'Am I like your penance of something? More importantly, what horrible thing did you do to deserve being turned into a frog?' Sally asked with glee. *If she couldn't get rid of him - consequences forbidding - she could mock him to her heart's content.*

Victor kept schtum. *He could keep her guessing.*

'Did you refuse to help someone like the prince from Beauty and the Beast? Were you a dog and had an affair just before your wedding like in the Prince Charming movie? Or did you find your princess and she refused to kiss your slimy *tuchis*[8]?'

'You do know your fairy-tales. Why do you hate them so?' Victor asked.

'None of your business, frog!' Sally bit back. 'And quit answering a question with a question. Jewish,' she pointed at her curly brown hair, 'we invented it.'

Victor shrugged. 'I don't care what your beef with fairy-tales is as long as you help me,' he said.

'You're going to keep haunting me until I help you, aren't you?' Sally asked.

Victor nodded enthusiastically. 'I cannot leave until I help you,' he said.

There was no escaping the damned creature! 'Just my luck! Everybody else gets a pretty fairy godmother and I get a frog!'

'But it means you are a princess...' Victor pointed out.

'And have been all my life, unfortunately...' she sighed. 'Only child, Jewish parents,' Sally shrugged.

'So the clothes - are you a very poor princess or is that a rebellion phase or something?' Victor asked.

She hadn't really thought about it that way. Perhaps the frog had a point.

'Let me just point out that whoever told you that T-shirts and jeans were suitable for leisure, smart casual AND formal wear should be shot on sight,' Victor said. *He could volunteer to help.*

Sally harrumphed.

Shooting his Charge was not an option. Unfortunately. 'So you do have money, you just choose to look cheap? Why punish yourself? It's not your parents who have to wear THIS!' the frog picked up a frilly blouse that would have made Austin Powers happy.

She'll be damned. The frog had a point. Again.

Victor had learnt that silence was not always a sign of agreement. In Sally's case, it was definitely a sign of quiet defiance. 'I could, of course, just wait until you went to bed and then do this,' he pointed at her favourite dress, 'to all of that,' he pointed at the closet.

She wouldn't put it past him to do exactly that. The frog had no brakes whatsoever. Out loud, Sally said, 'You wouldn't dare!'

Victor lifted his hind leg, 'You want proof?'

Salle shook her head. *One ruined dress was enough. If she agreed to a joint review, at least she could spare some of her favourite pieces from the frog's clutches.* 'IF I decide to let you anywhere near my clothes and IF I decide to allow you to advise me on which unfashionable items I could do without, then I decide IF I can or cannot live without them. And you will just comment and not destroy on sight, deal?' Sally tried to extract an agreement.

Victor nodded and tried to cross his fingers behind his back.

'And whatever I want to keep, I keep,' Sally said.

We shall see about that. Later. Tumble-drier accidents do happen. Out loud, Victor said, 'Sure, sure, now show me the stuff.'

Two hours later, Victor observed the carnage. Sally was passed out on top of her bed from all the anger, fighting and general hyperventilation over which clothes to keep and which to bin. When Sally had suggested they at least give the dated clothes to charity, Victor had reassured her that any self-respecting hobo would not be caught dead in what she was planning to bestow on them. Burning them had been his first choice, but he had no desire to find out how cops would react to a burning pyre in the middle of Gaian Manhattan.

The frog dragged the duvet across the girl. It was time to go inspect how his other charge, Charlotte was doing, but not before he got some fresh air. The first few moths from the magenta dress had unfortunately not been the last. Victor cracked a window for Sally. He hadn't fought her this far only to have her suffocate in her sleep on naphthalene.

Victor looked at the watch dangling from the tiny silvery chain around his neck. Between now and the morning, he had eight or nine Gaian hours to kill. This was a little more than one hour on Earth, no time at all to do anything. Meanwhile, he needed to think about different scenarios for how to lure Charlotte away from her destiny at the farm. He did his best thinking when killing something. It was time to visit Dialysis X. Time ran similarly to Gaia there. Eight hours of killing things would give him more than enough time to strategize and be back to continue taming Sally in the morning.

Someone observing an ill-lit stoop in the Village of a city strangely reminiscent of New York might have noticed a frog disappearing through a tiny green whirlpool with a small pop.

8. Guarding Grace
Gabriel

Gabriel saw Grace slip out, counted to ten and made his exit, promptly turning into a black cat to be less noticeable. The sooner she was home, the sooner he could drop the guard duty and concentrate on investigating who was after her.

Zigzagging the streets after her peppermint scent and shapely legs, Gabriel concentrated on his daily deductions. A day of observing anyone was usually indicative to reach a conclusion about who might possibly bear a grudge.

The only person in the coffee shop who didn't seem to be happy with her was her uncle. The rest of the customers, most of them regulars, did not exhibit any animosity towards her, quite the contrary. Grace always seemed to have an extra bun or cup of coffee for the elderly and a kind word for the surly teenagers. Undoubtedly, her uncle considered this kindness as wasteful and slacking, both eating into his profits, which was what made him grumpy. To his face, Grace tolerated his moodiness with smiles and kindness. She only occasionally banged her head against the wall in the kitchen afterwards. Gabriel concluded that even when nobody was watching, she preferred to bang her head instead of spitting into the coffees of rude people, which included uncle Tom.

Sneezing into his whiskers from the street dust, Gabriel followed Grace around the corner. After a day of observation, he found himself looking forward to spending an evening with her, getting to know her better. This girl was somehow the embodiment of all that was good, all that was worth living for, before the Crusades, before the horrors of the Middle Ages, before the envy and the greed took over. She was good through and through. Today, when she had taken a stroll around the block on her lunch break, Gabriel the cat had seen her stop to talk to a busker. The passers-by kept throwing coins into his satchel as she chatted to him about his hopes and dreams and encouraged him to keep playing at bars and other venues. When she finally said goodbye, she slipped him a five-pound note. The busker had looked after her as if he had seen a ray of sunshine.

Ducking a delivery boy intent on stomping on his tail, Gabriel recalled that the only person in the diner who she didn't seem to like was himself. Being liked had never bothered him. He could and would save beings from any dimension whether he liked them or not. It was rational to assume that it didn't matter whether his charges liked him back.

Still, for some strange reason it bothered Gabriel that he was the only customer Grace treated with coldness bordering on open hostility.

He suspected that after her relationship with Victor she distrusted single men being nice to her. *Who could blame her.*

Seeing Grace pause at her doorstep to fish for her keys, Gabriel ducked and clung to the wall. Making his way up to the window was arduous work on a full stomach. Gabriel persevered in cat form, assuming that neighbours would find cats climbing through Grace's window less suspicious than a grown man doing so.

He only remembered to turn back into the right kind of orange tabby when he caught his reflection in the window. Her hostility was distracting.

Gabriel decided that hostile or not, it didn't matter. The save wasn't complete until he found the culprit. The Watchers had found out nothing during the day. The Agency screens left no clues about the faceless assassin. After Grace fell asleep, he would have to do some leg-work, investigating in person where the shot had been fired from, with what, and, of course, by whom.

9. The Case of the Mysterious Ficus
Lanie

At the hospital, days turned into nights and nights turned into days with unwavering consistency.

A few days after the accident, Lanie felt a disturbance in her usual calm and saw a team of medics rushing into a room. Peeking over the threshold, seconds after the recognisable sounds of electrocution she saw a light wafting from the body of the old woman she had attended to just the evening before. The old dear waved at Lanie.

Lanie waved back. Then the strangest thing happened. A tiny fairy with translucent pink wings popped out from behind the old dear and across the room looked sternly straight at Lanie. She blinked away the accusation of not belonging there. The old lady took the fairy's hand and sped away to pastures new in a puff of light.

In the evening, long before it was bedtime, Lanie thought of Peter. She couldn't explain it, but it was he who was holding her here, allowing her to help him and other people, which is all she had ever wanted to do, really.

She smiled and appeared out of thin air in an empty room.

It was definitely Peter's room. The tubes were gone. The bed was made.

When she asked about him at the nurse's station, they told her he had woken up in the morning, they had conducted some tests, found him healthy and released him half an hour ago. One of the paramedics had volunteered to drive him home.

Lanie closed her eyes and thought what it would have been like, if she had been the one to take him home instead. She opened her eyes to a tastefully decorated living room. A white cat hissed at her, yowled and raced away.

As she followed the kitty into the kitchen, she understood the lament. Its huge feeding bowl was empty.

The cat sat in front of the bowl and looked at her reproachfully, every last hair on its tail puffed out.

Lanie poured a large dose of dry cat food into the bowl.

The cat didn't budge.

Right. If that bowl had been full of dry tit bits and the cat had lunched on that for nearly a week, no wonder it demanded some pampering. Lanie checked the fridge and found something better.

The ball of white fur attacked the deli produce with vicious single-mindedness.

Lanie changed the water bowl as well and noticed that the sink had paw marks on its sides. She wouldn't be surprised if the cat knew how to operate the tap.

She noticed a photograph on the fridge. Peter. With the white fur ball.

This was Peter's apartment.

Lanie walked around, taking it all in. A typical London bachelor's pad. Black and white decor except for the dark brown leather sofa, a couple of expensive-looking paintings, a few flashes of red and gold here and there. She thought that a bookcase in the corner of the living room and a potted plant on the window sill would make it cosier. In the enormous tiled bathroom she fantasised where her shampoos and toothbrush would fit.

As she was peering out the living room wall-to-ceiling window at the regal park below her, Lanie heard the scratch of a key.

Peter backed his way in through the front door, laughing and saying goodbye to someone.

As he turned, they both froze on either side of the foyer.

'Who the hell are you?' he asked sternly. The girl didn't look like a dangerous coke-head or a burglar, but she was in his apartment, uninvited.

The cat pranced to Lanie's side and sat down.

A woman stepped out from behind Peter. It was the same paramedic who had evicted Lanie from Peter's room. 'I know her. She's a volunteer at the hospital.' For some strange reason the woman was completely unwilling to volunteer the fact that this girl had dragged Peter from the river. The paramedic saw the cat, saw how close Lanie was to tears and tried to piece it all together, 'She is here to feed your cat.' The woman looked around and saw the spare keys in the bowl next to the front door. 'She probably took your keys to get in and then used the spare ones, returning yours.'

The cat leaned into Lanie's ankle and started to purr.

Peter smiled and stopped to pet the cat, 'Anyone who gets that kind of treatment from Kitty could not be a bad person.' Kitty's former mistress, on the other hand, had been a bad person. What else would you call someone who had adopted Kitty in an attempt to move in with him, but had left the critter behind as soon as he had told her he didn't see a future for them.

The paramedic made a face, 'Please, cats would be nice to anyone who feeds them.'

Kitty gave her a contemptuous look that suggested she should know better, turned and headed for the living room couch.

With peace established, the paramedic started to go, thought the better of it, turned, and kissed Peter on the mouth. Hard. She threw her parting shot straight at Lanie, 'See you later, gorgeous. You have my number.'

Unfazed, like pretty women smooched him all the time Peter closed the door, dropped his keys in the bowl next to his spares and turned to look at Lanie properly.

A strange girl in his apartment. A five feet three inches tall, cute brunette with eyes the colour of the Caribbean sea. Correction, a barefoot, cute, tiny brunette with those turquoise eyes in his apartment, but a stranger nevertheless. A stranger, he reminded himself, who had spared him the unpleasantness of coming home to a feral or, worse, a dead cat. 'Thanks for feeding my cat.'

Lanie smiled.

With eyes half the size of her face, she looked close to starvation herself. The least he could do was feed her before she went. 'Are you hungry?'

She shook her head.

'Thirsty?'

She shrugged.

Getting warmer, 'Tea?'

Another shrug.

Peter took off his coat and headed for the kitchen. As he passed her, he noticed the name-tag on her uniform 'Dolly'.

'Well hello, Dolly,' Peter tried to joke the girl into conversation.

He got a trusting inquisitive stare in return.

They sipped their tea in silence.

Kitty the cat got tired of waiting for them in the living room, sneaked into the kitchen and studiously ignoring Peter, hopped onto Lanie's lap. From there it jumped onto the table, plopping itself down sideways.

'Wow. Looks like Kitty has adopted you. You must be really something. She mistrusts strangers. Some days I have the feeling she doesn't completely believe she should trust me,' Peter said.

Lanie smiled. She rubbed under Kitty's jaw and the purring machine started.

'With Kitty's trust issues, I don't know how I am going to get her to like Alice,' said Peter, pouring 'Dolly' more tea.

Seeing a question in the girl's eyes, Peter hastened to explain, 'Alice, the girl who dropped me off just now, she saved me, you know. I was in a car crash. She was on the scene. Had to zap me a couple of times in the ambulance on the way to the hospital. If it wasn't for her, I would have been dead on arrival. So, when she asked me out, I didn't think it was a bad idea.'

Lanie kept petting the cat. 'Are you with Alice now?'

Peter looked up at the sound of her voice, 'You do know how to speak.' Not only that, but her voice was sensual and throaty, which was surprising for a tiny thing like her.

He offered to pour her some more tea and got a head shake in return.

On the table, the cat extended a paw with outstretched claws in his direction.

Lanie looked at the cat and then again at Peter, 'You didn't answer my question.'

Peter thought about it, 'Too early to tell...we haven't even been out on a date yet. Her driving me home doesn't quite qualify. If we start dating, I guess we might end up together...it's a possibility. I like her. She saved my life, you know...'

4. "Tea?"

The girl lowered her head and mooned over his cat. The cat was milking the attention from two humans at the table. A small compensation for abandoning it for days on end.

When the silence stretched beyond comfortable and the outside started showing signs of tiring from the day, as pleasant as the girl was to look at, Peter decided it was time to send her home, 'Shall I call you a cab, Dolly?'

Kitty hissed at him.

Moody bugger.

Dolly shrugged.

Peter was already dialling the cab company, 'What address shall I give them?'

Lanie looked him straight in the eye. Seeing those bottomless pools of despair, Peter almost dropped the phone.

'I don't have a home. I can get back to the hospital by myself,' was all she said.

The cat hissed again.

'What do you mean you don't have a home? Everybody has a home.' Peter hung up on the lad who was attempting to wheedle the address out of him.

'I don't remember,' the girl shrugged.

Looking into those green eyes, Peter realised she wasn't lying. 'If you cannot remember where your home is, why go to the hospital? Do you...live there? ...For the time being?'

Lanie shrugged again.

Sleeping at the hospital. That would explain why she was rail thin. He doubted free lunch was a perk of the volunteering job. God only knows when she had last eaten. He couldn't let her walk out of here into the night. That would be a poor thank you for taking care of his cat. Peter had a strange urge to take her hand. As he did, a sense of calm descended over him. The same kind of calm he remembered waking up with every morning.

'Why don't you stay?' Surprised at his own request, he tried to make his offer less ambiguous, 'On the living room sofa. Just for tonight? It's too late for you to go anywhere and to be honest, it's the least I can do as a thank you for feeding Kitty...?'

Lanie nodded, stood up and headed for the living room. Somehow, deep down, she knew that this was her last night with Peter. It was simple. He was alive and well. He had chosen Alice. His life was getting sorted. He no longer needed her.

As he was retrieving guest linen, he noticed an empty bookshelf in the living room and the ficus on the windowsill. Those had definitely not been there a week ago. In the bathroom he found bottles of shampoo and an extra toothbrush. Poor girl. For some strange reason, he wasn't even mad about the invasion of his lodgings. *Ha, this was probably what it felt like to live with someone - finding someone else's things among your own and not quite knowing whether you like it.*

As the house quieted down, Lanie lay on the couch, eyes wide open, nose deep in Kitty's long white fur, petting the cat that had established itself in the nook of her arm. She couldn't sleep. She couldn't remember having slept in a long while, yet she wasn't feeling tired. She had enjoyed her evening with Peter very much. There was so much she wanted to tell him, to discuss with him. She would give anything to be curled up next to him for one last time.

And so she was.

As she smiled down at his blissfully sleeping form she could see her weightless body starting to shimmer and slowly dissolve into the air. She felt airborne and free again.

Kitty was staring at her from the threshold of his bedroom door. It sat, deciding this was a more proper way to send her off.

With a final glance at Peter, Lanie let herself be carried off, away from Belsize Park and towards the obliviating unknown.

***

Out of the air, Lanie landed in a comfy leather chair in a huge office with a lazily revolving mirror. The mirror had a white and a black tally measuring something on either side. Somewhere, someone was singing something about witchcraft.[9]

The very affable man who reminded her of Morgan Freeman[10] slid the images of whatever he had been looking at on the glass surface of his otherwise formidable mahogany desk to the side, swivelled in his chair and smiled at her, 'How would you like to be a guardian angel, Lanie?'

The Boss let it sink in a bit, knowing she would say yes.

With Gabriel, his oldest and most loyal guardian angel dispatched on a long-term assignment moments ago, he would do well by training up a vanguard. Finding good souls like Gabriel and Lanie that did not join the ranks for atonement reasons was proving to be difficult in any dimension these days.

Seeing questions in her eyes, he continued, 'The perks are: a permanent job with immortality as the necessary boot. Doesn't pay much, but all your needs are taken care of. There is a retirement plan - whenever you decide to go after a minimum 200 years of service and then it's a straight ticket to the dimension of your choice. Drawbacks: you can never get in touch with anyone you knew in your previous life, but we don't have a problem there, since after the death of your parents you were pretty much a loner, except helping out in the soup kitchen. You enjoy helping people. This would be an ideal job for you. It also seems that by tending to the needy in your afterlife you have already informally started. Now, are you with me?'

Lanie smiled and nodded her assent to the terms of her employment. Something good came of bad things after all.

***

After he had dispatched Lanie to basic training with the Watchers, the greying man switched the monitor on his desk back on and enlarged the picture. He zoomed in on an old vagabond checking into a homeless shelter. The very same one that had cost Lanie her life.

It had been a means to an end, he kept reminding himself. A means to an end.

Lanie was perfect angel material. He knew he could persuade her to be an angel. All he needed for her to become one was for her to die.

So, driving a sick old man out of every safe haven he could find one night, refusing any usual good soul to give him food and shelter that day, making him desperate enough to go and take the money he needed by force was not the same as shoving Lanie against that dumpster himself. It had been an accident. A more or less planned accident, but an accident nevertheless. Who knew feeble men were so forceful in their demands when driven to starvation and despair?

It was difficult to recruit angels these days. This had simply been a means to an end.

The man shut off the monitor, catching his usual reflection of an Indian maharaja. With a quick habitual glance at the tally, he walked over to the window. The tally of white and black was almost even with the black one slightly up. What if he or any of his angels did nothing today to even it out?

From behind the clock in the Elizabeth Tower, known to all as Big Ben, the daily view of the snaking Thames on one hand

and Westminster Abbey on the other side never ceased to amaze him. Out of the real estate the Agency used, owned or otherwise occupied in London, this was his favourite. He had been right to relocate the Agency here 150 years ago, straight after the tower was built. Fitting anywhere and being an invisible part of anything had never been a problem. Neither had coming or going from the Agency to Earth or other dimensions unseen, unheard and unnoticed. People always saw only what they wanted to see.

He spun his chair, shivered and looked at the tally again, knowing what he would see. It was even. Barely. That was good enough for now.

Behind the revolving mirror he saw a grey staircase. He knew everyone else at the Agency saw the staircase leading to his office as white marble. That's what they wanted to see. White associated with the good winning, so they saw white.

Reality had a few more layers than just black and white.

On the days when good was losing, from his office the staircase looked pitch black to him. It still looked white for his guardians on the outside and thank goodness it did. He didn't need demoralised angels. The more goodness they saw and fought for, the less painful it was for them all to keep the balance.

But he could always tell, on a daily, hourly, minute-by-minute basis which one was gaining, the light or the dark side. He didn't even need to look at the tally or the colour of the staircase nowadays, he could tell by the feel of his office. Evil winning felt hot and dark and good winning felt refreshing and light.

It was the grey days, when things were even, when the air around him had the dewy feel of a misty morning, which should have made him happy.

Good will win. Good always wins. That's what his mother had taught him.

And here he was, destined to keep the balance because of what someone he had loved had believed aeons ago.

10. Cat

Grace

Grace listened intently for any mewing as she jiggled the keys in her lock. It was one in the morning. Grace was sure the critter was fast asleep. Probably on her pillow. Strays loved her lavender-scented pillows.

She pried the door open, flipped the switch and saw the cat.

It sat bolt straight, its tail curling around its hind legs and stared at her intently.

Gabriel was looking for any signs that after slaving away at the coffee shop all day Grace was dead tired and looking to just fall into bed into a dreamless sleep.

The sooner you sleep, the sooner I can get on with untangling the mystery of who is after you.

'Aww, you waited up for me!' Grace tentatively held out her fingers for the cat to sniff, a common courtesy. She had only respect for cats. They didn't really like excessive patting and scratching forced on them. Only after it rubbed its jaw against her hand did she stroke its chin.

Gabriel told himself he was just acting how an affectionate cat thankful to be saved from the streets and certain starvation would. But part of him was enjoying the attention and the touch.

Earth. To refrain from turning back into a human, he needed to get re-balanced at the Agency. *Often.*

Grace realised she had really been looking forward to coming home. 'Someone at home waiting for you makes all the difference.' Grace picked the animal up. She thought it weighed a bit more than when she had found it yesterday. The stray had been living off scraps before and had finally made it to kitty heaven of stable food supply and affection. Of course it had been gorging itself. 'My you're growing by the hour, aren't you? Good kitten!'

She put the cat down, next to its bowl. The cat pawed at the kibbles.

Gabriel looked at his reflection in the metal bowl. He had been stuffing himself all day, trying to watch over her in the coffee-shop. It seemed like he had eaten his body weight in snacks. That was the trouble with being on Earth - to seem human, he had to eat, something which he never did as an angel. At the Agency, in the eternal state of peace and bliss, there was never a need for food. In the bowl's reflection, the kitten looked like he had swallowed a miniature football. Gabriel had barely managed to wriggle his way into the apartment as the tiny crack under the window he had left open to get back was not too accommodating.

He turned his nose away from the bowl. The unappetising smell aside, kibbles was not an option.

Grace thought she saw the cat sucking in its stomach. *Must be her imagination again.* 'You know what? Something strange happened to me today,' Grace told the cat as she was biting into her sandwich. *Talking to cats was not the same as talking to yourself.*

The cat eyed her inquisitively.

'There's this guy.'

The cat perked up as if it understood her.

'Gabriel.'

The cat froze.

'I cannot quite place him, but he...kind of gives me the creeps.'

The cat looked down and put a paw over its eyes, thought about it a bit and finished the sweeping motion of washing its face.

'Well, you know I don't trust customers hitting on me,' Grace said to the cat.

The cat looked doubtful. *Had he hit on her? How? What did he do to make her think that way?*

'Well, of course, you don't know, having been adopted for less than a day...' Grace said. 'He wasn't doing anything bad in particular. No come-hither stares, no attempts at conversation or to catch my hand or any other body part. He just sat there...' Seeing the cat was not persuaded, Grace explained, 'You see, he just sat there and half-stared at me ALL day. This reminded me very much of Victor....'

Gabriel waited for the part of the story he already knew.

En route to the bathroom, Grace started switching off the lights, 'I used to have a boyfriend who had been a customer at the coffee shop. When we met, he seemed nice, at first. Later it turned out that he was....shall we say...not good for me and let's leave it at that,' she petted the kitten who had climbed the bath and was walking its precarious edge.

To console her, Gabriel put a paw out and touched her arm, telling himself this was perfectly normal behaviour for a rescued cat.

'Aww... I am glad I have such an affectionate cat,' Grace scratched him behind his ear. When the purr erupted from somewhere deep down his stomach, no one was more startled than Gabriel. He promptly shut up and nearly fell backwards into the tub.

Grace let go of her toothbrush, grabbed the cat and deposited it onto the floor, 'Safer for you there,' she mumbled through the toothpaste.

Gabriel agreed. It had taken him less than a day to adapt to a life form of his old dimension. That was fast regression indeed. He would need to go back to the Agency soon to avoid the bodily needs of cats and humans distracting him from his mission.

11. Copy Paste Jobs
Victor

'I didn't sign up to be nice,' Victor said popping his head into the Watchers' station.

'Oh?' Loretta looked at him above her horn-rimmed glasses, 'And, what, pray tell, did you think you signed up for?'

'Not this! Not another damsel in distress mission, that's just mean,' Victor complained.

'You mean being nice to a particular Southern belle you are guarding is getting to you?' the pixie smirked. 'Well, too bad. May I remind you, you are still on probation and on damsel missions of all kind until the Boss' say-so as per your original deal, so take it up with her,' the pixie was curt. No one disputed the Boss' judgement. Ever.

'Him,' Victor corrected her automatically, refusing to believe everyone saw the Boss differently, and added, 'And I will. It's about time my probation was over.'

The pixie tilted her head, 'You do know why your probation has been longer than for most guardians?'

Victor shrugged, 'Two years and counting and heck knows why.'

'Well, that for a start. Even after spending so much time at the Agency you're still...well...you, cursing and all,' Loretta said, trying to be subtle for a change.

'Don't know any other way to be and look who's talking,' Victor said, flipping drops of tea off the wall fountain, looking bored. Pixies were famous for their curses that could turn quite deadly, depending on the depth of emotion they were uttered with.

'All our other angels have adjusted just fine, except you,' the pixie poked him.

'If by 'adjusting' you mean zenned-out zombies, oh, pardon me, near-saints, then no, thank you,' Victor shuddered. 'And since I don't ever want that, I guess I'm not like other angels then.'

'You most certainly are not,' the pixie nodded, 'which is why the Boss thought she could trust you with two saves at the same time. Tell me, how fare your visits to Earth and Gaia? Feel the drain of Time as things happen five times faster on Gaia, do you?'

Victor harrumphed. 'It's a he as I have told you countless times and I suppose I have you to thank for the frog form? And you call ME vengeful?' Victor said.

Loretta nodded, 'I've only ever seen one angel that could compete with you in vengefulness and HE,' she poked him, 'nearly destroyed Earth with his dreams of justice and willingness to exploit the human condition. So we had to make a point that all Earthen religions remembered him to avoid the same mistake again.'

Victor didn't even bother swatting away the pixie's hand. It would be like kicking a child and whatever he had done in his life to women smaller than himself, he had never hit a kid and wasn't going to start now in his near-sainthood. 'Exploit the human condition how?' Victor asked, more out of idle curiosity than with any intent to follow in anyone's footsteps.

'At some point, when extolling vengeance this angel he stopped differentiating between good and evil. All it took was for some of his rescues to go awry. He took it rather personally. In time, these seeds of wrath led him to see and treat everything and everyone as just means to an end.'

Now Victor understood the frequent recalls to the Agency - to clear his head and re-base. If his underlying nature prevailed even in angelic form, then man was weak, and so was he. After all, that's what he had understood from Catholic school - temptation was all about helping someone reach for the right thing. *The question was - the right thing for whom?*

'Just so nobody ends up like him again, the Boss likes to vary the assignments. Too much specialisation is a sure way to narrow-mindedness. So, you see, it's all for a good cause,' Loretta said.

Victor harrumphed.

Loretta smirked, 'Nobody said you have to like the mission or your Charge. Is Sally getting to you?' She added tartly.

Victor harrumphed again. *It was a tough call, which one*

annoyed him more, the meek but clingy Charlotte or the opinionated stubborn Sally.

Victor huffed. 'How are these two special, then?' he asked. Thinking of Sally and Charlotte, for the love of him he couldn't figure out why were they important enough to be saved. *And such two bloody long-playing saves as well.*

'You need to rescue them from themselves,' the pixie said.

'These should be copy-paste jobs then, sweet,' Victor cracked his knuckles.

'Hardly, given how different the damsels are, but at least they are both in human dimensions. You do remember how to talk to human girls, Victor?'

'Easy as pie,' Victor nodded and noted down the coordinates.

'You wish. Remember, the save isn't complete until the Charge is absolutely safe,' the pixie said.

'I know, I know, although sometimes...ending them would be both, more just and more merciful if not for the damsel then for whoever she ends up with and her entire dimension,' Victor grumbled, thinking of Sally's unwillingness to follow his instructions without a huge fight.

'You have very interesting notions of mercy and justice,' Loretta said.

'Meaning?'

'Meaning you're rather...vengeful. Remember what you did to the *faux* Prince Charming who imprisoned the princess and tried to weasel his way into her favour so he could annex the kingdom she was about to inherit?' the pixie asked.

'Tell me, if there are frogs to disenchant, then someone has to enchant them, right?'

'You were only supposed to save the girl,' Loretta said.

'So the dude can go and try it out on another poor girl until he gets a kingdom of his own? Trust me, if he was brought up with the notion that he has claims to a throne, any throne, then he will never have given up. Now he has to actually work for it. If someone manages to fall in love with him while he's in frog form, he deserves a crown,' Victor said and threw a cup of espresso down the hatch.

'It's not your call to make,' Loretta said.

'Whose call is it then?' Victor asked.

The pixie looked at him like he was demented. 'As if you don't know.'

'Well, who died and made him the Boss?' Victor fumed.

'The previous Boss, thousands of years ago,' Loretta kindly offered, 'And technically, she didn't die, she just left to enjoy the rest of her immortality....somewhere. Back to the point, it's not your call to make and fingers crossed, it never will be,' she said.

He threw his black leather jacket over his shoulder and prepared to teleport. 'Well you or anyone else cannot make me be nice to them, if that's what it takes to get the job done,' he said just as a dark green cloud encircled him.

'Please, thank you and goodbye would be nice, once in a while,' Loretta mumbled. 'You can take the brute out of Essex and try to make him into an angel, but you cannot take Essex out of the brute,' she concluded with a snort.

'Sometimes we need a bit of a brute,' the Boss said from behind her.

'Maybe in Dialysis X, Xiaong Ra or Hel, where most of our angels would be at a loss what to do...' Loretta conceded.

'Yes, not everyone can handle the nightmare dimensions nor battling someone's worst fears as well as their own. You have to admit that on those rare occasions that we have let Victor depart from his traditional saves and let him loose there, he has come in handy,' the Boss mused, sipping on hot chocolate.

'He has, no doubt about it. It's just that when I see him relishing in the carnage and anticipating the trickery, it reminds me that within two years he has not perhaps changed as much as we would have liked him to,' Loretta sighed.

'You know beggars cannot be choosers, we take all and we need all kinds of angels, the reformed and the not so well reformed ones. Victor is useful precisely because he does not think like a completely reformed and serene guardian. The Agency simply brings out the best in all angels, so believe it or not, but the way he is, Victor is actually at his best,' the Boss said.

Loretta's mouth fell open, 'So, Victor's best is scary homicidal and use of brute force when things don't go his way, and we are ok with it?'

'At least he directs his homicidal tendencies to crisis situations and specific dimensions,' the Boss smiled, 'You have to give him points for how his ruthless calculation allows him to keep his cool.'

'But if he can be ruthless and cunning in the scary dimensions, what makes you think he won't act out in the peaceful ones?' the pixie asked.

The Boss didn't have to think about it, 'Same as everyone else, he has mandatory downtime at the Agency. He gets off on the high adrenalin of the more precarious saves before his next mission and being rational he knows full well not to enact carnage anywhere peaceful.'

'It also helps that we take it to heart to re-instruct him after he comes back from those dimensions not to use deadly force in a softie dimension,' Loretta mumbled.

'And I do appreciate everything you Watchers do for the Agency and the angels. But you do know, that while we can put them back together again when their bodies have been broken, the Agency does not offer a cure against character imperfections. There is no reforming him unless he himself wants to change,' the Boss said and turned to leave.

The Boss didn't see the glint in the pixie's green eye that didn't bode well for Victor. *Like any demand, the desire to change could be generated.* Victor needed a change of scenery. A save where he would not be able to use force. No more quick ins and outs, no more fly in, save the girl, beat up the bad guy or worse, then leave. He was already stuck with not one but two rescues where he would need to change someone's mind or life and hopefully learn something about himself in the process. She was going to teach him to be a better human even if it took centuries. With that thought Loretta got up and rewarded herself with cardamom coffee.

12. Charm School
Sally

Sally woke up, glad it was Sunday and vaguely remembering a weird dream she'd had. She had dreamt that a talking frog had caused a power cut in her apartment and tried to teach her how to dress. She stretched, yawned and opened her eyes to find a frog sitting on her night stand, inches from her face.

Sally screamed her lungs out, remembering to throw a pillow first.

'Calm down missy,' said the frog, gathering his limbs off the carpet.

'You're not real, you're not real, you are NOT real!' Sally kept saying as she pulled the duvet up to her chin.

'Well, no, I'm not. Enchanted,' the frog pointed at his body, 'remember? We discussed this yesterday. Do you often have amnesia in the mornings after consuming syrupy soft drinks with large quantities of pizza and do I need to go over everything we went over last night again?'

'Jesus, did last night actually happen? All of it?' *Including going over her entire wardrobe and binning most of it?*

The frog nodded.

Judging by her open half-empty closets and two huge black bin bags in the corner, the frog was right.

'Today, we're going shopping, so brush your teeth, grab your purse, we can get breakfast at the deli on the corner and off we go, chop chop,' the tiny green monster ordered from the floor.

'I had plans for today,' Sally said crossly.

'What, watching more slimy monsters annihilate other slimy monsters?' Victor mused.

Sally had meant to meet Harry for Sunday brunch. Judging by no messages on her answering machine, brunch was off just like yesterday's dinner. *Stinking Harry.* He was probably spending time with either his computer or another one of his flings, which made Sally madder than the frog could ever make her. That dreamy-looking geek was like honey to flies for seemingly all of the women in New York. Sally thought she could probably discount Harry from her day's plans.

5. 'Today, we are going shopping...'

'Fine, I didn't really have plans, but if I did everything every acquaintance of ten minutes suggested that I did,' Sally glared at Victor, 'then I could have been raped, mugged and killed by now.'

'A bout of shopping, is not going to end up in a mugging or rape or murder, I promise,' Victor sighed. *Not hers anyway.* Whether Victor managed to escape with his life was a different matter, judging by the crazy eyes of this fury. 'We have to get you something decent to wear,' he pointed at the near-empty closet and the black bin bags in the corner by the front door, 'and shopping will make you hungry, so we might as well eat first,' he shrugged.

Sally huffed, 'WE are not having anything or going anywhere.' Sally spat as she shuffled to the bathroom.

A minute later, Sally poked her head out and mumbled through her toothbrush,' It's a free country and you cannot make me! So far I'm the only one who knows I'm losing my mind and I'd like to keep it that way.' If this was really happening, she didn't want anyone to notice she was talking to...critters... like that girl from Enchanted when she had surfaced in New York.[11] Then again, good things happened to that girl later. Like hooking up with McDreamy from Grey's Anatomy.

When she angrily brushed her teeth, it dawned on her that she might be dreaming. This was all just a dream. And in dreams one could do whatever they wanted. In dreams, one could even go on a shopping spree and take fashion advice from a frog.

When Sally emerged twenty minutes later, still in her pyjamas, she thought that if she was going nuts, she was going to go nuts in style, 'So, since you're a self-proclaimed fashion consultant, what, pray tell, do you recommend that I wear – from the remains of my closet - to go shopping with you today?'

'Something simple and with pockets,' the frog stated, resolute. 'Simple because you're going to be trying on a lot of stuff in a lot of places and pockets so that I could come along to the dressing booths without hassle.'

'It's the 21st century, no self-respecting woman wears anything with pockets. You'll have to settle for the tote,' Sally threw back, just as resolute.

Mumbling that 'no self-respecting woman would wear anything Sally ever did,' the frog leaped into her closet.

'This, this and this,' he said pointing at her favourite jeans, a sky-blue T-shirt and an ornate leather belt, 'It's the best that I can do, from what you have. The good stuff we'll have to buy.'

Sally snorted and disappeared into the bathroom again. She would be changing in front of him when hell froze over. If the frog could talk, god only knows what else it could do, especially a frog who claimed he used to be a man once. She wouldn't put it past him to know how to operate the photo function on her mobile and then post embarrassing pictures of her on Instagram. 'You'd better not peek in the changing rooms either or else I will have to bury you then and there. Kill you and then bury you,' Sally yelled from her bathroom.

Victor was too busy picking out a tote to pay any more attention to her snipes. Now, bags Sally was good at. Whatever sense of style she lacked in clothes she made up for in spades in bags.

He picked a green beaded roomy one and positioned himself next to it.

'Green, seriously, you're going with green? Any particular reason why?' Sally couldn't help being sarky.

Victor saw his reflection in the hall mirror matched the bag. 'Shut it, missy, it goes with your blue top. Besides, it's camouflage. If anyone sees me in it or next to it, they will either not notice or think they imagined me. Now help me in, and off we go.'

Making a face at his comment of no one noticing – *as if* – as annoyed as she was, Sally was careful when she helped the frog climb into her bag. Partly, she didn't want him ruining her bag, slimy or not. Partly, as insane as it all was, she kind of respected him for giving her sass. The frog actually had the patience of a saint. Very few people she knew would not have snarked back at her mockery. Then again, no one she knew would dare to offer her style advice either.

'People won't see me because they only see what they believe in,' echoed the bag. Sally swore loudly. What was the frigging frog, a mind reader as well?

Yes, yes he was, but he wasn't going to tell her. Freaking her out in stages, that was the plan. Victor doubted he had to freak her out at all. This one seemed to voice all her thoughts, no mind reading necessary, thank you!

'You'd better NOT come out of that bag or else....' Sally hissed. Thinking of the changing rooms again, she added for good measure, 'you'll only come out when I tell you that you can – when I'm decent, got it?'

Trying not to squash the frog - much - she took the stairs

and headed for Barneys. That's what the frog had said last night, with plenty of sarcasm of his own, 'Barneys, not the Village, darling. We need mainstream, not your usually crazy picks.'

Sunny New York greeted them with honks and litter.

***

Five hours after Barneys, they were back at Sally's apartment. She was happy as a clam and Victor was cursing the Watchers while fiddling with her washing machine. This girl was a nightmare and not just to shop with. She liked nothing he pointed out. At some point in the dressing rooms he had to resort to shouting, pointing out who was the fashion consultant and whose dress sense sucked. He was probably a few grey hairs richer. Victor had a mounting feeling of doom about taking care of this Charge. It wasn't going to be as easy as pie. Going manual never was. So it was only just that he told the Magic Wand to tell her washing machine to shrink whatever old clothes she put into it. That should take care of the remainder of her ugly clothes.

Sally put down her bags and admired her purchases. The sexy red dress matched a red polka dot vinyl bag she had rescued from the frog's clutches yesterday. The black strappy mules with tiny beaded flowers were a concession to the frog. She had positively hated all of the shoes he had picked. His choice of shoes all had spiky heels. Sally could just picture herself toppling over and landing on her face. *No way.* She had seen Miss Congeniality, courtesy of Harry and his cheesy picks on their movie nights. She knew that falling on your face could actually happen and was more likely in heels. All of the dresses the frog had insisted on were either too short or too colourful or too demure or too flirty or *too something*. The frog could have his makeover but she was not going to look like a boring clone of all those Sex and the City wannabes. She had character and her own style. It didn't matter that the frog thought her style sucked which he told her repeatedly. When the frog had suggested she try on some floral prints, she felt like shoving something heavy into her bag to silence this Laura Ashley *aficionado* forever.

As a result of such creative differences, she hadn't bought much, disproving the misconception of men - *and, apparently also male frogs who used to be men* - that women were genetically disposed to shop.

Her closet still looked like she'd been robbed.

'Now the first thing we'll do...' Victor looked around Sally's apartment. There were too many knick-knacks for his liking. '... Ok, not the first thing, obviously,' Victor pointed at the pizza box and empty cans of Sprite, 'but one of the first...' Victor pranced around the apartment, assessing what he could throw out.

Sally tried to look polite. If there was going to be any re-decorating, she was going to kill him. 'You're just thinking up ways to get back at me for not listening to your professional shopper's advice,' she said. In a perfect world, the frog would lower his eyes in shame, admit defeat and clear out of here.

Not this frog. This frog didn't have a conscience.

Done with meandering through all the rooms and stopping at a safe distance from Sally and the ever-present bottle of what seemed to be her favourite beverage, Victor announced, 'We're going to get rid of all your mirrors!'

Sally's eyes dropped to slits. 'This really is payback, isn't it?'

Sensing the murderous intentions of this girl that, oddly reminded him of a Chinese demon statue, Victor adjusted his approach, 'It's not like I'm proposing to bin or lock away all of your cosmetic stuff, which, by the way, IS classy, but you have tons of it and tons is a little bit too much, if you ask me.'

'I didn't,' Sally said.

'Don't you know the less stuff you have on your face, the better you look?' the frog pointed out.

'In which universe?' Sally asked, clutching her make-up bag to her chest. She had to admit it was a little bit on the heavy side.

'In any of them,' Victor parried. 'I can let you review your cosmetics yourself, keep the good stuff, throw away anything that is older than six months. And just to prove to you that you don't HAVE to use every little gunk that you have, we are going to TEMPORARILY get rid of all your mirrors...do you have storage?' He looked all hopeful, knowing that although Sally was pulling that mutinous mule face now, eventually it would dawn on her that he was genuinely trying to help. As long as she didn't kill him first.

'How about I TEMPORARILY kill you, frog?'

Victor sighed. 'It's all those violent movies. You've got to stop watching them. Kill this and kill that. Do I have to teach you proper conversation as well? Or send you straight to charm school?'

Sally nearly choked on her Sprite.

'And you'll have to stop drinking those sugary drinks! Have some juice or milk or if you're lactose intolerant, have water for Christ's sake! By the way, water for me would be lovely as well, thank you!' Victor grumbled.

'Jesus, you sound like my mother! If you were a woman and Jewish, you would so bond with her over bossing me around,' Sally huffed but went to get him some water. After all, he had put up with her for five hours and helped her find a new favourite dress.

'You should listen to your elders, they are always right,' the frog said, lounging on the top of her duvet.

She put a vodka shot glass in front of him, 'Don't worry, it's not what you think. It's just that my Barbie house with all the miniature crockery and cutlery is at my parents, sorry!' Sally leaned closer looking anything but.

'Fancy someone trusting you to play with dolls. I bet you used them for autopsy experiments,' Victor retorted.

'Well, I had to know how they were constructed, didn't I?' Sally said before she could catch herself. Narrowing her eyes, she torpedoed in hovering over the low-rise living room table, 'So, you being bossy and all, am I assuming correctly that you're my elder? I'm all about helping the elderly,' her voice was all honey and almonds.

Sipping his water from the edge of the glass, Victor squinted at her, 'No guessing how old I am. All you need to know is I'm older and smarter and you should listen to me.'

Sally leaned back and fluffed a pillow, 'Yes, but how long do I have to listen to you, that's the trouble. I'm just trying to figure out how long do frogs live and whether I would have to deal with frog caskets and such…soon…' Sally was looking at him evilly, 'I have buried pets before, you know…' she said.

'And I'm sure most of them were dead,' Victor nodded sagely. 'You're being rather rude, you know, considering I'm actually trying to help you,' he said, the exchange bringing back angry memories of girls rudely resisting his advances when all he was trying to do was to be generous and protective.

'New Yorker…' Sally pointed at herself as if that made all the sarcasm and quips ok by definition, 'and no one asked for your help, remember?'

Having quenched his thirst, damning this dimension of reminding him of his deeds as a human, Victor sat down and sighed, 'That's a poor excuse for behaving badly and you know it. Your mother raised you better, I hope. Or if she didn't, I will have to teach you the basics of hospitality – like offering food and beverages to guests no matter how random BEFORE they ask you for it – and polite conversation as well I guess. For instance pointing out how long I might or might not have left to live is definitely NOT polite conversation, missy,' Victor said.

Sally found that despite being told off she was actually enjoying the conversation. It reminded her of Harry, her best friend since kindergarten who had no qualms about calling her stupid to her face either. The frog was actually fun, so she decided to offer an olive branch, 'Humanity is overrated anyway.'

The phone rang.

Sally glanced at the caller ID and sighed, 'Great! It's my mother!' The girl rolled her eyes and picked up the phone.

The frog was all ears. He might learn a lot about this reluctant Princess from her relationship with her mother. Perhaps he could enlist her help and then it could go much smoother.

It was much worse than he had anticipated.

After the third 'No, mother,' Victor watched Sally put the receiver down and start filing her nails. Without hearing what the lecture was about, Sally switched to 'Yes, mother,' and kept filing. When she was done filing, she took out bright green nail polish, at his thumbs-up showed him the tongue and kept doing her nails, spicing the conversation up with an occasional 'No, mother'. The receiver occasionally emitted a more shrill tone, but eventually it fell silent. 'Goodbye, mother,' Sally said and hung up.

No wonder he had trouble shaping this Princess Charming. The girl had no support system whatsoever.

When she hung up, Victor said, 'About your mother...'

'Don't you start, at least give me a breather first, after the conversation I just had!' Sally said and poured herself more Sprite.

'You call that a conversation?' Victor asked.

'What was wrong with it? My mother got what she wanted - to tell me off for whatever it was that I did or most likely didn't do and I got what I wanted - her off my back in the record time of...' Sally glanced at her watch '...33 minutes.'

'I'm pretty sure you said 'Yes, mother' at least a couple of times. For all you know you could have agreed to do things and you don't have the slightest idea what they were,' Victor pointed out.

Sally nodded happily, 'Yep, that's how mother gets the topics for her next rant. See, everybody wins!'

13. A Good Samaritan
Grace

After her night shift, Grace hoisted the black bin bag into the alley behind the coffee shop.

It was a few minutes past midnight. One last thing and she got to go home.

Uncle Tom had left long ago. On night shifts Grace was usually the one stuck with the honourable duty to close up after they were client-free. Aside from a couple of unruly customers nursing their beers outside the bar across the street, there was nothing disturbing the peace.

Grace stepped out.

The crystal crisp air made her shiver and pull her scarf tighter. She locked the door, making sure it stayed closed. As she was depositing the trash into the bin, she heard steps behind her.

'Oy, that's the cheeky moo that thinks she'z too d'mn posh to speak to us!'

Oh-oh.

Those were the City types that had been in the coffee-shop earlier to load up on food after some drinks and before some more drinks. By the looks of it, they had had a few unnecessary beers thereafter. They were also blocking her exit from the alley.

Grace stood up straight, with her hands on her hips and faced the three leering dishevelled gentlemen, whose red faces matched the power ties that were sticking out of their pockets.

Some sobriety arrived in their expressions. They almost looked afraid.

Ah-ha! Girl power!

Grace made a face and prayed to all the gods she knew. She hoped she looked stern and menacing, except she noticed that their eyes had shifted somewhere much too high above her, even considering to which heights her frizzy hair was able to climb on any normal day.

Was there someone standing behind her?

A strange, long shadow swallowed hers whole. For a brief

moment Grace thought she saw the shadow fold up a couple of insanely huge wings. She listened intently for the whoosh and heard nothing but bottles being kicked about in a street nearby. *Her wild imagination was acting up again.*

'Is there a problem, gentlemen?'

Grace didn't have to turn around to know who it was.

Gabriel.

Grace didn't know which was more disconcerting. The fact that he had been lurking in wait for her in the dead end of the alley and she hadn't noticed, or the fact that she had recognised him by his voice, given that they had only spoken twice and she had not been very polite. In any case, not polite enough to warrant any courtesy at all.

The bully stance of the 'gentlemen' had left for parts unknown. No wonder. Gabriel was six feet four and then some while they were pudgy to the point of the gym weeping for them.

'No, mate. No problem. Just saying hello, 's all,' the bullies seemed to find the pavement awfully fascinating and shuffled off, never turning their backs.

Grace nodded her goodbyes and headed off without a word, thanking the gods for the cleared alley entrance.

Gabriel fell in step right next to her, feeling good that he had been in the right place at the right time to avert possible danger.

Grace quickened her pace, but the boy just wouldn't take a hint. *Did he expect her to go out with him out of gratitude now?*

Lordy, did she have to get out of one pickle so she could end up in another one?

She was so not letting this one walk her home. She would prefer if sicko stalkers didn't find out where she lived.

'I'll just walk you to the corner of this street so they'll think I'm walking you home and then I'll be out of your hair,' the man offered, not unkindly.

Grace swore he could read minds. *Creepier and creepier.* She wished she was home, cuddling up to her red fur ball of a cat.

Gabriel wished he could get home to be that cat sooner rather than later. His gut screamed that he needed to get to the

Agency to re-balance. His ability to read Grace's mind, even in close proximity was already deteriorating. He didn't really need it, considering how much Grace was willing to share with the Cat, but it meant he was becoming more and more human with every passing minute. Which meant his angelic invulnerability to death and maiming was deteriorating as well and this was far more significant, if he needed to rescue her again. Mind reading could also become handy if, for some reason, she couldn't communicate verbally during the rescue.

Gabriel's head tried to reason with his gut that the real reason he wanted the liberty of being a cat was because animals got much more information out of humans than humans ever suspected. The humans that talked to their pets, anyway.

He stopped a few steps after they had turned the corner, doubled back and peeked.

'I thought they only did that in the movies,' Grace said, incredulous.

Ignoring her comment, he reassured her, 'They're still there, finishing their drinks. You're safe, no one's following you.' Gabriel waved at her and started off towards a tiny side-alley that seemed to have appeared out of nowhere.

Perplexed, Grace stared after him. *Maybe she had guessed wrong. Maybe he wasn't a stalker after all. He had just got her unstuck from something that had had all the promises of developing into a rather sticky situation. He hadn't asked for her number or tried to flirt with her. Yesterday or just now.*

Maybe he was gay.

Someone sputtered and coughed loudly in the distance and made Grace hurry home.

Maybe he already knew her number and even home address. If he was a stalker.

She shook all maybes off and started reprimanding herself, 'Grace, Grace, Grace, why are you still so warped that you automatically assume everyone is out to get you? Maybe he was just a good Samaritan? Why is that so hard to believe?'

An old gentleman crossed to the other side of the street to avoid the crazy girl talking to herself in the wee hours of the morning.

She was talking to herself. Again. A sure sign of stress. Not good.

She also knew perfectly well why her gut was screaming at her that something was wrong with this guy.

Good Samaritans helped when they happened on the scene RANDOMLY and did not hang around for two days so they could make a miraculous save.

Grace took two steps at a time up the staircase leading to her door. She was glad to get out of the night and into her warm, cosy home.

'Hello, cat,' Grace said as she entered her bedroom.

The cat eyed her from the window-sill.

'I saw him again tonight. Gabriel.' Grace took off her socks, smelled them at arm's length and threw them into the linen basket. 'He turned up out of the blue and actually kind of saved me from some really unpleasant blokes. I mean I would probably been able to handle it myself,' she thought the cat gave her a sceptical look and brushed it off as her imagination playing up again, 'Well, I might have, since I kind of know them. I have seen them at the coffee shop, but the strange thing is, they have never acted this way before.'

The cat gave her another sceptical look.

'No, really, up until tonight they have always been very polite and have tipped well and haven't said one cross word to me or anyone else but each other. So whatever they were drinking must have addled their brain. Maybe they tried absinthe and it brought out the worst in them...'

The cat listened intently.

'Well, I don't know what got into them, but Gabriel stepping in was handy. Maybe he isn't the sicko stalker I pegged him for?' Grace said cheerfully.

The cat wagged its tail once.

'Hey, don't judge. You've never been stalked...' Grace said and remembered that some neighbourhood boys had a fondness for chasing after cats, 'or maybe you have, but I'm telling you, the way he was holding the fort at the coffee shop the entire day yesterday was strange to say the least, if not down-right suspicious. At first I even thought he might be into drugs or an undercover cop, at best.'

The cat wagged its tail again.

Grace continued, 'Don't get me wrong, I'm glad to be saved and all...except it seemed a very strange coincidence that Gabriel just happened to be there today, in the *cul-de-sac* alley behind our cafe, well after hours but at the exactly the right time to step in. If he was waiting for me on purpose, maybe he IS a stalker, after all...' Grace said.

Gabriel sighed. The charges often tried to figure things out themselves. It was usually easier to tell them, if angels had to reveal their presence or gain their trust. Gabriel knew talking cats would look normal in the Enchanted dimension and in the Magic Kingdom, but not on present-day Earth. When in cat form, he had to endure and let the girl muse.

Grace thought she had just heard the cat sigh and wrote it off as her tired mind playing tricks on her, 'And just as I thought that I was safe, it was out of the frying pan and into the fire. I thought he was going to want to walk me home and maybe invite himself over. Except he escorted me only until the corner of the nearest street and then just...walked off, saying good-bye, of course.'

Gabriel was tempted to look at his watch, hidden under the fur. Instead, he looked at her wall clock. It was close to one in the morning again. He had to get a move on if there was any investigating to be done tonight. Last night he had turned up empty.

Maybe some misdirection would stop her from talking until the morning?

Gabriel did what cats do best - flopped on its back and produced its belly for scratching. *Perfectly good cat behaviour.*

Grace smiled and reached for him, 'I mean, he didn't even offer to walk me home or ask for my number or anything. Why lurk around until closing if you don't even ask the girl for her number, not once? Not yesterday. Not today. Gods only know how long he had to wait. No, really, why wait until closing, save the damsel in distress and then not make a move?'

The cat looked as perplexed as Grace felt. *Being a Knight in Shining Armour and saving her wasn't enough? She wanted him to be a Prince Charming? To save AND make her life all better? There was a good reason why he let others take the Prince Charming assignments. The girls always had too active an imagination. Over-thinking things.*

Taking the cat's silence for agreement, Grace said 'Exactly' and headed for the living room, with Gabriel in tow.

Grace turned the kettle on.

Tea. This was going to take all night.

Deciding to up the ante on the misdirection and distraction front, hoping this would take her mind off things, Gabriel rubbed its side against her legs and started to purr.

'Aww...that's sweet...' Grace buried her fingers into his soft coat. 'So was he. But maybe this is how he operates? Stalks you and saves you and leaves you wondering and then reappears, waiting for the girl to fall at his feet?'

The cat looked like it was about to bite her. *Did he really look like that kind of a guy?*

'Well, I don't think he's that kind of a guy. Because although he kind of acts creepy, there is something about him... I think I can trust him, you know...? Which is, of course how serial killers lure you in,' Grace concluded.

The cat wagged its tail and hopped on the opposite side of the couch. Gabriel missed short-term assignments. When you swept in and saved the day, you didn't have to think about how to make your charges trust you. They were grateful to be saved. Trust was assumed.

'If he were a serial killer and I'm not saying he is, but if he were, wouldn't he try to strike up a conversation and insist on walking me to my door, instead of vanishing mid-walk?' Grace mused. 'Unless he is a proper stalker and already knows where I live...' she said to the cat. It didn't seem like she was holding the conversation up all by herself. The cat was an active participant.

Gabriel thought he heard something outside and turned without trying to alarm his charge. He had to remind himself that he had to keep a lookout even at night.

Grace saw that something outside had caught the cat's eye. Probably a bird. The cat was just being a cat, looking out of the window. '...I kept checking all the way back to the house and I don't think he followed me.'

The assassin, however, might have done exactly that. Gabriel had to check out the surroundings. He hopped on the window sill.

'I'm pretty sure he didn't follow me,' Grace said, trying to reassure the cat, really.

It was a good thing he had transformed into different kinds of cats to escort her. The girl's instincts were good. Not about him being a serial killer, but she was spot on about someone following her. It was laudable for Grace not to trust people who behaved oddly. Still, this meant it was going to be difficult to get her to trust him. She already suspected him for a stalker. He had to make himself either a less visible presence as a cat or a rationally explained and friendly presence as a human. Or both. Soon.

'I would have spotted him anywhere, I'm sure of it. He's very hard to miss, tall, blond and handsome,' Grace told the cat.

The kitten stopped making goo-goo eyes at the pigeons outside and sat up straight.

Please say you trust tall, blond and handsome.

'Nowhere as lovely as you, of course,' Grace said.

The cat put a paw on her hand.

To Grace, somehow, that felt very reassuring, but it was also an oddly human thing to do. Grace scratched the cat behind its ear and the purring machine started again. 'Anyway, if I didn't think he was a stalker, given the fact that he kind of rescued me, I might be interested.'

The cat withdrew the paw. The purring stopped.

'Might, I said might, the jury is still out on this one,' Grace quickly corrected herself and patted at her lap as an invitation.

The cat shifted from paw to paw, thought better of it and gently found itself a place on her right thigh closer to her knee. He told himself that this was a better vantage point to keep an eye on the windows than the floor. *Or the couch. Or the windowsill.*

As Gabriel lay there, he allowed himself to relax a little when the girl stroked him. She had a gentle touch, not like some of his previous charges. He hated when people used too much force when patting him and animals in general. Through half-closed eyes, Gabriel kept a watchful eye on the room and beyond. With shooters and guys accosting her, one never could tell where the next tribulation would be coming from.

It was the evening of day two, well, actually, the very early morning of day three, and he was still nowhere in terms of figuring out who wanted her dead and why.

His investigation so far had given him nothing. When he had inspected where the shots had been fired from, all he had found was an automatic but professional, remotely controlled gadget. No fingerprints, no nothing. Maybe some kids had bought this online to try and have some fun and it all had been an unfortunate incident and not an assassination attempt after all?

Except, with a bullet aimed at her head at her precise height, he was sure that in the alley she had been the target. He had considered whether she could have been mistaken for one of her neighbours, disposing his or her garbage. A quick nightly prowl through the bedrooms and a visual approximation of height measurements of all dark-haired girls in her building and those adjacent confirmed what he already knew. There was no mistaking Grace for anyone else. Last night, two apartments had been empty, but a quick chat with the neighbours during the day on the pretext of purchasing a property in the area had revealed that single men lived in those remaining two apartments and none of them looked anything like Grace.

Gabriel had concluded that the assassination attempt on Grace had been personal. Which left him on 24x7 bodyguard duty, not much time to investigate and a whole lot of time to think.

According to Grace, this evening's altercation with the bullies had been strange. Gabriel wasn't sure this qualified as assassination attempt number two, but he was willing to seek out the lads and check. Tomorrow. While she was safely tucked away in the coffee shop, serving customers. If this had been another attack, he would also need to escort her home the next evening. Bad things usually came in threes.

Tomorrow he would also come up with a good story why he had been there all day yesterday and tonight after midnight. When his charges trusted him, they told him things, which made the saves so much easier. The faster she trusted him, the more she would tell him, the faster he would figure out who was after her, eliminate the threat and be done with this mission.

14. Angels and Residents Only
Victor

Victor appeared out of thin air in Tempest, a few streets from Aunt Mae's. The parking sign read 'Angels and residents only'. *Loretta and her pranks.* A Harley gleamed up ahead. Not his Harley, but he would soon rectify that situation.

All was quiet as it should be this close to midnight.

Victor groped around his neck. *Got it!*

The trinket caught in his palm - a tiny silver bike - emitted a low hum.

First things first. Victor lowered the toy bike onto the pavement. It looked squashable next to his giant biker boot. Victor glanced around, making sure no one saw him and pressed a button on his watch. A puff later, the bike was at its normal size.

He mentally thanked Loretta for her step-by-step transformation help. Had the bike transformed back with him, still dangling from the chain around his neck, he could potentially have looked as ridiculous as someone whose tongue had become stuck when licking an ice sculpture. He loved his bike but not that much.

Loretta had done an unusual kindness for a pixie. *Or maybe the pixies were a lot more misunderstood species than anyone knew.*

This sleepy street smelled of lilacs. A lazy bark up ahead was echoed by a couple more further away.

Victor looked at his bike. There was nothing to be done. He had to make an entrance.

Kicking it into gear, he roused the neighbourhood dogs who voiced their disdain together as if they had been a pack.

Charlotte heard Victor before she saw him. There was a distant rumble of what could only have been a motorcycle.

The devil was back!

She hopped up so quickly that she almost spilt her tea. Aunt

Mae raised her head from the crochet and tut-tutted at her.

'Visitors!' Charlotte exhaled, realising she had been waiting for him to return all day.

'Visitors? At this hour? That ain't proper.' Charlotte's joy ricocheted off her Aunt's resolute expression and the girl's face fell.

Aunt Mae carefully set her doily aside and went to the window. Peeling back the lace` curtain, she spotted the young man who had delivered Charlotte to her doorstep this morning coming up her garden path.

Ah.

'You can say hello on the porch, but please remind your friend that he should visit at more suitable times, when the day is still young,' Mae relented.

Charlotte nodded quickly and opened the door before Victor could even knock, 'Hello, I've been expecting you.'

Behind her she heard Aunt Mae hiss her disapproval at this admission she thought no young lady should ever make. Charlotte didn't care. She bounced in for a hug, surprising the heck out of Victor.

As he disentangled himself from his charge, Victor's stomach growled.

'Oh, where are my manners...would you like some refreshments?'

He would like a raw steak and a bowl of fries with ketchup, but he'd take whatever she would offer, 'Yes, thank you, that would be lovely.'

Remembering what Mae had said, Charlotte was pretty sure auntie would mind Charlotte letting Victor into the house, 'Why don't you make yourself at home on the porch and I'll be right back.'

Victor nodded. He didn't feel like making polite conversation with the auntie anyway, no matter how great she was.

He leaned into the railing of the porch and admired the stars. In Hyperion dimension he could hop from one star to another through hyperspace, which came particularly handy when chasing space bandits.

'They look like tiny fireflies pinned down, don't they?' Charlotte asked setting down a tea pot and a plate of savouries.

Victor harrumphed. 'Fireflies...I would expect girls to compare stars to diamonds.'

Charlotte handed him a sandwich she had rustled up. Victor attacked it with savage single-mindedness and stopped mid-bite. He didn't want to scare the girl. *Smaller bites, smaller bites.* He had to remind himself that that's what a proper Southern gentleman, well, *any gentleman* would do.

Charlotte tried not to laugh and pretended she didn't see anything, 'Well, I like comparing things to other things I have actually seen and I have never seen a diamond before...but I have seen fireflies on a hot midsummer night.'

Victor nodded, chewing. His stomach was easing up. *A girl who had never seen diamonds. Fancy that.* 'Well, they are like tiny shards of glass...'

'Stars?'

'Diamonds.'

She really wanted to ask him how come he knew and whether he had bought or given anyone something with diamonds in it, but she didn't really want to know the answer.

'I expect you have settled in nicely with Mae?' Victor asked.

'Yes, thank you for driving me this morning!' *And for saving me from most certain death!* Charlotte looked up, saw Victor glancing away and concentrated on playing with the tassel of the cushion on the porch swing.

How on Earth was he going to make her save herself and go to Italy? Before she changed her mind. Before she ended up back at the farm and back in front of a pitch fork.

A gust of wind ruffled the pages of the binder Charlotte had removed from the table to the swing and Victor automatically reached out to prevent it from scattering.

Half a page sticking out from the binder showed what he thought looked like a tail and a scaled paw. 'May I?'

Charlotte turned red but did not object.

Victor slid the page loose. A dragon in pencil was staring at him, looking half-alive. It could have been a not-too-distant cousin of the one he had killed just last week in the Xiaong Ra dimension.

Charlotte, still blushing crimson, shrugged, 'I had a bit of time on my hands...so I drew...'

This charge had hidden talents. Maybe this was her calling? Illustrator? Artist? This was definitely to be encouraged. 'It's a good likeness.'

Charlotte looked at him strangely. *What an odd comment to make.* 'Seen many, have you?' She could hear Auntie Mae tut-tutting at her mentally, for using sarcasm with a gentleman.

Damn, he had forgotten himself. 'Pardon me. I simply meant it looks lifelike. Good proportions, something that could have actually existed. And he has character.'

Charlotte glanced over his shoulder to see which one of her dragons he was looking at, 'Are you sure it's a he? Maybe it's a she?'

6. "Are you sure it's a he?"

Victor looked again. The dragon was not displaying any gender denominations. 'By the way HE is holding his head... this is clearly a battle stance...and look at his claws...no self-respecting female dragon would ever allow them to be so... unkempt.'

Charlotte giggled, 'Well...in battle it doesn't matter whether you are a male or a female dragon...apparently, females are even more vicious, so SHE could be a battle dragon...as for the claws... who are we to dispute what is dragon fashion?' She couldn't stop giggling. *This was such a silly conversation. She hadn't had silly conversations like this...well...ever.*

'Well, for me to be absolutely sure, I would need to see a comparison...draw me a male and a female one...tomorrow.' Victor rose to leave.

Charlotte was selfishly wishing he would not go just yet. Despite the long day he must have had. Seeing the fatigue in his face, she decided that since he had been chivalrous to come visit despite being tired, then she could be less selfish and let him go. *For now.* 'Yes, tomorrow. Thank you for visiting.' *And for saving my life.* 'Please come again.' *Soon.*

'Before I go...'

Charlotte's heart skipped a beat.

'When you say your dream is to go to Italy, how bad do you want it?'

Very. Charlotte's face must have telegraphed as much because Victor smiled. 'Then perhaps you should consider gainful means of employment and start saving up for that ticket,' Victor winked and bowed out, leaving Charlotte waving enthusiastically.

Auntie Mae observed a biker with an unruly Italian mop of hair bow like a proper Southern gentleman and walk curtly to his hell machine. The ratchet he made riding off into the sunset reminded her of aeroplanes flying over their fields in England during World War II.

At the end of the lane, Victor rode his bike through a wormhole straight into Gaian New York and materialised there as a frog.

15. A Secret Network of Cats
Gabriel

When Grace left for work the next morning, Gabriel followed suit. Day three of guarding Grace and he was getting good at climbing in and out of windows.

Gabriel escorted Grace to the coffee shop in the guise of various different cats to make sure she was not in any danger. He transformed back behind the dumpster in the back alley and waited for the familiar chime of the doorbell.

On autopilot, his hand reached for the sword between his shoulder blades. When his fingers grabbed air, he had to remind himself that here he was human. Swords and wings were present, but in another dimension, invisible to the eyes of locals. At least while his immortality shield was fully functional.

Before going in, he made a mental walk-through of his cover story. Right, the day he had spent at the coffee shop was his last day of freedom before starting work. He worked in the City, had gone out with his new colleagues yesterday, was passing by after midnight and had just happened on the unpleasant situation. This morning, he was here to get his coffee before heading into work.

There was only one slight problem with that scenario. He was still in his jeans and T-shirt.

Gabriel looked around for a door. Any door. He had already been in touch with Loretta and she had promised to provide.

He opened a door to what looked like a vegetable cellar and saw that a grey suit was hanging off a rusty nail.

Trust a pixie to come up with something like this.

Gabriel got dressed. The sky-blue male noose was slightly choking him, but his disguise had to be believable, so a tie was a must.

He was not going to spend all day smelling like cabbage. For a brief second he enveloped himself in a cleansing light.

Better.

The bell of the coffee-shop announced a new customer.

Grace looked up and saw her saviour from last night.

Gabriel was back, barely recognisable. He was suited up, his longish blond hair slicked back and what looked like a laptop bag dangling off his shoulder.

Good lord, he was one of those City boys!

As she plastered on a smile reserved for all customers - vacant but nice - Grace gleefully noted that Gabriel looked like he was not quite on friendly terms with the tie around his neck.

'Morning, Grace,' he said.

'Morning,' she chimed back, horrified at how fake chipper she sounded. *What's wrong with me? Maybe I'm just not good around would-be stalkers.*

'May I have one coffee with milk, no sugar, to go, please? I think I might be running late on my second day to work. The drinks last night until the wee hours of the morning with my new colleagues in a bar nearby didn't help.' Gabriel brushed back his already slick hair.

Grace busied herself with heating up the milk.

Drinks with colleagues after his first day at work. That was why he had happened to save her last night. So, perhaps not a stalker.

She realised she hadn't thanked him for saving her. 'Thank you!' she blurted out, sticking out the paper cup in his direction.

Taking his coffee, Gabriel smiled at her and Grace sucked in some air.

The smile on that man made her want things long forgotten.

'I thought it's the customers who usually say 'thank you' or is there something about this coffee shop that I should know?' he said and smiled again, concern in his piercing blue eyes.

Drawn to the icy-blue sparkle, Grace leaned towards him into the counter, unable to help herself. The smell of fresh daisies and sunshine made her dizzy. 'Uh, what?' Inwardly, she cursed.

How very eloquent. Seriously?

'You thanked me while I'm pretty sure I am supposed to be thanking you for my daily dose of coffee,' the guy looked amused and completely unaware of the effect he was having on her.

Grace thought she must look like a total ditz and cursed herself some more. She exhaled, regaining her wits, 'Thank you for saving me yesterday from those guys. I don't think I ever thanked you.'

Properly.

As that word echoed in her brain, she felt herself go hungry and not for food.

On the radio, a duet was trying to convince themselves to take it slow, that they didn't need to rush this, but just a kiss in the moonlight would be grand.[12]

Grace wanted to throw something at the radio for taking her own thoughts a notch further.

'My pleasure. Happy to help. I figured that since I kind of knew you, after spending my last day of freedom here, then looking out for someone who was kind enough to feed me all day was the least that I could do.'

Another perfectly reasonable explanation why he had camped out here all day two days ago. She wouldn't have chosen to spend her last free day in a random coffee-shop on the outskirts of the City, but that was her. So, just another City boy, maybe not a stalker after all.

This did not quite explain the lusting, but Grace was willing to cut herself some slack for now.

She noticed he was holding out his hand and realised he had been holding it out for a while. There was money in it.

He wanted to pay. And leave.

'It's on the house, Gabriel.' *That's the least she could do, right?*

He smiled again. She knew he would, which is why she had said his name. Maybe the lusting wasn't going to cut her any slack back.

'You remembered my name.'

She nodded.

Gabriel nodded back and turned to go, 'See you, Grace!'

She certainly hoped so, 'Bye!'

Leaving the coffee shop Gabriel briefly wondered whether Grace hadn't thought anything bad at all or if two days and full nights as a human had eroded his mind-reading skill and, consequently, his immortal protection and cloaking abilities.

Just in case, before he could recharge, he decided to stay in cat form. No *explaining necessary, should the hilt of the sword or tip of the wing show.*

Doubling back to the alley, Gabriel opened up the cabbage cellar to deposit the laptop bag. Besides the familiar waft of rotting cabbage, he was met with a loud ticking noise.

Gabriel saw the number 60 turn to 59. Without thinking, he grabbed his tie-pin, broke it in half and threw the incendiary device into the portal that opened and closed like a fish's mouth, destroying most of the evidence of assassination attempt number three.

By the look and weight of it, in less than a minute this little package would have wiped out the cafe and half a block of buildings around it, qualifying as a mere kid's firework in the Dialysis X dimension where he had sent it.

Gabriel shrunk into a grey tabby with white paws and wagged his tail in annoyance.

That had been close.

The bullet had been personal. The bullies, if that was, indeed, attempt number two, had also been personal. The bomb was a definite attempt even if it didn't fit the profile of a personal attack.

Had Gabriel not opened the door to the cabbage cellar the minute that he had, he knew precisely what could have happened.

Kaboom!

No Grace.

Gabriel himself could always be resurrected at the Agency within 72 hours after dying, provided there was at least something left of him.

Someone really wanted this girl dead.

Only a very unscrupulous or desperate character would wipe out a cafe full of customers in mid-London in the morning rush hour to get to just one girl.

Hearing uncle Tom's dulcet tones escaping the kitchen hatch, Gabriel the cat considered whether Grace and her entire remaining family were the real target. *Two birds with one stone.*

Stranger things had happened in his 12th century because of sizable and not so sizable inheritances.

Perhaps he was looking at it all wrong. Perhaps Grace's attempted murder had been only the beginning.

Conquer and divide. First, he would enlist Loretta to do some digging for him on the backgrounds and whereabouts of the bullies from last night. Gabriel dialled the Agency. That pixie could find fleas on a dog blindfolded with things screaming at her across five dimensions. She could do wonders in one 48-hour shift at the Agency. He could have an answer by the evening.

It was a good thing time flowed differently at the Agency compared to the dimensions it served. He was sure Loretta would be able to help him while only a few Earth hours snailed by.

All he heard in between his explanations was 'uh-uhs'.

'You'll have all I can find by the end of the day,' Loretta said before she hung up on him without even a 'goodbye'.

Gabriel sighed. Had he wanted grace under pressure, he should have phoned Daisy. Many mistook her efficiency for deliberate rudeness, but Gabriel knew better. He was sure the pixie would burrow in and leave no stone unturned in the lives of those bullies.

Meanwhile, he was going to investigate uncle Tom. Judging by his character flaws, it wasn't entirely out of the question that someone might wish him dead.

***

Looking at his mirror, next to which a tally of white and black was hovering at a flimsy balance, the Boss was reminiscing. He remembered recruiting Gabriel, one of the few guardian angels who had not joined to atone for their past misdeeds.

On the ancient radio sound system the Boss loved so much Robbie Williams was singing how an angel was contemplating his fate[13]. That's exactly what Gabriel had been doing when he had been called.

July 4, 1187.

The boy he had slain had been crying for his mother in the blood and the mud at his feet. The knight had looked at the pleading eyes, made a sign of the cross, nodded and drove his sword into the boy's heart on that hot July afternoon. A mercy kill.

Gabriel had followed Guy of Lusignan, the King of the Franks to the Holy Land. Trapped on the plateau near the village of Meskana the Frankish rearguard troops had been going without water for days until they broke through to the springs of Hattin. Here, their horses cut down by Saladdin's archers, they had been forced to fight on foot. Gabriel was leading the charge against the enemy, his men following him, still believing they could win, despite the odds. They had all seen worse. Until this youth of all but 12, dead at his feet.

Kneeling next to the tiny corpse amidst this massacre of the dead and the dying, Gabriel rested his head on the bejewelled hilt of the sword and looked up to his God. 'I haven't come here to kill children. How can children be infidels? I want to fight for what is right. There has to be a better way than this.'

The Boss had simply provided a better way for Gabriel to fulfil his calling. Fighting for good to prevail. Doing the right thing. Doing whatever was necessary. Gabriel had offered and he had taken him up on being a jack of all trades across different dimensions, saving one life at a time.

16. Hell's Bells
Sally

Victor materialised on Sally's kitchen table next to a giant cheese and pastrami sandwich as Sally was reaching for a bottle of Sprite in her fridge. He thought about kh-khming or tsk-tsking or doing something to draw attention to himself, but decided against it. Knowing how prone she was to screaming, he hazarded a guess that she might also be prone to anger over having to clean up the kitchen floor from her favourite sticky drink.

Sally turned to find the frog leaning on her sandwich and froze, 'Eeuw! Great! Now that you pawed all over it, I'll have to make myself a new one...'

Victor pointed at the bottle of Sprite and said, 'Enjoying your chemistry lesson, are you? I thought I ridded the apartment of all your sugary drinks.'

'I restocked them while you were gone. By the way, you owe me money,' Sally opened the refrigerator and started rummaging around.

'Frogs don't have money,' Victor pointed out to her back.

'Oh, yeah, I keep forgetting you're smooching off me,' Sally said happily stacking up another sandwich. Every time her back was turned, the frog threw the least healthy bits and pieces from the sandwich into the sink.

Sally caught him fingering a slice of cheese, 'Ah-hah! Stop that! Now you've pawed all over my second sandwich as well! What does a girl have to do to get fed in her own apartment?!? If you touch my stuff one more time, you slimy little sucker, I'm calling...I'm calling takeout!' She threw both sandwiches into the trash and picked up her white cordless kitchen phone, wielding it like a Taser.

'Your powers of observation suck, I'm not slimy, which we already established when there was no slime in your handbag after our shopping trip,' Victor said calmly, nibbling on a string of lettuce. *She probably had the lining dry-cleaned anyway.* 'I'm just trying to get you to eat healthier, that's all,' the frog shrugged.

'What's wrong with my eating habits?' Sally ogled him, her finger still poised over the phone, ready to strike as swiftly as a black Mamba.

Mumbling questions about what was right with them, the frog stared at her slyly, 'How long has it been since your last date?'

Sally frowned and reached for the take-out menus, 'What does that have to do with how I eat?'

Ignoring her question, Victor concluded, 'Too long, I reckon. What about the quality of your dates?'

Remembering all her crappy blind dates where the guys had stood her up or had walked off as soon as they had seen her or had simply told her within the first five minutes that she was not what they were looking for, Sally huffed.

'That bad, huh?' Victor munched on the cheese he had salvaged from the second sandwich before its trip to the bin. 'Well, can you blame them not liking you when even you don't like you?'

The sound of a dropping phone echoed off the stony silence. Sally looked like she was close to slapping him, 'Thanks for the 'assessment', buddy, but I like myself, well, on most days, thank you very much, and there are people who like me as well. Take Harry. It's this city and these morons who have a problem with curvy girls! Well, to hell with them! They don't deserve my company anyway!' she sniffed.

Victor flinched. He had used similar reasoning with those who dared to point out that his bullying and stalking was probably not the best way to make friends or treat lovers. To which he had responded that he liked himself fine when he really didn't and that people like Grace liked him as well. Except that it turned out that she hadn't. In fact, he had over-used the same line of 'those who have a problem with me don't deserve my time and attention anyway'. He had been blaming others for not being up to his high standards because they couldn't mend his flaws. Unfortunately, the realisation had dawned on him after his recruitment, so he had no way of making it up to those whom he had wronged or find out whether someone could actually stand the changed man that he was trying to become. *If there had only been someone who could have set him straight when he had been alive. Well, he could do Sally the favour now.* 'Blaming others won't help, missy. And if you like yourself on most days, that means you don't really like ALL of yourself on ALL days. Wouldn't you rather share your life with someone who truly appreciates you, just the way you are?'

'So my entire life sucks now, is that it?' Sally was close to crying. *And the day had started out so well. Day three without the Nazi frog. Now this insult on top of multiple injuries.*

Jesus Christ!

How on earth had she gone from this to that? Women! They were all nuts.

What could he say to make it understandable to this city chick?

Victor thought a little about it and tried to put it in the language he remembered city girls speak, at least the simple city girls from London and Essex that he used to know. Hazarding a guess that this New York beauty was no shrinking violet, Victor the frog offered, 'Wouldn't you like to get back into the saddle, so to speak? I mean it's been a while, hasn't it?' He would never dare speak like this to Charlotte, but he had figured out a long time ago that Sally was no Charlotte.

'What the hell?!?' Sally anger radiated off her like red mist.

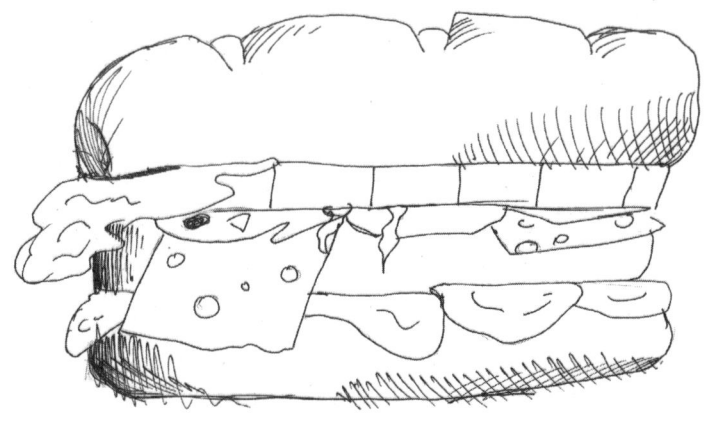

7. Sally turned to find the frog leaning on her sandwich.

Victor noted happily that at least the tears were gone, 'You know what I mean. Sex is a healthy part of life, not that you've noticed, cocooning yourself here with your world-annihilating movies.'

Sally was so scandalised she was choking on words, emitting only 'you-you' sounds. When she finally collected herself, she deflated as suddenly as she had angered. 'Why would anyone want to have sex with me, I'm not pretty and thank you for reminding me! Again!' *Dammit, she hadn't meant to sound all victimised.*

Ok, he knew she had body issues and she knew she had body issues, so there was no running away from it, but perhaps cold hard logic would work against the imminent water works, 'Even ugly people have it.'

A pepper mill nearly missed him, shattering against the wall, cracking up a tile, 'Did you just call me ugly, frog?!?!'

Victor looked at her like she was retarded, 'Doll, 'not pretty' means the same thing. You called yourself ugly first and I think you should stop doing that. Remember, if you talk bad about yourself, there are people who listen and they might actually believe you. If you don't love yourself, why should anyone else?'

Sally bent down and put her head between her legs. *Hell's bells, she looked ugly to frigging magic creatures who were telling her she was beyond hope.* 'You were gone for two days, I hoped I was rid of you. No such luck...' she said to the floor.

Victor reached out and patted her head. Carefully. He didn't want no flying lesson today. 'There, there, lucky for you I have just the perfect solution. You have to stop pitying yourself and start doing something about it,' he said.

Half an hour later, after Victor had given her the 'love yourself and practice saying one kind thing to yourself every day' and 'respect your body' talks as well as explained why sugary drinks were bad for her and why she should start eating healthy, Sally thought she had heard everything.

'You'll love the cooking channels. You're a visual learner and love TV, right? So watching TV would be the best way for you to learn how to eat healthy! And since we're on the subject of healthy...perhaps I could persuade you to go for a jog just now? Before dinner? Central Park is nice and close. I'm rather afraid about your safety if you do it later in the evening...?' Happy that he had finally gotten through to her, Victor was not holding back.

Now Sally really had heard everything.

The frog was going to make her run laps. Before dinner.

She didn't even have enough fight in her to issue a comeback on the safety point, that hers is not the one he should be worried about. As he started going over meal plans and offering other ways for her to exercise, Sally leaned into the cold comfort of her refrigerator and closed her eyes, all thoughts of food forgotten.

This Yoda was going to kill her with his good intentions.

17. The Dead Don't Sleep
Lanie

Loretta squinted her good eye at the newbie who had stumbled down the white marble staircase from the Boss' office and only then paused reality.

A pixie-sized barefoot girl, chewing on the end of a long strand of her dark curly hair stood in the middle of the Agency hall, her green eyes wide as saucers. Loretta contemplated whether to tell her to stand aside, but decided against it. *She might as well get the full gist immediately.*

Two seconds later, the girl was almost mauled down by a yeti.

The Boss sure was recruiting left, right and centre lately. How would this tiny thing ever be able to lift someone to safety? If she couldn't even stop a yeti dead in its tracks, how would she be able to stop armies to change the course of a war? Still, considering the Agency could never have too many guardian angels, maybe a pixie-sized thang was just what the doctor ordered. This one looked lost, though. Loretta gave her lip piercing a tug, adjusted her pout to make her facial expression a bit less scary - *hey it wasn't like pixies could help it...much -* sighed and went to help the newbie adjust.

Lanie was dumbstruck. Moments earlier a white fur ball the size of a small house had almost trampled her down. She also thought she saw a tiny woman with what looked like blue wings waft by. Another one, with purple wings, purple short spiked hair and what looked like quite a lot of piercings was hovering above, staring right at her. After she had accepted her new job, she had stumbled through the revolving mirror and traipsed down the staircase into this melee. Now Lanie understood how Alice must have felt going through the looking glass.

Amazed. Curious. Bewildered.

Everything was white. The staircase leading up to the Boss' office, the desks of the open-space call centre, the recreation room under the staircase, the corridors that led to gods knows where. Lanie spotted a man disappearing down one of those corridors, extending his wings mid-stride.

Wings.

Now that her job was to be a guardian angel, was she going to get wings as well?!?

Hovering inches from the dazed Lanie, Loretta got tired of waiting and gently khm-khmed. 'May I help you, sugar?' Loretta enquired as she arched an eyebrow propelling it high above her violet eye.

Lanie remembered they had had orientation in their first week at the university when things had not been very clear and that had made everything less fuzzy. 'Orientation?' she squeaked.

Loretta raised her other eyebrow over her green eye.

'Orientation around this...the Agency would be nice. I just accepted a job and the Boss was in too much of a hurry to brief me himself.'

Loretta patted her on the head, 'Oh, honey, She never ever explains anything to anyone. 'She's much too busy, not to mention important, don't you think?' Loretta explained to Lanie's goggle-eyes.

'She?' Lanie asked. *Maybe they were talking about two different Bosses? The one she had met looked male.*

'I see Supreme Goddess, you might see whatever figure of ultimate authority you worship,' Loretta said.

Well, Morgan Freeman probably had a lot of worshippers, having played God more than once. Lanie giggled. *Strange that her imagination had chosen an actor as the ultimate authority.* 'So, how exactly does this work?' she asked.

Loretta considered pairing this sweet thing off with Victor or Gabriel so she could work-shadow, but she knew full well that both of them were on long-term missions and not to be bothered for the time being. *Right, she would have to do the whole instruction herself. Fabulous.*

Seeing the face of the winged girl twist like a she had swallowed a whole lemon, Lanie did not expect anything good.

'Let's start with the important bits,' the creature briskly

pointed at herself, 'I'm Loretta. I'm a pixie. Daisy and I are in charge of fielding rescue calls to guardian angels. Daisy is the sweet one, she's a fairy.'

Since Loretta had said the word 'fairy' with such disdain, as if she had tasted washing detergent, Lanie decided to retain questions about fairies for later.

'Right, you take calls and assign guardian angels to....?'

'Charges. That's what we call those who beg to be rescued. Guardians do more than just guard, you know.'

Lanie nodded, but didn't know.

The vacant look in the newbie's eyes was a dead giveaway. *This girl had no clue.* Loretta gnawed on her lip, rolled her eyes and rattled off, 'Sometimes, what is needed is a Prince Charming...not to have and to hold, but to save and empower... get it?'

Lanie shook her head. *No, she didn't get it.* In all the storybooks, Princes Charming were the ones who rode in on a white horse, saved the day, saved the girl, married the girl and everyone lived happily ever after.

'Forget the storybooks, toots. It's a saving mission. Sometimes, we save the damsels from themselves. Restore their faith in men-kind, stress on the 'men', restore their faith in themselves...that kind of thing. We have a few professional Princes Charming on staff who can handle the disentanglement.'

Lanie looked quizzical.

'Means they don't get attached to the damsels. They just save. Get in, get out, charge saved, job over.'

That sounded a teeny bit clinical, but Lanie wasn't going to look her new gift horse of a job in the mouth.

'Then there are Knights in Shining Armour. These are even simpler than Princes Charming. We have a few professional ones and they are your basic rescue missions - from death, maiming, rape, assault, anything bad that can happen to damsels - this would be the stranger who helps them and is never seen again.'

Lanie was trying to figure out where she would fit in. She was neither a Knight in Shining Armour nor a Prince Charming.

She was really really hoping she wouldn't have to pose as a frog or some-such.

Loretta fluttered her purple wings in agitation of not having the newbie's full attention. *This one was a dreamer.* 'I assume you were recruited as a guardian angel, correct?'

Lanie nodded, 'Yep, that's my job. I know about the perks - immortality, retirement plan, etc. How about a job description?'

'Retirement plan?!?' Loretta couldn't help a snicker. 'Assuming you will ever retire, of course.'

Lanie perked up. *Oh, so the job was so much fun that she would consider never retiring?* Out loud she asked, 'Job description?'

Loretta looked at the excited newbie. *Either she was naive or she was suicidal.* Personally, Loretta thought all the guardians were suicidal even if they didn't know it. None of them ever made it beyond 500 years. Gabriel and the Boss were the only exceptions she knew. There were 63 dimensions. Anything could happen in 63 dimensions on a rescue mission. Especially in some of the wilder dimensions where some guardians ventured when the rescue missions became daily routine. Routine was a killer because it made angels careless. And that's what got them. Every time. Murder-death-kill. Inability to get back to the Agency to be revived within 72 Agency hours had taken more guardians than Loretta cared to remember. Yet she remembered every single one of them. Sometimes, the Agency was barred from reviving the guardian if the guardian had specifically given up their life not just to save someone from danger or certain death but to change the course of history, the latest case at point being their last Helreginne. Even mean-natured pixies had trouble explaining all of this to newbies. So Loretta didn't, allowing the guardian angels to find out for themselves. Eventually. The smarter ones started asking questions about why their predecessors had perished. *Too early for any of that for this one.*

Out loud Loretta said, 'Job description. Right. Take this pager,' she handed Lanie a funky pink wrist watch. 'See here, the text I page you with runs at the top. You can call me back by pressing the phone icon in the middle - if you have time and there is a need to clarify things, that is. There usually isn't.' Loretta glared at Lanie. 'If you need guidance on how to get somewhere, press the map icon in the middle, it is linked to the pager function and should pick up the address written there and link it to GPS without trouble, even across dimensions. Also works as a navigator for your transformative cocoon,' the pixie sighed, 'that's the thingy that forms around you and zaps you to other dimensions. All you have to do is think where you want to go. There are also three time zones shown at the bottom. You can adjust them to the two dimensions you frequent most and Agency time is already set. Any questions?'

'It's a smart phone with the absolutely minimally necessary functions! Thank you,' Lanie looked at the glitter girly watch like Christmas had come early.

'We call them pagers, on account of the main function that we use them for,' Loretta decided not to tell the newbie that the pager was a recycle. They always were. If she did, she would have to explain whatever happened to the previous owner of the item and she really, really didn't want to get into that at the moment. Loretta tagged Lanie back to reality from her naked adoration of her new toy, 'Your job would be to go to wherever I send you the second I page you. I can only pause reality for a short period of time, you know. If the text we send suggests there is time, only then would you have time to ring me to get the details. Mostly you just go blindly on faith to the scene to help anyone who has asked for any help.'

'That's my job - helping people?' Lanie was delighted.

'Yes, but on very short notice. Any time of day or night,' Loretta shot back. She hated doing the inductions.

'We don't sleep?' The newbie's face telegraphed genuine confusion.

Loretta looked at the tiny little lamb, 'No, honey, you're dead, the dead don't sleep.'

The poor lamb looked disoriented, so the pixie took pity on her, 'You have time off, of course and what you do when you have time off is up to you. Gabriel goes to jolly Valhalla. Victor usually goes for adventure tourism into the more...scary dimensions, like

Dialysis X or Xiaong Ra or the different variations of hell,[14] take your pick. You look like you would probably choose something more life-affirming even if tricksy like the Enchanted dimension or the Magic Kingdom or Avalon...'

Lanie's mind reeled. There really were other dimensions! She vaguely remembered the Boss mentioning something.

By now, Loretta was in auto rant mode, 'Daisy or I will call on you when you're available and IF you respond, which we surely hope you will,' Loretta made the IF sound significant enough in the hope that the newbie caught on that being on another mission was the only viable excuse not to answer, 'then you go where we tell you to go and you go from wherever you are and however you happen to look like. You'll either morph when you transport through dimensions or we provide a changing closet with more suitable attire – remember Harry Potter and the Room of Requirement – but only when there is enough time. The pager or smart phone as you named it links you to a wormhole, so don't lose it, ok?'

The clothes closet was the only thing that Lanie could relate to from her old life. *Morphing. Transporting through dimensions. Don't lose phone...erm...access to wormholes. Check. Check. Check.*

Loretta looked at her, convinced Lanie was getting everything a-ok. 'We won't usually call on you when you're in the middle of a rescue. We might when we see on the screen that you're very close to resolving the sticky situation and there is another sticky situation that warrants your attention.'

Lanie smiled, 'In the movies, the rescuers usually say, 'Listen, I really need to go but are you going to be ok now, do you have someone to look after you', yes?'

Loretta smiled, showing her pointy teeth, 'Precisely.'

Lanie braved it, 'The Boss mentioned something about prioritising certain dimensions...? Can you show me the screens, please, Loretta?'

The girl had remembered her name and she was polite. Points to the girl. 'And you are...?'

'Lanie.'

'Ok, pink-pager-Lanie, step into my office and I'll show you the wonder that is my world. Well, your world now as well.' Seeing the girl's eyes turn as wide as saucers, Loretta took pity on her. 'Since it's your first day, you can start it with a hot chocolate from the beverage machine in the corner over there.'

Lanie looked at where the pixie had pointed and didn't see a machine. What she saw was a liquid wall of what looked and smelled like coffee.

'The switch is just next to it,' Loretta felt she had given all the induction one could possibly need and stomped back to her priority screens. Reality had been frozen long enough.

At the wall, Lanie noticed there was only one button. She thought about hot chocolate and pressed the button. The wall emitted what she had asked for. All she had to do was take a paper cup from the stand and stick it under the stream. 'Cool fountain, they could use one at the soup kitchen I used to work for.'

Loretta harrumphed and mumbled something about there being too many artefacts that had changed hands across too many dimensions. Not all such 'borrowings' went well. The sale was never permanent, the artefact always returned to its home dimension when its owner died. Still, the Agency had to sustain the expenses of its angels somehow, hence the occasional peddling of artefacts.

As the pixie was showing her the 16 priority screens Lanie wondered whether 16 screens was really enough to monitor 63 dimensions. *Probably not.* Lanie realised not all dimensions were human. If these were only the priority screens....how many creatures died because there was no one to monitor and rescue them? *Probably a lot.*

Then and there Lanie decided that she was going to give up most of her free time to do her job. *If she never needed sleep anyway, why not dedicate herself to her new calling full-time? Saving more of those who deserved to be saved was a good thing.*

18. It's Alive!
Charlotte

'Hello kid, when are you moving to Italy?' Victor said as Charlotte looked up from her sketch. After spending a charming evening with Sally, he had run scenarios all Earth day and kept arriving at the same foregone conclusion. The girl needed to move countries.

How could he have sneaked up on her like this? She had totally missed the racket his bike had made. Out loud, Charlotte said, 'Oh, hello, I..erm…I didn't hear you arrive…'

Perks of materialising anywhere he wanted anytime. With all the hassle Sally was giving him in Gaia, Victor took the shortcut and just materialised behind Charlotte's house this time, leaving the bike on his chain. 'I parked further off so as not to wake everyone at this hour,' Victor said, 'then, I walked.'

On the table, lazily strewn across her portfolio of more and less vicious creatures, Victor spotted something that made his insides go cold. That triple pronged tail and that claw looked too familiar. Victor pulled the drawing by its corner. When he saw what he was looking at, his mouth tightened and he felt for a recent scar on his left arm, briefly exposing a swastika tattoo. He pulled his sleeve down to cover it up. Judging by the sharp intake of breath from Charlotte, he wasn't quick enough.

'When did you draw that?' Victor asked, looking at a red-eyed turquoise-scaled dragon. The same one that had eviscerated half of the volunteers Victor had managed to rustle up for a save in Dialysis X last week.

'Last week, why?' Charlotte asked, wondering whether there was a story that went with the tattoo and whether she had been rescued by a repenting former skinhead.

'It reminds me of someone. Did you draw this when you were particularly angry at someone?' *The thing had been vicious. He hadn't had time to get rid of the nasty scar yet.*

Making a mental note to quiz her knight in apparently not so shining armour about his strange choice of acquaintances later,

Charlotte admitted 'Now that you ask...' She blushed. *It was improper for a Southern lady to admit to be in a bad mood. Something about the devil made her tell it like it was.* 'I had a bad day last week,' *more like a bad few weeks or a bad year, to be honest,* 'So I drew a few of these overnight.'

'Show me everything,' Victor said, carefully setting the image of the now dead beast aside.

So, she did.

Victor surveyed the five drawings. Well, that probably accounted for the slew of new dragons in Dialysis X and Hel that the Watchers were grumbling about. The horn-back in front of him definitely rang a bell. Apparently, last week the dragons had just materialised out of thin air, as things sometimes did in those dimensions. No one ever wondered how or where things arrived from. Everyone at the Agency was fine with Hel manifesting everyone's worst nightmares that beings needed saving from. No one considered someone - corrections, someone's charge - may actually be the root cause of populating two of the scariest dimensions.

If what Charlotte drew came to life in other dimensions, they had a much larger problem than just saving her. He needed to save other dimensions from the darkest pits of her imagination.

Meanwhile, he had to get her to drawn nice, neutral things. Apples, tea pots, good people. A charmed life would also help. Lifting her from the farm was a good start. However, its proximity was not reassuring. She could go back there any time. All it took was one phone call from uncle Ted that he needed help at, say, harvest time. He had to put miles between Texas and this girl.

Briefly, Victor considered the easier option - letting the girl die. It would solve the dragon problem. How easy would it be to not fight for her? *Too easy.*

He sighed. Of course, he would finish the save. Perhaps her ability to draw things that came to life would come in useful for someone somewhere. Some day. Perhaps even useful for the Agency. Like Charlotte, Victor's life had not been a picnic. From early on, he had acted out, asserting himself where he could, hanging out with the wrong crowd. This one was a dreamer, she escaped into her art that just happened to come alive and terrorise. If instead of yelling at someone she drew a decapitation scene, gods only knew where and how that would play out for real.

A charmed life was the only antidote here. He had to get on with creating one for her real fast. Victor sighed again. *If he had to magick someone towards their happily ever after, he preferred to be a frog.*

Mistaking his silence and sighs for disapproval, Charlotte offered, 'I can draw other stuff, not just dragons. Tell me what you like...'

'No,' Victor said. Too forcefully, by the looks of Charlotte's trembling lower lip. 'I mean, if you're going to go to art school, they will probably start you off with boring stuff. Apples, tea pots, nice smiling people. Perhaps you should start practising drawing those first?'

'You mean like draw a hundred different takes of fruit and flowers and vary my style? Do an impressionist take and a cubist and...' Charlotte's eyes sparkled.

Victor was glad it wasn't from tears, she looked genuinely excited about the idea. 'Yeah, something like that.'

'I love the idea!' she said, jumping up and hugging him.

There really was no need for that. Victor disentangled himself carefully so as not to hurt her feelings. Getting the girl close to tears once in an evening was more than enough.

'There is going to be one problem, though,' Charlotte said slyly.

'What do you need? Art supplies? Paper?' Victor asked.

'Time,' Charlotte said and Victor tried to imagine whether he could get him on board. *Probably not.* He and Time[15] were acquaintances at best, it was Gabriel who had an in with this deity. 'I won't be able to draw too quickly, seeing how I've got a job,' she nudged Victor. 'Waitressing at the snazzy restaurant in town. They had a vacancy. Would you believe my luck?'

'Good girl, going to use your savings to buy that ticket to

Italy, are you?' Victor said and hesitantly patted her on the arm.

Charlotte instantly covered his hand with hers, 'Yes, of course! How did you guess?'

He'd been leading her up the garden path to find the solution herself. Now all she had to do was stay out of trouble and off that farm until she moved countries. He could speed up the wishing and wanting process somewhat. Tomorrow.

When hugging him goodbye, Charlotte decided to brave it. 'About your tattoo,' Charlotte pointed as Victor winced, 'You may have made some wrong choices, but you are not a bad man.' She held on just a little bit longer, tilted her chin up and closed her eyes, expecting a kiss. *That's the way it usually worked in the movies.*

Victor stepped away to be at arm's length from her. 'Thanks,' was all he said.

Charlotte opened her eyes. From the stare he was giving her she knew that he knew what she was trying to do. *The shame! No proper Southern lady would behave this way!* She pretended to pick some lint from her dress, 'I won't tell anyone. None of my business anyway. You're a friend and good people. Whatever you used to be about, maybe you've changed your mind about things. We all make stupid mistakes,' Victor caught Charlotte's voice breaking slightly. *Hers was a prime example.* 'I hope yours was something you can undo. I mean, they have ways to remove tattoos nowadays, you know...'

As Charlotte prattled on to disguise her discomfort, Victor just stood and stared at her with tired eyes, trying to control his anger over her bringing up his past. What was past, was past. The tattoo was a good reminder of things that should be left undone.

Well, this was awkward. What else could she say so that he wouldn't run for the hills? 'I'm sorry,' Charlotte said, hoping she didn't have to elaborate what she was sorry about. She wasn't sorry she did it. *She was sorry it didn't work.*

'Bygones,' Victor said and meant it. Charges falling for angels. Apparently happened all the time. It was the first time it had ever happened to him. Victor cursed under his breath. He missed the scary dimensions and he was sure scary things in those dimensions missed him right back.

Victor glanced at his watch. *Right. It was time to turn back into a frog to go teach a Princess how to be Charming. Again.*

He stood up to leave, 'I have to go now, please give aunt Mae my best.'

Charlotte had gotten used to Victor's sudden departures, suspecting it must be difficult to tend to businesses all over the country. *Why else did Victor have to travel so much?* She truly appreciated he spent as much time with her as he did, although she still couldn't figure out how to get him to pay her the attention she craved. Charlotte had decided to become the unobtrusive Southern belle, hoping he would eventually forget the first impression she had made as a gruff farm hand. So, instead of telling him off for being curt to the point of rudeness, she demurely waved at him as he mounted his Harley parked right up front. *How had she missed the ratchet of his arrival?*

19. Sprite-Free
Sally

The next morning Sally woke up to a Sprite-free apartment. She reached for the bottle she had left on her night stand. Gone. Sally wandered to the fridge to discover it no longer housed Sprite. Puzzled, Sally scratched her ear. She was sure she had stocked up. She had even told the frog so last night.

The frog.

It wasn't until Sally saw the bin bags near the front door, prodded them and heard the familiar clink of glass that it dawned on her.

Momzer![16]

Feeling like a bag lady, she rummaged through the trash bag. Empty bottles. He had poured it all down the sink!

Rat bastard!

Sally's work day was lost in conjuring more and less violent ways of making the frog pay for his sins. Little did she know, he already was. She kept slamming the receiver down whenever the phone rang. Whoever was calling will soon consider calling someone else directly or figure out tech support was not very supportive today. Either way, they would stop calling her. Sally was glad she had made a deal with the frog never ever to bother her at work. God forbid, he would try improve things here as well. He'd probably make her answer the phone. *Politely.*

On the way home Sally bought a small six-pack of her favourite drink. Cans were smaller and easier to hide. That'll show him. Quel *nudnik*[17].

20. No-Name Slob

Grace

As Grace was opening the tiny bathroom window overlooking the back-alley to save them all from the breakfast fry-up fumes, she noticed a grey tabby climbing into their cabbage cellar. *Did they have mice again? Oh, bother!*

Grace had been noticing a lot of cats of different colours and sizes around the City lately. Just yesterday, she thought she saw a striped alley cat follow her up her street at night. Probably on a night prowl for some romance. Her adopting one probably made her notice cats in general. Either that or there was a secret network of cats following her around as if to keep watch.

Grace shook off this ridiculous thought and went back to work, hoping that Gabriel might make an appearance in the evening.

He didn't.

After he had walked her home yesterday, she was half-expecting to see his friendly frame materialise out of nowhere at closing time.

Grace was chewing on the pen she used to write orders with as she kept glancing out the window every few minutes.

'Lay off the pen or Tom will make you run to the shop to buy a new one first thing tomorrow morning!' Emma, the cook, said, making Grace jump.

'Gosh, don't ever sneak up on people like that!' Grace said, swatting her with a kitchen towel.

Emma nudged the girl and asked, 'Looking forward to seeing your honey again, tonight?'

On the radio, ABBA sang about her honey thrilling and nearly killing her and how she wanted to know some more.[18]

Grace stuck out her tongue, 'He's not my honey, he's just a guy why saved me from an unpleasant situation and almost walked me home yesterday.' She scanned the street outside the cafe just the same.

No Gabriel.

'Uh-uh and I'm Missus Santa Klaus,' Emma said, putting away her apron.

'I don't know if he is even interested. With all of his caring for my wellbeing when getting me away from the bullies at night, he didn't seem to want anything from me. Maybe he is angling for friendship?' Grace said, hoping she was wrong.

'With a pretty girl like you?' Emma held Grace's face up by her chin, 'Dream on, sugar.'

'Well, most guys I know would have tried to take my hand or even tried to wheedle out an invitation for a night cap at my flat. Any normal guy would have at least asked me for my phone number! Not him.' Grace huffed.

'Maybe he just has proper manners and knows not to pester a girl after a nasty shock, putting her in a predicament of feeling obliged to say 'yes' when all she wants to do is go home and have a hefty glass of whiskey to steady her nerves,' Emma said.

'Perhaps you are right,' Grace nodded. *She hadn't thought of it that way.* She pretended to clean the counter while stealing glances at the darkness that now engulfed the bright spot that was the cafe. The counter was happy not to be rubbed down with brute force for once.

Having said their 'goodbyes' and exchanged their hugs, the ladies walked off in different directions.

Heading into the night, Grace noticed a grey tabby on the street corner. She wasn't sure, but it looked like the one she had seen this morning going into their cellar.

Now that she had a cat, she was seeing them everywhere. She hadn't noticed so many strays in the City before.

A secret network of cats or not, Grace made a mental note to leave milk out in the alley where she had found the kitten for the neighbourhood cats the next morning.

Her cat was waiting for her when she got home. Grace reached out and absent-mindedly scratched behind its ear. 'I saw him again this morning.' When the cat cranked an ear, Grace felt she needed to elaborate, 'Gabriel. The guy who was watching me all day the day before yesterday. Except he wasn't. Watching me. He was just enjoying his last day before whatever work it is that City boys do. He's a City boy, imagine? Mates took him out for drinks last night nearby, so that's why he was there. Yesterday. To rescue me. He came in for his daily dose of coffee on his way to work this morning. Didn't stop by later, though. Pity,' she sighed.

The story from this morning had worked its charm. No one in their right mind would be chagrined over not seeing someone they didn't trust. Satisfied, he climbed on top of a duvet that was lying crumpled on the red couch.

Noticing the cat had found a refuge on higher ground, Grace surveyed her flat.

Right.

Time to clean up a little.

She put in her earphones and started tidying.

The cat dutifully followed her around, watching her make one of the most futile of jobs merry. The girl danced, laughed and sang along horribly and off key, but with gusto, occasionally swiping him with the duster to get his attention.

Since keeping her away from windows was not an option, checking that no one was lurking outside proved to be quite a challenge.

'Do you want to know why I'm such a scaredy-cat, Cat?' Grace asked.

Gabriel suspected why, having been there two years ago, but was all ears wanting to hear Grace' side of the story. *Perhaps there is something we are missing about the life of this girl. The more she opens up to the cat or him in human form, the more clues he would get.*

'There was this guy, Victor. I told you about him. Charming. Gorgeous. Needy. Almost deadly. Because of him, for a while, I thought I was honey to flies for damaged men. Because that's how it seemed. Any creepy customer of the coffee shop would inevitably try to chat me up. Which made me make a rule - no accepting of invitations for dates from customers and no flirting. So two rules, I guess. Which doesn't mean the offers didn't keep coming. So, it's actually very refreshing when someone non-creepy and very attractive seems to want just my company, not a date, not a telephone number, not a discount because they know the waitress.' Grace straightened the cushions on her red living room couch. 'The guy I was telling you about was a bully. That's why I don't like to do things when pushed, by Emma or anyone else. I don't have to do anything I don't want to do.' Grace sighed, 'Of course, it can backfire spectacularly, like it did last year. Emma cured me of my severe case of reverse psychology in a day. After I'd been doing exactly what she wanted me to do while she was telling me not to do things. Now no bully can make me do something I don't want to do.'

Gabriel's disguise as a City boy had helped him approach all the bullies from the day before at their workplaces. Because of his considerable height and memorable circumstances of meeting him two nights ago, Gabriel thought he would have to use force to extract information.

Nothing of the sort.

They had all cordially greeted him, assuming he was a new colleague, trying to make his way around the building. Confused, Gabriel had steered the conversation to celebrations, drinking and the hottest most recently visited bars. The strangest thing transpired - none of the lads had a recollection of the night before.

They remembered going to the bar. They remembered drinking beer. Lots of beer. No absinthe. They remembered waking up in the morning with the mother of all hangovers and six hours' worth of blanked out memories in between.

According to Loretta's background check, none of these upstanding citizens had ever exhibited any signs of aggression. Rugby didn't count. Loretta had researched the bullies and found them to be perfectly normal family men who had never in their life been violent or abusive. None of the bullies had accosted girls, waitresses or single females roaming London streets at night up until that fateful night. For them to gang up on a girl had definitely been out of character. Almost as if not of their own volition.

Daisy, whom Loretta had enlisted to help, could not even fault the stars for their behaviour. Neither the constellations nor the position of Mars augured random aggression. Gabriel had asked if she was sure she had checked the skyline for Earth and not some other dimension at which point Daisy had hung up on him.

Great. This world was getting to him. He had managed to upset the most cooperative and understanding person he knew. He HAD to get back to the Agency to get re-balanced.

The lads could, of course, have drunk absinthe and that could have muddled their brains, like Grace had suspected. Gabriel was even willing to believe they then could have promptly forgotten about drinking it, and, consequently, about accosting Grace.

The problem was, the bar next door didn't serve any absinthe. Which didn't mean they couldn't have brought it along and shamelessly ignored the rules of patronage. Still, whatever they had drunk besides beer must have been pretty potent stuff to cause a memory lapse for all five of them and from the exact same time - around 11PM.

And that was the problem with this scenario.

As far as alternative explanations of how someone could do something out of character went, Gabriel knew angels with pretty decent hypnotising powers. Hell, even some humans he used to know were good at hypnosis.

What if someone had hypnotised these poor fellows into accosting Grace and then make them all forget about it afterwards?

Grace thought the cat looked perplexed. She sighed, 'You don't like bullies either, do you? Well, I don't blame you. Plenty of those out there who want to pull you by your tail, right? On the other hand, if it hadn't been for Victor's bullying, I would never have ended up where I did.'

To Grace, the cat continued to look puzzled.

Gabriel was thinking about a scarier possibility. There was a machine, procured from the Eerie dimension that could wipe out memories. The Agency had one. It was an antique that no one had used for a few centuries since the last time a guardian angel had requested a memory-wipe.

Perhaps someone had invented or, worse, transported a similar machine from Eerie to Earth?

Then their mysterious someone was obviously even more dangerous than they originally suspected. Then it became entirely possible and reasonable that such a person who had managed to elude them for three days now was perhaps also able to influence the minds of otherwise law-abiding citizens.

So far, he had been operating under the assumption that the assassin was local.

What if he or she wasn't?

In his 900 years of rescue missions, both the charge and whoever or whatever he or she needed to be rescued from had usually been confined to the same dimension. Most dimensions were not aware of the existence of other parallel worlds. Some humans did speculate about multiverses and parallel dimensions in literary circles, but most believed such speculations to be science fiction.

They were still all clueless as to who and, more importantly, why was after this girl.

Grace felt she needed to explain things to Cat. 'I wouldn't have ended up right here, silly. Happy and living my life just the way I want it,' Grace stroked its back. The cat let her for two seconds, then upped and left.

Too distracting.

'I walked away, you know. Then again, if he hadn't crashed into a tree two years ago, who knows, maybe I would have gone back to him.'

The cat wagged its tail in annoyance.

'No, you're probably right, I probably wouldn't have. Except he wouldn't have stopped asking. And while I can resist bullies now, two years ago, who knows, maybe he would have bullied me back into submission to give him another chance?'

The cat radiated disapproval and shifted from paw to paw. *Now really! Did the Agency have to worry about the battered wife syndrome where damsels they had shielded and saved were concerned?*

Gabriel decided to go with the process of elimination.

Hypnosis was more plausible than someone using a memory-wipe machine.

If the Boss' original hypothesis was correct and the assassin, whoever he or she was, was after Grace personally, then they were dealing with someone dark and dangerous with a serious grudge.

On odd occasions, ghosts did manage to escape Eerie and wreak spooky but usually non-lethal havoc across dimensions. The dangerous dimensions had live-in guardians who enforced entries and exits. If anyone dark and dangerous had escaped to the Earth dimension, the Agency would have been notified.

Also, he still needed to eliminate the hypothesis that someone was after uncle Tom or Grace's entire blood line.

The bomb at the coffee shop this morning was an impatiently desperate attempt at getting rid of Grace - the baddy didn't care whom he took out as long as he got Grace in the process.

Which brought him back to the most important question.

Why was Grace a threat?

Gabriel was so engrossed in his own thoughts he almost missed the invite.

Done with her cleaning, Grace was settling in for the night. She fluffed her duvet, adjusted the pillows and patted the bed beside her.

After a brief hesitation, the cat hopped onto the bed. Looking a little uncomfortable, it pranced around on her second pillow but finally settled down.

Scratching behind its ear, Grace said, 'You're probably wondering why I haven't named you yet.'

Gabriel had more pressing concerns on his mind so he pretended he didn't hear her.

'Well, I liked Holly Golightly's philosophy in Breakfast at Tiffany's - that nobody belongs to anybody, so that's why you'll remain a no-name slob, just like Cat in that movie.'

If Gabriel had been in human form, he would have shrugged his indifference. *He was going to leave after the rescue was completed. Perhaps it was for the best that the girl didn't get too attached to his animal form.*

Grace fell asleep with her nose against the cat's. As she closed her eyes, the lady above her, partial to chick flicks and soppy soundtracks put Sarah McLachlan's Angel[19] on. An owner of the same soundtrack herself, Grace didn't mind. She knew she wasn't in the arms of an angel and she shouldn't feel comforted by sleeping with a cat curled up on her bed, but she did.

Gabriel heard Grace's breathing slow down. Only then did he withdraw his nose from hers and relax.

With her every peppermint breath, a stray black curl on the top of her nose fluttered like a feather. She looked so peaceful. No threat to anyone at all.

21. A Little Side-Business

Boss

Having come in from licensing yet another artefact to yet another dimension, the dark-skinned man threw a cursory glance at the black and white tally. He already knew what the two columns lining his revolving mirror would show him.

Well, not HIS revolving mirror, if to be quite precise. It had been there as long as he could remember. The mirror was much older than the 2500 years that he himself had seen it dominate this travelling office. The revolving mirror had been there when he had been recruited as a guardian in 540BC. It had certainly been there in 187AD when he had taken up office from his predecessor, who had stood up from his chair, pointed at the tally, said 'Good luck' and walked into the revolving mirror, disappearing in a purple cocoon into the Unknown, an uncharted dimension that had started to look rather inviting lately.

Kelly Clarkson's heart breaking thank you ballad[20] switched to Florence and the Machine who started crooning about the devils in her heart and how she'd be dead before the day was done.[21]

As if. The man looked reproachfully at the speakers. *Really? Either the universe was commiserating with his mood or telling him off.*

It was probably the latter. He wasn't that fond of the universe lately. Then again, commercial missions were his least favourite kind. The Agency was at the forefront of artefacts, technology and diamonds trade to sustain itself and provide its guardians with whatever they needed to do their jobs. Everything was running like a well-oiled machine and someone had to make sure the machine kept running.

The Boss sighed. His cranky mood could be attributed to Gabriel not having any luck playing detective on his latest save.

He could step in anytime. He just didn't feel like it.

The Boss shook his head. He hadn't felt anything in a very long time. Angelic beings felt nothing but peace, although he could never tell with Loretta. Even hundreds of years hadn't ironed out her pixyish swears and sarcasm.

Peace was good. So why was it no longer enough?

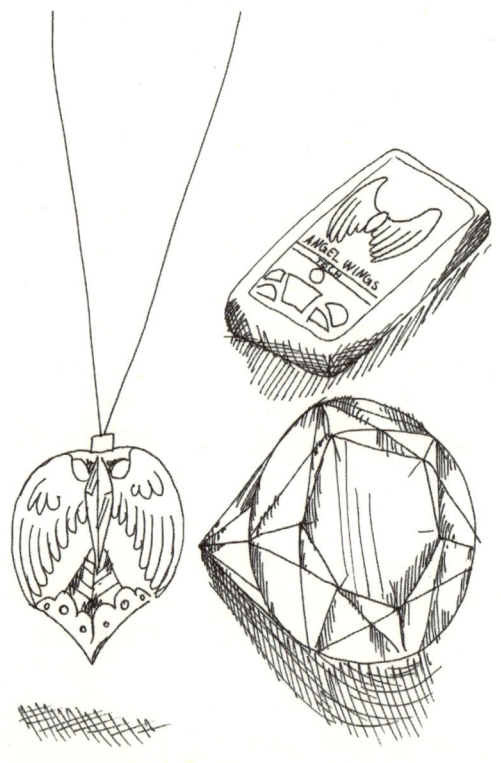

8. Everything was running like a well-oiled machine. The Agency was at the forefront of artefacts, technology and diamonds trade to sustain itself.

22. Walking on Sunshine
Grace

The next morning, Gabriel was out the window whilst Grace's keys still rattled in the door.

On her way to work, Grace felt light and happy to be alive for some reason. She whistled along to Walking on Sunshine,[22] which was appropriately playing on her iPod. She had a feeling she was going to see Gabriel again today. Just the possibility made her smile. She wished she had a daisy to pick at, guessing whether 'he shows up today and is interested' or 'he doesn't show up today, so he's not interested'.

Grace stopped at the grocer's on the corner from work to get a box of sweets, lingering for a chat.

'Hullo, chickie, need anything for the shop that Tom forgot to order?' the skinny, greying man asked.

'Not this time, Ed.' The shopkeeper always helped them out, whenever they were running low on milk or sugar or vegetables, which happened a lot more often than uncle Tom knew, since he preferred to under-stock. 'I'll just have the box of mini Milky Ways, please,' Grace handed him a ten-pound note.

'For your uncle? To keep him sweet?' Ed winked.

Grace nodded. Uncle Tom liked these sweets and she was feeling charitable this morning.

Ed handed her the change and said 'Emma should be in already.'

'I'll give her a bear hug from you, you big softy. You two are my inspiration!' Grace laughed. Despite no children, in their sixties Emma and Ed were still maddeningly in love.

Grace waved her goodbyes and left only to be stopped by the next shop owner at the next corner. While it paid to be nice to people, Grace simply liked chatting to the shop-owners who knew the tastes of their regulars and frequently tended the tills of their shops themselves.

The sun shone so brightly that Grace decided to stop in a small square and offer her face and palms up to the light. She closed her eyes and inhaled the scent of freshly mowed grass.

Biting her lip, Grace tried to filter out the honks of the London morning traffic and imagined that that's what kissing Gabriel would be like. He smelled like daisies and sunshine. She could only hope he kissed like a god.

When the time came and if he really was interested.

Grace briefly played around with the notion of braving the first move. *What if?*

After a minute all to herself, Grace left the tiny square happy and hopeful.

When she finally arrived at work, Gabriel was already sitting in his usual seat in the corner booth, looking anxious as he was waiting for his morning coffee. *Not that he needed any.* Waiting for tardy Grace was making his senses stand on high alert without coffee. *Assumption was the mother of all fudge-ups.* He had assumed she would come straight to work, as usual. Not today.

Seeing her come in, Gabriel exhaled with relief and waved. Worried that trouble might have found this girl again in brought daylight amidst the morning crowds of London, he had even dialled Daisy to search for Grace. The fairy had picked up, all ills forgotten. Gabriel silently thanked the lengthier time-span of the Agency as well as Daisy's sunny disposition. The fairy had reassured him none of the screens were recording Grace. He had requested that she zoom in, which Daisy did and assured him that Grace was on her way without anyone intending her harm.

Grace waved back at him and hurried behind the counter, stifling her deviant hopes and forcefully restraining herself from going over there to hug him. *What is wrong with me? One kindness of someone walking me home and I'm ready to throw myself at him?!?*

Gabriel was thinking.

He was not used to losing his charges and he wasn't planning to start now. He promised himself that from now on, he would be glued to Grace in cat or human form so as not to give the assassin another opportunity.

The Boss had been certain that Grace was somehow

important for Earth. Otherwise he wouldn't have dispatched his most experienced angel to deal with the situation. Hopefully with the help of the Watchers he would figure out soon exactly how.

Three days of guarding this girl had given him no insight into who could want her dead or why. Uncle Tom was gruff, but he and his family looked out for her in their own way. Grace got along with even the toughest customers and everyone in the neighbourhood liked her. She was easy to like. Of course, the situation with the bullies could have gotten out of hand, but even with all the memory-wipe conjectures, Gabriel still wasn't sure that it had been an attempt on her life. As far as he knew, only the shooting in the alley and the bomb in the cellar had been definite assassination attempts.

He was still waiting for Loretta to come up with uncle Tom's background check so they could assess whether Grace' entire bloodline was important.

Grace looked over at Gabriel sitting in his usual spot, blushed and had to remind herself that he had been in only twice and that assigning 'usual seats' was probably premature. She ignored her uncle's grumbling for being ten minutes late. Instead, she put the box of mini Milky Ways in front of him, patted his arm, ignored his stupor at her kindness and went back to the kitchen to give Emma her bear hug.

On the radio, Lady Antebellum was saying hello to the world[23].

Grace thought saying hello was only the polite thing to do after not seeing her rescuer for the eternity that had been 24 hours and headed over, grabbing a muffin along. *Someone who had done her the kindness of rescuing her certainly deserved a breakfast muffin.*

'Hello, Gabriel, I hope you like blueberry muffins,' she said and smiled. 'For the rescue. On the house.' *The smile was on the house, too.*

'Morning, Grace. Love them, thank you! And thank you for the coffee as well, although you shouldn't be giving me stuff for free. I'm pretty sure your uncle will deduct it from your wages,' the man smiled, melting ice-caps somewhere.

The auntie at the next booth pulled Grace's apron, 'Now I understand why this gentleman has been taking up my favourite booth for nearly an hour, all pins and needles and without ordering anything. He was waiting for you, dear.'

The radio confirmed that his empty arms were open and he was waiting for love.[24]

The old dotty winked at Grace, 'I hope you know that for a man, any man to get out of bed this early for a girl means he's sweet on her, sugar,' the lady smiled and stood to leave, oblivious that she had made Grace blush crimson and Gabriel to nearly choke on his coffee.

Gabriel could very well see how guarding a girl could easily be mistaken for affection. He smiled, dabbing at the coffee stains on the table in front of him, 'I have always admired the candour of that generation.' *Confessing he had been waiting for her could either backfire horribly or speed up their friendship.* 'She was right, of course, I was waiting for you,' he said simply and looked up at her.

Grace blinked. *Wow, a man who had no qualms about being honest.*

'You were?' Grace said, surprised.

'Yes, I enjoyed our walk the day before. You are a very easy person to be around.' *Well, she was.* This didn't make her an easy charge, but she was definitely not high maintenance, which helped with missions that took longer.

'Even when I'm scared?' Grace was surprised. *Being around her when she was all jittery and silent had put him at ease?*

'Even when you're scared,' he nodded.

'I enjoyed our walk, too.' Although he had just complimented how easy it was being around her, Grace felt tongue-tied all of a sudden. *Flirting took practice. Who knew?*

Realising she was still standing, he said, 'Where are my manners,' rose from the booth and motioned for her to take a seat across him, 'why don't you sit down?' Gabriel offered.

With regret, Grace had to decline, 'I'm sorry, I just got in and my uncle is already mad at me...'

Grace's reminder about her job made Gabriel remember that he had one to do as well. He sat back down, 'Perhaps another time.'

'Yes, another time would be lovely,' Grace nodded, relieved. She hadn't put him off, but his stern silence was slightly disconcerting. Taking a few steps, a crazy idea occurred to her and she decided to be bold and chance it.

She turned back making her hair fly everywhere. Nervously tapping her pencil on her pad, Grace blurted out 'If you'd like to go for coffee or tea or just for a walk after work today ... any other day ... I'd really like that...'

'Really?' Gabriel looked surprised.

Grace thought he had probably thought she meant to shoot him down completely. *Gorgeous AND unassuming.* 'Really,' Grace nodded. She only started smiling as she turned back to the till and saw Emma holding a pot of freshly brewed coffee, winking at her.

Outside their fishbowl of a coffee shop, the auntie was giving Gabriel a thumbs up.

Well now.

Gabriel wasn't sure whether they were on the fast track of becoming friends or whether she had just asked him out on a date. His experience with women dated back to the 12th century, so he couldn't be sure. He had, of course, heard from their Knights in Shining Armour and Princes Charming about the hazards of their missions. Damsels falling for their rescuers and some rescuers falling right back for the damsels as well. He had no intention to retire his angelic service to live happily ever after.

Gabriel had a different take on his calling.

Guardian angels were there to guard, not to fall in love.

He wasn't sure he had ever been in love. His first marriage had been an arranged one. He certainly didn't intend to fall in love or anywhere near it.

Making a mental note to ask Victor who liked the Princes

Charming assignments, Gabriel rose and dropped some money on the table for the coffee and the muffin, despite Grace having said it was on the house. Her grumpy uncle would deduct the cost from her wages, Gabriel was sure of it and he preferred not to cause any of his charges unnecessary discomfort. Financial or otherwise.

Gabriel waved his good-byes, receiving a nod and a smile in return. It was good to be trusted. Definitely made his job easier, although he had to steer carefully around the possible complication of the damsel in distress falling for her saviour.

En route to his fictitious job in the City and his real job to guard this girl, he decided to play it by ear. One thing he was sure of was that he would be here when this coffee shop closed tonight to meet her. After all, it was his job.

23. You Can Be A Waitress Anywhere
Victor

'Good evening, ladies,' Victor bowed slightly to Mae and extended a parcel to Charlotte.

'For me?' Charlotte sprang up, almost knocking over the table and eliciting a curt 'girl' from Mae. 'What is it?'

'Why don't you open it and see,' Victor suggested.

Charlotte spread art school booklets in Italian and English across her lap. A cathedral in Florence she recognised from her travel books was staring at her invitingly.

Victor noticed she held on to the brochure from Florence the longest. 'Firenze - that's Florence in Italian. There is information about scholarships there as well. You can be a waitress anywhere, you know,' Victor said. *He was trying real hard for her to say yes to being saved.*

Mae smiled at him.

Well, finally.

'I do believe you have our Charlotte's best interests at heart,' Mae said, fingering a doily in her lap.

Always did. Out loud Victor said, 'Yes, ma'am.'

Mae took the brochures from the unprotesting Charlotte. 'These are only for Italian art schools,' she said, folding her hands in her lap.

'Yes, ma'am.'

'Now, will you be escorting Charlotte to Italy, Victor?' Mae asked, a steely glint in her eye.

'Yes, ma'am. With your approval, of course, ma'am.' Victor said. *The save wasn't complete until the girl was far, far away from that pitchfork-loving cousin of hers. Preferably with a one-way ticket.*

'Oh, Victor, I don't know how to thank you!' *Except she did.* Charlotte jumped up, hoping Victor would catch her in his arms like they did in the movies.

Victor caught Charlotte and carefully disentangled himself from her bear hug under Mae's keen stare. 'Don't thank me. You told me your dream, what kind of a friend would I be if I didn't help you make it happen?'

Friends? He thought they were just friends? But what about all the late night visits? Well, three late night visits, but all in a row. It had to mean something! Charlotte covered her disappointment with a beaming smile, 'You're the best!' *What she had really wanted to say was 'I love you', but no proper Southern belle would admit her feelings for the gentleman before the gentleman disclosed his feelings AND intentions first.*

'Now show me what you drew today,' Victor said. Noting the sharp intake of breath from Mae, he had the good sense to finish with 'please'.

'On my break I managed to draw an egg, a white egg...' Charlotte was off, chatting away happily about the intricacies of drawing a white egg without using the colours white and black.

'Charlotte, perhaps you can tell Victor about your visitors as well?' Mae nodded.

'Oh yes, some old friends from school came to visit earlier this the evening, just before you...'

'Much earlier,' Mae intoned.

Victor smiled to ease the tension and looked at his watch. He had been here one hour, which meant seven hours had passed in Gaia. Evening visits it would have to be. A day on Earth was a week in Gaia. His other charge was much more work, so he had to make full use of his days and early evenings aka most of the Gaian week without sleep as it were.

Meanwhile, Charlotte had moved on to commenting on how lovely the clients of the restaurant were, who had come in with whom and how the other waitresses had given her good hints on how to get people tipping.

Victor nodded and mh-mhed at appropriate intervals at Charlotte's soliloquy to keep up the conversation. He glanced at his watch again. He could stay another hour, then say his goodbyes and be back before the day was out in Gaia where he would have to start persuading Sally to change of her own free will and for her own good all over again.

'You're such a good listener,' Charlotte pounced in for another hug. *Friends hug, don't they?*

Victor carefully disentangled himself. The girl looked close to bestowing a kiss on him and popping a foot. In his human life, Victor would have welcomed the constant hugging. Heck, he would even have probed his luck with a little bit of a grope of the girl's backside. Maybe even in front of the old broad who would probably be too scandalised to admit she noticed anything.

In his angelic form, Charlotte's clinging was annoying. *Somehow needy wasn't sexy.* Maybe that's why he used to change girls like socks as soon as they fell for him and boy did they fall... *Maybe that's why Grace left when he had become too controlling and needy?*

Victor sighed. He had never been in a situation of such a protracted save that he had ever had to think about how to be the good guy AND avoid charges falling for him. *Maybe he should ask Gabe for a few hints and tips?*

Taking Victor's sighing as her cue, Mae rose to leave. 'I will think about it,' she said. Not seeing comprehension in either of the faces before her, she elaborated, 'About my approval for this gentleman to escort you, should you decide to study in Italy, girl. Now before I retire for the night, let me have a word with Victor. Meanwhile, please be so kind and clear the table, Charlotte. Thank you!'

Charlotte held her breath. *Mae was going to talk to Victor on her own? Whatever for? Was she going to try and scare him off?*

Seeing the frozen statue that was Charlotte, Mae said, 'Nothing to be afraid of. We're just going to have a little heart-to-heart, that's all, child.'

Great, she had gone from girl to child in less than a minute. Charlotte smiled hesitantly and started cleaning away the dishes. With any luck she could dawdle out on the porch long enough to overhear at least some conversation.

Mae walked Victor down the garden path in the general direction of the street.

Victor got a sense of being escorted off the premises.

Mae didn't stop until she was next to his bike.

He WAS being escorted off! Victor smiled. The auntie had excellent protective instincts, too bad they didn't work long-distance and against her closest relatives.

'Victor, I have only one question for you,' Mae said.

Victor nodded, 'Yes, ma'am.'

'What are your intentions towards my Charlotte?' Mae asked and pursed her lips.

None whatsoever except saving her sorry ass. Out loud, Victor said, 'ma'am, you have nothing to worry about.'

'Now, when a boy says I have nothing to worry about that is exactly when I do start to worry,' Mae said.

Victor wanted to say, *Look, lady, I just want to help.* Instead, he said, 'ma'am, I'm just seeing through that she gets her dream. I have no aspirations beyond her schooling.'

Mae huffed, doubtlessly wanting to say something about the kind of schooling she was worried about and refraining from the comment as too crass.

'Just paying it forward,' Victor said. *Well, he was.* 'Someone once helped me and that made all the difference. So it's my turn to do the same kindness for someone else.'

'As long as we have an understanding that you behave respectfully,' Mae said.

Victor thought of all the names he had called Sally in Gaia to get her to grasp what or rather who was right in front of her. He had been completely different with Charlotte, which was why the going to and fro between the dimensions was even more tiresome. 'Have I ever given you cause to suspect otherwise, ma'am?' Victor raised an eyebrow and mounted his bike. *Before returning to Gaia, he had to pop by the Enchanted dimension to recharge the wand. Covering all Sally's mirrors overnight had depleted it to five per cent and he needed it handy. Just in case.*

'No, I guess you have not,' Mae said. Her pursed lips telegraphed 'yet' loud and clear.

24. It's Just Coffee
Gabriel

As planned, Gabriel came into the coffee shop just as Grace was finishing her evening shift. He waved and sat down in a booth by the window, casting worried glances outside.

Grace didn't know why Gabriel keeping an eye out bothered her.

Maybe he was keeping an eye out for a female someone?

Yes, he had asked her for coffee, but it was just coffee. Maybe it was just something to say while he was waiting for someone better to come along? Maybe he had already met someone at work today and that girl was about to show up any minute now? Maybe Gabriel had just returned to the coffee shop because it was convenient, not because she was there?

She had already put her apron away, but decided to take him on as her last customer for the day anyway.

'Hello, Gabriel. What'll it be?' she said, putting on a smile but still thinking about potential other girls he might be waiting for at this time in the evening.

Gabriel smiled at Grace and her breath caught slightly. 'Would you be so kind and have coffee with me?' He motioned at the seat opposite him.

'Right now?'

Gabriel nodded and smiled.

'Right here?'

Another nod.

Grace was so surprised she sat down. *Well, not the place she had thought he'd take her for coffee, but why not?*

Someone on the radio informed them there was more to this, promising she can make it out and that she wasn't alone.[25]

Two cups of steaming coffee appeared in front of them as if by magic. Grace wouldn't have noticed if uncle Tom had come and personally brought them. She was too busy staring into Gabriel's deep blue eyes.

'Thank you, Emma!' Gabriel said and nudged Grace's cup closer to her, 'Coffee?'

'Erm, sure, yes, thank you,' Grace took the cup, praying her hands wouldn't shake. *She was feeling like a prize idiot, flaking out like this over a simple invitation for coffee. And at her own shop, of all places!*

Gabriel sipped his drink and gave her all the time in the world to come out of her stupor. *She had gone awfully silent over a simple kindness. Hadn't anyone ever been nice to this girl?*

'Gracie, stop flirting with the customers and settle your shift. Now!' her uncle yelled from the back of the shop.

With the coffee left for dead, Grace scurried away, blushing wildly and muttering, 'I wasn't flirting.'

Judging by the way her uncle treated her and by the scars Victor had left, Gabriel came to the logical conclusion that people being nice to her was not something Grace experienced on a daily basis.

Uncle Tom might be a brute, but he wasn't on anyone's hit list. Yet. He had a few debts, but they were to the banks, which are generally not known for blowing up their debtors and their places of business as a means of collection.

Gabriel dialled Victor.

'If it isn't the chiefest of them all, as I live and breathe,' Victor said. There was such a loud honk from a car Gabriel had to pull the phone away from his ear.

'Ouch! I'm near deaf, so you must have incurred permanent hearing loss, wherever you are,' Gabriel said.

'In New York traffic on Gaia, the second Earth,' Victor said and something in the background went splat.

Gabriel ignored his curiosity stabbing him repeatedly and said, 'I need to run something by you.'

'Shoot,' Victor was all ears. It was unusual for Gabriel to consult with other guardians.

'As an ex-villain and our most vengeful angel,' Gabriel started.

'Hey, if you're going to start name-calling, this conversation is going to be very short.' Victor huffed.

'Yes, you've certainly come a long way...' Gabriel nodded into his phone.

'If you're about to add 'my young padawan', I'll hurt you when I see you next,' Victor growled.

Ignoring the Star Wars reference, a movie Victor had introduced him to, Gabriel smiled, 'I'd like to see you try.' At boot camp when training up the battle skills of new recruits Gabriel had discovered Victor's strength near-equalled his own, except he had 900 years of experience on his side.

'My battling skills have come a long way since boot camp, big guy,' Victor boasted.

'Yes, yes, I know all about your trips to Dialysis X on your spare time. Now will you help me or not?' Gabriel asked.

'Fine, I'll help. But for future reference, I prefer to think of what I do not as revenge, but doing wicked justice,' Victor huffed.

'And that is precisely why I need you. You can still think wickedly, can't you?' Gabriel asked.

'Are the twin World Trade Centre towers still standing in Gaian New York?' Victor said which Gabriel ignored. They had wasted enough precious time on idle chit-chat. 'Say someone would attempt to wipe out an entire family...' Gabriel said.

'One family unit or the entire bloodline?' Victor specified and swore loudly. 'That was not meant at you,' he told Gabriel and refused to elaborate.

'Let's assume either, so give me both scenarios,' Gabriel said, 'who would you start with?'

'The kids,' Victor said without hesitation, 'to avoid the procreation and revenge problem.'

'Ok, what if there are three kids, two from one family and their cousin, sole survivor, no parents?' Gabriel elaborated.

'If the two are family and can be taken out both or the entire family at once, I'd start there, then take out the remaining relatives one by one, until the last remaining member of the family, the cousin,' Victor said. 'Fancy that, my knowledge of friends and schoolmates from the London underbelly finally came in handy.'

'So, if you were trying to destroy the entire bloodline, not just one person from this family, you would go after the family, not the loner first?' Gabriel asked. 'That would make sense.'

'Why do you ask?' Victor enquired.

'Someone has been trying to eliminate my charge a few times. She's the sole survivor, no parents but she has an uncle and two cousins,' Gabriel said.

'If someone is repeatedly going after the loner, ugh, they are gunning for the loner, not for the bloodline,' Victor said through gritted teeth, swore and hung up to the background noise of screeching tyres.

So Grace WAS the real target. And after all the checks the Wacthers had run, he still had nothing useful.

Besides Victor who was now dead and annoying and the guys from two nights before who were alive but harmless, no one had ever accosted her. No one had ever even harboured a grudge against Grace.

By the looks of it, whoever was after Grace, was after Grace only. The bomb in the cabbage cellar meant this person was either very unscrupulous or very desperate or both. Which meant Gabriel had to find him, fast.

Or her.

For a brief moment, Gabriel considered the resources that had already been used for this single save and wondered whether Grace was just a red herring, a damsel put into deliberate distress to distract the Agency from something far, far more important.

Gabriel texted Loretta, asking her to check whether things had gone unusually quiet in any particular dimension across the board.

If Grace was the common denominator and background checks on her life had produced nothing, he had to go to the source. He had to get the information out of her. Maybe something she noticed. Maybe something someone said to her. Maybe she had said something to someone and that someone had taken offence of undue proportions. Maybe they didn't know everything about her life.

Gabriel decided it was time to make it all about Grace if he were to solve the mystery of who would want her dead and why.

As Grace was putting on her coat, Emma appeared with two cups of coffee and two muffins to go, 'Here you are, for your walk. You are walking her home, aren't you, honey?' Emma gazed up adoringly at Gabriel. The man was built like a god and gods were good enough for her Grace.

'Yes, ma'am,' Gabriel said, taking the coffees and pocketing the muffins.

'And polite, too,' Emma stage-whispered to Grace, making her blush.

Grace tried to pay for the coffees and the muffins and Emma waved her off, 'My treat.'

When Grace gave it another try, Emma took her gently by the arm, 'It's just coffee, poppet. Let someone take care of you for a change,' she said, making goo-goo eyes at Gabriel, who was waiting at the open door.

Grace smooched Emma on the cheek, 'Bye, Ems!'

'Bye, sweetie. Safe journey!' Emma waved them off.

Outside, it was raining cats and dogs. Typical London weather. Unearthly sunshine in the morning and buckets of icy rain the same night. Not the best weather for a walk, but bar a favour from a weather goddess, it would have to do. 'Shall we?' he said, offering her his arm.

Grace nodded, quieted by the rain.

At the nearest newspaper booth, Gabriel said, 'Just a minute, if you please,' popping into the shop next to the Monument underground station.

The radio from the shop reminded Gabriel that time was only borrowed.[26]

Outside, Grace wondered whether cigarettes or the evening paper really couldn't wait until he had walked her home. Rain always made her crabby.

Gabriel emerged and opened a huge black umbrella above her.

A flower pot fell from the first floor balcony, jostled by the jerky motion of its owner who got spooked by a loud noise from the apartment. It bounced off Gabriel's umbrella and crashed harmlessly into the gutter, managing to neatly avoid people, cars and bikers.

Oblivious to having avoided injury, Grace smiled at Gabriel. 'Thank you, this is very considerate of you,' she said. *It wasn't quite the same as making the rain stop, which would take a miracle. Instead of miracles, she would settle for being taken care of.*

Gabriel looked up at a horrified woman who was holding up a cigarette, looking down at them.

Had that been a coincidence or another attempt?

If he discounted the bullies and this was attempt number three, the attempts were getting feebler.

9. If it was another attempt, the attempts were getting feebler.

'Ready to go?' he asked and Grace nodded.

They fell into step on the pavement before they reached the next corner.

'Do you have a favourite route home?' Gabriel asked, knowing the answer. Except this morning, Grace had taken the same route every single day.

'How much time do you have?' she asked.

'Aeons', he said.

This cheered Grace up immensely, 'Then we can take a longer walk. There are some parts of the City that I haven't seen in a long while.' If a simple admission that she was important enough to invest aeons of time in could cheer her up so much, maybe the man could perform miracles as well. Maybe he would take her mind off the rain and the memories it brought.

Gabriel nodded. Good. More time to quiz her about her life. Balancing the umbrella under his chin, he took both coffees from her and pointed at his back pocket. 'If you would be so kind as to extract the muffins, please?' Gabriel patiently waited until Grace had taken back her coffee as well.

'What about your muffin?' Grace asked as she bit into hers.

'I can have it later, don't worry,' he said, shielding her from the passers-by as well as the rain.

As she started walking, she offered him a bite of hers, 'That's the least that I can do in exchange for you getting me home in a more-or-less dry state,' Grace smiled weakly. She hoped he would recognise her feeding attempt as flirting.

'Thank you,' Gabriel stopped and took a small bite. 'You are very kind. To me and to your customers. The way you are with people, have you always wanted to work somewhere you can be of service? Is that why you chose waitressing?' he asked.

Grace sidestepped a lamp post, 'I didn't exactly choose to be a waitress. It kind of happened,' she shrugged.

Sensing a story there, Gabriel pro   mpted, 'Do tell.'

Grace considered whether there was any harm in divulging certain facts about her life to a near-stranger. A nice stranger who had saved her twice - from the bullies and now from the rain - but a stranger nevertheless.

The past was the past. She couldn't change it. She opted to divulge some truth, 'I'm just really bad at saying 'no' to people,' she shrugged. 'I was training to be a vet, when uncle Tom asked me to help out at setting up his coffee shop, so I did. That was two years ago.' That was her version and she was sticking to it.

The Globe theatre towered over them in quiet agreement.

Two years ago in Earth time Gabriel had recruited Victor. *Had she dropped out of school because of what had happened to him?*

'The shop seems to be set up well and to be honest, while you are great with people, I think you might be wasting your nurturing talents on waitressing. Why doesn't your uncle hire someone, so you can go back to vet school?' Gabriel asked instead.

Grace eyed him warily and steered them towards the Millennium Bridge, 'You aren't one of those management consultants, are you?' she asked.

Gabriel laughed and shook his head. 'I'm only a baby consultant, just starting out, I wouldn't know any Jedi mind tricks yet.' Of consultants. He knew plenty of Jedi mind tricks he had picked up from other dimensions.

'We haven't discussed me going back to school. I'm not sure they'd want me back or that I could afford it,' she said, tossing her empty coffee cup into the bin.

'Is that the real reason?' Gabriel gently asked, folding the umbrella. It had stopped raining.

Grace cast Gabriel a sidelong glance as she emptied the crumbs from her muffin onto the Thames sidewalk for seagulls to find. *You had to hand it to the boy, he was very good at asking all the wrong questions.* The real reason Grace hadn't had this conversation with her uncle was because she was afraid of change. Afraid to say yes to something important. The last time she had said yes before the waitressing was to Victor's proposition of him moving in. She should have said no to both - to going out and him moving in. Like with the waitressing, she hadn't really wanted to do any of those things. Victor had been so charming and uncle Tom had been in real need and she was a fool. 'I'm just really bad at saying no to people,' Grace shrugged, reluctant to rehash the past. The past was what it was.

For a fleeting moment Gabriel had a feeling that her inability to say no to people in need or people who wanted something from her would probably make her a good guardian angel. Someday.

To lighten the mood, Gabriel suggested, 'Imagine, if you did go back to vet school and graduated, you could start your own clinic some day. Perhaps you can rescue a few more cats?'

The edifice of St. Paul's Cathedral sneaked up on them, humbling her as usual.

'How did you know...' Grace fell silent. *How did he know about her ever having rescued a single cat? Maybe he was a stalker after all.*

Gabriel picked off an invisible lint off her sleeve and said 'Cat hair,' showing a long reddish hair to her. 'My grandmother's favourite cat used to sleep on my head when I was a kid, so I know their secret tell-tale signs. You don't strike me as someone who would go and buy a thoroughbred on purpose or for show, so you probably adopted one off the street.' He smiled, since this seemed to put her at ease.

'Aren't you a regular Mister Sherlock Holmes...' Grace eyed him suspiciously, biting her lip.

Laughter was the best cure against careful suspicion. 'Well, there must be real perks to waitressing, if you are loathe to leave it behind. Do tell, is it the huge tips or the adrenaline of dodging grabby male customers?' Gabriel asked.

Grace blinked and giggled, 'Oi, at least my training as a veterinarian comes in handy - feeding the animals.'

Gabriel smiled. He enjoyed making her laugh. 'Which ones do you love more - animals or humans?'

She didn't even have to think about it, 'Animals. When I was a kid...' Grace paused, swallowing hard, 'I was around horses and dogs a lot and I used to bring home any manky injured animal I could find. My parents didn't know what to do with me except suggest becoming a veterinarian. I have been dreaming of being a vet as long as I can remember,' she hushed. Easy-going with the customers, Grace became tongue-tied when it came to sharing things about her own life. There was a good reason, too. She didn't want anyone pitying an orphan and there had been plenty of those who had tried.

'Well, since you love animals so much, fancy going to the zoo some day?' Gabriel asked. He didn't even know why he said it. Just to cheer her up, perhaps. He wasn't planning to stick around for long. With any luck, they would resolve Grace's problem in a few days.

To his surprise, Grace accepted with a quick nod. The street where Grace lived was a few blocks away. Grace's pace was slowing. Gabriel suspected she didn't trust him to walk her even to her corner.

Grace didn't want to go home just yet. She had taken the longest detour possible. She didn't want their conversation to end. Besides Emma from work, in years Gabriel was the only one who had taken an interest in what SHE wanted to do.

She surprised both of them by turning the wrong corner, away from their end destination. *I just hope he doesn't notice we're going around in circles.*

Gabriel felt the need to reassure her, 'Don't worry, I'm not some crazy stalker. I just like your company.'

Grace regained her senses, fell into step at his side and managed to laugh, 'You do know that that's exactly what a crazy stalker trying to earn my trust would say?'

He looked at her curiously. She had trust issues. Given her experience with Victor, he wasn't surprised. Still, it made him want to say some choice words to Victor even if he was atoning for all his sins already. 'You don't trust easily. I get it. Someone must have hurt you a lot. I don't want to hurt you. I just want to walk you home safely.'

Grace's laughter died. Apparently, besides Emma Gabriel was the only person who dared talk to her about things that made her uncomfortable.

Gabriel was sorry he had been so direct. He liked her laughing and she probably didn't do that enough, 'I'm sorry. I didn't mean to upset you.'

Grace shrugged, 'You didn't. There is no point of getting upset at the truth.' But it was disconcerting that someone who had known her for only a few days could see she had issues.

'Besides work, what do you do for fun? I just started a new job and I'm new in town, so I'm trying to find stuff to do....any tips?' Gabriel tried to change the subject.

'You mean besides the zoo?' Grace stuck her tongue out at him and steered them back to her street.

They were nearing Farringdon underground station. Again. Their walk was almost at an end and so was the banter. Gabriel was sure that Grace would wave him off at the corner. Buying time, he stopped, 'I know you don't know me very well and I am glad you trusted me enough to let me escort you almost home this evening.'

Grace nodded and walked on. She did trust him. She didn't know why, but she did. The man didn't seem to want anything from her besides her company. The entire conversation tonight had been around her, her likes, her dislikes, her life. All she knew about him was that he was a City boy, that he was thoughtful and kind and liked her muffins. She knew nothing about his life or how he came to be that way. As trustworthy as he was, she wasn't prepared to have a conversation about 'teas' or 'nightcaps' or 'coming up for a minute' or 'using her loo'.

As Gabriel had suspected, Grace bid her goodbyes at her street corner. Fortunately, the street was well lit, which guaranteed her safety in crossing those last few feet to her door.

25. Sure Thing

Lanie

After going through the rigmarole of explaining about how immortality works, the importance of pressing the right button on her 'pager' slash watch slash smart phone no matter what before lights out so they could find, retrieve and revive her and a little about the tools Lanie could use on her missions, Loretta decided orientation was over. It was time for Lanie to get stuck in. 'See here, I'm going to unfreeze reality by pushing this button and then I'll send you off on your first rescue mission.'

Lanie looked slightly shocked, 'Already? You're not going to let me follow anyone or train me properly or anything?'

Loretta shrugged, 'You'll learn on the job, same as everybody, we're understaffed, anyone who has the patience to train you is on a mission and, besides, there really is no time to train you up, so boot camp will have to wait. And since you have to start somewhere, you can start here and now.'

Lanie looked fearful.

The pixie ruffled her purple hair, 'Don't'cha worry, I won't send you on a suicide mission or anything difficult, let's find you a nice bog standard rescue, shall we?'

Lanie was pretty sure even bog standard things can occasionally go horribly, horribly wrong, but then remembered that she was already dead, so the worst had already happened and she had nothing to lose. Well, except apparently when she couldn't get herself resurrected within 72 Agency hours after being killed on a mission in any dimension. Only then would she cease to be and never come back to how she was now - dead but here. That was one of the few essential things she had remembered well from her talk with Loretta. The Agency hated losing their angels.

Meanwhile her smart phone slash watch beeped. Lanie looked at it and it flashed with a simple message '!Rescue!'.

Loretta was tapping her foot at her, 'I activated it since you're now on active duty, so when you see this message without mission details, it means you should call the Watchers - that's me and Daisy - as soon as possible.'

Lanie pushed the phone button and dialled Loretta's pre-programmed number. Looking into Loretta's violet eye she said, 'Hello?'

Loretta demonstratively clicked her headset and yelled into Lanie's ear, 'Enchanted dimension, Klaus, you have his coordinates, go!'

'Sure thing,' with those words, Lanie felt herself being sucked into a tunnel of blue light.

Loretta almost wolf-whistled. *Wow, that girl was a quick learner*. She had never seen a wormhole appear even as she had been stating the name of the dimension, much less opening and closing as a perfect cocoon of light around the newbie. *Well then, this one had all the makings of becoming as good as Gabriel someday.*

The first thing that Lanie saw on the other side of the light was a frog.

The frog nodded at her and hopped off with what looked like a wand dangling off the chain around his neck.

Lanie told herself that this was an Enchanted dimension, so the frog was probably someone enchanted, and it was perfectly normal for him to say hello in this way.

Frogs saying hello had never factored into her life as something normal before.

She would probably get used to the absurdity of things someday. She just hoped that 'someday' came soon.

Right, Klaus.

She looked at her smart phone slash watch slash pager. Funnily enough, it seemed to be working here. A very smart phone.

She tapped the map button on the screen. The shortest route to her charge popped up as a red arrow.

Lanie wondered whether she was meant to walk to where she needed to go.

The red arrow crawled out of the watch, looked at her reproachfully and pointed back at the phone, blinking quicker.

'You don't have time to walk. I suggest you fly,' Loretta's voice said and Lanie realised it was her watch and not the arrow talking.

At the agency, Loretta, nearly forgetting to freeze reality, sat back to enjoy the show.

Would the newbie figure out how to fly or would she need to send another, more experienced angel?

*10. Frogs saying hello had never factored into her life
as something normal before.*

Lanie nodded.

Fly.

Right.

How?

If only she had wings.

Lanie felt something rustle at her back. Her shoulder blades felt slightly uncomfortable, so she flexed her shoulders. The rustling increased.

As she turned to see where the rustling was coming from her nose was instantly buried in a bunch of white feathers.

Darn, she did have wings.

Well, there was only one way to find out whether they could carry her.

Lanie opened her wings wide and felt herself soar upwards.

Holding her phone firmly in her palm, she merely thought of needing to reach Klaus quickly and already she was halfway there.

Neat.

At the screens, Loretta smiled her pointy smile. *The newbie WAS a quick learner.* All she had to do was imagine things in the Enchanted dimension and she got them. Which was partly why Claus was in trouble in the first place. Loretta was pretty sure she hadn't told Lanie anything about this dimension. So, the girl had figured things out for herself. Good for her.

Lanie arrived at where the arrow was pointing.

It was a gorgeous day, the sun was shining, the wind made the tops of the aspens ripple like night-time static on the TV, animals of all colours were roaming around in Disney-like fashion, unafraid of man or guardian angel. The only thing that looked odd in the picture was a murky puddle in the middle of the road.

The arrow disappeared with a 'poof' but not before climbing out of the phone, once again, arching itself at an impossible angle and pointing at the puddle.

That was Klaus?!?

Right.

She could see the urgency. With the sun shining brightly,

this hot summer day would soon cause the puddle to evaporate. Lanie guessed evaporation, even a tiny bit, was not a good thing for Klaus.

How would she go about saving a puddle?

Mopping him up was not good. Some moisture...erm...some part of Klaus would be lost in the tissue or in whatever she used to mop him up.

It would have to be a clean rescue.

If only she had a plastic Tupperware container.

A see-through re-seal-able plastic container appeared in her hand.

Apparently, anything she wished for in this dimension, materialised. She had to remember that in order to avoid wishing for the wrong things. Or scary things.

She wished for a large syringe and a plastic spoon and started on the scoop-up mission.

Having collected Klaus into the Tupperware, she sealed the container off to avoid Klaus evaporating, made sure there was no liquid left in the syringe or on the plastic spoon. She put her tools down next to the container on the asphalted ground which looked so out of place in the otherwise rustic surroundings.

Was she meant to take him back to the Agency to get him disenchanted?

Hang on.

If she could have anything she wished for in this dimension, perhaps she should just wish for Klaus to regain his true form and save him a trip to the Agency? Now, why didn't she think of that before?

With a loud pop the container was gone and a slightly dishevelled Santa Claus was sitting on the road in front of her.

'Thank goodness, child, I don't know what would or could have happened had I remained a puddle for much longer. The sun was starting in quite mercilessly,' he inspected his red coat, 'ah, golly, the sun did manage to do some harm. Look! The coat is half an inch too big for me now.'

He extended his hand and Lanie helped him up. He

doubled it as a handshake, 'Santa Claus, pleased to make your acquaintance. And you are?'

'Lanie, your guardian angel for the day,' Lanie couldn't help smiling. She had just rescued Santa.

The jolly bearded man gave himself a once-over and started dusting off his coat, 'If only I had not listened to the goat...'

Lanie stifled a giggle and wondered whether Alice in Wonderland had also found everything incredibly funny while also thinking she was going mad.

'The goat, sir?'

Santa stopped fluffing his coat, 'You see, I was vacationing. The Mystic North gets a bit tedious now and then, especially just before Christmas, too much work you know, so I come here or go to the Magic Kingdom to enjoy a bit of a fairy-tale existence. Enchanted dimension! Who knew the goat was enchanted for a very good reason and out to do mischief! Anyway,' Santa carefully considered his words, 'he...tricked me...into wishing... to know how it felt to be a puddle and there I was - a puddle. And puddles have no thought, so I couldn't wish to be back to my normal self, hence your rescue mission.'

They had walked almost to the end of the road that ended abruptly in the bushes. Lanie spotted a sleigh under a fir tree.

Santa beamed, 'That's my ride. Well, thank you again, Lanie, for saving me. I don't know what I would have done without a guardian angel today or without the Agency, for that matter. Imagine if there were no angels or the Agency...horrible, horrible thought... Best not to think of such horrors, they might materialise somewhere, we are in the Enchanted dimension, after all... Ooh, look at the time! I'm off now. Missus Claus will not be happy, no siree. She'll be as mad as a thousand squirrels for me having missed half a day here. It was a day before Christmas when I left, fed up with all the preparations, so I'm afraid I completely missed Christmas, which means we now have to turn back time, which is always fraught with consequences of someone remembering. Someone always remembers and then we have stories about ground-hog days and some such...'

Lanie couldn't quite hear the end of his muttering as Santa together with his sleigh evaporated with a pop and a wave.

Lanie laughed out loud. She had just saved Santa. Curiouser and curiouser, as Alice would say. While Lanie was pretty sure it was still mid-July on Earth, she wouldn't be surprised if it was Christmas somewhere, in some dimension. Maybe with Christmas in different dimensions it was like with seasons on Earth - while it was Summer in Europe, it was Winter in Australia. Seasonal Christmas and turning back time probably explained how Santa managed to visit all children on Earth and in other dimensions in the space of just a few hours.

Despite Santa's warnings not to think about dangerous things, Lanie idly wondered what would it be like if there was no Santa. In any dimension. No Christmas. No gifts. Lots of disappointed boys and girls. Or would the dimensions rearrange themselves as if Santa never even existed? It would be a new world order. *Cancel that, she didn't want a world, any world without Santa.*

Right. Time to get back.

Lanie wished to be back at the Agency and through the tunnel of blue light she went again.

Lanie materialised in front of Loretta who didn't look very pleased, 'You were supposed to bring him back! Now what do I tell the Boss about Christmas? The man goes and gets trapped, quite by his own fault, and now Christmas is ruined for quite a few dimensions.'

Lanie patiently waited until Loretta had let off the steam, 'You can tell the Boss that Santa promised he would make it all good. It would involve turning back time to redo Christmas eve and he said there might be consequences, but he promised Christmas is back on.'

Loretta nodded reluctantly. 'Groundhog day.' Judging by her first rescue, the newbie was probably a good find.

Lanie stretched, 'Frankly, he seemed to be more afraid of his Missus giving him hell than of anyone else, including, I'm guessing, the Boss.'

Loretta nodded, 'Who do you think is in charge of preparing everything? All the gifts for all the good girls and boys in all the dimensions based on the list she gets from the Boss? Who doubles as the nine reindeer guiding Santa's sleigh on the night? Wouldn't you be upset if all your hard work went down the drain because SOMEONE forgot himself at play-time and failed to simply show UP on the night?'

Lanie's eye-brow shot up, 'Really? Missus Klaus does all that?'

'Yep,' Loretta summed up.

'Why the reindeer?' Lanie pried.

'Someone has to, considering all the eggnog being left out at Christmastime,' Loretta shrugged. 'Fine, that was an ok first save, I can trust you with some more easy stuff before you can get battle training in boot camp.' The pixie turned to the screens, fishing for another non-violent save.

Lanie briefly wondered whether Santa had gone gallivanting before and they had had to resort to a Groundhog day on Earth more than once already during Lanie's own lifetime. She did remember having a nightmare as a child that Christmas was cancelled and waking up on the morning of Christmas Eve to find everything perfectly alright. Out loud she asked a more pressing question, 'Boot camp?'

***

As the pound keeper was thrusting around a cage with a wire collar, in the corner, a short-haired brown Dachshund was silently praying for any help.

The wire collar was something they brought out every once in a while and those dogs were never seen again. Jack doubted they went to a new home.

New homes came with new collars and new people taking dogs from their cages. To new homes.

A girl stepped out from behind the pound keeper, 'Can I have him?'

The keeper shrugged and retreated, 'Saves me the trouble of putting him down.'

Lanie made smooching noises at the dog, 'Hello, puppy! Want to come with me?'

Despite the fear, Jack's tail started wagging. *Usually the wire collar and pound keeper were a duo. Maybe with this girl, the wire collar didn't mean what it usually meant?*

Lanie extended a new collar towards the dog, 'Want to come with me?'

New collar!

New collar!!

New collar!!!

The pound keeper would not waste money on a new collar just to lure him to his death. The cheapskate was feeding them only once a day.

New home!!!

Jack sniffed the collar, then the girl. She smelled heavenly. Jack let the girl put the collar on and they started walking.

When they were in a safe distance from the pound, the girl stopped and squatted down to Jack. 'This is going to sound ridiculous, but I'm your guardian angel.'

Guardian angel - yes, yes! The girl had saved him from imminent death, she could call herself anything she liked.

'I know that you can understand me and that in this dimension animals pretend they cannot speak, so they don't freak out the humans. I am not from this dimension, you can speak freely around me. Everyone else will hear you barking, but I will understand what you're truly saying.'

Easy enough to check.

'Jack! Jack!' Jack said.

To anyone but Lanie that had sounded like two barks.

'Jack? Is that your name? Pleased to meet you, my name is Lanie.'

Gosh, she did understand him!

'Why did you save me?' Jack asked, trotting next to Lanie.

'You asked for any help and popped up on our screens, so they sent me to help,' Lanie said.

'If you're an angel, are you dead?' the dog asked.

Lanie smiled and nodded.

'So now you can live forever? Sweet deal! Can I be an angel, too?' The dog hopped up and down. *Dog life was way short.*

'I would have to ask the Watchers...' Lanie said.

'Ask! Ask!'

'Very well, I will, but you do know that immortality comes with a price?' she asked.

'What? What? What do I have to do?'

'You would have to serve.'

'How long?'

'At least two hundred years or so I'm told and then you can take retirement to the dimension of your choosing,' Lanie related what she remembered from Loretta's induction.

Two hundred years!! 'I can live and serve for two hundred years. Count me in!'

'You want to start now? I was thinking of finding you a nice family with a kid and a garden...' Lanie said.

'No thanks. I've already had a nice family with a kid who adopted me from the pound only to ship me back a month later. The kid developed an allergy. They never knew. Before that, my owner took a new wife and we didn't get along, so she 'lost' me on one of the walks. As if. Drove me to the woods and left me there. So thanks, but no thanks, I'm all done with being a temporary toy for humans. I'd rather do something meaningful with my life,' Jack said.

'The Agency was considering taking you on as a guardian anyway. After your...short...life span was over. I guess they wouldn't mind bringing you on board now... We are severely understaffed...' Lanie mused.

'I don't need a little more life to agree to serve as a guardian. I can start serving as a guardian now. I have excellent references - I've never bitten anyone in my entire life!' Jack said.

'If it was up to me, you'd be hired, but I don't make the recruitment decisions, so let's ask the Watchers, shall we?' Lanie said, picking Jack up. She wasn't sure her cocoon would carry them both and prayed the entire dog materialised alongside her if she just held him. The Cheshire cat's floating head had always scared the bejeezus out of her. *Oh well, they would both find out soon enough.*

***

Lanie had never seen anything like this before. Billows, ridges, streams and mountains of white stretched before her as long as the eye could see until this magical terrain met the lavender sky under the twin suns. Further away Lanie could see a peninsula of white arches of waves edging away.

She was standing on a cloud.

The terrain in this dimension was gorgeous and also very deadly for travellers who occasionally got lost here. Once they fell off, they turned into the cloud shape of the being they had been in their dimension.

Lanie remembered how she had admired clouds in the shapes of dragons, butterflies, birds and even humans when she was a kid. Now she knew that these funny shapes had been beings who had either fallen off or been pushed off the Cloud that was occasionally visible in the Earth dimension.

Lanie squatted and looked down.

It was a good thing she hadn't suffered from vertigo as a human and that all angels were immune to it. Below her, the clouds ended abruptly after a sheer drop of 50 feet. A tiny black dot was cliff-hanging off the bottom tip.

Engaging her wings, Lanie spearheaded down, the dot growing into a giant elephant toy that only blinked at her as she reassuringly smiled at it.

She took a good hold of the critter, but it held tight with its trunk as if glued to the last ridge of sanity.

Lanie projected calm and peace and love from her heart like Daisy had taught her, 'Honey, let go and I can help you get to where you need to go.'

The toy elephant whimpered and shook its head.

'I know you are afraid, but I'm not a hallucination, I will catch you and nothing bad will happen to you, I promise,' Lanie reassured.

She sensed the elephant wasn't reassured. A thought, not her own, came to her that something bad had already happened, otherwise the elephant wouldn't be here.

Telepathy with toys? Really?

Lanie hoped she could handle someone else's thoughts in her head.

'I know that you're not supposed to be here, that something happened that you cannot explain, but let's get you off this cliff and you can tell me all about it so I can help you, ok?'

She thought she sensed a nod and held on tighter as the elephant let go of the cloud.

Lanie propelled them swiftly and slowly upwards, 'There, see, I'm holding tight and you didn't fall and you're going to be alright.'

Lanie sensed such misery that she almost let go in surprise. *Was the elephant miserable because it knew it was not going to be alright or because she had managed to save him?*

After she deposited both of them on more or less solid ground in the middle of the Cloud, she had to ask, 'Tell me, what happened? How did you end up hanging from there,' she pointed below them.

The toy looked at her with something that was a cross between reproach, hurt and scorn. Ever since childhood, Lanie had always found it intriguing how even the least animated toys could project emotions.

The storm of thoughts that hit her was unreadable. Now that the elephant was out of peril, no one could accuse him of thinking slow.

'A bit more slowly, please. I'm new to reading minds,' Lanie smiled apologetically.

Then she heard the toy's thoughts. It was like someone was whispering half phrases in her mind.

Taken from its home amongst dozens of its brothers and sisters...wrapped and gifted...to a human child...punched and torn and put in dark basements for storage...afraid...missing the kid...thrown into the dumpster when the parents were moving house...not knowing what had happened to the kid...crying for help as the lid of the garbage truck was closing...last thought being of the heaven in the sky that humans spoke of...stuck in between the sky that looked nothing like the human one and grabbing hold of the cloud at the last minute.

Lanie noticed that the elephant's thoughts quickly transformed into a film in her head. She could probably even guess what had happened to the kid. He or she had grown up and moved out and the parents had been cleaning the basement and thrown out a large toy that had been taking up too much space. Well, thank goodness, the toy had not deliberately walked off the cloud. Eccentric Santa she could handle. Suicidal toys, she wasn't so sure.

'Now let's get you to your heaven, this is just in-between land,' she said and stood up.

Human heaven. He wanted to go to human heaven.

'Why? Don't you want to see your brothers and sisters again?'

Human boy. The elephant wanted to see the human boy again.

Ah.

That could also have been the reason why the parents and not the kid had been cleaning out the basement.

Lanie wished there was grief counselling for toys. She had done it for humans back when she had been one.

'I cannot help you there, but I know someone who can, shall we go see her?' If anyone could, Daisy would sort him out. Lanie knew that bringing charges back to the Agency was not protocol, but she was out of her depth here, she had no choice.

Lanie and the elephant materialised at the Watchers' station seconds later. Daisy waved hello at the toy as if she had been expecting him.

'You wouldn't believe how many we rescue from the clouds doing a similar thing, going after their masters to human heaven,' Daisy looked sad, 'but the clouds they make if we miss a rescue are so pretty...' she brightened up again.

Before Lanie could say a word, a door opened straight into the Watchers' station and from a backdrop of a dimension sliced in half between Disney and Adams Family, a golden-haired god of a boy walked in.

'Hi, Freyr,' Daisy said, batting her eyelashes at record speed.

The teenager nodded a wordless thank you slash hello to

Daisy, walked to the elephant and held out his hand. Lanie could sense the joy the toy was emitting. It was nearly jumping up and down with excitement.

So this had been his master? He looked quite alive to Lanie.

As the two started walking back to the boy's dimension, Daisy chirped, 'Bye, Freyr!' and gone they were.

Incredulous, Lanie turned to dopey-looking Daisy, 'Why couldn't he have taken the toy along in the first place? It had been trying to go to human heaven since that is where he believed his master was and he looked quite alive to me.'

Daisy looked at her pointedly.

Oh.

'So, he's dead and now a guardian, so what. He could still have taken the toy with him.' Lanie's mouth moved into an unforgiving stubborn line.

'Honey, Freyr has plenty to do in the dimension he guards along with four other guardians. Four. Even Hel has just one guardian. Eerie needs four to keep the spooky stuff at bay across dimensions. Freyr simply didn't have time to dwell on people or things he left behind when he took up this permanent assignment,' Daisy patted Lanie's hand, which was always oddly comforting.

'How did he know to pick the...' Lanie wanted to say 'ollyphant', which is what she had called elephants when she had been little, '...elephant up from here?' As far as Lanie remembered, she hadn't uttered anything out loud, the elephant confessing where he had wanted to go had been a conversation held only in their minds. Was Daisy a mind-reader?

'The toy just looked familiar...' Daisy shrugged and kept tapping at the screens.

'You knew Freyr when he was a kid?' Lanie's eyebrow shot up. 'I thought fairies and humans didn't mingle.'

'We don't,' Daisy said, concentrating very hard on the priority screens. The tapping increased.

'So how come you know about his toys?' Lanie asked, genuinely interested. 'Were you sweet on him or something?' The thought of Daisy being sweet on anyone to the point of noticing their belongings was certainly intriguing.

The tapping stopped. 'Or something. If you must know, the Boss had been watching over Freyr for a while before he was recruited. I just happened to watch a lot of recordings of him for her. Since he was not a save, he didn't pop up on any of our screens, I had to go through a lot of CCTV, video tapes of neighbour's kid's birthdays, you name it, I looked through it,' Daisy said.

'Why?'

'To see if he was good guardian material. Especially for a dimension such as spooky Eerie.'

Daisy's reluctance to admit anything roused Lanie's suspicions, so she had to ask, 'No love affairs between Watchers and humans?'

Daisy shook her head. The tapping started again.

What about humans and guardians?

'And none between humans and guardians either. You would have to become human again for that. By the time two hundred years of your service pass here, anyone you loved in your dimension will be long gone, honey,' Daisy said and patted Lanie's hand.

To avoid dipping back into her dark thoughts about Peter, Lanie decided that hot chocolate was an allowed distraction and went to get them both a cup from the wall.

26. Learning the Language
Victor

Victor cursed when he materialised in Tempest, Texas. He continued cursing, using all the swearwords in all the languages he knew. If he had to behave like a perfect Southern gentleman for a few hours, there would be no cursing, so he was getting it out of his system. Probably looked like he had Tourettes. If there were anyone nearby to look. Or hear.

The dusking street was empty.

Whether it was from all the cursing or from the stress of traipsing between two dimensions without proper food, water or sleep, Victor felt parched. He hoped he would get lemonade when he got to Mae's.

Before Victor managed to ring the doorbell, Charlotte opened the door and pounced in for a hug. Trying not to get strangled from her enthusiasm, Victor nodded at Aunt Mae, 'Evening m'am.' Disentangling the hands of his charge from around his neck under Aunt Mae's reproachful stare, he said, 'Evening, Charlotte' and accompanied it with another courteous nod.

Charlotte looked so hopeful, so happy to see him. From inside, someone on the radio was drawling in southern sing-along how even angels fall.[27]

Rubbish. No one was falling anywhere or into anyone. He had a job to do. Prep her for Italy and off she goes and he is free for other, hopefully swifter missions where he can finally kick some ass.

Victor could feel the bad boy in him starting to itch from all this wholesome goodness. Thank gods for New York, the land of sarcasm where he could unleash his dark side with Sally who seemed to be immune to cruelty. Here, he had to be good. Only four days back on Earth and four weeks in Gaia and he was turning back into his old self.

Well at least he didn't have to listen to the constant noise in Charlotte's and Sally's heads anymore! The more human he became, the more his mind-reading ability deteriorated. *And good riddance!* Well, until he re-balanced at the Agency anyway.

He didn't want to become who he had been. He knew that much. Victor took his frustration and anger and shoved it deeper than ever. It could stew there a bit while these good people were being kind to him.

'Come see what I drew today at work, come see,' Charlotte was dragging him to the table out on the porch with Aunt Mae tut-tutting her disapproval at such lack of manners.

Victor nodded at Aunt Mae again. The lady was a proper Southern lady. She made him feel right at home, even when she was tut-tutting around or even at him. *If his mam had tut-tutted even a little at him instead of watching his dad beat him senseless for every single little thing he had done wrong, maybe his human self would have grown up to be every bit as good as Charlotte did. Boring but good.*

'Charlotte! Lemonade...' Aunt Mae reminded, disappearing into the kitchen.

'Oh, yes, yes of course, one moment,' Charlotte made sure Victor was sitting comfortably at the table, slid her portfolio at him and darted back into the house to get the drinks.

When she came back, she continued her monologue exactly where she had left off, oblivious to Victor's moodiness.

Victor was admiring Charlotte's drawings of apples and pears and various kitchen utensils with a smile that could have made crocodiles envious. Four days in with Charlotte and four hellishly long weeks with Sally, he was starting to suspect the Watchers had an agenda, sending him on two particularly long-playing saves. He had never stayed in his former dimension and another, Earth-like dimension for this long without recharging. *Why wouldn't the stupid girl move? She would be far from her pitchfork-wielding family and living her happily ever after and he could go kill something in Dialysis X. On a save, of course.*

It wasn't until she stopped talking and looked at him with eager eyes did he realise he had lost the plot of the conversation entirely. She had probably asked him a question. 'Sorry, toots, deep in thought.'

Slightly scandalised about the 'toots' but trying not to

show it, Charlotte repeated her question, 'Would you drive me tomorrow when I go pick up the art supplies I ordered?'

She had money to waste on supplies instead of saving up for the ticket to Italy.

Looking at Charlotte's stricken face, Victor realised he must have said it out loud.

'Even if I saved for a year and lived entirely on Mae's charity, the tips from the restaurant won't be enough to cover a return ticket, not to mention art school costs an arm and a leg. I simply need to find alternatives closer to home,' Charlotte said, looking mortified that she was discussing her finances with him. *Proper ladies never discussed money with gentlemen. It was distasteful.*

'Buy a cheap one-way ticket when there are airline sales and there are scholarships,' Victor threw back. 'Didn't I give you the information about those already?' *Honestly, the girl was killing his patience which was already mortally wounded from his encounters with the ever-charming Sally. The only way to keep her from repeat forking was to put thousands of miles between her and farmville. Even a visit back could end poorly since there was no predicting what the stoned boy would do in retaliation of having to work.*

'What about my family?' Charlotte asked.

'What about them?' Victor retorted.

'I couldn't just leave them and go off to do something I like, even love. What if they needed my help?' Charlotte said.

The sheer pig-headiness of the girl!

Victor felt his fists clench.

Her family, the people closest to her treated her like dirt, like a slave, letting her work for food and a roof above her head and still she had no ill words to say about them. Some Stockholm syndrome.

'You know, they took me in when Pop died. They're all I have left. I am grateful that they took in an extra mouth to feed when it couldn't have been easy, tending a farm and putting Andy through school. Orphanage was an option, and they chose to take me in. They chose to take care of me. So I chose to take care of them. They just have a special way of going about it.' She looked up at him, pleading for him to understand, afraid that he wouldn't.

Something in the way Charlotte said it made Victor's throat close up. He had heard someone else say those same words time and time again.

Grace had said she chose to take care of him because he had chosen to take care of her. That he just had his own way of going about it. If you could call bullying her, controlling her every move and being over-ardently jealous as ways of caring about someone. Charlotte, like Grace had no one left in this world. And the people left certainly took their liberties.

'Besides, they're all I've got. You play the cards you're dealt,' Charlotte shrugged and smiled.

Victor wondered whether Grace, like Charlotte had been afraid to be alone and that was why she had chosen to be in a bad relationship rather than end it. Completely without anyone's support, no matter how he had treated her. With their parents gone, Charlotte and Grace must have feared loneliness a great deal to choose to withstand the kind of treatment their nearest and dearest were inflicting upon them.

For the first time ever Victor had the urge to go and apologise to Grace for the way he had treated her. Except he couldn't. The Watchers had explained to him the rule of no contact with previous life, which he had thought of as convenient so far. If she thinks he is dead, seeing him and hearing an apology would just be too confusing.

Persuading this charge was taking too long for Victor's liking. His fingers were itching to use the now recharged magic wand. He was almost tempted to organise everything by magic, if it hadn't been something Loretta had said, 'Only use the magic wand in emergencies. It doesn't take kindly to be called on to do menial tasks.' He had found out the hard way, nearly depleting it when he had used it to pour Sally's Sprite down the drain and cloak all her mirrors.

So, instead, he had to try the sap approach chicks digged, 'If you keep thinking of others first, that's how your life is going to play out. What if you went and became a famous painter and could help them even more? Or do you prefer to stick around here, find some community college and probably end up in obscurity? How likely are you to paint if you need to help out at the farm at your every spare moment?'

After a hefty silence, Charlotte asked, 'So you suggest I go and live in Italy for a while?'

How about for always? 'Yes, how about for six months or a year? You've heard of exchange students? People go and study abroad all the time. You could learn the language, go to school, start painting.' *Marry an Italian, have loads of kids and settle down there. Avoid death by pitch fork.*

'Learn the language?' Charlotte beamed.

Was she going to repeat everything at him now? Before his patience eroded completely, Victor went for the distraction her drawings provided. 'Why not, I could teach you, I promised, remember?'

'I remember,' Charlotte said. He had promised to teach her the first time they had met. *She could hardly believe that it was just four days ago! In just a few days this devil with a halo knew her better than her family whom she had lived with for a year.*

Charlotte felt like tearing up, 'Will you excuse me, I'll get some more lemonade.' She had done plenty unladylike things in front of the devil. She wasn't going to cry, though.

When Charlotte came back, Victor rose to meet her, 'Let me help you with the tray.' Amongst the fuss of pouring, Victor put Charlotte's drawings on the swing, keeping them away from harm of potential spilled glasses.

From the doorway, Mae observed the boy taking great care with something that meant a lot to Charlotte.

'Aunt Mae, would you join us for lemonade, please?' Victor asked holding a chair out for her.

The boy was thoughtful, too. Mae nodded and set herself up on the porch in one of the sunny spots.

The porch had seen many a good lemonade party. Certainly those where there was as much laughter as today. Perhaps even those where Florentine art was the focal point of discussion, but none where a Southern gentleman tried to teach the ladies Italian.

Later that evening Aunt Mae caught up with Victor just as he was getting on his bike. She had sent Charlotte upstairs to get a shawl. 'Victor, I thought about what you said yesterday...about Charlotte going to study art and painting in Florence...' Victor looked up at the old lady mussing her handkerchief. 'If she got into that school you suggested and if she got a scholarship, I could perhaps contribute a little towards airfare...?' Mae smiled.

Victor nodded, 'It's settled then.'

Aunt Mae threw him another smile and walked back to her porch with her head held high.

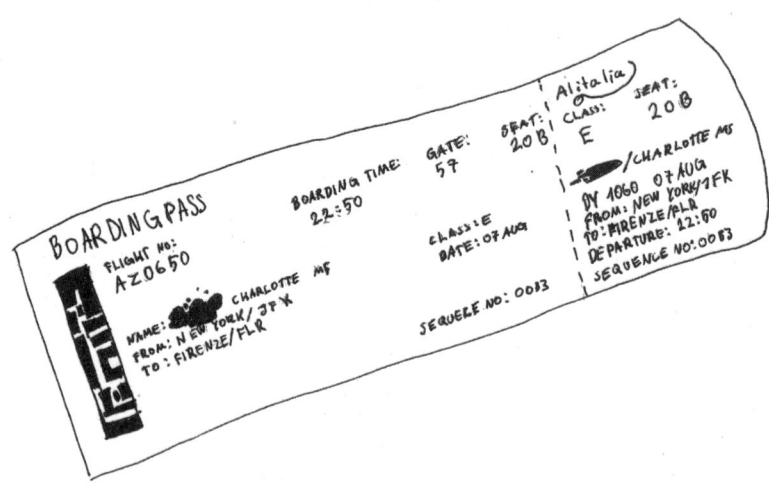

11. „It's settled then."

27. The Long Shot
Grace

Gabriel the cat dashed back through the window and into the hallway ahead of Grace's arrival just as he had done on the previous three nights.

Grace exhaled loudly as she closed the door behind her. 'That went well, I think,' she said to the cat who was waiting for her in the hallway. She picked it up and smooched it on the nose. 'Missed me?'

Mistaking the cat's stupor for expectation, Grace waltzed around the lobby, laughing, 'Hungry? I'm starving! The blueberry muffin helped keep off the hunger, but I haven't had a bite since lunch!'

Grace put the cat down gently and went to the kitchen to make herself a snack.

Looking up from around her ankles Gabriel watched her load up a tray full of all sorts of goodies. *All of that would fit into this skinny girl?* Meanwhile, in the Earth dimension, unlike at the Agency where no one remembered food, his stomach grumbled.

Grace looked at him, startled, 'You're hungry, as well, aren't you? Did you wait for me to get home so we could eat together? How sweet.'

If cats could make faces, this cat would definitely have made one. He had been too busy saving her all day to grab a meal. Eyeing her ham and cheese sandwich, the cat sighed and went to see about his kibbles.

Grace headed for the kitchen to check whether she needed to refill his bowls.

The bowl of dry kibbles looked untouched.

Grace looked the cat in the eyes, 'You haven't eaten anything today, Cat.'

If only she knew. Day one, when he had been buying meals throughout the day not to give an excuse to be booted from the cafe for taking up space had been a picnic compared to the last few days. Aside from the muffin and coffee in the morning and this evening, he had had no time for food.

'Did you miss me, is that why you're not eating?' Grace asked.

If kibbles was all there was, he would have kibbles. Ah well, life evened itself out - good meals on a thoroughly leisurely day, kibbles for his hard work today.

Despite his efforts he hadn't found any traces of the assassin in the coffee shop cellar. It looked pristine. The Watchers weren't able to tell him either, how or why they missed this attempt on Grace's life in the first place. Loretta had mumbled something about Grace's being not the only save. The rest of Gabriel's day was spent following Grace's every move. He also made a routine of checking and double checking all the places she frequented for hidden incendiary devices - her apartment, the coffee shop, the shops along her walk to work. That was a lot of checking and running around. Keeping an eye out for snipers and dodging kids and cars when in cat form had kept Gabriel on a constant move.

Grace's own stomach grumbled loudly. Graced with a metabolism of athletes, she could eat half her fridge and still look slim and be hungry. Her model acquaintances hated her.

Grace made herself a sandwich as the cat hopped up onto the table top. It was his favourite spot in the entire kitchen.

Grace noticed the cat's interest in her ham and cheese. 'Well, cheese is almost milk, so maybe you are used to eating cheese? And ham...? No harm in offering...' Grace had to admit that if the kibbles didn't smell that great to her, maybe the cat was not too keen on them either.

She ripped off a slice of cheese and put it on the table next to the cat. On a second thought, she added a sliver of ham.

The ham was gone in less than a second. The cheese was executed next. The cat turned its gleaming eyes on her tray.

'Oh, so that's what you prefer? Human food? Well, alright, I don't mind sharing.' Not thinking twice about it, Grace grabbed a saucer from the kitchen cabinet and headed for the living room with the cat in tow.

She set the saucer next to her own plate and watched the cat hesitate. 'Hop on, kitty, it's ok,' she patted the table next to the saucer.

Ripping her ham and cheese sandwich in half, she diced the ham and the cheese into smaller bits onto the saucer, leaving herself the remnants of the buttered bread.

The cat hopped onto the low dining room table and sat next to its plate, thought about it for a second and zeroed in on the food.

They both ate in silence for ten minutes.

Grace kept stealing glances at her cat. *Yes, by now it was her cat, even if he didn't know it. Of course, her cat would be the one to eat human things off a human plate.*

'I have a cat and apparently, an admirer,' she said polishing off her sandwich.

The cat's ears perked up.

'What else would you call a hunky City boy who keeps turning up at the coffee shop for his morning coffee and to see me almost home at night?'

A guardian, that's who. The cat wagged its tail once.

'I don't even know why I haven't let him walk me to the door,' Grace said.

The cat eyed her wearily.

'He does have lovely blue eyes and he's built like a god,' Grace said, shredding another slice of ham onto the cat's plate.

The cat sat up straighter. *He had to finish the rescue before this girl fell head over heels for him.*

Grace nodded, 'Believe you me. I mean, I don't know a lot about him. Not even his last name! He is such a gentleman. Manners from a whole other era, really. Do you know what he did? He opened the coffee shop door for me while he nodded his goodbyes to the remaining customers. Whoever does that at our day and age? Also, he asked me for my preference of our route back. Most men just walk. And...and...while we were walking, he kept to the street-side of the pedestrian walkway. A proper gentleman, I'm telling you. Reminds me slightly of my dad, to be honest. But he can't be that old. He's just been brought up proper. At first I thought he was doing it on purpose, trying to impress me. Except it all comes out so naturally. When I made a comment about mollycoddling me when he steered me carefully around a puddle, do you know what he said?' Grace waited for Cat to respond.

Cat was listening intently.

'He just looked at me blankly and said every other person would have done the same to save the lady the trouble of wet feet and ruined shoes. Whoever talks like that nowadays?'

Gabriel made a mental note to adjust to the language patterns of the modern Earth.

'You know, maybe his upbringing dictates long courtship? But even then, he could have already indicated somehow that he was interested and that we are, in fact, courting. Not a peep. What if he really only wants to be friends, after all?' Grace asked Cat.

Cat wagged its tail in annoyance. Honestly. Damsels in distress. They always over-thought things. Things were never either/or, sometimes the third logical alternative was that the guy didn't want anything from the girl. In Gabriel's case, just to protect her, not to be her friend, not to be her lover, just make sure she lived to see another day.

Meanwhile, Grace continued, 'The fact that I don't know that much about him makes me think he used to be special ops. The way he is built and how he steered me round people and traffic and how he doubled back and peeked whether the guys followed us the other night. It would also explain why he is so tongue tied about his past. As a trader in the City, he cannot tell me much about his current job either. So, imagine, he was saying virtually nothing and I kept prattling on, like you wouldn't believe - about my life, my hopes, my dreams. I know I thought he might be a stalker, but when you actually talk to him, somehow, he has this demeanour of tall, blond and trustworthy. If you saw him, you would probably trust him immediately. He's ... decent, you know?'

If this girl hadn't seen much genuine kindness from her nearest family, perhaps decency was also something she didn't see often. He put his paw on her hand.

'I know, I know, I should be more careful with strangers,' Grace said, eating off the cat's plate since it seemed he was no longer interested in his food. 'But still, I somehow trust the reason he gave for being there last night to rescue me from the drunken lads. The situation could have easily gotten hairy, you know. If it hadn't been for Gabriel.'

Interpreting the cat's stony silence as doubt, Grace asked, 'Or....Do you think it's possible that Gabriel made a deal with them so he could step in and make me trust him?'

The cat looked at her like she was deranged.

'Probably not. It would be very 'Enough' of him.'

The cat shifted from paw to paw.

'You know...that movie where Jennifer Lopez plays a waitress and a guy arranges his friend to insult her so he could save her and briefly romance her, except he falls for her and marries her, but then still cannot help himself and is abusive until she runs away with their daughter and eventually kills him to break free...?'

The cat stopped shifting.

Grace shook her head.

She was explaining her reasoning and retelling the plot of a movie to a cat. As if it understood or cared.

Except it seemed to listen to her and she didn't want to bother Emma with any of it. As much as Emma loved her, she would be disappointed that after two years of her listening to Grace's doubts and boosting her self-esteem, Grace was still at square one. Self-doubt and distrust of men.

Since the cat wasn't judging or running for the hills, Grace continued, 'Anyway, minus the marriage and the arranged meeting over insults like in the movie, that was pretty much the scenario of how I met Victor. One morning, a long time ago, he was sitting in the same corner booth that Gabriel favours. He flirted with me, asked me out, stupidly I said 'yes' and a whole lot of misfortune followed. Which is why I have trusting issues with perfectly nice men nowadays, not allowing them to walk me to my door. Since Victor had been a customer, then Gabriel taking an interest in me made all the alarm bells go off. For fear of history repeating itself, you know?' Grace said, pouring milk into a saucer for the cat and into a tall glass for herself. Drinking milk before bedtime had been strangely comforting since childhood.

Gabriel mentally thanked Victor for making this save unnecessarily complicated. *Building trust took time. Time that they didn't have.*

'Oh, don't you make the same face Emma usually does when I'm wondering about the intentions of another hunky suitor,' Grace said to the cat. 'I mean, he SEEMS like a very nice man. I just sense there is more to him than meets the eye.'

Like a pair of wings and an immortal soul.

'I have to admit, he looks very yummy. The whole tall, blond thing and his muscular build make me feel safe. The longish hair and blue eyes telegraphing genuine concern for other human beings are slightly at odds with his otherwise assertive demeanour, though. He seems to generate trust easily, almost too easily. While for a consultant it may be a learnt skill, I've fallen into that trap before, you know?'

Grace looked outside. No change compared to their walk. The sky was depressingly grey. 'It's still raining. It must be the soggiest day of this summer out there right now...' She sighed.

To keep her maudlin thoughts at bay, Grace switched the TV on, skipping the daunting news and looking for an upbeat music channel.

A lovely red-head was singing that this life was as fragile as a dream and nothing is really as it seems.[28] Grace switched to VEVO where Katy Perry was wondering whether her alien love interest was the devil or an angel, but already begging him to lead her into the light, even if he was from a different dimension.[29]

Grace tsk-tsk-ed. As if. *The girl was being rash. What if he led her somewhere that was even worse than her apocalyptic now?* Still, VEVO was pretty perky, she decided to keep it on.

'Back to our conversation, Cat,' Grace said plonking onto the couch. She patted the duvet. The cat hopped on it. 'Let's analyse this, shall we?' Grace thought she saw the cat roll its eyes. *Must be a trick of the light.* 'I know Gabriel is no Victor, they are completely different, it's like heaven and earth...or heaven and hell more like it... Maybe...just maybe I don't want things to proceed too quickly. I mean, a girl never wants to leave an impression that she is too easy, does she?'

Walking her to her door would have meant she was an easy catch?!?

The cat lay down and put a paw across its eyes. Gabriel wondered which out of the two of them had been brought up in the 12th century.

'After all, if to believe Emma and my uncle, all the guys are after one thing,' Grace was flicking through the TV channels again, since the music channel had taken a romantic turn.

Gabriel almost shook his head, but thought better of it. Not normal cat behaviour. Still, the girls in this day and age! *Not all the guys were after one thing!* He certainly wasn't nor had he ever given her reason to believe he was.

'Oh, don't you look so shocked,' Grace told the cat. 'Yes, he is a gentleman and no, he hasn't made any passes at me,' she said as she paused to watch Julia Roberts in a wedding dress, on a horse, bolting[30]. 'Not that I would mind...' she muttered, pulling up the duvet.

Stunned, the cat fell off the couch, but landed on its feet, looking like someone just told it that mice were made of tofu.

Grace hoped it was at her choice of movie and not because of her confession.

It was perhaps too late to try and avoid his charge falling for him. Gabriel was stumped. *He hadn't DONE anything for Grace to be attracted to him!* Strangely, Gabriel's human side was doing a small happy dance somewhere deep down. His angelic side was screaming at him to return to the Agency immediately. Once there, he would be restored to his senses, so to speak. Be on permanent neutral, devoid of all emotions. Only then could he keep his distance and avoid setting this girl up for failure.

'I haven't felt ditzy around anyone. Ever. But yesterday morning...I had to hold myself back from hugging him. I was so happy he came back to the shop to see me. And did I tell you about his baby-blues and his smile? Gawd ... his smile could melt ice caps ... he makes me forget the world and the troubles in it, so sue me if I admit he looks jumpable to me,' Grace huffed.

Loud drumming behind the window made the cat sit up and made Grace peek outside.

A wall of rain.

Grace's shoulders sagged and she sighed loudly, her happiness evaporating with every rain drop tap-tapping on the window. She muted Julia confessing something to Richard Gere on TV. 'I hate it when it rains,' she said and drew the blinds shut. 'Drizzle I can handle. Drizzle didn't rob me of my family,' Grace shivered and reached for the duvet.

The cat perked up its ears.

With the duvet trailing behind her, Grace proceeded to light all the candles she could find.

Grace found lighting the tea-lights calming. 'We were all thinking of going to a concert or recital or something and in the end, they did go... My parents... It was raining just as hard. I'll never forget the doorbell and what news it brought...had it ripped out when I got older...it reminded me too much of that night...'

Grace still remembered the rain drip-drip-dripping from the policeman's coat onto their hallway carpet as he imparted the news.

Looking into his concerned face, Grace had only heard sound bites, '....steep curve...country road...water puddles....attempted to break...glided on water...tree...died instantly...sorry for your loss.' In those few simple words, the people closest to her had ceased to exist.

'I don't remember much after. The drudgery of burial arrangements, shaking hands with the few relatives that had turned up for the funeral, sorting out my inheritance - it was all a mute blur.' Grace had just followed uncle Tom and signed whatever needed to be signed, shook hands that needed to be shaken and dressed in whatever was laid out for her.

'For months after, whenever I closed my eyes, I was back in

that hallway, in front of the policeman, seeing the wall of rain behind him... Every time I woke up I hoped it was just a bad dream and would run into my parents' bedroom only to find it empty. Every time, it brought back the horror of the moment when I realised that I would never see my mom and dad - the laughing, the lively, the crazy-dance-at-two-in-the-morning, the cuddly and encouraging and loving mom and dad – ever again.' Grace told the cat from the corner of her red couch and peeked from under the duvet.

She was sitting amid a sea of candles.

Better.

A low rumble outside augured a storm.

Grace pointed at the TV, 'Julia isn't doing it for me tonight. If I put a better feel-good movie on loud enough, I won't hear what's going on outside, what do you think?' Grace asked the cat.

The cat looked sceptical.

'Well, maybe an action movie, then...' Grace said and went to sift through her DVD collection. She found the first Terminator movie, 'Oh good, the music in this one will definitely drown out the rain,' she said and popped the DVD in as the cat made a face. 'We're watching this,' Grace pointed at the TV, 'take it or leave it.'

The cat sat down at her feet.

'Good,' Grace settled into the red couch.

Knowing what was to come in a few minutes, Grace paused the DVD when Sarah was biting Kyle and went to make herself another sandwich.

'That Sarah girl, she's really not that bright, you know,' Grace told the cat, shredding ham and cheese for it. 'She has already had a run-in with the cyborg that obviously wants her dead and if the dude was there for the specific reason of rescuing her and her only, couldn't she conclude a bit quicker that he might possibly be telling the truth, no matter how crazy it sounded?'

Nibbling at the savouries, Gabriel made a mental note of Grace's preferences to be told the truth in case he ever needed to involve her.

'Although I have to admit, there was never a sign that there was something off with the world, that something was about to happen...everything seemed perfectly normal...well it always is until stuff happens, doesn't it?'

The cat munched on.

'About that...I cannot quite describe it, but for the last few days I have been feeling that something is not how it is supposed to be.'

The cat's ears perked up.

Grace thought that in cat world that was probably the equivalent of a raised eyebrow and kept going. 'I don't mean all of the tsunamis and accidents at nuclear power stations, although judging by the news on the soap-box radio at work, there has been a pile-up of that lately. I mean there is something strange going on with MY world, you know?'

The cat stopped eating and pawed at her, meaning to encourage her to go on.

'It all started with the City boy camping out in my coffee shop all day and him just happening to be in the vicinity to save me from the drunken lads. These guys, they have been to the coffee shop many times and they have never given me any trouble before. I even checked whether it was the full moon and look,' Grace pointed at her kitchen calendar, 'it's not. It's all somehow too convenient, too coincidental, too...strange, you know. Gives me the heebie-jeebies...'

The cat licked its paw, done with the food. He had to hand it to the girl, she had good instincts.

Grace returned to the TV.

The cat crept towards the extra pillow on the opposite side of the couch. *A few more days and it would all become clear. He could keep Grace out of harm's way without reinforcements for a few more days.*

Grace scratched him behind his left ear, 'You are a good listener, Cat.'

The cat looked up at her, its eyes semi-closed in scratchy bliss.

12. 'You are a good listener, Cat.

Well, you are,' she reassured as it settled into its pillow.

An hour later, when the rain had slowed to a petty drizzle, Grace was nodding off and Gabriel was letting her.

Before Grace fell completely asleep, Gabriel heard her say, her voice thick from sleep, 'I feel for her, Sarah...normal girl turned hero to avoid something really bad from happening...I feel like that all the time...that bad things happen...and that no matter what I do, somehow the good is not winning anymore... and...I'm supposed to do something about it...dunno what though...' She yawned and was off like a light.

The cat caught the duvet with its claw and dragged it across Grace's bare legs to cover her up for the night. He then pushed the button on the remote to switch off the TV.

Could Grace be a hero destined for greatness in this dimension? It was a long shot, but worth investigating. Gabriel made a mental note to call the Watchers ASAP.

There was a loud sigh from under the duvet. Grace turned on her back, exposing a mess of hair across her face.

Gabriel checked his surroundings, the outside and returned to the couch to guard Grace.

At night, all the crossness that Grace armoured herself with against menfolk frequenting the coffee shop fell away somehow. Lying there, peaceful and quiet, Grace reminded him a little of Daisy, their ever-happy fairy.

She was kind. She was generous. She was...perfect. Gabriel remembered how her dimples came out every time she laughed together with a customer. How she waited while an old regular counted out the money for the bill for her cup of tea in pennies, helping the old dotty to open her coin purse so she wouldn't have to struggle with her shaking arthritic hands. Losing her would be like letting the sun eclipse forever. Fine for some worlds, but devastating for this one. Devastating for his world as well.

He was shifting from paw to paw, trying to figure out the best vantage point for keeping guard and to establish how proper it was exactly to sleep so close to his Charge.

Looking at sleeping Grace, Gabriel realised he wanted more out of life than just to serve. He stopped mid-shift.

Wait a minute.

All Gabriel ever wanted to do was to serve. Until now, it had been enough. He had never thought about love as something that could or should have been part of his life. Part of his experience.

He still had his wings and eternity, but that was no longer enough.

What would it be like, keeping just one person happy, not the entire humankind or all 63 dimensions or the powers that be?

Being around Grace and being back on Earth for only a few days was making him human again.

Serving wasn't enough? He himself had started wanting things for himself?

Shocked at the thought, Gabriel decided he needed to lie down.

Selfishness in an angel?

That had happened once before and didn't end well for humankind.

No, no, no. Better perish all such thoughts. He needed Valhalla, Victor, the Boss, Loretta, anyone to talk some sense into him. *He needed to get away from Earth. To get rebalanced. So as not to endanger his mission.*

Except he couldn't at the moment. He couldn't risk Grace waking up to a cat making a phone call or disappearing into thin air. Gabriel couldn't really decide, which would look worse in a dimension so low on magic as Earth.

While Gabriel was fighting whether to go or stay, Grace reached out and cuddled him up into the nook of her arm so close that his face came up to hers, making the decision for him.

Gabriel fell still. *Well, proper was out of the window now, but this was a good vantage point for watching out for whatever could go bump in the night. No re-balancing at the Agency just yet.* As Gabriel watched Grace sleep, he had a strange feeling that right about now, he would prefer to be in human form.

28. A Grey Day of Peace
Boss

The Boss looked down on weepy London and considered whether it was the rain that was getting to him. Things should have been peachy. It was another grey day, a balancing act briefly achieved, an agreement temporarily struck between good and evil. So why was he feeling out of sorts?

It had been five Earth days and Gabriel had still not figured out who was after Grace. Victor had saved Charlotte way too easily and was simply procrastinating before that save was properly over. Juggling saving two girls from themselves was not quite as complex as the Watchers had intended for his next level of training, but Victor was tending to two saves in two different dimensions with vastly different timespans. That was plenty complex.

A male voice was assuring him on the speakers that someone could see the pain and the love in him, that the angels and devils burn inside all of us.[31]

Annoyed, the man twitched his fingers and the music started calling out to all new angels[32], which sounded more appropriate. Lanie had been a good find, but even the man himself could not help but notice how lately all his recruits had come from Earth, once his dimension.

He had entombed himself in this ivory tower to keep an eye on everything. Doubling the Watchers' screens across the glass surface of his otherwise mahogany desk was his latest attempt to keep things in check. Nothing he did seemed to be making a difference. He had recruited, saved, trained and battled. He didn't sleep, he didn't eat, he didn't rest. Luckily, the pan-dimension Agency operated in suspended time, where natural laws didn't apply.

There were no wins to celebrate.

No joyous jumping over lives saved.

There was no sorrow, no unnecessary death.

The Agency and those passing through it *en route* to their next save were on permanent neutral. Guardians were required to periodically take up residence, however brief, in Agency quarters to keep their senses. Recuperating after particularly trying or lengthy missions was a must so they could keep doing whatever needed doing, no questions asked. Staying in any dimension for long made even angels lose their calm.

And they needed their calm. To preserve their balance, they had to be devoid of emotions, wants and needs. These usually got in the way of doing the right thing in any tricky situation.

Pain. Love. Feelings.

Once, decades of staying at the Agency had done wonders for his no-judgement attitude and level-headedness. The most he managed to stay in nowadays was hours, if not minutes.

The Agency was devoid of all emotions, needs and wants. However, it did nothing to nurture his sense of accomplishment.

The job required him to keep the balance and preserve the existence of all known dimensions.

When all you feel every single day is peace - wins, ambitions and even emotions are unnecessary.

Staying at the Agency even for a few hours was like tapping into unlimited peace.

Lately, that peace had started to feel a lot like emptiness.

The Boss reminded himself that it was him and him alone who had elected to be permanently stuck in the 'Neutral' gear. Well, as permanently as he chose. He could choose to shift out of the neutral gear and leave or just decide to stop being an entity altogether. After he selected his successor.

The man found Israel Kamakawiwo'ole's 'Somewhere Over the Rainbow'[33] on YouTube, sighed, opened up the drawer of his desk and did what he usually did to keep hopelessness at bay.

His smart phone showed him all the creatures he had saved and all the guardian angels he had recruited over the years, one by one in random order.

Grace smiled up at him. The young woman he had seen picking up Gabriel-the-cat was hardly recognisable in this girl of thirteen. That time, too, the tally had been perilously tilted towards evil winning. The only screen blinking for a save was transmitting the face of this girl looking out of a car nearing a corner on a winding wet country road in the middle of the night. Some local idiot had parked his tractor in a blind bend for five minutes, which was all it took for him to get booze from an accommodating neighbour and for a family of four to downsize to an orphan of one. The tally had pinpointed her to be saved, not all of them. Quick to believe he could do magic, she had asked him about it later, at the penthouse apartment the Agency kept in London. Why had he saved her and let her parents and her baby sister burn to a crisp? Instead of answering, he chose to erase the entire event from her memory and deposited her back at her home to wait for the police to arrive. He had done his duty. He had saved who the screens had told him to save.

Lanie smiled up at him. She was turning out to be one of his best angels yet. Which did not excuse the way he had recruited her.

Annoyed, the Indian-looking man flipped to the next picture. Gabriel.

Now that had been a sensible decision. And no flop in recruitment either. When a crusader for Christianity offers his life up for service of the greater good, it is foolish not to take him up on such an offer.

Some more and less scarier creatures, pixies, fairies, yetis, unicorns, dragons and other more and less magical creatures from all kinds of dimensions alternated on the screen in his palm. His success stories, his warriors, his victims.

The man shut down the display, unable to shake the feeling that no matter what he did to shift the tally in favour of the greater good, he wasn't making much of a difference.

The tally mocked him by allowing the black tally hover inches above the level of the white one. Evil was winning today.

Lately, evil seemed to be winning on most days.

How could that be?

Good always wins. Always.

At least that's what his mother had taught him when he had wept over the beheading of one of his mutinous uncles thousands of years ago in the kitchen of a long forgotten Hindu palace. It was strange how this belief lingered while the teachings of his father to just do his duty and put his family first had wavered. He had decided to be a guardian and not take the throne instead of his banished brother Vijaya, leaving the dynasty in tatters. At the time, he had told himself he had accepted a greater calling, that saving entire dimensions was more important than saving one family or one country.

It was time for another personal mission, another save. If he couldn't save the universe and its existing 63 known dimensions and a few unknown ones, then he would do what would make a difference – save a single life. One at a time. So what, if he aged a little compared to his age at death every time he went to the extreme dimensions. He was willing to pay that price. He could still retire before he looked and moved like he was a hundred.

It was time to go to Dialysis X and then Eerie and maybe even to Hel for good measure, not necessarily in that order. He could do scary, spooky and the certifiable dimensions. Or he could go straight to Hel and end their civil war that had started after a successful assassination attempt of their guardian, their queen, Helreginne.

As the cocoon of silvery light took him, YouTube mellowed to How To Save a Life[34].

29. Bored
Sally

In the frog's absence, Sally was so bored, she decided to go for a jog before it was completely dark.

Now, her lungs burnt, her feet ached and she was sweaty-Mac-Sweatison from head to toe. After running what seemed like only half a mile.

Her shower lasted twice as long as her jog, which Sally considered was only proper. *Relaxation was important.*

Sally attempted to sit down on her living room couch with one towel around her and another around her wet hair. She had to throw magazines, a few stupid pillows and a pizza box out of the way first.

Sitting down, she surveyed her surroundings. In the bleak light of day, her apartment did look cluttered.

Damned frog had been right. Wherever it was. Gone for a week, TRUSTING her to make the right choices. Pfff.

Sally picked up the receiver. 'Harry, I swear to Jesus, if you won't return my calls today, I will start calling the morgues,' she said, 'or your mother,' and hung up.

She leafed through an old magazine and switched the TV on. Jamie Oliver was showing off his culinary skills, trying to persuade her that she, too, could cook a fabulous meal in just 15 minutes.

As if.

She abandoned the TV but was loathe to leave the horizontal position on her couch. Snuggling into her mushy decorative pillows helped to ignore the burning pain in her legs, her lower back, her neck, heck everywhere!

Although pretty much any movement hurt, at least all the burning was keeping her warm. If only there was someone she could yell at to bring her a book, a magazine, tea, biscuits, anything. Where was the frog when you needed it? Not that she had any biscuits. She was sure the frog had got rid of biscuits and any sweets she might have had stashed anywhere... Even if by some miracle she had biscuits anywhere, fat cacne the frog would agree to bring her any. But maybe it would? As a perk for the hard decision to exercise. Not without a lecture, though... Strangely, Sally kind of missed the lectures.

30 minutes later, she awoke with a start. *She had nodded off! A teensy bit of exercise and a gulp of fresh air...well, fresh... ish...and this was her reward? Lights out? Oh well...*

As she stumbled towards her bedroom, she didn't even have the strength to kick at the stuff on the floor that was hindering her slumber. *Tomorrow. I'll clean the apartment tomorrow. And call Harry's mother. And go for another jog. And maybe even watch a rerun of Jamie cooking...maybe he has a recipe for something simple, like pasta... Tomorrow.*

30. True Friends
Charlotte

Charlotte didn't want to admit it to herself but she was falling head over heels.

She didn't want to say anything to her friends who had visited earlier, except they had pried it out of her somehow that there was a tall dark stranger in her life who apparently contributed to her looking happy and healthy and dreamy. Scandalised that she didn't have a single snapshot of them together, they immediately sicced her to get proof or be called a liar.

'Oh, may I?' Charlotte said and snapped a friendsie of both of them, not really expecting Victor to say 'no'. 'Darn, this one didn't turn out well, you are a blinding blur, must have caught the glint of the setting sun...' Charlotte flashed Victor a shy apology of a smile and fumbled for a re-take.

'If you don't mind, I would be very much obliged if you didn't,' Victor said and gently lowered Charlotte's outstretched hand.

'Whyever not? How else am I supposed to prove to my former classmates that you exist? You pop by at such hours that it's no longer proper for them to visit with me, so they cannot meet you in person. They doubt that you exist at all.' Charlotte omitted two facts. That the reason her schoolmates wanted his picture was because they were under the impression that he was Charlotte's beau. And that it wasn't just her friends pointing out he was never around at daytime, but that it was Aunt Mae who had told her not just on one occasion that the times Victor kept were not proper for a gentleman to visit.

'Why do you need to prove anything to them in the first place?' Victor asked.

'Don't you think it's important to have friends?' Charlotte responded with a question.

'You didn't answer my question, but I'm going to let that one go. It is important to have friends if they are good and true,' Victor said, 'and these are few and far in between, so when you find them you should keep them.' He knew first hand, having seen the sad turnout of zero people at his own funeral at the Watchers' station. 'Are these former classmates of yours true friends? Are they important? Tell me!'

'Well, now that I live in town, they can come visit. They've visited with me twice already this week so we can catch up on everything that has happened since we graduated a year ago and...and...they are being nice to me!' Charlotte said, fingering the leftovers of the cake she had bought for their tea party that had cost her an arm and a leg.

Victor looked at the quite obviously bakery-bought cake. 'How much of the money you earned this week by waitressing did you spend on entertaining your classmates?' he asked, not unkindly.

'All of it,' she confessed after ten seconds of silence.

'Did you squirrel away any money for your trip to Italy?' Victor asked, knowing the answer.

'Not this week, but I'm going to start saving from the next one, I promise!' Charlotte argued, feeling flushed.

'Unlikely, if these so-called friends of yours are going to keep coming around,' Victor concluded. 'Tell me, where were these people during the past year when you were having a tough time? Did any one of them come visit you on the farm? Did they even call and ask how you were doing?' Victor continued the interrogation. Being cruel was the only way to get through to her.

Charlotte shook her head 'no', red to her roots. 'But Annabelle had a baby - it's real fussy - and Bette was busy working and her boss is a horror of a man...'

'And now that you are conveniently within their travelling comfort zone, they deign to come and eat the cake you buy for them with your savings so they can complain about their life?' Victor was merciless.

'Isn't that what good friends do, listen to each other?' Charlotte asked, remembering how Bette had complained that the cake wasn't her favourite and told her she should only buy fresh-made on the same day.

'Yes, and if they had listened to you at all, true friends

would be baking cakes for you, so you could save up to go live your dream. True friends would also not bother you with their negative stuff, especially if they knew that the life of a farmhand must have been just as tough if not tougher than what they had to deal with,' Victor said. 'Tell me, how much time have you spent drawing this week?'

Charlotte was taking a deep interest in the layout of the porch floor. 'Not much,' she said quietly. *Not at all.* 'But they liked my drawings, they said so.'

'How long did they stay?'

Too long. Charlotte had had to practically yawn in their faces to get them to go home and she had been far too tired to sketch a single wing after clearing the dishes.

'True friends support each other and each others' dreams and are not time-sucks,' Victor said.

'So you think I should stop seeing them?' Charlotte asked, crossing her arms.

Victor thought hard about the message he really wanted her to get, 'No, I don't want you to end up as friendless as you were the whole of last year. All I'm saying is that if you need time to draw and have money to save, you should craft the terms of those friendships and ask them to honour your time so you can do stuff that is important to you. You might be surprised to discover who sticks around and who doesn't after a candid conversation like that.'

'Victor, may I have a word?' Mae said, opening the front door, drawing a shawl close and waving toward his Harley.

He could swear the old broad was always lurking nearby, hanging on every word. How else would she know when precisely to intervene and send him packing? 'Of course, ma'am,' Victor said out loud. 'Good evening, Charlotte, see you soon,' he said and rose to leave.

Soon? How soon? Charlotte bit her lip and hid her extended arms as Victor respectfully bowed away from her hug. *Did he have to be such a darn gentleman? Well, she wouldn't be head over heels otherwise.*

'Victor, may I ask a great favour of you?' Mae asked.

'Of course, ma'am,' Victor said.

'I wanted to consult with you about something...' Mae fingered her shawl, 'One of the ladies at the parlour who is quite computer-savvy mentioned to me today that there is a website where one could get cheap tickets for intercontinental flights... I was thinking about that trip to Italy... Charlotte's birthday is coming up next month...' Mae looked up at him and blinked. She reminded Victor of a heron, looking just as delicate and careful. 'I was wondering...perhaps you could take a look on that wonderful smart watch of yours...?'

Finally! 'Of course ma'am!' Victor tapped his watch.

Mae slipped a piece of paper from under her shawl and handed it to him, 'My friend gave me an address to look up on the computer. Can you really access any web address directly from that?'

'Yes, ma'am', Victor said. It had taken him inception-like manoeuvring to make the computer-savvy acquaintance of Mae's notice the information in the first place and he had to rely on her good spirit to go and tell everyone. Not to mention the lengths he had had to go to in order to coax Mae to that parlour.

In a couple of taps, he was in. The cheap flights were all bought up. Victor fingered the trinket around his neck. The phone screen shimmied once and produced a grand sale.

Thank you, magic wand!

Best of all, there was a one-way flight ticket that was clearly the cheapest. Flying the day after tomorrow.

Victor showed Mae his phone.

'Oh, would you mind reading that for me, dear?' Mae squinted myopically.

'Of course, ma'am,' said Victor and read the results out, line by line. 'It appears that the cheapest option would be to fly to Florence for two hundred dollars. One way. The day after tomorrow.' he concluded.

'That might be a problem...' Mae said.

They didn't have even this kind of money?

'I mean, I do have the money,' Mae produced a weathered

envelope and clutched it to her chest, 'It seems like a bit of a rush, that's all...'

Victor smiled, 'ma'am, I don't see it as a problem. Charlotte is a quick packer, I've seen it myself. And she does seem to have made up her mind, don't you think?' he asked.

Mae nodded, 'What I meant was - would we be able to do everything in just one day? Buy the ticket, pick it up...'

'Ma'am, I don't mean to be rude, so please excuse my interruption. Buying a ticket takes mere minutes nowadays, everything is electronic, the passengers even check in for the flights themselves online and print out their own boarding passes...'

Mae blinked, 'That sounds very complicated...'

'If you'll allow me, I can take care of it all for you - buy the ticket, print it out and bring it over tomorrow,' Victor offered.

Mae looked hesitant. 'If we do manage to procure that ticket today, would you be able to escort her on such short notice? You would have to buy the ticket for yourself, I'm afraid it would wipe out all my savings, if I contributed...and I cannot presume...'

He didn't let her finish, 'It would be my pleasure.'

Mae nodded, 'Thank you!' She opened her envelope and counted out two hundred dollars in ten dollar bills, diminishing the content of the envelope by half. From the way she clutched the remainder of her savings to her chest made Victor realise exactly how much she would miss the money. *She had only known him for five days. Thank goodness, he wasn't a con man.* He was sorely tempted to caution her against trusting strangers too quickly, especially with her savings. 'Thank you, Victor!' Mae said and the envelope disappeared under her shawl. 'Thank you for doing this, for organising everything and for going with her! As much as I will miss her, this is her dream and I am glad that I can help a little. It will be a wonderful early birthday present for Charlotte.' She grabbed his arm. Her bird-like frail hand clasped his wrist firmly. 'I do believe you have her best interests at heart,' she said and turned to go.

Heart had nothing to do with it. Charlotte's best chance of survival was what this save was all about. That and making sure she avoided drawing nasty things that came to life.

Victor checked his watch again. He could probably squeeze in an hour at the Agency. Sally and Charlotte could both do without him for one measly hour. His temper was showing. He was due for some re-balancing, even if it didn't work on him as well as it should have.

31. Keeping the Balance
Gabriel

Gabriel woke up with a start in the early hours of the morning when Grace shifted slightly, realising he had slept through most of his watch. He cursed, which in cat language translated to a series of hiccoughs and hisses.

Damnation!

Five days in the Earth dimension with human food and without popping back to the Agency and he was adjusting to human life and sleep patterns. Going native and becoming near-human was not good for a guardian.

Wagging his tail in annoyance didn't help but it certainly relieved the tension.

After Gabriel escorted Grace to work, from the alley behind the coffee shop, he paged the Watchers requesting to pause reality for an hour and monitor Grace so he could recharge at the Agency.

Daisy obliged.

One Agency hour later, Gabriel sprung up from the guest room bed. He stretched his wings and noticed there was someone in the adjacent cot.

Victor popped on one elbow and waved hello. 'Did you get deaded, maimed or did you go native?' he asked.

'Native,' Gabriel was brief, 'You?'

'Same, unfortunately. Two long parallel saves, one on Earth and another one in an Earth-like dimension and I start turning back into a human and not the nicest of humans, if you remember.'

Gabriel nodded. He remembered. He also noted that Victor was currently stationed in the same dimension Grace was being hunted. Could this be a coincidence? After all, there was a thin line between coincidence and fate. Out of curiosity, he asked, 'Whereabouts on Earth?'

Victor yawned, 'In the States - first Texas, now moving to Italy. Finally! As if being stationed in the New York where the

Twin Towers still stand on the alternative Earth is not enough. Time runs five times quicker on Gaia. I have no time to sleep in between the saves,' he yawned again.

It didn't matter that one of Victor's missions was in another Earth dimension. With the angels' transfiguration and transporting abilities, Victor could have crossed dimensions, much less continents and states in fractions of seconds, unnoticed.

'Say, you've been around for aeons. Any tips on how to make your Charge NOT fall for you?' Victor asked.

'I thought you were used to dealing with Damsels, including how to avoid romantic attachment and that's why you prefer the Knight in Shining Armour type of saves?' Gabriel said as he folded his wings and pulled on a new white T-shirt.

'Well, the short-term saves yes. I think the Watchers stuck me with two long-term missions on purpose. The Princess is fine, she has a love interest and it's really tough to fall for a frog, but the Texan girl...I fear she's starting to get all goo-goo eyed over my usual attire...' Victor gestured at the black denim biker outfit in the corner.

'Even with your usual attitude?' Gabriel smirked.

'My usual attitude is what is encouraging her even more. Talk about good girls falling for bad boys...'

'I thought we cured you of that, angelic re-balancing and all,' Gabriel lifted an eyebrow.

'To a point, mate, to a point. You can take a boy out of Essex, but you can never take Essex out of the boy,' Victor said and got dressed, folding his dark purple wings in the process.

'Let me know when you figure it out, I might have a similar problem on my hands...soon...' Gabriel said.

Victor nodded.

The angels said their goodbyes. Gabriel padded to the Watchers' station barefoot, ignoring the icy floor. The world made sense again, tranquil and calm. All it took was an hour. An hour and he was able to forget what a mess of feelings being human was. As much as he was enjoying a not-so-obvious

whodunit he had to untangle when saving Grace, the fact itself
that he was enjoying her company spoke volumes. Returning to
his angelic self restored clarity of thought.

Gabriel decided to check.

Daisy?

Standard check that you can read minds again?

Yep.

Done?

Done.

He could read minds again, provided the proximity was
close enough. Filtering one voice out of thousands at a distance
was feasible, but took up too much energy and concentration.

He felt his usual calmness returning.

The thoughts were also fewer and none of the circular kind
of what would happen if he didn't manage to find out who was
after his charge.

*Grace was just a Charge. As much as he would love to
complete every mission successfully and keep his service record
spotless, sometimes things didn't work out. The angels could
always only do their best. So would he, come what may.*

Gabriel remembered what Grace had said before she
fell asleep the night before - that she felt like she should do
something to prevent bad things from happening. He decided
to check just in case.

He peeked into the Watchers' station, 'Hey Daisy, remember
you once said something about near-dream states being
somewhat prophetic? Any chance Grace could be destined for
something spectacular, to do something to prevent Evil from
triumphing in her dimension and that's why someone is after
her?' he asked, finishing buttoning his shirt. *The hero theory
was probably a long shot, but it warranted at least discussion
if not investigation.*

'You mean there is a possibility that someone has figured
out what it is that she could change in the Earth dimension and
that's what they are trying to prevent from happening?' the fairy
looked up from her frozen screens. 'Does she have any special
powers?'

'Besides being really good with people and very down to earth? No, not that I know of,' Gabriel admitted.

'Well then, you've answered your own question, haven't you?' Daisy beamed, turning back to her screens.

'Still, I'd like us to be thorough,' he insisted. 'Can you show me the recordings of all of her assassination attempts, please?' Gabriel asked, glancing at his watch. Still 15 minutes to go until time unfroze on Earth and he had to be back to guard Grace.

'Sure,' Daisy flipped a file from the archive to one of the screens, 'here you go!'

Concentrating on the video stream, Gabriel retrieved the scene with the drunken bullies. None of them looked like they were plotting to accost Grace. It just happened. When they saw her, they zeroed in and then it was Gabriel to the rescue.

'Why can't we SEE who the assassin is?' Gabriel harrumphed, after he watched the shooting and the bomb in the cellar video feed again. Both recordings started after the contraptions had already been put into place.

Daisy sighed, 'I didn't make the recording rules for the 16 priority screens. The way the archived history function works is the screens record the distress event in REAL time from the moment the intent of the perpetrator forms until the moment of the save, not before and not after. The screens only start recording from the time intent forms in Grace's own dimension. If there is no intent yet in the dimension she's in, the screens don't record. Only a limited amount of time gets recorded. Otherwise our archives would require a dimension of their own.'

'Why can't we use the forward function to see if whoever is after Grace will try again?' Gabriel asked, hopeful this would provide the easy and obvious solution.

'The future forward function works with probabilities. We are missing the key denominator of who the assassin is. Without feeding it into the probability matrix, I can only see what would happen to her in the future if she doesn't die,' Daisy explained.

Watching Grace appear in the alley with a black bin-bag, Gabriel commented, 'Judging by the video, we also only tape the charge, but not the assailant.'

Daisy shrugged, 'Again, it's the rules and I didn't make them.'

Gabriel frowned, 'So what you are saying is whoever is after Grace forms an intent to attempt to assassinate her once in a while, but is not keen on killing her all the time?'

'Seems so,' Daisy said, 'At least we're not dealing with someone who is obsessed with her.'

'Worse, we're dealing with someone for whom it looks like... random fun,' Gabriel darkened. 'Can we see when the next attempt is going to be?'

Daisy shook her head, 'No, not until he or she intends to try again. And even then a picture of whatever Grace is doing at the time will flash on our screen for just a couple of minutes before the attack. I can try and freeze time and ring you to give you a heads up..., but to be honest, tending the other priority screens is also important.'

Gabriel nodded and said 'Thanks' completely ignoring the fairy's last remark. 'The shooting, the bullies, the bomb in the coffee shop cellar, everything had been remote operated,' Gabriel was thinking out loud. 'If the assassin tasked someone else to set this all up and that someone didn't know whom they were targeting, would that kind of intent show up on the 16 priority screens?'

Daisy forgot she was miffed at the archangel ignoring her pointy remark. 'I don't think so. Our saves and rescues are usually highly personal and direct, which means so are the assaults.'

'The fact that whoever it is has chosen an indirect route only means he or she is a calculating coward and does not mean it is not personal,' Gabriel said. 'If it's personal, maybe it is someone from her life, just not from her most recent past.'

Daisy shrugged, 'Perhaps.' She really did have other rescues to attend to.

Gabriel sighed. *He would have to go back and review all of Grace's recent and not so recent interactions - from any source he could find.* 'Can you get your hands on any material - video, paperwork, audio - about Grace and her life for, say, the past 10 years?'

Daisy sighed, 'I knew you were going to ask me that. I'll have Loretta start with CCTV and Google.'

'In case of video feed, filter out the boring bits of eating, sleeping and walking in between, please.' He had come to enjoy living those boring bits by Grace's side, so they were not that meaningless, but he had to be efficient in reviewing the material.

'Send me the footage when you get it, I can review it while watching Grace,' Gabriel said. 'Perhaps then we can find out who doesn't necessarily see Grace frequently enough to be constantly reminded they hate her and want her off the planet.'

For now, Gabriel kept schtum about the other thought Grace had voiced - the feeling that somehow the good was losing. It was the same as the bad winning, which was out of the question.

The Agency always managed to keep the balance. They had kept the balance for thousands of years. That was their job. That's why the guardians did what they did. That's what he was here for.

To keep the balance. To make sure the tally was always even.

'I hope we will see you at the Agency more often,' Daisy said, her hands never leaving the screens, 'your home dimension ... you need to recharge...'

'Just done.'

'...More often,' the fairy finished.

'Don't you trust me becoming a little bit human again?' Gabriel asked. *It wasn't like he was going to give up his calling.*

Daisy eyed Gabriel inquisitively, 'It's not about trust, it's about diminishing the probability of success of the save - should you become fully human, you lose your immortality, remember? This has been the longest you have spent in your old dimension after being recruited, hasn't it?'

Gabriel nodded.

'What's it been? A thousand years?' the fairy asked.

'Nine hundred,' Gabriel said, 'Why do you ask?'

'What if you turned completely human and weren't able to

protect her anymore?' Daisy asked, 'or worse, fell in love with her?'

'Grace is just another charge. This is just another rescue,' Gabriel said and frowned.

Daisy looked him up and down, 'You know, I think I believe you. For now. Because you've just recharged. Now, shoo! I have work to do.'

Gabriel remembered how high the tally of evil had been just before he had jumped in to save Grace. *That had been temporary. He had made sure of it. He always made sure.*

He would save Grace if this was meant to be. If it wasn't, it was probably for the best and the universe would find other ways to restore the balance.

With that sense of calm comfort, Gabriel headed back to assume his duties. As he was teleporting back to Earth, Gabriel saw Victor emerge from the Boss' office, wave at him and head downstairs towards the Watchers' station.

32. Ever That Bad?

Victor

Back at the Watchers' station, Victor saw Daisy reviewing the scene of Andy nearly forking Charlotte. Just as she hit save, he pointed at the frozen screen and deigned to ask, 'Don't you think it's too early to archive?'

'Have you bought her the ticket to Italy?'

Victor nodded.

'Is there any likelihood she will change her mind between today and tomorrow?'

Victor shrugged.

'I'm sure she'll go. I have time on my hands now, so I'm archiving now.'

Victor tilted his head back at the screens, 'Was I ever that bad?'

'Did you ever try to kill Grace with a pitchfork?' Daisy countered.

Victor shook his head.

'Anyone else you tried to murder?' she asked.

He shook his head again, 'No, I meant, was I ever that BAD?'

Daisy raised an eyebrow, 'Define bad?'

It was Victor's turn to stare, 'Are there different levels of evil, some more acceptable than others? I think I missed that lecture.'

Daisy shrugged, 'Ever heard of yin and yang? Someone I rather like and respect says that sometimes a little bad goes a long way towards making something good.'

Ignoring the philosophy of good and evil, Victor wanted a specific answer to a specific question, 'Ok, let me ask you in another way - was I ever as short-sightedly destructive as that pitchfork-wielding idiot?'

Daisy shook her head, 'Controlling - yes. A coward - that too, maybe...'

Victor's ears went hot.

'You may have been...and I'm not quite sure past tense is quite warranted here...a self-obsessed jerk bordering on the manic...'

Victor's eyebrows crawled up his forehead. *Did he have to ask?*

'...but never psycho-sociopathic, if that's what you're asking.'

Victor's eyebrows kept crawling.

Undeterred, Daisy continued, 'If you hadn't been the way you were with Grace, she might never have got scarred for years and maybe she would just have met a slightly nicer version of you and not...' the fairy shut up, realising she had said too much.

'Finish, the sentence, fairy,' Victor said, 'what's past is past, she has a new life now, I get it.'

'Fine, then she wouldn't have met someone way nicer than you who deserves her more.'

That stung, especially since Victor had got used to Daisy being the non-judgemental one. *So, Grace was dating someone.* Victor wasn't sure how he felt about it. Despite what he had said about the past being the past, Grace had been his most defining relationship. Possessiveness reared its ugly head for five seconds only to be silenced by fairness. 'Well, as long as I don't know the guy and it's not like I plan to watch them together and even if I did, I'm sure you wouldn't let me, not that it matters. What can I do - haunt her from beyond the grave?' Victor shrugged.

Daisy kept a straight face. All those nights playing poker with the Boss over thousands of years finally paid off, now that she was bluffing.

'I guess she deserves happiness,' Victor admitted grudgingly. Possessiveness took cowardice by the hand and went to tie another not in his stomach.

'Damn right she does, now go rescue Sally from the bodily harm she is about to do to herself by exercising too hard. If anyone can get her to treat herself nice, that'll be you.'

'Why, because I say please and because of my otherwise charming persona?' Victor threw the fairy a smoldering smile.

'No, it's your level of sarcasm that happens to be the only language that she understands,' Daisy retorted, flapping her wings at him 'Now, shoo! I have work to do.'

33. Role Models

Sally

'So, what have you been up to while I was away? Besides ruining my work,' the frog said to Sally from behind her as she screamed into the bathroom mirror.

'Stop sneaking up on me like that!'

'Stop ruining my work like that!' Victor mimicked her. 'Why on earth did you uncover the mirror?' he pointed at the polished four squares.

'Just how do you suppose I floss? Without a mirror I can't see whether I have something in my teeth or not,' Sally said.

'Can't you trust people to tell you?' the frog enquired.

Sally turned her finger gently at her temple, 'Are you stupid? That's exactly why people floss. To avoid being embarrassed by others pointing out they have spinach in their teeth.'

'Good girl, did you eat spinach while I was gone?' Victor asked.

'No...' Sally said.

'Then you shouldn't have worried, should you?' Victor concluded.

Sally looked at him like he was retarded. He probably was. 'You are missing the point,' she said.

'You had a point?'

'Dental care is important,' Sally said.

'You can use the reverse camera function on your phone as a mirror. You carry that one everywhere, don't you?' Victor said resolutely and went in search of black tape.

'You were gone a week, I was kind of hoping you'd have the sense to stay gone,' Sally said when he returned, a little glad he was back. She had discovered she missed stupid conversations like this.

'No you didn't. Otherwise you wouldn't have exercised and cleaned,' Victor said.

'Stalk me, did you?' Sally asked, loathe to admit she had done things to get his approval.

'Nope,' Victor tapped his nose, 'powers of deduction,' he said.

'I only did those things because I was bored,' Sally said.

'Bored? Don't you have friends?' Victor asked.

'Harry's been AWOL,' Sally said, her face darkening.

'If you don't have any friends but Harry, how about making some new ones?' the frog asked. 'You could get to know your neighbours, for example. Friendly neighbours always watch out for each other, don't they? Can be a lot of help if you're mugged when opening your front door,' Victor said. *So he'd heard.*

'Not in New York they don't. The neighbours of a school friend of mine called the cops on her because she put an empty baby-buggy out on her balcony for half an hour in February while she was cleaning the apartment.'

'Don't you think they were right to be concerned about the baby, had it been there?'

Sally harrumphed. She had told the story many a time and every time everybody laughed. She hadn't thought about the neighbours calling the cops out of concern, not malice. *Still, the neighbours, if they had been really concerned for a child, could have walked over and enquired themselves. Which is precisely what people in New York didn't do.*

'Do you even know any of your neighbours?' Victor asked.

'No,' Sally said.

'Then how do you know they're more of the calling-the-cops kind than the lend-you-a-cup-of-sugar kind?' he asked.

'You wouldn't allow me to borrow sugar anyway, so what's the point?' Sally asked tartly.

'You know what I mean. You're passing on a chance to meet nice people, perhaps even role models. For instance, do you know the old lady opposite you?'

'There's an old lady living opposite me?' Sally asked, genuinely surprised.

'How long have you lived in this apartment?' the frog sighed.

'Ever since I graduated, so seven years,' Sally said.

'She has lived here all her life,' he said, 'meaning - she predates you.'

Come to think of it, she had spotted an old dotty meandering about the day she was moving. Harry had nearly tripped over her cane, carrying boxes in. Out loud, Sally said, 'So what?'

'What if she's nice?' Victor asked.

'Again, so what?' Sally asked.

'Maybe she could exert some positive influence on you. I'm not going to be around forever, you know,' the frog said.

'Excellent news! When are you leaving?' Sally countered.

'Not anytime soon. The outside,' the frog looked her up and down, 'is progressing nicely, so almost taken care of, the inside,' he tapped the side of his head, 'will definitely take more work.'

Sally was speechless. *A frog had just looked her up and down like she was prize cattle and commented on her sanity!*

'You have no friends besides the constantly AWOL Harry and your relationship with your mother leaves to be desired, so by my calculations, yes, you do need a role model,' Victor said. 'Badly. Now, close your mouth dear.'

Sally's eyes dropped to slits, 'Did you just comment on my sanity, frog? I see my therapist once a month, thank you very much, I don't need any more psychobabble, especially not from you.'

'You are seeing a therapist?' Victor asked, 'About what?'

'As if I'd tell you! These sessions are private,' Sally said.

If she was already in therapy, maybe he would have help where her inner makeover was concerned. Then again, if she'd been in therapy for years, the present state of her did not quite encourage Victor. 'Are you sure it's working?'

Sally threw a pillow at him, 'More or less. My relationship with my mother is a little bit better now that I've learnt to cope with her, which is only fair since she's the one paying for the sessions.'

'Therapy is not the same as having a role model, you know,' the frog said.

'I know, but if you are suggesting that I go befriending neighbours, why on earth would I start with the old bag? Why would I want someone so close to the grave as a role model? Role models should be my own age.' *Like the hot guy upstairs.*

Too bad he had a live-in girlfriend.

It was Victor's turn to tap on his temple, 'By definition role models are people you aspire to be like, which means they should be more experienced, which usually implies they have to be older than you,' he said.

'If I want to be like someone, I'd rather look at my successful peers. Too bad my class doesn't have a single genius of the Steve Jobs calibre...' Sally mused.

A good example from an elder was not going down well. Perhaps pity would work better in getting Sally on the rocky road of benign human relations. Sally did have a wicked tongue but deep down she was really kind at heart. *Really deep down.* 'The old bag across the hallway... She used to be a teacher, you know... All her family is gone, she's all alone in this world... She still volunteers at the shelter... And did you know it's her birthday today?' Victor finished with his *coup de grace.*

Sally fell quiet.

'She's turning ninety,' Victor said. *By the looks of Sally, pity was working way better.*

'I could bake her a cake,' Sally finally suggested.

Unexpected, but nice. Out loud, Victor said, 'You could...are you going to?'

Sally nodded, 'I'm baking her a cake. I can do a Pavlova, Jamie Oliver's style... What if she's lactose intolerant or allergic to strawberries?' Sally's shuffle towards her kitchen halted as she was trying to figure out which cake she could bake that would not push the old bag closer to, or, worse, into the grave.

Victor didn't have the heart to point out that those would be the things she would know, if she had bothered to get to know the lady.

***

A successful three-hour trip across the hall later, Sally was back in her apartment, feeling great. She'd made Emmeline's day, surprising her with her cake. The lady had invited her in and contrary to Sally's fears, her apartment did not look cluttered or smell like moths and cat pee. Quite the opposite, it was neat and much tinier than Sally's and it had paintings of flowers everywhere. Emmeline had said everyone needs a hobby and enquired about hers. Sally was too ashamed to admit she didn't have one, so she lied that she was still trying this and that.

The frog had been right, once again. Talking to someone, making their day made Sally feel good. It was good to be needed.

'Wishing you'd done that a lot earlier, aren't you?' the frog said from behind the couch.

Sally didn't even flinch, 'It was too much to hope you'd clear off by the time I came back. Of course you'd want to know how it all went,' she said.

'Oh, I know, how it all went,' the frog said. Pre-empting Sally, he added, 'Yes, I watched you from the window. What else was I to resort to since you didn't take me with?'

'Now was I right and is she or is she not good people worth knowing?' Victor asked.

'Well, duh, anyone her age would have to be kind to survive,' Sally retorted.

And there goes that mouth again. Out loud, Victor didn't say anything. *Sometimes, silence was a much better educational tool than people realised.*

A stretch of silence later, Sally said, 'Oh, don't you try to make me feel bad, I was just in such a good mood.'

The frog shrugged, 'No one but yourself can give you permission to feel bad, you know.'

'Eleanor Roosevelt's quote is actually 'No one can make you feel inferior without your consent', smarty-pants,' Sally bit back.

'Eleanor was right. So why are you consenting to let yourself feel inferior? Could it have been something YOU said that you think you shouldn't have?' the sly frog hopped closer.

'Bite me,' Sally replied.

'Not a chance. You may have scrubbed up nice, but human flesh is not as tasty as all those zombie shows would like you to believe. About tasty...' Victor made a face.

Did she forget to offer refreshments again? 'Did I forget to offer you refreshments again?' she asked.

Victor nodded.

Sally's mood was considering taking that downhill climb and making it into a lunge. 'Fine, what would you like?' she bit off, heading for the kitchen.

'Water, please.' *Sometimes a little praise went way longer than a biting remark.* 'You did ask me rather nicely, though, thank you.' He hopped after her.

Praise from a frog. 'My pleasure,' Sally said from the insides of her fridge, her back telegraphing anything but. She slammed a water bottle in front of the frog and reached for a glass off the shelf, tempted to slam that one down, too.

Victor reached up and gently took the glass from her, 'Thank you!'

'Oh, shut up! Why are you being so nice to me? I forgot about hospitality again and you're thanking me regardless,' Sally said.

'You shouldn't be so hard on yourself. So, you forgot to offer me refreshments. So, you forgot to take an interest in your neighbours. But you're learning to care, aren't you,' the frog said.

'You make it sound like these are all things that any normal human being should already know how to do and that makes me feel...not normal,' Sally complained.

'You're talking to a magic frog, you AREN'T normal!' the frog beamed. 'Now tell me why you're really upset.'

'I'm upset 'coz you made me upset!' Sally bit back.

'No, you're not,' Victor said with conviction, 'Permission... Eleanor...remember?'

'So you're saying I'm upset at myself?' Sally asked.

The frog nodded, 'Now tell me the first thing that comes to mind...'

'Mirrors,' Sally said.

'What about them?'

'I cannot see myself and I'm forgetting what I look like or how to match things?'

'Lazy lies, I've seen you take photos of yourself to see what goes together, dig deeper,' the frog said, leaning on the water bottle.

'I feel like the clothes are baggier on me but I cannot see

if I've actually lost weight with all the exercising you've been making me do,' Sally finally confessed.

'Ah-hah!' the frog raised a finger, 'Before you started exercising, did you LIKE to look at yourself in the mirror?'

'No...'

'So, looking at yourself in the mirror did not make you feel happy?'

'No, look, I've always hated the way I look, brown button eyes, too close together, matching brown hair, too large mouth and too large cheekbones, besides, I seem to have developed curves at precisely all the wrong places...'

'I thought we've talked about not talking down to yourself?' the frog said and tsk-tsked. 'So, basically, looking at yourself didn't make you happy before, correct?'

Sally nodded.

'But not looking doesn't make you happy either?'

Sally nodded again.

'So, why do you think looking into the mirrors NOW would make a difference?'

Because I think I might look a little bit more fit thanks to you. Out loud, Sally said, 'I don't think it will, I just want to test a theory.'

'If your happiness is so hung up on how you look, why didn't you do something about it earlier than at the ripe age of thirty?' the frog asked.

'Because at the ripe age of 16 my mom offered to pay for a whole range of plastic operations - nose job, eye-lid-lift, boob-job, ass-job, tummy-tuck, arm-and-leg-lipo, you name it, she had it on the list. My own mother told me I was unattractive unless I did all of those things. Had I done all of those things, it wouldn't have been enough. Some of those rather painful things need doing again and again and again. Tummy-tucks don't last, a nose job might,' Sally said.

'So, to spite you mother, you did nothing?' Victor asked. *At least the girl had guts.*

'Yep, I learnt my lesson - my mom's happiness was about how I look. Painful operations and constant self-doubt - that's not happiness, that is self-torture. If I was going to be unhappy anyway, it was easier to leave things just as they were. And if I couldn't be happy, mom could be right there with me, so I took the money mom was planning to spend on all those operations and bought Harry a car,' Sally said.

Suddenly, all the body-issues and dress sense made perfect sense. 'So you hated your body because your mom made you feel inadequate, but you are no longer hung up on how you look?' Victor asked, begging to differ. 'Why would you miss mirrors, then?'

'I didn't say I no longer care how I look. I care. I'm just not big about showing it,' Sally tried to joke her way out of a conversation that was becoming too serious too fast.

This conversation was going nowhere. The frog noticed an old photograph on Sally's windowsill and tried a different tack, 'Who's this then?' he asked.

'My grandma. I found the picture when I was cleaning,' Sally said, glad they were done talking about her body issues. The photo had always been there. It had just got buried under the gazillion magazines she kept shoving into the alcove, meaning to and never reading later. She wasn't fessing up to the frog about this, though. He already looked down on her for having a bad relationship with her mother. If she confessed to have forgotten her grandmother, she would never hear the end of it, she was sure.

'She is gorgeous,' Victor said and meant it.

'Yes, a *shiksa* that married my grandfather against his family's wishes. The Jewish side of my family only accepted her after she converted. At age 70, after granddad had already passed on. When my great grandmother, her mother-in-law asked her why she did not consider pleasing her with a conversion during her late husband's lifetime, my grandmaman replied that she wasn't aware that she was under the marital obligation to please anyone but her husband.'

So that's where Sally got her mouth.

'Later when I asked her the same thing - why at age 70 - she told me that she had needed that much time to make up her mind about who was going to have her soul when she died.'

'You sound like you admire her,' the frog said.

'Look at her! What's not to admire? She was drop dead gorgeous!' Sally said. *Nothing like me.*

'Looks aren't everything. Besides, there is no such thing as an unpleasant-looking woman, there is just improper clothing and bad manners,' Victor said.

'You should tell my mom that,' Sally muttered.

'Besides her looks, how was she?' the frog asked.

'Kind. She was kind,' Sally remembered. *Grandmaman wouldn't have to be told to go bake a cake for her neighbour. She would have known all the neighbours' names, their kids' and grandkids' names and birthdays.* 'I've never heard her say an unkind word, not a single disparaging remark, even about my family who did look down on her all her life. She always said 'thank you' and 'please'.' *Unlike her generation.* Sally herself sometimes forgot to say thank you and please. 'She never made me do anything I didn't want to. Instead, she gently guided me to discover what I was good at and what I really wanted. And she taught me to stand up for myself. With words, not fists.' When the frog made a face, Sally confessed, 'Believe me, there are a lot of boys where I grew up who have had to have a rhinoplasty later in life.'

When the frog still made a face, Sally felt the need to explain, 'Lots of broken noses...'

The frog put a paw up, 'Why does that not surprise me?'

Sally ignored his comment, lost in her memories, 'She was the only one who could ever stand up to mother. Or anyone else, for that matter. She used to say that it was her cross to bear to have raised such a headstrong but conventional daughter.'

It sounded like grandmaman was the only layer of protection Sally had had against mother dearest. 'Sounds like you don't need to model your life on someone successful who is your own age. You already have a far better role model,' Victor nodded towards the photograph, 'your grandmother.'

34. A Chance Meeting
Grace

When Grace entered the coffee shop, she knew immediately that today was the day Emma was baking her magic apple cinnamon pie. The cinnamon lingered, making the air around them taste sweeter and people behave better. Grace sensed Emma had added a tinge of vanilla today.

A red-head in the corner booth where Gabriel usually sat glanced up and snatched a few raspberries from the plastic container in front of her that Grace was sure they didn't sell. The red-head popped the raspberries in her mouth, stuck the horn-rimmed glasses back up her nose and buried herself into her laptop.

After their late night walk, Grace was a little disappointed Gabriel wasn't at his usual seat in the morning. *Well, it had been pretty late when they had parted ways and the City boy did work for a living.*

Inhaling the scent of cinnamon and vanilla and seeing fresh raspberries always made Grace remember home, the way it had been before the car accident. In front of her, the café till transformed into their kitchen. As she inhaled the vanilla deeper, she could see how dad was snatching pancakes from the pan over her mom's shoulder and how mom was playfully swatting at him. Grace still remembered the tiny wrinkles and the golden wedding band on the hand that put the plate of pancakes in front of her. Mom used to arrange them sometimes as flower petals and sometimes as three overlapping circles and sprinkle the toppings liberally, making the entire kitchen smell like cinnamon and vanilla.

And raspberries.

Grace smiled at her happy memories. There was magic in the air. Not that she believed in magic. She might have, had her entire family not burnt to a crisp 12 years ago.

Happy to start the day, Grace put on her apron and disappeared into the bowels of the kitchen to help Emma.

'How was your walk yesterday, honey?' Emma asked her, handing Grace her apron.

'It was alright,' Grace said and shrugged.

'Just alright? He didn't make a pass? Are you disappointed?' Emma queried, putting a kettle on and nudging Grace towards the corner-booth where the red-head was waving at them frantically.

Grabbing her pad and pencil, Grace shrugged, 'He was nice and the walk was nice and he didn't make a pass, which is fine because I didn't let him walk me to the door anyway...'

'Whyever not?' Emma asked.

Grace shrugged.

'Scaredy cat,' Emma patted her on her shoulder.

'Well, I have good reason. And, AND, you know how keen guys are to ferret stuff out about the exes, why we broke up, etc. But with this guy, it's this giant thing we don't talk about. Ever. Like they never existed,' Grace said. 'Another red light for me, I'm afraid.'

'Maybe to him it doesn't matter if they did, honey?' Emma said putting a slice of her pie on a plate for Grace.

'Meaning he is completely indifferent to me?' Grace asked.

'Honey, anyone who walks you home after night shifts cannot be indifferent. Meaning - he knows you must have had someone in your life before, but it doesn't matter at all because we all have a past,' Emma said.

'Yes, that is very well in theory but in practice the question remains - why hasn't he made a move?' Grace let the question hang and went to tend to the red-head who had occupied Gabriel's usual seat. With any luck, the read-head would leave soon so by the time he would pop by, his usual booth would be waiting for him.

'How may I help?' Grace uttered her usual greeting to female customers. With males, especially the ones who looked her up and down, she preferred to use 'What'll it be, mister?'.

The red-head grasped her by the hand, pulled Grace to sit down next to her and said, 'I think it's the other way around, sugar.'

Grace blinked back her surprise, 'Pardon me?'

The red-head stuck out her other hand, 'I'm Della. How would you like to earn a 50-pound tip today?'

Grace shook Della's hand, 'Grace, pleased to meet you.

Money is always welcome. What do you need?'

Della beamed, 'I need someone - a definite assigned someone - to look after me while I write here all day. And I need that definite someone to keep that brute,' Della gestured at uncle Tom, 'away from me. His hovering is disrupting my thought flow and don't even get me started on his choice of tobacco...' Della wriggled her nose.

All that for 50 pounds? Easy money.

Before Grace could nod, the shadow of uncle Tom loomed over both of them, 'You come in late, girl, and then shirk off your job, talking to your friends?'

Grace tried to get up, but Della held on to her. The red-head looked sternly at uncle Tom, 'Sir, I mean you no disrespect,' her tone telegraphing otherwise. 'I'm a writer and this place seems to have a good vibe.' Della looked pointedly at uncle Tom, noting the exception to the rule. 'So, I'm going to stay here most of the day, eating, drinking, and bringing you some business. I might even tell some of my friends about this charming place and you'll have more good tipping customers in the future.' Della peeked at Grace's name-tag on her apron, 'Grace here looks like she could handle looking after me all day, but I haven't had the time to tell her what I want, so how about you let us chat for ten minutes in exchange for my all-day custom. Deal?'

'No deal. If she sits here with you all day...'

'Not all day, just ten minutes so I can give her my instructions, although chatting to people IS very inspirational.'

'Either way, who is going to work?' uncle Tom stared the silly girl down.

'You have hands,' Della pointed.

Astonished at such gall, uncle Tom was speechless for a second.

'Listen, let me sweeten the deal for you,' Della said reaching into her purse. She pulled out a 20-pound note and put it on the table, 'If you let Grace briefly listen to my instructions so she won't bother me throughout the day later,' seeing greed glistening in the man's eyes, Della finished with 'your lovely establishment can keep this money as a tip. Whatever tip I choose to leave her,' Della nodded at Grace, 'will be extra. This would be on top of everything that I manage to consume. Deal?'

'Fine, but she sits with you for just ten minutes and then she works,' uncle Tom turned and left, remembering to pocket the 20 and muttering something about snooty girls with writer's block but money being money.

Della made a face, 'Charming. Now where were we?'

Grace nodded, 'Deal! And by the way, I apologise. That brute is my uncle.'

Della cocked her head to the left, assessing uncle Tom once more, this time from the behind, 'I see…that explains his predisposition to tyranny if not outright slavery where you are concerned. She jotted something down on a napkin, 'Ignore me, I'm just making notes I can use later, I think your uncle could prove a very useful specimen of a prototype for one of my books. Now then, keep bringing the tea and biscuits and when you see me fidgeting more than usual, slip a salad in front of me, fork only. If I ignore you, please don't mind. When I get into the flow, I tend to shut out the world, but a girl needs to eat, so I will eat whatever you put in front of me. Just put light, nice things in front of me and tea, lots of tea. A hot meal sometime around four PM would be nice and when I need the loo, I'll just up and leave the table, so could you watch over my stuff while I'm gone?' Della beamed at Grace.

'That's it?'

'That's it! Now we still have eight minutes, so do tell me about yourself, Grace. Can I call you Gracie? There's this move called Miss Congeniality where the main character goes undercover and is given the name Gracie Lou Freebush, I've always found that enchanting.'

'Considering you just said you were going to ignore me most of the day, for a 50 quid tip on those rare occasions that you do remember I exist, sure, you can call me Gracie or whatever you can remember to call me. What's your book about?' Grace asked, steering the conversation back to Della and enjoying the cup of coffee Emma had brought her.

'It's a fantasy about an author struggling to finish a book by deadline when Time itself comes to the rescue…'[35]

35. Check Lists
Sally

After two weeks of exercising through sweat, tears and swears, Sally was still not convinced on the frog's 'love yourself and respect your body approach'. She had to admit that following the frog's, well really Jamie Oliver's, instructions had made her feel better. The power of proper nutrition, the frog called it. Having caught her once or twice with sugary drinks, the frog promised to put a hex on her. Sally didn't know whether he could, but fell in line just in case. She didn't want to end up as a magical creature next to the frog. Being human was hard enough.

A semi-starving human, thanks to the frog's healthy meal pointers. When she had seen Jamie Oliver's 15 and 30 minute meal shows on the cooking channel, she resolutely opted for those instead, explaining to the frog that diets and meal plans won't work while learning how to truly cook healthy might. The smug thing had been much too content at this turn of events.

A shower later, Sally was lounging around in jeans that felt too loose and a T-shirt that wasn't so tight anymore.

Before she could made herself a snack to reward all her hard work, a much too familiar and annoying voice asked, 'Sally, what makes you happy?'

Sally jumped, 'Where the hell did you crawl out from?'

The frog waited stoically for his answer while Sally mumbled something about no luck that his week's long absence was permanent. 'Fine, fine, I know! Hello, how are you, would you like something to eat or drink?' she spat out.

'No, thank you and is that the way your grandmaman would have greeted guests?' the frog asked.

Sally groaned, 'None of your talks, please! I've just been to the park, jogging, like you ordered, you slave driver, I'm tired and hungry, so not today, ok?'

The frog edged an unlit candle closer to her, 'I've prepared a light snack for you in the kitchen, go get it and by the way, I'm really interested about what makes you happy.' Victor was giving himself the creepie-crawlies with his chipper tone. 'Everybody wants to be with someone, right? Hypothetically, what does your perfect man look like?' *I'm a skirt and eye-liner away from turning into a girl.* Victor kept smiling, as far as frogs could and tried not to grind his teeth.

Resigned that the creature from hell was not going to let her lounge around in front of the TV, Sally sighed and went to the kitchen. 'Celery and apple salad? Really?'

'You'll live and like it,' the frog countered, 'Now quit stalling. Perfect man?'

Sally took the plate back to her living room, sat down and started playing with her food. Eventually her hunger got over her repulsion towards celery. Chewing on her first mouthful she said, 'Well, if we are speaking hypothetically here, I want perfection. I want to be deliriously happy with a guy who's six feet tall, size 12 shoes wouldn't be bad either, ideally, he has to have brown hair, brown eyes, Jewish would be good, someone who treats me right, also, he should never ever talk over me, he should have a good job, a white-collar one, and he has to be polite, manners are important, you know, he's educated, of course, a man who fits me, fits my life, adores and worships me,' Sally made it all sound non-negotiable, kicking up her feet, carefully avoiding the candle he had just lit.

Sally's best friend and the love interest the Watchers were trying her to take notice of was half of those things. *A perfect cue to introduce Harry.* 'Don't you already know someone like that?' Victor asked slyly.

Sally looked at the frog who was sunning himself on her living room table like he was demented, 'Well, if I did, don't you think I would be with him by now?'

With this attitude, not necessarily.

'What about Harry?' Victor asked.

'What about Harry?' Sally snorted. 'He may be my best friend and all, but he's a *shagetz.* That's why our friendship works so well.' When the frog shrugged, Sally explained, 'He's non-Jewish.' When the frog still shrugged, Sally explained some more, 'My mother will never accept a non-Jew as a choice for a husband, so being friends with Harry is harmless.'

Hopefully not as harmless as you think. Besides, your mom will come around after a few beautiful grandkids.

'What if he converted?' the frog asked.

'Not Harry. Besides, he only dates *shiksas* and *zaftig tsatskeles* at that,' Sally said. When the frog shrugged, Sally explained again, 'Non-Jewish ... erm ... well-endowed bimbos.'

'What if you converted?' the frog asked.

'Would you stop with the nonsense already? I don't see him that way and he most certainly doesn't see me like that,' Sally said.

Victor decided to drop the subject for the time being. 'So, you've assessed everyone you know and have found them wanting, not wanting to cave on any item of your check list? Instead you sit and wait around wishing your perfect man would just... appear?' he asked, munching on half the sandwich he had made for himself and had had to wrestle away from Sally whose salad had disappeared as if by magic. The Earth dimension was quickening his metabolism.

'Hey, show some gratitude by not being rude to the person who feeds you!' Sally shot back with bite, 'Besides, I date. I've been on two dates. This year.'

'And since you're alone those didn't go too well, I surmise and now it's already summer, so you need to put a move on. Which brings us back to the check list you have concocted in your head. Don't you think having requirements of how a guy, your guy, is supposed to be, look like, behave, etc kind of defeats the purpose?' Victor wondered.

'What purpose?' Sally asked.

'To fall the frigging heck in love, of course!' the frog yelled. Girls were so slow sometimes.

'Oh...that.'

'Yes, that!'

'Well, that's where you're wrong,' Sally adjusted her jeans that kept slipping off and decided to go get a belt instead. 'I don't have a problem with falling in love. I have a problem with staying in love.' *Not to mention the guys staying, but she wasn't about to divulge quite everything about her love life to a frigging magical creature she'd known for four weeks.* Tucking in her leather belt, Sally decided she didn't care for the subject so it was time to change it, 'The run today was amazing, who knew there were so many squirrels in that park! Imagine,

I'd never have noticed, if it were not for you making me run!' Sally thought she sounded like a chipper cartoon-character, but hoped that another cartoon character would not notice.

'Stop changing the subject.' Victor zeroed in on her.

'The subject? What subject?' Sally bounced on the living room couch, trying to look sweet and innocent and failing miserably at both.

'Love...? Your perfect man...?'

'Oh, I know my perfect man already....we're going to meet somewhere in a NYC diner and he's going to sweep me off my feet and we'll live happily ever after.' Especially if she wore that fantastic red dress. Sally was in such a good mood from actually owning a piece of clothing that didn't make her look frumpy that she almost believed her life-long dream herself.

'And the lucky guy is....?' The frog prayed that Harry's number had finally come up. Mission accomplished, magic wand and frog disguise hung up for good.

13. „*I want to be deliriously happy with a man who fits me, fits my life, adores and worships me.'*

'Why, Johnny Depp, of course, he's funny and a bad boy turned good parent, he's purrrfect! And newly single and available,' Sally's eyes acquired a dreamlike quality behind her ever-present specs.

Victor swore. *Fools like her was why he had never been short of a date. Tell them what they want to hear and they're all yours. For someone who hated fairy-tales this girl sure had concocted a ridiculous one bordering on the hilarious for herself. She was never ever in a million years going to find love this way.*

Looking at Sally's shocked face Victor realised he had said it all out loud.

'You rat bastard! Get out! Better yet, *ver dergarget!*[36]' Sally yelled and threw a pillow at him.

Victor spent the next ten minutes hiding and ducking. Sally's anger seemed to be growing with every throw and her aim wasn't bad. She had exhausted soft toys and pillows and was moving on to something that could actually hurt when it hit. Sally picked up her favourite Tiffany lamp, hesitated, thinking why she would ever trash something she liked, put it down and yelled, 'Fine, if you won't go, then I will!' She grabbed her purse and stormed out, evicted from her own apartment by a frog.

'Now wait a pea-picking minute, missy,' Victor yelled after her, spilling down her front steps and into the night street, ignoring that someone might take an interest in a shouting frog.

New York ignored him right back. So did Sally who was already a distant dot a block away. Well, a bit more exercise wouldn't hurt her, Victor thought and lingered on the sidewalk.

Moments later he was almost hit by a half-eaten hot dog that was flying towards him in a short miss of the trash bin. Almost, but not quite. Congratulating himself on his reflexes, he watched the hot dog miss the trash bin, as predicted, and land where Victor had been standing a second ago, if he hadn't stepped off the curb.

Straight into the path of the yellow taxi cab.

Rolling over the bump that was Victor, the taxi pulled to a stop and let out an old dotty with a walking frame.

Five minutes later, Victor was still lying under the right front tyre of the cab, tap-tapping his annoyance at triple the speed of movement of the old lady from the safety of a protective bubble. During those five minutes Victor had had time to call Sally all sorts of names, accept his own fault of nearly getting deaded and miss Charlotte. *Bless the magic wand.* It had formed a transparent but hard as nails bubble around him when danger had hit. Victor suspected the wand, being sentient, had really formed the bubble around itself and he was just an innocent beneficiary, but who was he to mind. It saved him from having to be reassembled at the Agency. Having been deaded a couple of times before, he had been lucky enough to have been spotted by the Watchers within the 72 hours window, otherwise it would have been permanent oblivion, bye-bye afterlife.

Sally would eventually come home. He wasn't deaded yet. So the only truly disconcerting part of those past five minutes was him missing Charlotte. She was clingy, but she was nice. He chalked such temporary insanity down to the comparison of the level of abuse he got from Sally. Add his former self coming back in Sally's charming presence, and there was only one logical conclusion. He had been in this dimension for too long. Since Sally wasn't under immediate threat from herself or anyone else, Victor decided to pop over to the Agency for a few hours to get his head back straight. This stroppy charge would eventually cool off and come back.

She had to. It was her apartment.

Mere hours later when back at Sally's, Victor heard a commotion outside the door. Someone dropped the keys about ten times, and a raspy voice that would have made Deep Throat envious uttered swearwords that would have made Charlotte blush. Finally, Sally stumbled in, swaying at about five on the Richter scale. She proceeded to her bedroom, knocking over her favourite Tiffany lamp in the process. Victor sighed. He was sure she would find a way to blame him for it in the morning.

On her way to oblivion, Sally encountered some shoes that didn't get away from her quick enough and kicked a bag like it was a soccer ball, 'Getting to my bed is getting to be an extreme sport,' she mumbled, nearly falling over. She managed to pirouette, gracefully fell face first onto her bed and started snoring almost instantly.

Victor tut-tutted. He could have magicked her a large bottle of water on her night stand, but decided against it. This turn of events was an excellent one. The maximum that he would do to help the Princess was to cover her up so she wouldn't catch a cold.

In the hard light of the morning, Victor heard groaning from under the duvet. A leg emerged and felt for the floor.

'*Oy vey*...[37] No spinning...good...' under the protective cloak of the duvet, Sally was trying to remember what she had drunk last night. She had started with a bottle of red wine. Then had come three cocktails. And five shots. There had been something else afterwards and it clearly hadn't been water.

Victor marvelled at how inarticulate humans could be the morning after binge-drinking.

'I'm so hungover that I think I'll have to come down the bed backwards to stop the world from spinning,' the duvet said.

'Sally, look at the state of you. You obviously don't love yourself at all, but it has given me an idea,' Victor chirped and the duvet that had been slowly sinking to the floor froze mid-ooze, dreading what was coming.

'Sally, I think we're going to give up alcohol next,' the frog declared triumphantly.

'Now you're just being mean,' the duvet said and revealed the glory that was Sally. Her squiggly hair was doing a successful Medusa imitation and her panda eyes were telegraphing how far from glad she was to see the world in general and the frog in particular.

'I bet you won't be able to go a month without alcohol,' Victor offered, thinking he was being kind. Alcohol took 21 days to leave the system. A proper detox would be going completely tee-total forever.

'Are you insane?' Sally wanted to throw something at him, but that would involve moving one of her two right arms and she wasn't up to fighting the painful and cruel world at the moment.

'Your side of the bet is that you WILL be able to go one month without booze,' Victor said, not unkindly. 'If you win, you get a bottle of Sprite,' he tried sweetening the deal.

With all the other horrors that the frog was exercising on her, Sally resigned herself to the situation, 'Deal!' All she wanted was some peace and quiet. 'As long as today...you leave me alone.'

'I'm just trying to look out for you, you know,' Victor said.

'If this is you looking out for me, who needs enemies,' Sally muttered. *More than peace and quiet she wanted Nurofen. Or Solpadeine. She would even take Ibuprofen or Paracetamol. Hell, she would even take Aspirin. Lots and lots of it. Which would involve crawling to the kitchen. Or asking the frog to wheel a bottle of something over here.* 'If you want to look out for me, bring me painkillers. Lots and lots of painkillers.'

'Deal.' After he would get her the pills and lots of water to get her re-hydrated, he would pour all the alcohol she owned into the sink. Then, he could spend the rest of this day planning Charlotte's arrival in Italy. Everybody wins. Well, maybe not the alcohol.

36. Trivial Moments
Gabriel

Gabriel was keeping a watchful eye on the coffee shop from the alcove of the bar across the street. According to Daisy, without exceptional powers Grace couldn't be destined for great things. Maybe she was going to get these special powers any minute now and that's what the assassin was trying to prevent?

Gabriel observed Grace waving smiley goodbyes to some regular customers, puffing stray curls away from her face. Gabriel smiled when she smiled. Her smiles were contagious, whether you were a shop keep, a hungry customer, a busker or an angel. Grace was attentive and kind. She was also an orphan, except for her uncle and he didn't count. No boyfriend.

Wait a minute. Solitary, unattached people whom everybody loved were prime candidates for becoming guardian angels.

Grace's empathy for people and critters alike could make her an exceptional guardian.

If two Earth years ago Grace had died instead of Victor, Gabriel knew he would have recruited her without hesitation.

Hold it.

Was she destined to become a guardian and the reason why someone wanted her dead was to prevent that from happening?

The only thing was - they were going about it all wrong. If Grace was earmarked to become a guardian, when she dies, she would just materialise at the Boss' office and be made an offer that was very hard to refuse.

In fact, if any of the guardians had already earmarked Grace as a potential guardian angel, the only thing the Agency had to do was to wait for her to die. The assassin would, in fact, be helping them recruit her, not preventing it.

Blowing her to smithereens with the cafe and half the city block didn't fit the theory. Her physical body would have been beyond repair. There would have been nothing left of her to recruit.

This train of thought was not helping him find the assassin.

As much as he would enjoy seeing her join the Agency, this sweet girl had her whole life ahead of her. She need not die just yet.

That couldn't be it.

Gabriel tried another tack. Maybe she knew something or had unsuspectingly overheard someone at the coffee shop that had warranted a contract being put out for her? As wild as conjecture as this sounded, they were running out of suspects, so any new theory was a good theory.

Gabriel crossed the street to be closer, in case the assassin should strike again. Having finished the routine inspection of all the venues Grace frequented half an hour ago, he was keeping an eye out.

From outside the fishbowl that was the coffee shop, he saw Grace chatting away to a red-headed girl in the corner booth when Loretta called.

Without any niceties, Loretta started in, 'The tally evened itself out. Whatever Grace did or didn't do during the last ten minutes is good, she should keep doing it. What did she do?'

'She's at work, talking to a red-headed girl.'

'Hang on,' Loretta used the fast forwarding future option, 'After meeting this red-head, I see a lot of dinners and girls and...oh, I see...'

'See what?' Gabriel asked, both hopeful and sad the mystery was finally almost solved.

Loretta laughed, 'Well, you'll be pleased to know that now we finally know why someone is after Grace. She's meant to move in with this girl and meet her other friends and keep them all grounded.'[38]

'How would that make a difference in this dimension? The Boss said that the life and death of this girl would permanently change the face of Earth and perhaps even the Agency.'

Loretta just laughed again, 'The girls she is meant to keep at bay are mortals coming into their magic Goddess' powers. They need someone to believe them as they discover their newfound powers but also someone to ground them and prevent them from doing too much damage. You know how low Earth is on actual magic at the moment? Not just beliefs? Their meeting is a good thing. Your Grace, without a smidgen of magic herself, is the guardian of magic in this dimension and by proxy, in all the others.'

Grace, a guardian of magic?

Out loud, Gabriel said, 'So, I guess Daisy was wrong. She is important even without any special powers.' It made Gabriel wonder what else the Watchers had been wrong about. 'Just to be clear, she was always meant to meet this girl, this future Goddess? That all the death threats were simply an attempt to stop this moment from happening and now they should cease?'

'Yes, yes and yes,' Gabriel could feel the pixie nodding away, happy to have finally solved the mystery.

'But it's so trivial...' Gabriel realised he had said it out loud.

'Never underestimate a moment. No matter how trivial it seems to you, it might actually change someone's life,' he could almost hear Loretta pursing her lips in displeasure.

Gabriel remembered how Loretta came to be a guardian and then a Watcher and apologised. Had it not been for a certain Thumbelina seeing something as trivial as a book for the first time in her life the night before her wedding to the Faerie Prince, the Agency might be missing one excellent Watcher. As it happened, opening a ridiculously ordinary story-book about extraordinary worlds had been the magically trivial moment that had irrevocably changed this pixie's life.

Loretta snorted and hung up. In pixie terms, he guessed he could consider himself almost forgiven for his short-sightedness.

Well, at least he no longer had to review ten years' worth of Grace's life to establish the culprit.

Gabriel was left standing outside the coffee shop with his ear still glued to the phone and with an incomprehensible feeling of pity that his mission was over. A very small part of him was glad that this lovely vivacious girl would get to live countless years until she was recruited.

14. 'Never underestimate a moment.'

37. Possible Has Nothing To Do With It
Lanie

When Peter woke up it was still dark outside. He got up to go to the bathroom. As he was washing his hands, he noticed that Dolly's toothbrush was gone. So was her shampoo. She had probably packed up before she had gone to bed.

The cat was waiting for him outside the bathroom door, looking reproachful.

'Well, thank you for finally gracing me with your presence, Kitty. Schmoozing up to strangers, you should be ashamed.'

The cat gave him a look, wagged its tail once, which could have meant anything from 'I'm annoyed at you' to 'follow me', and trotted into the living room.

Loathe to disturb the last few peaceful hours of sleep the girl was going to get in probably a long time, Peter hesitated.

As he peeked into the living room, he saw the cat sitting on a made-up sofa.

No book-shelf, no ficus and no girl anywhere in sight.

The only evidence that she hadn't been a figment of his imagination was a book of fairy-tales by Hans Christian Andersen, lying on the coffee table, left open at the story of the Little Mermaid. He didn't even know he owned that book.

Deep down and for reasons he couldn't entirely explain, he missed her.

In the morning rush, instead of heading to work, Peter found himself heading towards the hospital. On foot.

As he saw the hospital building towering afar, a pair of eyes the colour of the Caribbean sea made him stop dead in his tracks in front of a tiny church.

His volunteer girl was laughing at him from a picture with a black frame that graced the awning.

The dates underneath the picture read: 20.05.1992-07.07.2011.

A memorial service was about to begin. Mourners were being ushered in.

She had been just 19 when she had died on the day of his traffic accident.

In the picture, her hair was windswept, creating a crazy wave of a glossy dark mane.

Peter had a flashback to an Undine pulling at him when he had been struggling with the seat belt underwater. He remembered how the creature had dragged him to the surface semi-conscious. He remembered how she had smiled in relief when he had finally coughed up river water and started breathing. He thought he had imagined it all.

That face. He remembered that face now.

It was the same face with those huge turquoise eyes that was laughing up at him from this sad poster. Why on Earth couldn't he have remembered that yesterday, when she had been in his apartment? He could have thanked her better than by offering her tea.

Yesterday. At his apartment.

That could not have happened.

According to the poster she had died a week ago. He must have imagined it. No, no, Alice had seen her as well. So either he had imagined nearly dying or he had imagined seeing her yesterday.

That was just great - he had two crazy theories to choose from.

When the usher asked him, how he knew her, he made the choice, 'I was the last person she saved.'

Peter sat down in the last pew, next to an old man who seemed to be wearing hospital PJs under a huge coat, probably borrowed.

Peter could only make out scraps from the eulogy. 'Orphaned at an early age...after the death of her adoptive parents at age 17...volunteering at a homeless shelter...Lanie was loved by everyone whose life she touched...'

Lanie. Her name had been Lanie. The volunteer's uniform with the 'Dolly' name-tag attached had probably been borrowed just like her entire last week.

The old man next to him sniffed, 'The girl was a saint.

Volunteered at the hospital down the street. Held my hand and wheeled me to procedures the whole of last week when my pains were at their worst.'

Peter shook his head. 'She couldn't have. She died a week ago.'

The old man looked at him reproachfully, 'You of all people should know better.'

'Why?'

'She kept watch over you at night. I saw her. One night I couldn't sleep so I was walking the halls. She was cuddled up next to you on the hospital bed. And I don't think it was just that night either. I reckon she did it all the nights you were in there. At least she did it all of last week when I was there.'

All of the last week that she had been presumed dead.

The old man lifted his eyebrow, 'I thought you knew her. I thought she was your sweetheart.'

Peter shook his head again.

'She sure took a shine to you, though, watching over you like that. Goodness of her heart. Pure goodness.'

She hadn't really been there, had she?

Other people saw her, so she must have been real.

He shook his head, 'It's impossible. She was dead.'

The old man looked at him like he was an idiot.

She had been dead and had still looked after him? 'How is that even...possible?'

The old coot patted his arm, 'Who said what happens has to be logical? It just happens. Possible has nothing to do with it.'

He remembered the sense of peace he had felt in his coma and when he had finally woken up. The same sense of peace he had felt when he had taken her hand back at his apartment. Yesterday evening. A lifetime ago.

Had she really been watching over him at the hospital?

It had to have been her. She had been there. In spirit.

This explained the appearance and disappearance of the bookshelf, the ficus and the toiletries in his apartment. All things connected to her vanished poof into the air when she had finally gone.

Lanie had saved him from drowning and nursed him back to health and fed his cat and now she was gone.

Peter stood up. He needed air.

As the tears started falling, he tried to convince himself it was because of the blinding sunlight and not because of the unbearable and inexplicable sense of loss he was feeling.

Lanie was gone.

Could he ever have held on to her?

Bereft and defeated, Peter leaned into the door-jamb next to Lanie's poster.

'You alright? You look kinda shaky.' The old man he had spoken to was shaking so badly he was barely keeping himself upright.

Peter nodded into the door, mumbled his thanks and waved the man to continue on his way.

The vagabond gathered his assortment of borrowed or found clothing about him, nodded goodbye and steered himself back to the shelter. On his way, he passed an alley by the Strand that looked strangely familiar. Then again, all the alleys in this city looked strangely familiar to him.

38. Just Friends

Grace

When Grace's ten minutes were up, uncle Tom made a point of coming up to Della's table and pointedly staring, 'Back to work, Grace.'

As she rose, Grace noticed Gabriel on the phone outside the coffee shop, looking sad.

She filled a takeaway cup with coffee and went to the door. As he stepped in, on the radio, ABBA began to sing about not looking too deep into those angel eyes because he'd take her heart and one day she'd find out he's wearing a disguise.[39]

Gabriel looked incredulously at the till that housed the sound equipment. He knew that it was a spectacularly bad idea for him to get in touch with his humanity which could create the complication of falling in love with Grace. Hence, the re-balancing act this morning. Now, the universe was trying to communicate to Grace not to fall for him either?

In any case, there would be no falling from any side. His mission was over.

'Hey, I cannot stay long, I'm already late for work, just popped by to say hi,' he said as she handed him his morning coffee. He tried to give her some money for the coffee, but she refused. 'Thank you,' Gabriel said, turning to leave.

'It's the least I can do when you've clearly overslept because of our long walk yesterday,' she smiled and waved.

'Grace! Stop flirting!' her uncle bellowed from the innards of the kitchen.

She stuck a tongue out when he couldn't see and winked at Gabriel, hoping he'd be there in the evening to walk her home again. Then and there she decided that this time she would let him walk her to the door.

The glass door closed shut between them.

It seemed an appropriately final gesture. Gabriel knew that it would hurt her, him not being there tonight to escort her home. Any explanation would either be a falsehood or he would need to delve into explaining the Agency to her. Guardians were not allowed to do that unless their cover was blown.

Gabriel smiled, mouthed one more 'thank you', raised the coffee cup and walked away, leaving Grace's life forever.

The radio rejoiced it felt so much better now that he's gone forever.[40]

Before Grace could reach the kitchen, Della tugged at her sleeve and dragged her back to the corner booth, *en route* handing uncle Tom a fiver and mouthing 'I forgot some really important stuff.' Practically bouncing up and down on the soft red vinyl, Della demanded, 'Who's the dish?'

Grace noticed Emma turning down the volume of the radio so she, too, could hear better. 'He's just a friend,' Grace said.

Emma tsk-tsk-ed from the kitchen at such a blatant lie.

Grace glared at her.

Della kept prodding, like a cat playing with a mouse, 'So, you wouldn't mind if I took an interest in him, would you?'

Now Grace glared at Della. *What was it with people sticking their noses where they didn't belong?*

'Ah-hah! Thought so. You're sweet on him, you are!' Della clapped her hands together like she was five.

'Fiddlesticks,' Grace mumbled and coloured to her roots, 'I thought you promised to ignore the world when you wrote...'

'Not when such prime specimens for hero prototypes are roaming the streets...I'll use him somewhere...in a book...or maybe several...now tell me all about him so I don't have to imagine too much...' Della continued, raising her perfectly manicured hands, 'Mitts off, I do promise!'

Luckily, there was nothing to tell. Grace wasn't sure she believed Della's promise, given how easily she broke the one about ignoring the world when writing. For the first time in her life, Grace thought that the piece of advice from her model friends was sage - never introduce your beau to your single female friends until the boy has proposed or even better, married you. This girl was certainly fickle and Grace knew nothing of her relationship status. Fickle, but fun and certainly entertaining.

By the end of the night, after Della had managed to get them to change the radio channel ten times and their menu as well, on paper and off, uncle Tom looked as incensed as he felt. His growls had stopped Della's re-decoration attempts, but had not stopped her from showing the potential decor on her laptop to Emma and Grace. At closing time, Della said she had loved the food, the drink, the decor and the people and had got some good writing done. She patted uncle Tom on the cheek and said she would be back first thing tomorrow morning for fresh ideas and fresh coffee. The look on uncle Tom's face was priceless.

Grace decided that fickle or not, she'd keep Della around for pure good old-fashioned fun.

39. Even Frogs Have Secrets
Sally

When Victor materialised in Sally's apartment five Gaian days later, the television was emitting a soppy song on high volume.

He peeked into the living room and saw Sally wiping away tears as Julia Roberts was being romanced by some floppy haired guy in a garden as the girls in the background kept singing that the guy said it best when he said nothing at all[41].

'It's so completely like you to like your men silent,' Victor commented as Sally screamed. Ignoring her, he hopped on the table, carefully avoiding a punnet of raspberries and muted the television with his hind leg, 'You cry over soppy chick flick movies,' Victor pointed to the tissues peeking from between the couch pillows where Sally had stuffed them, 'My, my, have you always been a big softy and no one noticed?'

'Wha...what are you doing here?' Sally managed.

'Sugar, I'd like to say I live here, but we both know that ain't true, so, let's leave it at I'm visiting, shall we?' the frog offered and angled in for the raspberries. Thank goodness it wasn't pizza. He was secretly proud she had taken his advice to eat more sensibly, but he wasn't going to tell her that. He would praise her when she deserved it. After she got her prince, Harry.

Eyeing the cheeky frog with suspicion, Sally enquired, 'Where did you go again? You leave for four, sometimes five day stints and I have no idea where you are or if you're coming back.'

'Missed me, did'ya?' the frog sidled up to the raspberries.

She swatted at him with her handkerchief, 'As if. I thought I was rid of you, thanking my lucky stars you've disappeared forever after passing on all your wisdom.'

Tsk-tsking at the ingratitude and popping a raspberry in his mouth, the frog shook his head, 'Sticks and stones, love, you don't get rid of me that easy,' *at least not until she saw the light*, 'I'm not done with making you into a human being yet,' Victor reached for another raspberry as the evil girl snatched the punnet away.

'Funny – very funny – coming from a frog and you didn't answer my question, buddy, no raspberries for you until you do,' Sally said, triumphant.

Victor exhaled. No rest for the wicked. After all the things he was doing for her, she wasn't even going to feed him for his efforts, 'Fine. Your hospitality still sucks, so I cannot leave.' He flicked the sound back on, hopped on a cushion and settled in to ignore her until this flick ended.

Sally was slightly scandalised that he would rather starve than take the bait. She decided to prod him some more. 'I know why you came back!' she said triumphantly.

'Do tell, why would I voluntarily succumb myself to your reluctant presence, oh fair one,' Victor said.

'Because you're still a frog!' Sally said and took a raspberry.

Victor had the urge to laugh hysterically, 'And what, pray tell, has changed since last I saw you?'

'Precisely nothing. Which is why you had to come back. You still need me to disenchant you. I'm part of your atonement, remember? And stop with the Shakespeare act, will ya?' Sally said.

Victor considered the proposition. Disenchanting was part of his legend, true. It was what he had asked her to help him with in order to get to help her instead. In a way, helping her and every other charge that the Watchers threw his way WAS penance and part of his atonement.

Satisfied with having silenced the frog for once, Sally decided to push her luck a little, 'So, you're not going to tell me where you went?'

The frog shushed her as Julia was professing her love to a man in a bookshop, 'We ain't married, so back off, woman.'

Making a mental note to frame her questions differently in the future, Sally prodded, 'I don't remember you speaking with a southern twang before and look at all the 'ain'ts' and 'sugars',' she countered slyly.

'You're a regular detective, cannot get anything past you,' Victor continued with a New York accent. He had to watch it. Spending time with Charlotte certainly had its appeal, but he had to remember to switch characters when he switched Charges.

'Hedging your bets, in case helping me doesn't work out for you?' Sally prodded.

'Your intuition astounds me,' the frog said, staring into the TV. *He did have two charges. It was a good thing he didn't have to save either of them to be disenchanted.* 'Even frogs have secrets?' she tried one last time.

'Yup, even frogs have secrets.' And Victor was not a frog which Sally did know and he kept forgetting.

Five minutes later Sally took pity on the critter and moved the raspberries closer to him.

Victor decided that frogs have no pride and proceeded to flick the berries using his tongue from the safety of the couch.

'Eeuw...' Sally said as Victor hushed her motioning at the TV where the man with a floppy hairdo was propositioning Julia at a press conference.

When the movie was over and Victor had finished all the raspberries, thinking the moment opportune, he turned to Sally, 'So, what does it take for you to fall in love?'

'Not that again! This is a conversation I don't even have with my friends, what makes you think I will spill my guts to you?' Sally was indignant.

'Harry is your only friend and I can see why you would not want to have that conversation with him. But you'll have to talk to someone...eventually...and I come free while therapy is not cheap,' Victor shrugged.

The frog had a point, 'Fine! You told me my expectations were unrealistic. What, pray tell, would be?'

'Well, not expecting romantic movies to come to life would be a good start,' Victor said.

'I don't expect anything like a movie to happen to me in real life, I just like soppy romantic movies, thanks to Harry,' Sally groaned. This conversation was definitely something she didn't want to have.

'Harry, Harry, tell me more about this Harry that I've been hearing so much about,' the frog looked inquisitive and decided to try a direct approach, 'Would he fit your checklist?'

'God, no. He's my best friend and I just don't see him that way. He would be the first one to tell me to ditch my checklist and just live a little,' Sally made a face.

'What's wrong with living a little?' Victor asked, 'Sounds like sound advice to me.'

'Precisely! Too sound, too rational, which is why Harry might be a cute IT geek and all, but he's too rational for my taste. I need sass, I need adventure, I need...'

'A reality check,' Victor interrupted her, 'You have sass enough for the both of you, I'm sure. Do you really need the male you? Ever heard of opposites attract?' He tap-tapped his foot, neatly missing the empty punnet.

'Well, if that were the case, Harry and I are simply meant for each other. We're as different as you can get,' Sally sneered, thinking the joke was obvious.

'Maybe that's not such a bad idea, ever thought of that!'

?!?

Clearly not.

Victor sighed, dangling his feet from the table, 'ok, ok, let's not go into epic mythology here. Let's start with something easier...'

'Wait. Why do you think me and Harry getting it on would be as impossible as..what did you call it...epic mythology?' Sally was curious.

Victor shook his head. He had meant something quite contrary – to give her a pep-talk based on mythology and epic love stories of opposites attracting, but perhaps it was fortunate that Sally had taken offence. Reverse psychology seemed to work on her. 'Well, you said it yourself, you're too different, besides I'd rather start with weaning you off...'

'Hang on, hang on, we're not that different, Harry and I,' Sally interrupted him.

'Manners, Sally, it's rude to interrupt! As I was saying, I'd rather start with weening you off checklists...'

'We both like the Yankees!' Sally said triumphantly, ignoring the frog completely.

Victor sighed. Rudeness aside, at least they were getting

somewhere. Mumbling how there was no stopping her, he put his brightest smile on, 'Great! What else do you have in common?'

Sally thought about it, 'We've been friends since we were five, so I've known him for practically my whole life, we went to the same university, we're both apolitical and both like pizza. Now are you telling me that this is enough for a long-lasting relationship?'

Victor thought she'd be surprised by how much less marriages during the Second World War had been based on, but decided not to goad her. With her reverse psychology trigger, she would swing right back. It would be safest to leave the discussion be and have her stew on it on her private time.

Victor yawned. Five weeks on Earth and even with a couple of stretches at the Agency, his humanity was truly getting to him. 'I'm not going to argue with you, I'll let you figure it out for yourself, but you do know that long-lasting relationships are about common interests and doing stuff together and having something to talk about, and not needing but wanting to share your life with someone?'

He let the thoughts hang in the air, shrilly pierced by Sally's phone ringing.

Deep in thought, Sally reached for her phone, 'Yes mother, no carbs.' Victor thought that was rather an interesting way of saying hello. 'Mom, Mom, listen, I'm done with carbs anyway. I'm actually on something called a paleo-diet, where you only eat meat and veg,' Sally listened with surprise at how the usually demanding tone of her mother softened from full-demand-mode down to just animated, 'uh-uh, uh-uh, uh-uh...Ok, mom, no, I'm eating a salad. Uh-uh... I have to eat something after I've just exercised...' She almost lost her hearing at the shriek, 'Yes, mom, EXERCISED...yes, really, for a month now, yes, I'll keep it going this time,' Sally sighed. *Benefit of doubt. That was all she asked. Benefit of doubt.* Considering the countless diets and gym memberships she had cancelled in her life, maybe that was a lot to ask. 'What's that you said? Am I eating properly and exercising because I found someone? No, mother, I'm doing this for myself, not for a guy.' Sally listened intently at the reply. 'No, mother, once I get my make-over done, you're not dragging me to a *shadkhen*[42], no not even the millionaire one.' She listened to the reply. 'Uh-uh. Uh-uh. Nothing is ever good enough for you, is it? The powers that be or YOU forbid I be happy.' 'I did NOT take our Lord's name in vain! How did you even...' Seeing the pointlessness of the conversation, Sally said 'I'm gonna go now. Good-bye, mother!' Sally hung up while her mom was still talking. That was usual.

What was not was that for the first time ever Sally hadn't slammed down the receiver. She wanted to. Especially after the last lamenting comment of 'With all this effort, I have high hopes that you'll get married to a nice Jewish boy. Soon.' She had actually managed to be almost civil to her mother and vice versa. She wasn't going to tell the frog, otherwise it would turn into a relationship-guru next and Sally wasn't sure she could manage any more change happening to her this month.

40. Doubts
Gabriel

At the Agency, Gabriel was attempting to resume his duties. Attempting being the operative word.

When he had knocked on the Boss' door, silence had been his answer. According to the Watchers, the Boss was on a personal save mission in Dialysis X. Again. That's where all the daredevil angels went when they were slightly tired from easy saves. According to the Watchers, the Boss had been frequenting that dimension a lot lately - a clear sign of their usually serene leader needing variety.

Gabriel surveyed the halls from the top of the white marble staircase. Angels kept appearing and disappearing on missions in cocoons of various shapes and colours. Gabriel knew all of them, having recruited about half. The Watchers were fielding the calls and keeping an eye on the screens of the 16 priority dimensions, freezing time when necessary. Necessity being either getting food or drink or helping someone in the sick bay, which was rare. Everything looked normal. Everybody kept busy.

Why was he having trouble volunteering for...well... anything?

He was entitled to a day off after a protracted save. A save that had somehow become his most important save across the past 900 years. And not only because Grace was the keeper of magic on Earth and potentially across dimensions.

So far he had never waited this long to delve head first into another rescue mission.

If the pixie was right and Grace and Della were destined to meet, then from the point of view of the would-be assassin, the damage was already done. The meeting had already taken place. There was no point in anyone going after Grace anymore. This meant there was no need for him to hang around protecting her. For some strange reason, that didn't sit well with him.

Something about saving Grace didn't feel right. Despite his realignment earlier this morning and despite his mission being over, Gabriel was still thinking about the who behind the why. After all, the identity of the would-be assassin was still a mystery.

If Grace was important as a guardian of magic on Earth and by proxy across dimensions, who on Earth or elsewhere would want her dead?

Daisy popped out of the Watchers' station and took his sleeve, 'Do you mind helping out while the Boss is away?' she pleaded, handing him a tablet that was blinking red with all sorts of pending notifications.

'Sure. Any new recruits I should know about?' Gabriel asked, taking the gizmo.

'Lanie and Jack, the bios, photos and commendations for saves are all in there in a separate folder,' Daisy said, speeding off.

The rest of Gabriel's day was spent resolving administrative issues - from approving applications for retirement of some Princes Charming who had fallen for their charges to deciding which new technological gadgets on offer were to be commercialised in which dimensions. At the end of the day, Gabriel knew he had been right in deciding against volunteering for a promotion.

The Boss had summoned both him and Victor to his office a few weeks ago, looking drawn and tired, his thousands of years etched as dark shadows under his usually alert eyes that had lately been losing their sparkle. The meeting had been brief. The Boss had asked both him and Victor to consider helping him find a worthy replacement.

Agency heads usually trained their own replacements, so this had been a strange request. For a brief moment the Boss had looked Gabriel straight in the eye. Gabriel had had a strange feeling that the Boss expected him to volunteer. Although his poker face never betrayed him, from the way he waved both angels off after a long pause, Gabriel could sense that the Boss was not pleased his eldest compatriot had not jumped at the opportunity.

Today, it seemed like the Watchers were keeping him at the Agency on purpose. As the most senior guardian angel after the Boss, he could understand. With the Boss' protracted absences, the Watchers wanted someone more experienced around, should something go terribly amiss. From how the Watchers were delegating to him on administrative as well as important matters, Gabriel had a strange feeling that deep down they had already decided who the next head of the Agency was going to be.

Not if he could help it.

Helping the Boss find his replacement - sure. Even training the new replacement up - absolutely. But stepping into the Boss' shoes - no way. Especially not after the day of trying to fill these shoes, no matter how successfully. Dead boring admin gave Gabriel a toothache. He was a man of action. Avoiding taking on his nobleman's duties was precisely why he had volunteered to go to the Holy war in the first place.

Hold it.

Grace was good with people and keeping the coffee shop running despite her uncle's mismanagement attempts. She would undoubtedly make a formidable guardian.

Maybe Grace was destined to be the Boss' replacement?

She would just need to die in the Earth dimension to become a guardian to become eligible to be the Boss-in-training. Yes, granted, Bosses usually served centuries before they were chosen, but what if...?

What if the Boss had asked not only him and Victor for their thoughts on who could become his replacement? What if the Boss had asked the Watchers as well?

The Watchers were known for their prowess at calculating the odds of any situation. Perhaps they were simply securing a bigger pool of worthy candidates for the Boss' replacement position?

What if the Watchers had been behind Grace's assassination attempts all along?

Loretta knew that Grace was important for balancing magic on Earth and everywhere else. Sanity dictated that even if the Watchers had been behind the assassinations, their futile attempts would now have to stop. The risk of unbalancing magic across dimensions was too big.

Gabriel could vouch for Daisy's priorities being straight, but he never knew about Loretta. Especially after the misguided incident where the pixie had switched an X-ray to make a perfectly healthy but slightly maudlin girl think she had a condition she didn't really have, all because the pixie thought the girl could use an incentive to live.[43]

What if Loretta prioritised having a new head of the Agency over everything else? The stubbornness of pixies was legendary. What if the pixie carried on with what she thought was the right thing to do? It was she who had told him why Grace was important for Earth and she had been the one to confirm his mission was over.

What if she did that on purpose?

Gabriel looked in on the Watchers' station and only saw Daisy on duty. The evil genius of the pair was nowhere to be seen. Gabriel had a nasty feeling that keeping him at the Agency all day might have served a completely different purpose - to keep him away from looking in on Grace.

The angel checked his watch. It was nearly midnight in Earth time. Hoping he was wrong about Loretta, Gabriel teleported to the alley behind the coffee shop. As he straightened his jeans and T-shirt, he thought that walking Grace home for the last time would give him the peace of mind he needed. If everything was really alright, one last walk would be a more appropriate goodbye.

If becoming a little less immortal again was the price he had to pay, so be it.

A thorough check of Grace's surroundings revealed exactly what he had hoped to find - nothing. *Old habits died hard.* With certainty that this was the last he would get to talk to her in a long while, Gabriel headed for the coffee shop.

41. Suspicions
Gabriel

'Ready to go?' Gabriel asked as he stuck his head through the front door to the coffee shop. The grandfather clock in the corner struck midnight.

All done, Grace turned and smiled at him from behind the till, making all of his worries and woes melt away. She grabbed her jacket and headed for the door that Gabriel was holding open for her. Passing by, she accidentally brushed up against him.

His scent made her dizzy enough to stumble. Daisies and sunshine.

Gabriel caught her by the elbow and Grace felt a jolt of electricity at his touch.

The radio promised he'll catch her whenever she would fall[44] and promptly switched to promising he can be the one, that he would never let her fall even if saving her sends him to heaven.[45]

Grace blushed to her roots. Hoping he hadn't noticed, she quickly walked into the dusk, aware that Gabriel was following right behind her.

Steadying her, Gabriel held on for a couple of seconds too long. Enough to feel the heat of her skin and sense her heart race like a hummingbird. Enough to want to smell her hair and not want to let go. Gabriel's heart started to race, matching hers, reminding him he had been human, once. Gabriel withdrew his treacherous arm.

Why was it that his re-balancing from this morning was wearing off in seconds around this girl?

He should check the sick bay. The re-balancing pod could be broken or its battery depleted. Another worry on his list made his mouth draw into a thin line.

For a while, they walked the ill-lit streets in silence.

Grace kept stealing glances at Gabriel, trying to decide whether to rebuke him for being impolite and not saying 'hello' when he had walked in or to ask him what was wrong. In the end, she did neither. *Sometimes, it was best to let people be and they would eventually come around telling her everything anyway.*

Gabriel radiated worry, steering Grace carefully around street corners and holding her back at the red pedestrian light even though there was no visible traffic.

Grace enjoyed the way he gently touched her shoulder or upper arm when he did that. Always respectful, always the proper gentleman. If it wasn't for his stern expression, she would have liked to take his hand, put it on her shoulder and hold it there for the entire walk. Her wild side kept coaxing her to step in front of him, put her hands on his chest and kiss him on her tiptoes to shake him from his dark thoughts. Dark didn't become him.

Grace stopped so abruptly an elderly gentleman would have mauled her over from behind, had Gabriel not pulled her close from harm's way.

Backtrack. She had a wild side that wanted to snog him?

He was holding her so close, she could smell daisies and sunshine again. Grace felt her knees go weak. Gabriel holding her did nothing to keep her wild side at bay.

Grace blushed crimson and told herself to get a grip. She noticed that Gabriel's expression hadn't changed. Grace was half glad and half offended he hadn't noticed her embarrassment at such close proximity.

How on earth was a girl to start a conversation about whether the guy was interested in her or not? From the way they were frog-marching and not talking it seemed he was performing an obligation, rather than enjoying her company.

The thought made Grace angry. She wanted to slap him silly and head for the nearest tube station. Him steering her round the next puddle made her reconsider. *Maybe he really did care if her feet got wet or not. Which meant maybe he really did care about her?*

Streets crept by as the silent duo treaded the husky London night.

When there were only three more traffic lights to go and Gabriel hadn't spilled the beans on what was eating him, Grace really started to worry.

Was this the last time she was ever going to see him? She hadn't been very welcoming or flirtatious around him. *Maybe he had gotten the idea SHE wasn't interested? Why else was he escorting her like she was a distant relative and not a well-liked one at that?*

Oh gods, what if he didn't even want to be friends?

Emma had told her time and again to be more direct about what she wanted - whether it was to be left alone or to get answers. She needed answers.

'Gabriel, can I ask you something?' she started tentatively, touching his sleeve.

He looked at her like he was seeing her for the very first time, 'Yes?'

Grace's heart sank. Just that look was confirming her suspicion that he wasn't interested. *He had already forgotten who he was walking home! All his kind gestures, all his caring - it wasn't meant for her, he would have done all that to any feeble old lady he was helping to get home safe.*

Swallowing back her disappointment, Grace decided to brave it, 'I said - can I ask you something?'

He nodded, 'Sure, go ahead.'

'You're somewhere else today. More quiet than usual. Is something the matter?' Grace asked, thankful there was a roundabout way to ask personal questions she didn't know if she wanted answered.

Besides someone wanting this sweet girl dead and him suspecting one of the Watchers was behind it in a misguided attempt to recruit them a new Boss - no, nothing. None of which he could tell her. 'I do apologise that I haven't been paying more attention to you. I was lost in thought.' Gabriel uttered.

Grace nodded, 'There seems to be a lot on your mind. How was your day at work?' Grace asked, praying his worries were work-related and that he wasn't keeping his distance from her on purpose.

'Lots of admin, which was tolerable for a day, but it did feel like someone was trying to pressure me into a...promotion,' Gabriel decided to be as truthful as he could be.

'Promotion? That's early on. You must be very good at what you do. Why don't you want a promotion?' Grace asked, thankful it WAS work-related.

'I would simply be the wrong man for the job,' Gabriel said and shrugged.

He saw Grace stop at the bottom of the stairs of a too familiar doorstep. 'This is me, thank you for walking me home tonight,' Grace said, looking miserable. *Why hadn't she taken a longer route home? Sure, they would have reached here by one in the morning, but she could have wheedled more information out of him. She should have started asking him stuff sooner.*

'Thank you for trusting me to walk you to your door. I hope we can have coffee again sometime.' Gabriel knew he was talking rubbish, saying things he didn't mean. *This was their last walk. There would be no more coffees, no more walks, no more anything. He couldn't help himself. He wanted to keep her there a few minutes longer.*

Still, his time was up. She was safe for the time being. It was time for him to take his leave.

His watch beeped. It was Daisy ringing him. Probably another rescue. Gabriel ignored the call. He would talk to the Watcher first thing after this goodbye.

Grace nodded and as she turned to go, he gently pulled on her sleeve, 'Grace?' He wished she wouldn't go just yet. He would take a few precious seconds of being near her, if a few precious seconds was all he got.

She paused, her heart skipping a beat, unwilling to go either, 'Yes?'

Gabriel was grasping at straws, so he thought he might as well ask the charge herself the most obvious question left unanswered by his analysis of the attempts on her life, 'Has anything strange happened in your life lately?'

Besides meeting him, forging a strong belief there was a secret network of cats watching over her after she adopted one who she felt was becoming her best friend? No, nothing.

Grace started to nod just as her front door exploded above them.

Seeing the splinters coming at her, Gabriel grabbed Grace

and sheltered her with his body. He was virtually indestructible, she was not. His wings extended instantaneously to protect them both, ripping through his tailored shirt. Grace would have marvelled at their gorgeous span and iridescent colour, had she not squished her eyes shut as soon as he grabbed for her.

'Assumption...fudge-up...mother...string that in one sentence...' Gabriel swore under his breath, still holding Grace tight. He had assumed that checking everything twice would do it.

He had scanned the entire house half an hour ago, before he went to the coffee shop to meet her. During their walk, someone had managed to rig the door with explosives.

He should have known better. Assumption was the mother of all fudge-ups. Thank goodness for the re-balancing act at the Agency this morning – it had restored his inviolability at the expense of considerably but not quite eroding his humanity. Five days of humanity without the reboot and neither of them would be standing here now.

Had he not stopped her, she would have been much closer to the door when it had exploded.

Gabriel dusted Grace off.

Still hunched over, she opened her eyes and thought she saw a shadow of huge wings on the pavement, amongst all the billowing dust.

Great, not only was her hearing gone, she was also seeing things. She had no clue she could have a concussion without having hit her head.

Grace turned and found her nose in Gabriel's chest.

Well, this was...solid, but not hard enough for her to get a concussion.

They both looked up at what had minutes ago been a door of her semi-detached house.

All Grace could muster was, 'Oh, my.'

Gabriel decided now was as good a time to tell her as any, 'Someone is trying to kill you.' He let go of Grace and tried to look reassuring while pointing out what was bleedingly obvious at the moment. He still probably needed to do some convincing since Grace didn't know about all the other attempts.

'I know,' Grace said, shaking off the rest of the door, briefly wondering how it was possible they were both still alive.

Gabriel paused. 'You know?' *Perhaps she DID know who was after her?* 'Do you have any enemies?' Any that the Watchers' careful research hadn't managed to unveil.

Grace shook her head no, 'It is bleeding obvious. Judging by the strange things that have been happening to me...especially lately...I wouldn't put it past the universe to try to...'

'Assassinate you...?' Gabriel finished her sentence.

Was it this simple? The balance of the powers needed her dead? Why would the tally then suggest she needed to be saved? Gabriel scratched his head. He had never heard of the Universe to try and rid itself of someone before.

Ever.

'Yes. I cannot find another explanation for it,' Grace was now looking at her lovely home that had a gaping hole in the facade, sticking out like a broken tooth on a Barbie. 'Gods, it will take ages to repair this.'

Not if he could help it. 'I know a certain carpenter who can perform miracles in impossible timescales.' *Well, he really did.* 'I'll arrange it to be fixed by Monday. Meanwhile, you,' he dusted off some splinters from her back, carefully avoiding her rear, 'are staying somewhere safe.' And he was going to sleep on her floor, on her ceiling, on her window sill, outside her window in the rain, if he had to. But first, he had to get her out of here, before whoever was after her could try again. Before he could figure out why.

Meanwhile, he had more research to do. On the Universe, Grace's life, the consequences of magic getting out of hand on Earth and across dimensions as a result of Grace perishing, on everything. If the Watchers were behind this after all, he could only trust his own detecting efforts.

With a last look at her house, he asked, 'Do you have anything in that apartment that you absolutely cannot live without?'

'The cat!!!' He had to physically restrain her from running in after the cat that wasn't there.

'The cat is fine.' For someone so tiny, she was putting up quite a fight.

He heard sirens in the distance. Some vigilant neighbour had called the police. Good. 'We need to go. Now.'

'I'm not leaving without the cat,' Grace mumbled into his chest in between sobs.

Gabriel sighed. 'Wait here. I will go check. But if the cat has scrammed, will you then go?'

Grace nodded, eyes as wide as saucers.

Gabriel ran into the building, moving quickly and listlessly through the rubble that had been Grace's apartment, keeping an eye out for her. This wasn't difficult, given the rather airy view from the facade. Knowing full well the cat was not there, he made a quick circle around the flat, calling out for 'kitty'.

Gabriel's phone rang. 'Daisy,' Gabriel said inspecting the door and nodding at Grace who was starting to shiver from shock.

'What happened?' his ear-piece said.

'That's what I wanted to ask you, actually,' Gabriel said sifting through the rubble. 'I checked her apartment 30 minutes ago...'

'I did try to call...' Daisy said, 'I didn't see it coming at all. The screens showed nothing. The bomb detonated less than 60 seconds after the recording started and I tried to call you. You didn't pick up and I couldn't freeze time on Earth while you were there! Whoever it was got in and got out in less than one Earth minute. Did you forget to put the protective spells on against outside intruders?' Daisy asked.

'They were on,' Gabriel said grimly, knowing where this was going.

An inside job.

Gabriel didn't even have to say it. This level of preparation... the assassin's intent should have been clear long before the bomb had been attached to her door.

'How?' was all that Daisy asked.

Choosing to take her question to mean what had happened, Gabriel summarised, 'Judging by the extent of the destruction...'

Gabriel looked around. The blast had wiped out most of the hallway, killed the windows and left the living room looking like a half-bitten sandwich. '...Our assassin used Semtex, probably one kilogramme of it and attached it to the inside of Grace's front door. The blast was directed at Grace standing outside of the door, so it had to be a ready-made directional shrapnel charge. Plus, judging by what I cannot find,' Gabriel kicked the rubble looking for a pre-attached blasting cap and disposable remote receiver and finding none, 'it looks like a pre-manufactured device that was installed in under one minute.'

'So, we are looking for someone who knows their way around bombs, knew he would have a window of about 30 minutes after your last check and can get in and out of apartments in less than one minute?'

'Including the bomb-set-up time,' Gabriel finished.

'Including the set-up time,' Daisy agreed.

'Looks like whoever it is also knows our recording rules, including about intent...' Gabriel grabbed for whatever clothes he could find that were not scorched beyond belief.

'...That the screens start to record those who want to do harm from the time they decide to do harm...' Daisy finished for him. 'Unbelievable!'

'Precisely,' Gabriel said grimly.

This looked like an inside job. Unless someone at the Agency had accidentally said something to someone they shouldn't have and this someone was magical enough to know how to appear inside apartments with ready-made bombs.

'Worse, they probably also know the Agency's resurrection rules if they were aiming at complete annihilation, just like with the cellar bomb. If I hadn't stopped to ask Grace a question, it would have taken us a couple of seconds to get up the steps. At the door we would both have gotten the full impact of the charge. There wouldn't be enough of anyone left to resurrect. Those few seconds and going back down the steps had made all the difference.'

Gabriel checked that Grace was still shivering on the pavement and noticed adjacent houses were sporting a few lit windows. Neighbours were finally waking up to see what had gone kaboom in the wee hours of the morning.

They had to leave.

Passing the door Gabriel realised WHEN exactly the bomb had detonated.

Grace hadn't touched the door.

The bomb had been rigged to work not on contact but by remote detonation.

The remote-controlled device must have been on a few seconds time-delay.

Which meant only one thing.

The assassin had been within a line of sight to detonate.

'I have to get her out of here,' Gabriel said and hung up. If the assassin was near, they knew they had failed.

Keeping eye contact with Grace, Gabriel darted out, shaking his head, 'No body. No cat. It must have let itself out through the open window when whoever it was rigged the door.'

Grace looked like she didn't trust his word on this one.

The sirens sounded like they were around the corner.

Gabriel took Grace by her shoulders and started steering her away, 'Look, we need to go now, for your own good, in case whoever is trying to kill you tries again.' *If they were desperate enough they could try to finish the job this very moment with whatever came in handy.*

He wasn't going to say that out loud and scare the girl beyond her wits. 'Do you prefer to wait around here for the police and spend the entire evening answering their questions or do you want to spend the evening figuring out who is trying to kill you and why?'

Grace blinked the tears away, forgetting to argue that this was exactly the job for the police.

Gabriel looked at her quivering lip. *Poor kid. She was in no state to make decisions. He would have to make them for her.*

'The cat is alive, it's just not at the apartment, which is a good thing,' he said softly, guiding her away into the recesses of a tiny side street that she had never known was there.

She let him quick-march them away, his hand across her

shoulders with sirens bellowing directly behind them. This wasn't strictly a dream come true, him with his arm across her shoulders, but given the circumstances, beggars couldn't be choosers. Grace leaned in, not daring to look back. She hoped he was right about Cat. Accepting her fate of being rescued by Gabriel once again, Grace mustered, 'Wh-where are we going?'

'Somewhere safe.' *That's all she needed to know for now.* 'And switch off your phone, unless you want to be summoned to the police station to give a statement,' he added. *He would take the battery out when they got to where they were going.*

Grace did what she was told. *At least he didn't make her throw her phone away, like in the spy movies.*

Gabriel led them down the steps of an underground station Grace never knew existed around this corner either.

They alighted at Kensington Gardens. For a brief second Grace wondered why she felt so much at ease with this City boy who she had met only five days ago. Maybe because he hadn't actually wanted anything from her, not her time, not her money, not even a freebie coffee at the coffee shop.

When they stopped in front of a white stucco mansion, the Italian-looking 50-something doorman greeted Gabriel with, 'Good afternoon, Mr St.Croix.'

Grace felt slightly uncomfortable, realising she knew nothing about Gabriel, his lifestyle or background. *At least now she knew his last name.*

Gabriel nodded back and smiled, 'Afternoon, Tony.'

The place looked awfully pricey. *That's what happens when you let someone else make decisions for you.* 'Look, if this is a hotel, I cannot afford it,' she said.

'It's not a hotel, I have an apartment upstairs,' Gabriel said and ushered her towards the door, looking all solid and reassuring.

Grace inhaled and looked like a frightened bird, 'You've brought me to your home...I couldn't possibly,' *not after knowing him for just a few days, she really couldn't take advantage of someone whose mobile phone number she didn't even know,* 'maybe I should go and stay with my uncle or Emma...?' she said, stepping back to the curb even though the doorman was holding the front door wide open.

Something had her running scared again. 'Grace, are you sure you really want to do that?'

She pictured her uncle's shoe box of a flat that he shared with his wife and two teenage sons and squirmed. 'I could stay on their floor...'

'And put them in jeopardy?'

Grace inhaled sharply, 'Jeopardy?'

'Whoever did...that,' Gabriel made a 'kaboom' motion with his palm, '...obviously knows where you live. What are the chances they would also know where you work and who your next of kin and best friend are? You might be putting your family and Emma's in danger, Grace.'

She would never do that to Emma and Ed and while uncle Tom and his lot were not her favourite family, they were the only family she had left. 'Wouldn't I otherwise be putting you in danger?' she decided to enquire.

'This,' Gabriel gestured at his solid, old, marble-halled building, 'is probably the safest place in London for you right now.'

Grace nodded but Gabriel could see she didn't quite believe him.

As she stepped through the door that Tony was patiently holding for them, her feeling of foreboding shifted up a notch. The Albanian knot in the middle of a black and white circle on the floor looked familiar. Sos did the crystal chandelier bathing the lobby in yellow starry Christmas lights. The black rectangles of door awnings made the lobby look infinite, while the winding white marble staircase as well as the 1930s elevator looked like something out of a long-forgotten but very familiar movie.

'Have they shot a lot of movies in this building? A bit of Hercule Poirot, maybe?'

What a curious question to ask, Gabriel thought, 'No, why?'

Grace shrugged, 'It just looks really familiar.'

They had stopped in front of the elevator. Gabriel opened his mouth to object but closed it again. *Impossible. This was one of the few Agency safe-houses in existence in the Earth dimension. She couldn't have seen it. The only way for her to see it would be to have actually been here.*

The elevator took them up to the penthouse. Because of his manners - he actually had them as opposed to the posh wannabes roaming the City - Grace always suspected Gabriel was well off. She never suspected how well off until now.

Gabriel opened the green door of the apartment and offered to take her hand.

For some inexplicable reason that gesture was also too familiar. Except she remembered it having been a darker hand that had been proffered.

Something in Grace's expression puzzled Gabriel, 'What's the matter?'

She looked half cross and half lost, 'I....I think I have been here before.'

Gabriel flicked on a switch and the foyer immediately stretched to end with a door. 'In this building?'

That door... 'In this building, in this apartment, in this hallway.' Grace was fairly sure that should they turn left there would be the living room with French windows overlooking a park and a black grand piano in the middle with a giant crystal vase with white flowers on top of it.

They turned a corner and there it was. The French windows, the park, the vase, even the white flowers and the grand piano, only a white one, an elegant speck against the backdrop mishmash of black and white monochrome.

'I have to sit down,' Grace said before Gabriel caught her *en route* to the floor.

Grace was eyeing the next room under the belly of the piano. She saw a familiar book shelf spanning the entire wall in the study next door, just as she knew she would.

'I have been here before,' she said so quietly Gabriel almost didn't hear her. She told him about the park, the windows, the piano, the vase, the flowers, the bookshelf and the dark hand offered to take her beyond the awning of the front door.

'I can even tell you that in the study next door,' she motioned in the general direction of it, 'there is an ornate silver picture frame on an oak dresser.

Gabriel peeked - from where she was sitting on the floor she couldn't see behind the corner into the next room. He stood up and as he reached the corner he saw a letter desk with a black and white photo framed in decorative metal. He took the picture with him as proof.

'Maybe you're clairvoyant?'

Grace threw her head back and laughed until she cried, 'Well, if that were true, I should have seen my front door being blasted to smithereens before it actually happened, right?'

He gave her the photo. *This did not make sense. Had some other guardian angel brought her here before?*

She handed the frame back to him, 'And this is the man who brought me here...when I was 12. After my parents had died in a car crash.' *Twelve years ago.*

Gabriel took a good look at the photo this time. *It couldn't be. Could it?*

The man in the 1930s stylised photo was looking sideways. It was a face Gabriel recognised. A face he saw at the Agency every day. The face went with clothes from the Arthurian era. At least for Gabriel.

His Boss.

'He didn't look like that then, of course.'

'Are you sure it was him?' Gabriel asked.

Grace took the photo. The black and white shot was of an Indian-looking regal man, dressed in a grey coat with a bowler hat and a walking cane. 'This photograph looks really old... beginning of the 20th century...look at the car next to him...I mean...the man I remember looked like that...but 12 years ago the man in this picture would already be dead...maybe I don't remember him,' she pointed at the photo, 'maybe I remember his son or grandson or something? Maybe they are just related and look very much alike? Who is this man anyway and why do you have a photo of him in your apartment? Who is he to you?'

Gabriel knew this was probably the best opportunity he could ever have to tell her the whole truth. *Except he wasn't going to.*

Gabriel tried to think fast on his feet. *Whom would it be appropriate to have pictures of in his apartment?* 'He's an old family friend and as far as I know he doesn't have any relatives, sons or grandsons or nephews.' *Well, that part was true. He didn't know the Boss' family or even which dimension he was from.*

'But how could he have showed me into your family's apartment 12 years ago?' Grace looked puzzled.

Gabriel let yet another golden opportunity pass him by to tell her about the immortality of guardian angels. Instead, he settled for a lie, which he thought was probably better than the truth and certainly better than nothing at all at the moment, 'He couldn't have.'

More importantly, why had the Boss never mentioned he knew Grace, if he had himself saved her 12 years ago? Could he have forgotten? Maybe he didn't keep tabs on everyone he had rescued like some of the other angels Gabriel knew.

Too many questions.

Gabriel lifted Grace up from the floor and carried her to the armchair. She was as light as a feather when she didn't struggle. 'I'll get you some water,' he said and headed for the kitchen.

'Get me a new life while you're at it,' Grace muttered when Gabriel was out of earshot. *Something strange was going on. Besides the oddness of her having been at this apartment 12 years ago, someone was trying to kill her. Fancy that.*

Grace pinched herself. *Nope, she wasn't dreaming.*

Gabriel was back, offering her a glass of water.

She gulped it down and fell silent.

'A penny for your thoughts?'

Grace wasn't ready to share. Her stomach growled.

Gabriel lifted an eyebrow.

'Yes, I almost get killed and my stomach decides it wants food,' Grace tried to make light of the situation.

A cursory inspection of the refrigerator and the kitchen revealed a whole lot of cans. Canned tuna, canned pasta, canned lentils, canned beans. The kitchen was stocked with everything that would not perish for years. The counter spotted a bowl of sugar and a mill of salt. 'Not proper food but this'll do,' Grace said.

The intercom rang and made Grace jump. The can of beans she had been holding rolled under the living room sofa.

'I asked Tony to kindly provide us with take-away food and took the liberty of opting for Chinese,' he said.

Grace nodded.

'I'll go get it,' he said.

When Grace nodded again, Gabriel turned and left.

A man of few words.

After retrieving the reluctant can from under the sofa, Grace put it back into the kitchen shelf where it belonged. Curious whether all of the drawers housed canned food, she opened a few. Nope. Proper knives, forks, pristine kitchen towels. The kitchen looked ready for someone to use it for the very first time. *The cleaning lady did an awesome job here.*

15.'I have been here before.'

The wine rack housed a selection of random CD-s – Beyonce's single Halo[46], The Red Jumpsuit Apparatus' Your Guardian Angel[47] and Depeche Mode's Angel of Love[48] were the most recent releases. She picked up the familiar soundtrack from the movie 'The City of Angels'. Grace remembered watching it on the television with Victor. He had gotten bored and told her to shut it off, but she had secretly bought the soundtrack and used to play Alanis Morissette's Uninvited[49] and Sarah McLachlan's Angel[50] after particularly bad rows. After Victor had already stormed out of the apartment, of course. These songs aptly described the relationship of the main characters of the movie.

From the back of the shelf, she fished out two cassettes from 1997 – one was U2's single 'If God Will Send His Angels'. [51] The other was Robbie Williams' single 'Angels'[52]. *Surprise, surprise.*

When she opened the next cupboard stacks and stacks of CDs were staring at her lying in disarray amidst cassettes across what looked like vinyl albums. Seeing 'Earth Angel' by The Penguins[53], she didn't even have to guess. More songs on the same variation. Picking up 'Ella Sings Gershwin', Grace traced the first song on the first side of the 1950 vinyl album - 'Someone to Watch Over Me'[54], one of her parents' favourites. She remembered watching mom and dad dancing around to it in their living room on Saturdays.

Right. If she had to guess, then the owner of this apartment was preoccupied with one particular subject. Just a tad. She would never have figured Gabriel to be a nutter for angelic stuff.

Grace noticed that the door of a narrow drawer compartment under the oven was not properly shut. A laptop bag she had seen Gabriel with was preventing it from closing. When she opened the drawer, a hefty manila folder slipped out and disintegrated into a pile of flying sheets.

Oh, bother.

Out of curiosity, Grace picked up a sheet of paper and saw her own smiling face staring back at her. From the shot of the camera, it appeared to have been taken in the street from across the coffee shop. Grace leafed through the rest of the folder. All the other papers were also ALL about her.

Gabriel HAD been stalking her!

***

When Gabriel returned to the apartment, laden with plastic containers an eerie silence met him. He put the bags down and called out, 'Grace!'

Nothing.

Had she gone out?

Grace was standing in the middle of the living room, holding a manila folder, staring at him in disbelief and fear.

She had found the file he had been collecting about her life with the help of the Watchers. Judging by the stormy look Grace was giving him, he should have put it in the vault, but now was the entirely wrong time to think about that.

'I don't know what's going on and I don't know who the hell you are or what you're playing at, but you'd better start explaining before I call the police,' Grace waved the manila folder in front of his nose. She was too mad to consider he was twice her size, that no one besides Tony-the-doorman downstairs knew she was there and that instead of explanations he could do whatever he wanted to.

Gabriel sighed. *He had always known he wouldn't figure it out without her anyway, which would eventually mean he would have to fill her in. About everything.*

The question was, would she believe him?

'You wouldn't believe me if I told you,' he sighed and sat down on the cream sofa.

'Try me,' she spat back and remained standing.

Please, please say you are an undercover cop and you have been sticking around to suss out whoever had planned the bombing and that's how you knew it would happen, but hoped to prevent it and catch the bad guy and that the explosion was a whoopsie.

Except she knew from her cop friends they would never jeopardise her by not letting her know she was a sitting duck.

'Please believe me when I say that I mean you no harm,' Gabriel entreated.

Grace thought about it for a moment, 'Well, considering

you have saved me twice and are about to feed me, hopefully not with poison, we can assume that as established. The true question is why.'

'Four,' he said.

'What?'

'Four times. I have saved your life four times, five, if you count the flower pot, not that it's important.'

'It's important to me! And what do you mean four? There were those drunks in front of the coffee shop when I don't know what could have happened and my apartment today...'

'There was also the time you were taking out the trash and found the cat. I had to turn into the cat so that you would bend down to pick me up and the bullet someone shot at you from a remote-control operated gadget across the street would miss you. Two days later, a bomb was left in the basement of the coffee shop that would have blown you and your City block to Kingdom come if I hadn't sent it off into a much more harmless dimension. Your apartment today makes three definite assassination attempts. The altercation with the bullies could also have ended badly and while it qualifies as someone wanting to do harm, I'm not quite sure it was an assassination attempt. The flower pot could have been an assassination attempt. It would have fallen on your head, had I not opened an umbrella on our walk two days ago. The worst you would have ended up with would have been a concussion, so I doubt it was really an attempt on your life, but there you have it,' Gabriel said in one go.

'Wh-what?' Grace slid to the floor. The angel noticed this was something she did as default as if her legs stopped carrying her whenever she was stressed.

'You...YOU were the cat?!?' was all she said.

That was the only thing she had registered?

Gabriel nodded.

Somehow, she believed him instantly. Images of her stroking the cat to sleep and waking up breathing into its fur swam into Grace's mind. *Oh Gods, she had talked to the cat about liking Gabriel.* Grace flushed scarlet. 'Why you....you....'

Ignoring that Grace was turning crimson, Gabriel admitted

freely, 'Me. That's why I knew that the cat was not in the apartment and that it was fine...as in not dead.'

Right about now, Grace wished against all her animal loving instincts that the cat had died.

Turning into animals, dismantling bombs, being in the right places at the right time... 'Wh-what are you?' Grace stammered, retreating from him crab-fashion on the floor until her back came up against the cold wall. 'That guy, the guy who first led me here after my parents had died, he WAS the same man as in the photo, wasn't he?'

All of a sudden, Grace remembered how cool Gabriel's skin had felt to her touch when he had sheltered her from the blast which had left him completely unharmed, although they had both been standing much too close. Ignoring the turning into animals bit, but factoring the impossibility of someone from the 1930s looking the same age some 60 years later, a horrible thought occurred to her.

'You...you're a vampire, aren't you?'

Gabriel sighed. *The modern malaise of popular television shows and movies.* 'No. Not a vampire. Have I tried to suck your blood even once?'

'No.'

Well, he hadn't. Despite the cat sleeping on the pillow next to hers. Plus Grace was quite sure she remembered Gabriel having a heartbeat when she had her nose pressed up against his chest. *But what else could explain the longevity of certain individuals?*

'Are you a god?'

Gabriel tried to keep a straight face. *He hadn't been called that before.* 'No.'

Before her head imploded with any more wild suppositions, he kindly offered, 'I'm a guardian angel. Your guardian angel for the time being.' Pointing behind him in the general direction of the Boss' photo, 'And the guy in the photo is my Boss who acted as your guardian angel 12 years ago.'

'So I didn't imagine seeing wings on the pavement. Today or the other day in the alley when I was being bullied?' she asked.

'You saw the shadow of my wings?' The girl had astute perception.

'Aren't I supposed to?'

'Not many notice. Or if they do, most people convince themselves they must have imagined things,' he replied.

She shrugged, 'Well, I'm not most people.'

No, she was not, he had to admit that.

He braced himself for the inevitable barrage of questions. Maybe even tears. Even the ones they picked for guardians sometimes went into shock before they started believing what was happening. He occasionally had to restrain various beings from beating him up or incinerating him with their breath as a result of a nervous hiccough. He was thankful they were on Earth and Grace as per Loretta's assurances was not a magical creature but simply a guardian of magical creatures of this dimension.

Propping herself up against the comforting cold white wall, Grace felt slightly better. She had to process this. *Well, the guardian angel story explained Gabriel's interest in her. Sadly, not the kind of interest she was hoping for. The angel thing also had to be why she trusted him. Because despite him having snooped on her, she trusted him still.*

There were still some things that needed explaining – like turning into animals and ability to throw bombs into other dimensions *and other dimensions*!

What had Conan Doyle said via his immortal creation Sherlock? When you eliminate the impossible, what remains, however improbable, must be the truth?

People had guardians. Uncle Tom was hers until she came of age.

Why couldn't she have a guardian angel?

'Ok,' she said.

'Ok what?' Gabriel asked.

'Someone is trying to kill me and you are my guardian angel. Now what?'

'You accept it all, just like that?' *That was a first.*

Grace shrugged, 'Why, did you lie to me or something?'

'No, of course not, but usually people...'

Grace didn't let him finish, 'Well, I guess I'm not a usual girl then.'

'So you keep telling me.' *He was prone to believe her.*

A little bit of more proof would help, though. 'It would completely, utterly and irrevocably convince me if I saw your wings, though.'

Gabriel sighed. Right there, she was back to being just an ordinary girl. *The damsels, they always went for the wings. Very well.* 'Ready?' Gabriel asked, positioning himself in the middle of the living room.

Ready for what?

Three metres of majestic white wings erupted from Gabriel's back, extending above the piano on one side and the cream sofa on the other side in a whoosh that reminded Grace of wet laundry.

'Wow, very 'X-Men: The Last Stand',' was all she could say, admiring the view from the floor.

When Gabriel raised an eyebrow, Grace elaborated. 'It's a movie about genetically mutated...erm...evolved people with special powers.' *Such a shame. Just when she was starting to consider him as good boyfriend material.* 'You really are an angel,' she said with a sigh.

Huge grey eyes were looking trustingly up at him from the floor. Glad he didn't have to do any more convincing, Gabriel simply said, 'Yes, I am.' He folded his wings to make space in the apartment. Outside, the sun came out. When it hit his wings, they sparkled iridescent.

A monosyllabic protector. Fancy that. Grace smiled weakly, 'My dad always used to say - Accept everything, fear and expect nothing and be prepared to be pleasantly surprised. So that's what I've decided to do, ok?'

'Ok,' Gabriel felt slightly awed by this tiny girl. 'Pleasantly surprised?'

She nodded, 'After...four or according to you maybe even five assassination attempts...staying alive would be a pleasant surprise.' Grace looked up at him and smiled.

For some strange reason Gabriel felt pride at Grace keeping her cool.

'Did you have them out when you were sheltering me from the blast?' Grace asked, reaching for the tip of his wing closest to her.. 'Is that why you don't have a scratch on you? They are not just feathers, are they?' she stroked the ones she could reach, 'But they are so soft...'

Grace's touch felt like skin on skin. Gabriel blushed, feeling himself go warm all over. 'Hard as marble, when I need it,' he managed.

'So, what do we do now?' she asked and held out her hand.

He pulled her up. 'Now we eat.' He pointed at the canisters of take-away food. 'You can help with the plates or do you prefer to eat out of the boxes?'

Grace nodded sagely, 'Boxes.'

'We need forks or do you prefer chopsticks?' Gabriel started for the kitchen and heard a shuffle as light as a feather. When he turned, Grace was on the floor, passed out cold.

Gabriel sighed and went to deposit Grace on the cream sofa, hoping she would regain consciousness at the smell of food.

42. What A Difference A Day Makes
Lanie

For the very first time since she had started her new job, Lanie was having time off. Loretta had insisted that a 48-Agency-hour shift was more than enough for starters and Lanie had not dared to disagree. Just this once.

Since she hadn't travelled to all 63 dimensions yet, she was having trouble picking which one to make her home. She hadn't had time to pop over to the Mystic North to see Klaus and admire the Northern lights while she was at it. She had no clue whether it was as uninhabitable as Daisy had told her. It couldn't be that horrible if Gabriel chose it for home. She decided to inspect all the variations of heaven[55] and the Magic Kingdom as well before she decided on a more permanent residence. Earth would always remain her home, but she was barred from it for a while. Agency rules. Lanie told herself it was probably for the best. If she had to go back there now for a save, she would be...too homesick.

Meanwhile, Lanie had stayed at the Agency, in one of the guest bedrooms that occasionally doubled as an infirmary. Daisy had reassured her that this was completely normal, that most new recruits stuck to Agency lodgings for the first few weeks.

Well, at least something was normal even if there was nothing normal about her job or the Agency.

Lanie had gotten used to dodging phones, spears, axes and other artefacts handed out for rescue missions as well as wings being extended by various beings mid-stride on their way to rescues, before, mid and post-transformation. She had also gotten used to her own wings appearing at a mere thought and was experimenting with their colour. Daisy and Loretta's bickering and everyone slightly fearing but revering the Boss was as normal to her as having a morning coffee had once been.

Lanie had even gotten used to not feeling tired or sleepy or overwhelmed when travelling across dimensions and time zones. There was only so much wonder that the mind could take and not boggle.

Today, she had nothing better to do but hover over Daisy's

shoulder in the control room on her precious hours off. Lanie tried telling herself she was just going to see which dimension to go visit, but she knew she wasn't quite being truthful. She didn't need to look at random ones on Daisy's screens to help her decide. She already knew which dimension she wanted to visit most and that's precisely the one she shouldn't visit at all.

Daisy had agreed to let the newbie hover over her shoulder for half an hour off-peak. All newbies did this sooner or later. Any minute now this poor lamb would ask to be shown her own family or loved one left behind. They all did. Until they learnt they had no time to watch over their former family and loved ones. Until they learnt to just answer the rescue calls and use their in-between-time to be entertained by their favourite pastimes in their favourite dimensions to forget. All fairies understood family and love, so Daisy could relate, but it didn't make her any less sad watching the newbies learn the hard way.

The fairy was curious about who from her former life this no-name orphan would want to spy on. Her file said she had no living relatives and no boyfriend. No one, really. Which was probably why the Boss had considered her a worthy candidate. Her background and that big heart of hers.

Daisy decided to ease the lamb's pain. The sooner the pain started, the sooner it was over. 'See here, this is London, Earth dimension. That's here you were from, right, doll?' Daisy asked pointing at one of her screens, showing Tower Bridge lit for the night and one of their angels talking down yet another jumper.

Lanie leaned forward and seemed to be making swiping motions with her hand.

Daisy tsk-tsked at the humans and their penchant for touch-sensitive technical toys, 'Now that we have London in the palm of our hand, is there anywhere in particular you want me to look?'

'Belsize Park area, if possible?' Lanie seemed a bit embarrassed by her request. Hoping against hope, she wanted to check if she could still feel something, anything at all or whether angelic numbness had already set in. Given how quickly she reached lack of awe, perhaps not feeling anything also came with the job. Permanently.

Daisy figured that by the looks of her, Lanie had had a secret sweetheart. *Maybe her life had ended way too early.* The fairy patted Lanie's arm. *This would definitely hurt then.* No matter if the loved ones left behind were still grieving or had already moved on. It was hurtful to see them in either state.

'There!' Lanie was pointing at a tall, dark, handsome man exiting a townhouse.

Definitely way too early.

Or maybe not.

A red-head in nothing but a rumpled male shirt waved at a man from the doorstep of a posh semi-detached house, thought better of it, ran down the stairs and laid a smacky kiss on him.

Lanie had been gone only one Earth day. *Maybe the Boss got Lanie out just in time. Unless this was a brother that no one knew of.*

Daisy looked over at Lanie. *Not her brother, judging by the look of horror on Lanie's face.* She crumpled like she had been slapped.

Lanie recognised Peter as well as the paramedic. The same one that had shooed her off his bedside the very first night. The same one who had kept mum about Lanie dragging Peter from the river.

She had no right to feel jealous. Peter had been unconscious the whole time she had been there at his bedside, watching over him, wishing him well, trying to heal him with her presence. He only knew her as the annoying girl who had crashed in his apartment and fed his cat.

So why did Lanie feel like the Little Mermaid? Someone who had found the man of her dreams, given her all so he could live and then this love of her life had chosen someone else, which qualified Lanie as only mild entertainment?

Why did it hurt so much?

Seeing Lanie's eyes start to water, Daisy switched the screen to New York, 'Honey, as much as losing you hurts, the life of those you loved does go on. For some, it happens sooner, for others it takes more time. After a while the guardians don't want to see the life and the loved ones they have left behind. No one that lives forever wants to see their loved ones age and die. Or find love again with someone new. This,' Daisy motioned at Lanie's face, 'is exactly why we don't let newbie angels go to their old dimensions for saves or recreation for at least five Agency years. To avoid angels doing anything stupid to the people they used to love. Show themselves, try to explain their new state... We also suggest the newbies don't even look at their old dimensions on screen. Like you, they all want to check up on their families and love interests...'

'But seeing my former dimension is my only emotional link to my former life...' Lanie whispered, 'I feel like without this I would have no emotions at all...'

Daisy nodded. *That's what made them angels.* Out loud she said, 'Oh, honey, of course you'll have emotions. Good ones, trust me. From jobs well done, from experiencing good things on your days off...' Daisy saw Lanie's expression and shut up. Fairies could never lie too well. Daisy had a sinking feeling Lanie had just realised what the drawbacks of her job were.

'...But I will never fall in love again...' Lanie's voice trailed off.

'No, honey. You will never fall in love again. You wouldn't have the time. We do lose very many Princes Charming to their job, but you're not male. It's only logical that they are bound to fall in love with someone they save and empower...eventually.'

Lanie nodded, 'Daisy, how long stand-by time do I have left?'

Daisy looked at Lanie's phone, which was counting down, 'You have two more Agency hours.'

'May I go to the Mystic North, please?' Lanie really wanted to see Klaus again and maybe even meet the missus. Those two were probably good company in and outside of Christmas.

Deep down something inside Lanie protested. She wouldn't be good company herself. She needed to stay away from people for a while. She needed to observe happily-ever-afters more than she needed good company at the moment, 'On a second thought, I'll go to Magic Kingdom instead.'

'Sure thing, honey.'

Lanie checked her pink watch.

As the perfect pink whirlpool sucked Lanie in, Daisy took a

rescue call from Magic Kingdom. A Knight in Shining Armour was required, so she yelled after Lanie, 'Rescue someone for me while you're there? And keep the visor down!'

A fraction of a second later, Lanie was gone.

'This is exactly why I never show them anything even when they beg. And they do beg,' Loretta said, materialising in the chair next to Daisy in all her Goth glory.

***

Lanie couldn't really understand what Daisy had yelled after her about the visor until she was looking through the slits of one.

She tried to lift her arms and heard the screech of metal.

She was in full body armour and judging by the whinnying and fidgeting under her, also atop of a horse.

Right. This is what Daisy had meant. She was literally charging in as a Knight in Shining Armour. Very shining armour, by the looks of it.

Lanie was pretty sure Knights were supposed to be male.

The damsel undoubtedly would be expecting a knight and not a maiden. That's why Daisy had told her to keep the visor down.

She'd better keep the name of this Knight anonymous. The damsel could conjure a name of her rescuer herself afterwards. She was sure Magic Kingdom was not so enlightened as to welcome maidens saving maidens, if even the heroic tale of Rapunzel managed to be bent and twisted so as to ensure a Prince had saved her and not the other way around. If the Kingdom could not handle Rapunzel[56] rescuing herself and a boy from the Enchantress, she understood the need for the helmet. A girl saving another girl had to remain secret even if for all practical purposes that happened left right and centre in the Magic Kingdom not to mention elsewhere.

She was going to have to pretend to be a mute or just grunt in reply as means of communication. *Lovely.*

Where was the damsel then?

A scream away, as it appeared. With a dragon cornering her.

Apparently, Lanie's day off was over but she had gotten her wish to end up in Magic Kingdom after all.

By the looks of it, there was a new fairy-tale in the making. All the known stories already had Knights or Princes assigned to them and their names were very well known. Guinevere had Lancelot[57], Snow had Charming[58], Belle had Beast[59], Sleeping Beauty had her Prince[60] and the Little Mermaid's Prince was also a well-known heir to the Danish crown even if that story didn't end happily in Hans Christian Andersen's original rendition[61].

The screams were growing louder.

Right.

What did she have? A horse, armour, a sword, apparently, her voice on permanent mute to avoid blowing her cover and not much more.

The damsel was in distress. The dragon was approaching, slowly but approaching nevertheless. Pretty soon its fiery breath would cause the damsel being BBQ-d to a shishkebob at the stake to which she had been fastened, undoubtedly by charitable villagers wishing to escape the same fate they were consigning the damsel to for all their sins.

Lanie lumbered off the horse, very inelegantly. She congratulated herself on not getting stuck in the stirrups and grabbed the reigns to keep the animal close.

Sod this. She wasn't going to slay the dragon. With the armour, she couldn't even extend her wings. Lanie wasn't even sure her wings would carry 30 kilograms of metal, much less the bucket of metal on her head. What else was there?

She wished she wasn't this hot and that the armour would just fall away, leaving the helmet, the men's clothes on her back and the sword dangling from her hip.

With that thought, the strings attaching the armour to various parts of itself unravelled and she was left there standing in boy's clothes and the helmet. The horse wriggled its ears at her, but otherwise didn't even flinch.

Ah, excellent! Wishing for things also worked in this dimension. Now what?

While it was tempting to wish the whole situation away,

it wasn't very sportsmanlike. Besides, Lanie wasn't sure the damsel wouldn't be a casualty and she would certainly hate the dragon to become one. Also, if she just wished for a solution now, the situation might repeat itself some day until someone came and resolved it for good. Lanie hated bad karma coming back to bite you.

What if she tried talking to the dragon? Find out what its problem was.

As far as she knew no one had ever attempted that before in traditional fairy-tales.[62] *Maybe they were just hugely misunderstood, even if slightly largish, creatures? As unlikely as that was, for the lack of other options coming to mind, it was worth a try.*

This option, however, would involve talking.

Lanie had a look-see at the damsel and saw her slumped at the stake, thankfully passed out.

Perfect.

The dragon thought so too, as it crept closer and tried nibbling at one of the ropes holding the girl to the stake.

'Hey, what are you doing?' Lanie asked the dragon.

The dragon stopped chewing the cord, turned and blinked, surprised there was anyone there to witness its dark deeds.

It had understood her. The better. Even if this was probably likely to end up a one-way conversation, it was good to know she was talking to someone sentient and not a thoughtless, blood-lusting beast.

Lanie holstered her sword, 'You can understand me.' *A statement, not a question.*

The dragon nodded with the last of the rope snaking away from between its teeth.

Now came the tricky part. Finding out what it was that it wanted. Lanie decided to go with the obvious.

'Are you hungry?'

Another nod.

Despite evidence to the contrary, Lanie hoped the dragon was not partial to human flesh. Or angelic for that matter. She spied a saddle bag on her horse and wished there was some bread and apples in there. The bag filled out with the shape of a French baton and two apples before her very eyes.

Lanie loved the Magic Kingdom.

She reached into the bag and took out an apple. She also stuck the baton under her arm for good measure.

The dragon carefully angled closer.

The horse started going backwards.

'Wait. The horse is scared. Let me tie it to this,' Lanie pointed in the general direction of the stake that was still holding the damsel firmly captive, 'And then I can share my meal with you. Deal?'

Another nod.

Lanie did as promised and walked a safe distance from the damsel, the horse and the stake with the dragon waddling in tow. When the damsel was thumb-sized, Lanie stopped, thought a bit, unfastened her sword and put it down on the grass.

There. A gesture of good will.

The dragon seemed unperturbed by the sword. Probably because it was the size that the beast could comfortably use as a toothpick.

Having fed a few stray dogs when she had been alive, Lanie thought she could try doing the same here. After all, so far, the dragon hadn't shown any ill intent. Well, if she were to exclude almost nibbling on the damsel before.

'Want an apple? Just don't bake it while it's still in my hand, ok?'

The dragon made a noise resembling metal rumbling in a huge barrel.

Was this chuckling?!?

Lanie held out her hand and a pink tongue gently licked the apple clean off her palm.

The dragon sniffed appreciatively in the direction of the bread baton.

Lanie broke off a piece and they repeated the song and dance. Lanie broke off a bite of crust for herself, realising that all this hoopla had made her hungry and quickly in this dimension.

Right.

She had to take a chance even if it all backfired horribly and the dragon shishkabobed her and ended up going back to devour the damsel later.

She had to ask, so she did, 'Do you eat meat?'

The dragon shook its head.

That was a 'no' then. *Curious.* 'Now that we've broken bread, established you understand human speech and are, in fact, a vegetarian, do you mind telling me what you were trying to do back there, scaring that poor girl half to death?' Lanie hoped it wasn't all to death as in the distance, the damsel remained completely and utterly still.

The dragon seemed to be thinking.

'Well, if you cannot speak human, how do you communicate?' Lanie felt stupid for even asking. *If the dragon couldn't tell her what its problem was, how was it going to tell her how it communicated?*

A tail poked Lanie in the ribs hard enough that she almost fell over. 'Hey, gently, if you please!'

The dragon had the good sense to look sheepish.

'Well, I suppose this probably was gentle for you, wasn't it?'

The beast nodded.

It then extended the tail and with its spear-like tip drew a rectangle on the ground between them.

The dragon looked deep into Lanie's eyes.

Lanie shrugged. It was trying to tell her something but so far, she wasn't following.

A huge wind engulfed them. Lanie started to look for weather signs when she realised the gust of wind had come from the dragon sighing.

'Ok, I'm not getting it yet, but don't give up, please continue,' she encouraged.

The dragon swished a few quick swizzles on the ground with the tip of its tail and when Lanie next looked, inside the rectangle there was something round with sticks going everywhichway, a shrub with more sticks going everywhichway but only southwards and something that looked like a cloud in the sky.

It was a drawing.

The dragon had just drawn the sun, a cloud and a tree.

'Pictures? You communicate by pictures?'

Another nod.

'Well then this is going to take a very long time, isn't it?'

The dragon shook its head in the universal sign of 'No.'

The tip of the tail travelled - very very carefully this time - to Lanie's head.

'Pictures in the head? You're a telepath?' *Why was she not surprised.*

The dragon nodded, looking cheerful.

'Ok, so if I ask you again what were you trying to do there with the girl, can you tell me by showing pictures in my head, yes?' Lanie thought that luckily, she was already dead, so whatever the dragon projected into her mind and at whichever force was not going to kill her. *Hopefully.* She had seen The Matrix and knew that sometimes when you died in another reality and believed it, you could very well stay dead. Permanently. She knew that if she got deaded and didn't get rescued within 72 hours, she would be *kaput.* Just in case, she held on to her pink wrist watch.

The dragon nodded again.

'All right. Show me. Gently.'

The tail rose in a sign of a warning.

The picture of two apples materialised inside Lanie's head. Then one of them vanished.

As good a test as any. 'You want the other apple?'

The animal nodded.

'Very well,' as Lanie fed the dragon her second apple, she briefly wondered how long vegetarian dragons could go without food, how much did they need for sustenance and how long this one had gone hungry. *Probably long, probably a lot and probably awhile. Still, it looked pretty docile and it had behaved rather reasonably.*

So far.

'All right. Now, please show me. Gently.'

And then it did.

The pictures that assailed Lanie's brain told a tale she didn't expect to see. There were sheep, lots of sheep. Dragged away from the pastures by the dragons to...a castle? The dragons had a castle of their own? Or a dungeon. Then again, the dragons didn't discriminate, they dragged away pretty much anything that was larger than a dog. Mostly, it seemed pretty random - the dragons snatched their pray but didn't eat it. Instead, they flew awhile doing what seemed like push-ups with their paws - either that or then it was random twitching - and put their prey down either where they had originally found it or if villagers with pitchforks had already started to assemble, then deposited their baggage a few kingdoms away. This seemed quite pointless.

Lanie tapped the side of her head, 'I don't need the entire story[63], just this story, please,' she motioned at the stake and the girl.

The dragon emitted a huffing sound that almost blew Lanie off her feet.

'Easy there!'

Another huff but this time, Lanie only got the hot wind in her visor and quickly closed her eyes to shield them against the flying sand.

Next, the dragon showed her a movie of villagers tying the damsel to the stake.

Tufts of random shrubbery swam into view just as one of the villagers administered a slap to the screaming damsel to shut her up.

The dragon had been spying from the nearby forest and had seen the girl being tied up.

Lanie tried not to judge, but it occurred to her she might have been mistaken about the dragon's intention and vegetarian preferences.

It looked like the beat had showed up early and waited patiently for its lunch.

Lanie thought she'd try something, hoping telepathy worked both ways.

In her mind's eye she pictured the villagers, the damsel at the stake and the dragon eating the damsel by swallowing her whole.

The dragon bellowed its hurt feelings, making the briefly roused damsel pass out again.

Lanie cringed. 'Fine, fine. You are a vegetarian.'

A nod.

'I believe you and I'm sorry! I know now that you don't eat people, but I think everybody here still thinks that you do, right?'

The animal nodded and sniffled. Then it looked at Lanie and in her mind's eye she saw how the dragon's own kind had bashed at it with their tails and wings and made it leave. The next image was of the dragon very carefully nibbling at the damsel's ropes.

Well, that was a surprise. 'You were trying to save her, to help her escape?'

A nod.

'And you told your kin what you were about to do and they didn't agree?'

Another nod.

Lanie could only conclude one thing, 'Are you a girl?'

A couple of very quick nods. Well, as quickly as the dragon's giant head allowed her.

Heck, this new fairy-tale was kinked from the start. A girl had already tried saving a girl before another girl, masquerading as a knight had arrived and botched the rescue.

'Right. How do we turn this into a fairy-tale worth remembering without you...' Lanie pointed at the dragoness, '...getting slaughtered and without her...' Lanie pointed at the damsel in the distance who was showing signs of stirring, '... getting a whiff of the fact that I'm a girl...'

The dragoness snorted.

'...well I am, deal with it! I didn't bat an eye lid when you said you were female...' Lanie continued, 'and in this rather modern tale of girls rescuing girls... how exactly do you propose we give everyone their happy ending?' Briefly, regret surfaced that Lanie herself would never get her happy ending, but she quickly shoved it back where it had come from.

The dragoness shrugged.

Right.

Lanie had always known she would have to figure it out for herself. That's why she was a guardian angel, well, at the moment a Knight in Shining Armour who had found her mission slightly...mutated.

'Right. You,' she pointed at the dragoness with what remained of her French baton.

The dragoness sniffed at it.

'Still hungry? There you go,' Lanie surrendered the baton and picked up her sword, twirling it around in the air a few times for fun. 'Ok, I'm going to try something and please don't be offended. Play along, alright?'

The dragoness looked at her quizzically.

Lanie kept twirling her sword, 'You need to go away, fly away, ok? And it needs to look like you got scared and I rescued the girl.'

The dragoness flicked her tail.

Lanie coughed to get her voice as deep as possible. For anyone out there who might dare look Lanie yelled, her voice as low as she could manage it, 'Get thee hence! Shoo! Go away!'

In her mind she was sending the dragon apologies and promises to come back and sort out the rest of this story sometime later. *She could do that on her time off.*

The dragoness nodded, took a few steps back and then took off with its giant wings causing a minor tornado in its wake.

Lanie kept twirling the sword.

What remained was to convince the damsel the Knight had chased away the dragon.

Twirling the sword helped.

Somehow Lanie doubted that without proof of slaughter, the villagers or the damsel wouldn't believe there had actually been any slaying.

She raised her sword, shook it at the departing dragon and yelled, 'And don't come back!' while in her mind she sent the huge creature a picture where she affectionately hugged its neck.

All she needed was to keep this nice, professional and anonymous. On permanent mute. All she had to do was cut the damsel down and ride off into the sunset.

When the damsel finally came to, she was free but had no one to thank but the dust that was billowing after her no-name rescuer speeding away on his noble steed. Undoubtedly in a hurry to save other damsels. The girl sighed. The valiant knight who had saved her from the dragon could have at least stayed for a kiss.

As Lanie was beaming herself back to the Agency from the safety of the forest nearby, she vowed to come back some day to sort the dragon's story out. If dragons were vegetarians and girls didn't get eaten, why were the villagers still bringing them for sacrifice? The girls were disappearing somewhere to be presumed dead and Lanie hoped to find out where, how and why.

The rescue, if Lanie could call it that, had helped her mood somewhat. Sure, she wouldn't find true love. Ever. But she could give others their happy ending.

Plus, she could talk to dragons.

The Magic Kingdom might become her favourite dimension yet.

Then and there Lanie vowed to herself to stop peeking at the Earth screen and tell the Watchers to warn her not to look, if by some random chance they were observing her home town while she was visiting them.

16. 'Ok, I'm going to try something and please don't be offended. Play along, alright?'

***

The Boss earmarked the girl dragon as a potential guardian and congratulated himself on choosing right. *Lanie had been a good pick.*

The Penguins started crooning Earth Angel[64] on his speakers.

He nodded at the speakers.

Yes, yes she was.

The question was, was she quite ready to let go of her former life and being human?

The Boss thought about the scene he had witnessed at the Watchers' station.

Could it be? Could three of his best angels be tempted all at once?

Charlotte was Victor's temptation.

Grace was Gabriel's.

Could Peter be Lanie's?

He hadn't meant to turn this into a tournament. It was chance that when Charlotte's plea had come up Loretta had sent Victor. And that Charlotte just happened to be a mission that required a bit of presence. Enough for Victor to get attached.

As for Gabriel, a Grace would have happened sooner or later. In Gabriel's case much, much later, but the more time they were spending together, the more attached he was getting. Also, what better way to see if Victor had actually learnt something over the past two years than to allow Victor's mentor to protect and fall in love with Victor's ex-girlfriend?

How very interesting. How very interesting indeed.

43. Confessions
Gabriel

The steam coming from the rice and vegetables that Gabriel had unpacked was circling elegantly towards the vent. Gabriel took a spoon and ladled some of the mix into the bowl in front of Grace, opting to eat civilly. They had crockery and cutlery here that had been begging to be used for decades. He wasn't going to deny them such a simple wish.

'Eat something,' he ordered Grace, not unkindly.

'You sound like a Greek mother,' Grace said and sniffed the food. The piles of yummy stuff in front of her made her mouth water. Grace reached for the chopsticks. 'Aren't you going to have anything?' she asked, noticing his place mat was empty.

'Angel,' he pointed at himself. Since this produced no reaction, he had to explain, 'An angelic state is a state without needs and wants.'

Food half-way to her mouth, Grace squinted her eyes at him, 'Without desires?'

Gabriel nodded.

Grace sighed. *Just her luck. I finally find the man of my dreams, someone I could fall in love with and he turns out to be a guardian angel. She should have known this hunk was too good to be true.* To deflect herself from self-pity, Grace concentrated on eating, feeling her curiosity return with every bite she took, 'Tell me more about my assassination attempts.'

'Not much to tell,' Gabriel said.

'Humour me.'

Gabriel sighed.

'There was something about a flower pot... and you aren't sure have there been five or four attempts...?' Grace said.

'Yes.'

'What was fishy about the flower pot?' Grace asked.

'I had to open the umbrella to change the trajectory of a falling flower pot, which would otherwise have dropped onto your head,' Gabriel said.

Grace nodded. 'Before the flower pot, you say there was a bomb in the basement of the coffee shop?'

'That I dispatched into another dimension where it would be harmless. Not so much here, it would have taken out half a block and you with it,' Gabriel explained.

'And before then, there were...'

'The bullies,' Gabriel reminded her.

'Yes, the bullies, otherwise also known as quite alright City blokes who I know and who have never accosted me before but who were apparently brainwashed by a mysterious hypnotist into scaring me silly,' Grace said.

'Or worse,' Gabriel offered.

'You don't know that,' Grace said.

'Unfortunately I do,' Gabriel countered. 'Otherwise, why would someone take the trouble of erasing their memories for a specific night?'

'Do you know what binge drinking does to your brain?' Grace asked, incredulous that such an easy explanation had not occurred to...HER guardian angel. She had trouble thinking of him as not human.

'Does binge drinking have the tendency of erasing the memories of four individuals from precisely the same moment in time and until the same precise moment in time?' he asked.

'No, but that is not necessarily proof of intended murder,' Grace said.

'Neither is a falling flower pot, but the potential of it landing on your head and killing you is enough to trigger a saving response, at least from me,' he countered.

'And I am truly grateful for that, don't get me wrong,' Grace said. 'It's just odd that someone wants me dead and...for what reason, exactly? What have I ever done to anyone?'

Gabriel frowned, 'Unfortunately we still don't know that. We have investigated every possibility from the first attempt...'

'The shooting in the alley where you pretended to be a cat,' Grace offered helpfully.

'Yes, from the shooting. Remote operated set up, no witnesses, no nothing. Just like your apartment, which someone rigged with a ready-made bomb in less than one minute. We've gone over your most recent past to try and find someone with a grudge, nothing, no one.'

'We?' Grace didn't mean for her voice to come out in a squeak, 'You mean there are more of you...watching over me?'

Gabriel shook his head, 'Just me for now. The Watchers were gathering intel via...other channels.' *Telling her how much video feed they were able to collect about her life via CCTV before the data gathering was aborted due to her having met Della would probably put her guard up again. And he needed her calm and talking so they could figure things out together.*

'The Watchers?' Grace said nearly choking on her food.

'Daisy and Loretta, our resident fairy and pixie who take turns watching over those who need help across dimensions,' Gabriel volunteered.

'Ok...' Grace bit on her lip. *Fairies were real. Pixies, too. She wasn't the only one being watched.* Absent-mindedly she shoved some more vegetables and rice into her mouth. 'Mm, this is tasty,' she mumbled in between mouthfuls.

'How many dimensions are you watching over, besides Earth?' Grace asked, loading more food into her bowl.

Gabriel smiled, happy she was eating. Fed Grace meant a calm Grace. '63 known ones and a couple of unknown ones probably as well,' he said.

'Which dimension are you from?'

Gabriel sighed. They were back to questions about angels. 'I was originally human, from Earth.'

'But you opted to serve and live forever?'

'Yes. Or I can retire when I decide I have done enough.'

'And even with all the spying that you and the Agency does, even after my apartment got bombed, you don't know who is after me and how he keeps eluding you?' Grace asked.

'Or she,' Gabriel said. 'Which brings me to the elephant in the room. Grace, I know I've asked you before, but considering all that you know now, think again, please. Do you have enemies, someone who would bear a grudge - for years - or on an impulse, someone who would want you dead?' he asked.

Grace finished her food, licked her chopsticks and eyed the bowl. She wanted to lick the bowl as well and would have, had she been home. In fact, she had licked plates, forks, knives and bowls in front of her cat but now that her Cat was sitting in front of her as a man, a very attractive and very unattainable man she had a crush on, she didn't dare lick anything. 'Umm...I don't think I've done anything in my life to piss someone off enough to want to kill me. Even Victor didn't really want me dead. He just wanted me all to himself.'

Gabriel nodded. The silence stretched.

Wait a minute. No questions about who Victor was or what he had done? 'You're not going to ask...' Grace stated.

Gabriel shook his head.

'Of course, you had to research my life. You already know who he is,' Grace concluded, 'although I've never told you much about him...'

'You didn't tell the Cat much...' Gabriel said as Grace frowned.

'Why are we even discussing this? Why would he be a potential suspect? As far as I'm aware trying to do me harm would be slightly difficult from beyond the grave...' Grace looked at Gabriel who was living proof you could do plenty of good after death.

Gabriel sighed, it was time to come clean, at least in small increments, 'I was there.'

'There where?'

'In the bar.'

'What bar? With the bullies?'

Gabriel shook his head. 'No, the day Victor died. THAT bar.'

Grace's heart skipped a beat.

Silence hovered and stretched itself thin.

'During my reunion?' Grace finally managed.

A nod.

'You were on a mission?'

Another nod.

'Did you see him press a gun to my head?'

Another nod.

'And you didn't think that warranted jumping in and saving me?!?'

Gabriel looked uncomfortable, 'It wasn't a saving mission, Grace.'

'What kind of mission was it?' Grace asked.

'A recruitment mission,' Gabriel confessed.

'You were there to recruit....me? To become a guardian?' Grace's eyes turned into saucers. *How could he sit in front of her now explaining how he had gone out of his way to protect her when two years ago he would have been just as happy to recruit her off this Earth?!?*

Unfathomable.

'I see. It seems I have a lot to learn about the logic and morality of angels. So what did your boss say when you failed your mission that time?'

'I didn't fail,' Gabriel said very quietly.

'Wh...what?' Grace stammered, thinking back to the Twilight Zone series and hoping she wasn't in a situation where it would turn out she had long since been dead and not known about it.

'I did recruit a guardian that day. My instructions were not specific. I wasn't told it had to be you.'

'Do I assume correctly that you have to be dead to be recruited as a guardian?'

Gabriel nodded.

Like a snake, worry started uncoiling itself at the pit of Grace's stomach. *Maybe reaching out from 'beyond the grave' was true not only for Gabriel.* 'Gabriel, whom did you recruit?'

Gabriel didn't say a word. He didn't have to. All those involved knew precisely who had died that day.

'Victor?' Grace stood up and backed away from him, 'You recruited Victor?!?'

'I know it looks...unfair,' Gabriel started.

'To say the least, the likes of him...I don't even know if he's even capable of doing nice things for other people, much less save them instead of bullying them...' Grace closed her eyes. *There was no justice, her worst nightmare had become...an angel. If she was ever recruited, she would have to work next to Victor, see him again, remember him again.*

'There is justice, you know. He keeps doing the jobs where he gets to save women from the likes of who he used to be. He's changed,' Gabriel tried to comfort her.

'Tell me you have lobotomised him and given him an entirely

new personality, please? The one that doesn't remember who I am.' Grace said sarcastically.

Comforting wasn't working. Gabriel decided to take another tack, 'Not really, but think of it this way - since I recruited him, you are the one left alive.' *It could have gone the other way around.*

Grace seemed to have understood that as well. 'For now and not for long if we don't figure out who wants me dead. I know you said he has changed, but could it be Victor, reaching out for me from beyond the grave?' Grace asked.

'Technically, with Victor there is no such thing as 'beyond the grave'. It cannot be him, he has two simultaneous saves to take care of at the moment, he wouldn't have the time. Besides, he doesn't know about us being called to guard you.'

'But, you're simply assuming, you don't actually know? You said things were done remotely, well some things at least - the automatic sniper thingy and...someone rigged my apartment door in less than one minute. Is there any way for him to drop things out of nowhere to land into specific locations in this dimension - like flower pots, bombs into basements, that kind of thing? And pop by in person for a minute to attach a ready-made bomb to the door?'

Gabriel paused. Victor was in the same dimension as Grace. He had ruled out Victor because HE himself wouldn't risk endangering two charges to try and make someone else's life hell. Victor was a whole other cup of tea from your average angel. He did have a weird sense of justice. Maybe he blamed Grace for the abrupt and untimely end of his life and had decided to get even?

'Dropping' he could do. Dropping something from the USA to the UK in the same dimension or even popping in personally would only take Victor seconds. 'Dropping in could explain why the intent to kill you wasn't showing up early enough for us to get a glimpse at whoever was after you...' Gabriel said out loud.

'Intent, what intent? What are you talking about?' Grace enquired.

'There are time limits for how long in advance we know that someone wishes to do someone else harm. Usually, beings who feel they are in need of help, just ask for it. Their request flashes up instantly on one of our 16 priority screens. When someone has no idea they are about to be accosted and if they are important enough for their dimension, we get a signal they might be in danger. One of the screens starts recording their life from the moment whoever is after them forms an intent to harm them. The Watchers' screen starts recording the situation from the time the harmful intent forms until the save is complete.' Gabriel explained.

The fact that her life was being recorded somewhere made Grace inhale sharply.

Gabriel didn't notice and continued, 'I did consider that whoever was after you did not hate you permanently, otherwise they would be thinking about you all the time and their intent to harm would show as a constant. We did consider a possibility someone was doing this...just for fun.'

'Just for fun? Just for fun?!? Are you saying some rat bastard is out there, getting his kicks from trying to off me for FUN?' Grace was shouting and hyperventilating at the same time. Not a good combination.

As she started sagging to the floor, Gabriel caught her with a practised gesture and sat her down gently, handing her a paper bag from the take-away food. He waited for her to calm down before he asked, 'Do you think Victor is the type to...have fun like this?'

Grace kept breathing into the bag. She never thought this would actually be calming. Leaning into the cold marble of the kitchen surface was also reassuring. A few minutes of hyperventilation and she was able to gather her wits, 'Victor... he was more possessive than lethal, I think. From what he said of his exes I seem to remember his usual defence reaction was to start despising them as human beings after the break-up. He would not go out of his way to harm them. Whatever or whoever he despised, he no longer wanted to touch or have anything to do with.'

'Perhaps you were special in some way?' Gabriel asked, hoping that the answer to that question would be 'no' and knowing better.

'I don't think so. Most of his live-in relationships lasted about two years, our break-up was right on the mark.'

'But he did come after you a year after you broke up. Were you aware if he did anything like that with any other ex?' Gabriel asked, regretting that after speaking with Victor he hadn't tasked the Watchers to research his comings and goings more properly. He could be their assassin, after all.

'I am not aware, but let's look at his potential motive now, shall we?' Grace offered, 'I mean it's been two years since his death, he's been a guardian angel all this time, right?'

Gabriel nodded.

'Why would he suddenly remember me and want me dead?' Grace asked.

'To have you working by his side,' Gabriel blurted out. *If the idea of working together with this girl was appealing to him, it might be even more appealing to Victor who had loved this girl zealously enough to violently pursue her.* Gabriel was ashamed of his thoughts. As good an angel as she would someday become, he would rather see this lovely girl live out her entire life as she was destined to.

'You think he is so reformed as an angelic being that he now understands right from wrong, perhaps even regrets some of the things he did, but would still be selfish enough to wish to hoist his company on me for all eternity?' Grace looked incredulous. 'A simple apology would do, thank you very much.'

'Now that you mention it, perhaps not. Victor would know it would be the wrong thing to do, precisely because it would be unpleasant for you. As an angel, a slightly vengeful one, but an angel nevertheless, he knows better. At least I hope he does. It would only be temporary anyway - if you disliked working side-by-side with him you could always quit and that would be that, his actions would be thwarted,' Gabriel said as Grace nodded.

Gabriel looked at her curiously, 'You would really settle just for an apology?' he asked.

'I'd settle for not being hunted,' Grace said, 'But yes, from Victor, an apology would do.'

'You don't hold a grudge?'

Grace shrugged, 'All hard feelings - and by hard feelings I mean the fear of him - disappeared with his death. The dead cannot apologise. It was pointless to hold a grudge. Which doesn't mean I would like to renew the acquaintance. Even if he is an angel now. So, if it's not Victor, who else is really good at being sneaky, knows all the rules and could want me dead for a reason only they know?'

Instantly, Gabriel thought about Loretta who embodied all of these things, except as long as he knew her, she was also terribly good at succeeding. She wouldn't have botched the attempts up, especially since she was at the controls. Unless she was botching them up on purpose and this was all part of pixie fun. Still, it was worth a check.

'And if he sor she knows the rules about intent, maybe they are not doing it all themselves, but asking others who don't know me to set it all up? Would that show up on your screens?' Grace asked.

'No, it wouldn't...' Gabriel said.

'Maybe someone just put a pan-dimensional contract out on me, although for the life of me, I cannot figure out why...' Grace said, almost cheerfully. *In the space of an hour she had gone from believing in angels to admitting the possibility that whoever was after her might not be human.*

Gabriel processed the proposition. Their mysterious assassin had remotely accessed a sniper rifle, near-perfectly timed not one but two bombs and probably made that lady nudge a flower pot. Lest he forgot the ability to either hypnotise or wipe people's memories for specific periods of time.

Gabriel could think of a few guardians who could do all that. What he failed to understand was why. This had to be a major vendetta, because using others to do their bidding without any questions asked, without knowing or caring why or who the intended target is, was quite simply, too costly. A lot of money could buy a lot of obedience. So could loyalty.

Was it Loretta, after all in a misguided attempt to recruit Grace? Gabriel wouldn't put it past her to try and engineer a solution to find someone to step in for the Boss. Logic dictated that in order to succeed, the Watcher should have sent a more junior angel to tend to Grace's save. *Except it wasn't the Watchers who had sent him.*

Perhaps the manner of the saves and introducing Grace to detective work was somehow part of her induction process to the angelic world?

Gabriel sighed. They weren't any closer to solving the puzzle than before. 'I don't know.' Remembering his unkind thoughts about the Watchers and Victor, he said, 'I do have a hunch and I'm going to check it out while you wait here.'

'You're leaving?' disappointment rang thick in Grace's voice.

Mistaking it for fear, Gabriel nodded, 'Don't worry. You are quite right. I should get reinforcements while I am away...in case it is someone other than who I am going to have a nice chat with.'

As Gabriel started dialling, Grace turned her back on him and turned on the tap. She was going to do the dishes. At her apartment and at the coffee shop, she always started on the dishes when she was nervous or thinking about something. There certainly was a lot to think about. She put a cling film on the bowl of now cold food and stuck it in the fridge. She could have that later. Before she went to bed.

Someone was trying to kill her.

She would think about that tomorrow.

Right now, the more important bit was that the gorgeous man she had a crush on was sadly, unavailable.

Unless she died.

Were inter-angelic relationships even allowed?

Maybe that's what Victor was after?

Except she would burn in hell before she got back together with him, angel or not, and he had to know that.

Was dying such a bad thing, if it meant she could be with Gabriel?

That is if he wanted to be with her. So far, he had given her no indication that he was interested. All of his actions could be interpreted as those of a guardian angel caring for his charge.

As Gabriel was still on the phone, Grace decided to have a

shower. A hot shower was exactly what would relax her after the evening she had just had.

The chequered floor of the bathroom reminded her of her childhood. The floor of the bathroom in her parents' house had been tiled out the same way.

Grace looked at her feet and thought she saw muddy hands and knees of a child. She thought she heard the rain outside, pelting against the window. Grace looked in the mirror and a younger version of herself was wearing a torn and singed dress. She had been so excited to be going for a drive with her parents to attend her sister's recital.

Had she gone?

Grace looked at the bathroom floor again and wiggled her pedicured red-tipped toes. The mirror showed a girl in her twenties with frizzy hair, not a 12-year old with soot on her face.

She had been in this apartment before. The Indian-looking man, Gabriel's boss had brought her here 12 years ago.

Had she gone on a drive with her entire family?

Had he pulled her from the burning car and brought her here before he returned her to her parents' place to wait for the police to arrive in order to tell her she was now an orphan?

Grace massaged her temples.

Why didn't she remember what she had been doing on that fateful afternoon? It could, of course be the result of the post-traumatic-stress disorder some of the therapists she saw at age 12 told her she had developed because of the shock.

She wasn't sure her hands and knees HAD been muddy.

Maybe she had stayed at home like she remembered? Maybe she hadn't been in that car? Why would this apartment feel familiar then? Why had the elderly gentleman saved her all those years ago only to make her forget it had ever happened?

Why didn't he save her family?

Would Gabriel also make her forget everything that had happened, once his mission was over? Would she have to forget him tomorrow?

44. City of Dreams
Charlotte

Charlotte was in shock. After Mae had surprised her with a pre-purchased ticket at breakfast yesterday, she had packed for all of five minutes, mostly agonising over which sketches to take with her and which to leave behind. Mae had forced her to go to town and pay her respects to the town folk. They had passed uncle Ted at the grocery store and Charlotte extended her best wishes to aunt Flo and Andy via him, saving herself a trip to the farm. Charlotte wasn't sure she would be missed by anyone but Mae.

Early this morning, she had taken a ride on Victor's Harley to the Houston airport, passed through the customs and boarded a plane to cross a continent. Thirteen sleepless hours later here she was.

Stepping onto the tarmac in Florence, Italy with Victor by her side.

Coming down the stairs, Charlotte had extended her hand, hoping Victor would be chivalrous enough to take the hint and escort her down like the princess she felt. He had looked at her, taken her shoulder bag full of books and had stomped down the stairs. *Well, that was chivalrous, too.*

An airport attendant wheeled Victor's bike round to meet them.

'You sure do have connections,' Charlotte said.

'Like you wouldn't believe,' Victor said and smirked.

Charlotte looked up at Victor and smiled. *A week ago she hadn't even known this man.* She had been at Auntie's merely a blink before she was propelled into the insanity of her dreams of an independent life coming true.

And here she was. In Florence. The city of her dreams. In the flesh.

Charlotte pinched herself.

Nope, she wasn't dreaming.

She had so many plans. To see the Uffizi gallery and the Da Vinci's drawings that she had so far only read about. To draw the Duomo[65] and the Palazzo Vecchio. To eat real Italian pizza!! To buy a cheap bicycle and go discover the city. After all, Victor wasn't always going to be there to ferry her around on his bike. He had agreed to escort her to Italy and see her settle in, but she wasn't sure how long he would stay before he had to tend to his business back in the United States. She wished he didn't have to go. *Wouldn't it be great, if Victor stayed with her in Florence... for as long as they both should live.*

Victor was observing the girl, all starry eyed and dreamy, quiet and happy. *They were close. Very close.*

He steeled himself against the naked adoration he saw in her face. The girl was besotted. Victor knew he should probably do something about it in terms of dissuading her from her affections but that was an extra mile on this mission and with Sally getting on his last nerve, he was all out of extra miles.

'Where to now?' Charlotte asked, leaned on his bike and batted her eye lashes. *Not that it had any effect.* Charlotte coloured to her roots. *Pining after a boy was one thing. Actively throwing herself at him, quite another. She should be ashamed.*

As if.

Not when she had so little time left to win his affections.

'Let's find you a place to stay and then see about that art school and scholarship,' Victor said, checking his bike was alright and carefully un-gluing Charlotte's hip from it in the process.

Charlotte stepped back, looking hurt.

Victor pretended not to notice. Function over emotion. They had to move. He looked at the trinket hanging from his neck. The wand's purple stone had turned red. *Hunh, low battery. One use of the wand on Earth and it was nearly depleted?!?* He would now have to pop by the Magic Kingdom to get the wand re-charged. In Gaia, Sally still needed work. *A lot of work.* Any more meandering here and there might not be any time left even for a quick drink in Valhalla. *Damnation.*

Perhaps he could ask the Watchers for some assistance in magicking Charlotte's admission and funding. The sooner he got those sorted, the sooner he'd be gone for good.

45. Happens to the Best of Us
Sally

Sally was sitting in her bathroom, trying to do her make-up. Trying being the operative word.

The frog was allowing her to get dressed to the nines in order to walk to the corner deli. This was ridiculous, of course, but it was also the first time the frog - also known as her personal shopper, personal trainer and her personal Sadistic Yoda - let her do anything besides learn about proper nutrition and exercise. She was wearing the red sleek dress he had helped her buy a month ago. It felt a little loose, even though she had bought it two sizes smaller than she usually wore, as per his instruction. Goal orientation he had called it. With all the mirrors scotch-taped in the apartment, it was really difficult to tell how it looked. She wasn't going to ruin her manicure and claw at the bathroom mirror.

When she had pointed at her face and enquired how on Earth she was going to do her makeup, her personal devil incarnate told her to stop *kvetching*[66]*,* fished out her camera from her bag and held it up with glee. *A frigging mirror function on the camera was all she had been allowed to keep. A frigging camera!* Sally tried having a peek of herself in the new dress in the phone camera, but the frog had done something to it, so all she could see was close up of the red colour. Vibrant red that filled the entire mirror.

This was no use. Not knowing was probably better.

At least the shoes were a consolation. Black mules with tiny Swarovski dragonflies on them. Sally wiggled her toes. She didn't need a mirror to see the shoes were gorgeous and complemented the dress perfectly.

Since she couldn't inspect her look with one last glance in the mirror, Sally simply grabbed her red polka-dot bag that was beckoning invitingly and headed out.

'I have to TRUST you I am *farpitzs*[67]! That's a lot of trust, so that you know!' she hissed into her bag.

Descending from her stoop she had to hold on to the railing

for dear life. The shoes, as gorgeous as they were, were not her usual height. Standing up in them made her want to keel over either head first or bum first. It wasn't until the frog had suggested retracting her shoulders and leaning back a little that the weight had distributed evenly enough for her whole frame to straighten out.

A few steps down mischief hit. *How could it not. She was all dolled up.*

'It's all your fault,' Sally hissed into her handbag, trying to understand how she had been so ditzy as to tie the bow on her ankle so loose that she was now standing beside her right shoe. Sally hopped on one leg and wriggled her toes to restore some blood supply. This was clearly a mistake. The shoe slid off her toes, rolled down the steps and straight into the path of an elderly gentleman.

The gentleman hastened to pick up the shoe and offered it up to her, his eyes a-glitter.

'I fell off my shoe,' was all that Sally could muster as an explanation.

'It's quite alright, it's quite alright, dear. Happens to the best of us,' said the gentleman, who was quite happy to fuss over her, sitting her down and tying her bows.

'Thank you,' Sally's gratitude was genuine. She had only ever heard of strangers being kind to strangers in the movies that were taking place in lands far, far away from New York, so this much attention to her person and her shoes was a little novel.

'My pleasure, always happy to help a pretty girl out,' the gentleman bowed, kissed her hand and bid her goodbye.

Pretty? He thought that she was pretty?

Sally had to find the nearest shop window. *Fast.*

'Now you're going to go to the deli on the corner, buy your healthy lunch and come right back, you hear?' the flailing bag squawked as Sally quick-marched, feeling more confident with every step, now that the bows on her shoes were properly tied. 'And for chrissake, walk slowly, more ladylike, have I taught you nothing?' Victor thought if she didn't stop marching he was going to be too queasy to enjoy any brunch at all.

She shoved some jaw-dropped teen aside and went for the glass reflection of the nearest shop window. A gorgeous voluptuous smoldering brunette shaped like a guitar and then some was staring back at her, 'Wow, you were right about the dress, it looks really nice.'

The frog whispered from the bag, 'With the right undergarments, everything does, honey.' At least it did according to the girly magazines Sally had forced him to read. She had insisted it was only fair that he suffer a little since she had to suffer a lot exercising and giving up things like mirrors and Sprite.

When they returned to the apartment two hours later, Sally was dazed and Victor was as happy as he was hungry. She had ignored his orders, of course. Nothing new there. After the deli, where she had been lavished with attention and compliments Sally thought she would milk it some more and went to Vittorio's. By the looks of it, this evening Victor was going to enjoy the deli meats alone, which he didn't mind since he had gone hungry while Sally had been enjoying herself. Vittorio had practically swooned at the sight of her and then dragged her into the kitchen to try various dishes his mamma was making. Victor had hissed at Sally not to pig out and ruin all their hard work. To be fair, she had refused to have dinner, excusing herself with being full from all the small delicious bites. To mollify Vittorio she had promised to come back soon. Victor was glad his elocution lessons had not gone south either.

'So, how many telephone numbers did you get?' Victor asked, peering over Sally's shoulder at the pile of napkins in front of her. He had specifically instructed her not to give out her own number. That way she would have a choice of whether to call the guy or not. Not to mention that she wouldn't have to sit by the phone and wait for the guy to call her.

'Five, I think,' Sally was dumbstruck. *Whatever the frog had done to her, had actually worked.* She felt like a rock star and judging by the numbers men, boys and restaurant owners had been practically throwing at her, she must look like one as well.

Victor nodded, happy. *It was time.*

A green light was blinking on Sally's answering machine. Victor wandered over and pressed the button with his hind leg.

'Hey, Sal, it's Harry. I haven't seen you in a month, which is way too long if you ask me. You've cancelled all of our movie nights and no one's seen you at the bar either. What's up? If you've hooked up with a guy, time is ripe for you to present him for inspection, don't you think? Meet me at our bar tomorrow night, say 8-ish? See you there!' Click hum.

Victor nodded. Time was definitely right. 'You're going,' he told Sally, who happily saluted him, ignoring all the unashamed lies Harry spewed on her answering machine. *SHE was the one that had cancelled their movie nights?!? - yeah, right!*

'But not before we buy you another great dress,' her personal mini-Hitler finished.

For the first time in a month Sally smiled warmly at the frog, 'Yes sir!'

17. "I fell off my shoe."

46. Trust a Pixie

Gabriel

Gabriel closed the door to Grace's bedroom at three in the morning. Grace had asked him to stay and watch over her until she fell asleep. He missed the comfort of the pillow, but since the girl now knew about the cat, taking liberties was out of the question. So he had stayed in the armchair by the bed and talked to her until she had drifted off. He had encouraged her enthusiasm about Della, the newbie goddess and decided not to overwhelm Grace yet with the fact that she was destined to be a guardian of magic on and off Earth. He had also promised her that he would make sure the apartment was safe before his stand-in arrived to keep watch outside her door.

He had magic-proofed her window and ventilation duct with the same protective spells against intruders that Loretta had dug up for him from the Magic Kingdom and the Enchanted dimension for her apartment. The only other way into that room was through the bedroom door and whoever it was had to go through Gabriel to get to Grace.

Standing in the middle of the living room, hearing the ticking of the clock, Gabriel wondered about the puzzle that this save had turned into.

Continuing attacks on Grace after she had met her fate could mean someone was purposefully keeping him on this mission. Was Grace a red herring, destined to distract him from something far more important elsewhere? If he hadn't been on this save, where would he have been instead? What if Grace was simply a distraction?

Four beings knew about Grace. Gabriel, the Watchers and, of course, the Boss, who had dispatched Gabriel on this mission and forgot to mention he had rescued Grace himself once before. Then again, the Boss had only had seconds to hand Gabriel his instructions. But he did have oodles of time to get in touch later if he had wanted to fill him in that he had saved Grace once before himself. If it was, indeed, a piece of the present puzzle.

Did Victor know the Agency was keeping a look-out for her?

Was Loretta trying too hard to recruit them a new Boss?

Or maybe this was an unknown player and then the question was whom had the Watchers or the Boss told about Grace? Maybe whoever was after Grace was someone who knew about the Agency and had somehow managed to infiltrate it?

Too many questions.

He had to start somewhere and some things were better done in person.

Gabriel was going to start by interrogating the Watchers. If they were not at fault themselves, maybe they told someone? So far, their communication had been patchy and mostly over the phone.

What if the Agency's phones were tapped and that's how an external party got their information?

Maybe undermining Gabriel preserving magic across dimensions was a way to demoralise the entire Agency?

Gabriel didn't want to contemplate the logical alternative - that it wasn't a random being trying to erase Grace from existence, but that it was, in fact, an inside job.

If the Watchers were not at fault, he would speak to the Boss. At this point, any ideas were welcome. Poring over every single detail with someone else might take a while, but it might also yield better results than him struggling to figure out things on his own. Whoever it was could have made mistakes. Tell-tale mistakes that could lead to his or her or its discovery. Gabriel had no problem swallowing his professional pride to ask his Boss for help to figure out how to save Grace. The situation warranted it. Grace's life was more important than his pride.

Watchers first.

Three heads were better than one. Besides, he could always trust a pixie to spot knavery.

At this point, any help, any clue was precious. For the first time in his 900 years, Gabriel felt like he was running out of time.

Gabriel tap-tapped his watch. His backup was due to arrive any second now. He didn't want to weaken Grace's chances of survival while he was away. Backup was required.

As Grace was in the Earth dimension, he needed someone used to being a human who wouldn't know Grace to wish harm on her.

This meant that out of the two latest recruits, he could use only one.

Lanie.

Before calling her, he had briefly thought if she could have orchestrated the assassinations, since she also originally hailed from Earth. Grace and Lanie were even from the same city. Gabriel couldn't believe that with her bio, Lanie could be the assassin. Lanie's treachery would involve firstly, purposefully leading an exemplary life not knowing whether she was going to be offered a chance at being a guardian angel. Second, somehow she had to set up Grace's first assassination attempt without being detected and then die herself on purpose soon thereafter. Had she been detected, it would have weighed against her and she would never have been offered to serve as a guardian. Third, even if she had managed to do all that and get recruited, she would have had to continue with the assassination attempts extremely covertly while learning how to be an angel.

Impossible.

Lanie could simply not be corrupt. Good people were good through and through. They didn't have momentary lapses of judgement, they didn't go around trying to kill someone with pigheaded consistency. Besides, he was pretty sure Lanie didn't know about the Agency and how it worked before she was recruited.

Gabriel was aware that if Grace was a red herring, then calling Lanie in meant two guardians would be kept away from something more important.

For the past 900 Earth years he had never summoned other guardians for help in mostly harmless dimensions. One guardian angel was usually enough.

Not this time.

Gabriel tried to remember what the Boss had said when he had handed him this charge. Someone wants Grace dead and it could alter the face of this entire dimension.

He had no choice. He had to get to the bottom of all of this. *Personally*.

Lanie had let the phone ring for a long while before she picked up. It turned out she had been subbing for the Watchers at the screens.

That was not good news.

Both of the Watchers were conveniently off duty at the moment?

Lanie had said something about Daisy and Loretta having to run crazy overtime and handled the training, so they were badly in need of some rest.

When Gabriel had explained that he needed her to step in on his save, Lanie started looking for other available guardians. Gabriel had to come clean and tell her that he would only settle for her as she was the only one he trusted at the moment. Sadly, what had made the difference was that no other guardians were currently available.

Mumbling something about the Watchers' station been fitted with software that translated barks to all the working languages, Lanie had finally agreed to go get someone else to tend to the screens.

Minutes after he had fully explained the situation to Lanie on site, Gabriel appeared in the Thumbelinas' dimension to go verify a certain pixie was where she said she would be.

***

A tiny thumbelina with prominent pixie ears peeked into Loretta's hut.

So this is how the Weird One lived. No one ever dared visit her, although plenty of kids from the Flower had tried to peek into the Weird One's house while she was away.

She was away a lot. Every time they had been nosey and tried to get in, a weird loud beeping noise had scared even the bravest away. The noise stopped as soon as they scattered, but it made it such fun to try again. And again.

This little thumbeling of the mature age of five finally had a decent excuse to nose around. She had been sent with an important errand as soon as the Weird One had arrived.

The Weird One's house was a mess. Everything was too... neat. Even the books were organised and hanging on some wooden contraption on the wall.

Books! The Weird One had books! How medieval.

Everyone knew no good ever came from reading books, just like no good ever came from working. That's what the old'uns called what the Weird One did when she was away from the Flower. Pixie life was supposed to be all about frolicking, mischief and fun. Not for the Weird One. She had actually been overheard to mumble that she preferred working to staying home.

Working! And with humans out of all trixsy species, ppfff!

Clearing her throat, the thumbelina braced herself for the famous wrath of pixies when interrupted *(pixus interruptus)*, 'Ahem...'scuze me...'

Loretta looked up from her book and eyed the kid above her glasses.

Fascinated by the contraption on the Weird One's nose, the kid almost forgot why she was there.

Not being yelled at was rather shocking as well. The Weird One was....well...weird.

'Is there anything in particular I can help you with, child?'

The young pixie snorted at the 'child', instantly regaining the famous pixie arrogance *(pixus arrogancia)* 'As if. A human is here. We can only assume it's one of yours,' the kid spat with scorn.

'Angels. Not humans. Angels.'

'Whatever.' Loretta wasn't sure whether it was an obscene gesture or a simple pointer of a direction that the kid flipped when off she went, singing the last of her message as she pranced away, 'Outside.'

Sighing, Loretta put the book away. So much for a day of rest and relaxation. She glanced out of her window. Miles away, Gabriel seemed a normal size for a human.

Right, she'd better go outside, otherwise he would be peeking into every single house until he found her. She already had a bad reputation, she didn't need years of reproachful and embellished accusations about how 'her' horde of humans once came to disrupt their carefully planned festivities.

Everyone was home, having lunch pollen, and there was no one in sight, but pixies liked to embellish, so the tale would be spun until it would become completely miraculous to the point of improbable. Goddesses forbid someone was in labour anywhere and the kid would not be born translucent blue. Loretta would never hear the end of it. Plus she didn't want the outcast kid thus born to be thrust upon her to raise. How would she explain it at the Agency? 'I found this kid in a basket floating down the river and would now like to raise it myself?' Very Moses, but wouldn't work at the Agency, not to mention it would put a considerable kink into her working arrangement.

Loretta fluttered her purple wings in annoyance (*pixus disgruntus*) and flew to the roof to roll out the unwelcome carpet.

As Gabriel approached, she waved at him lazily.

'Morning. I need to talk to you,' said the giant towering over Loretta's humble hut, his eye the size of her window.

A gust of sweet-scented torrential wind would have blown Loretta off the roof if she hadn't clung to her chimney.

'Tone it down, will ya? If there was a time to use telepathy, that time is now!'

Gabriel gently shrugged.

'Near-human, are you? Telepathic ability all gone? Well, I'm not deaf, I can hear you when you whisper. So, whisper, please! Otherwise my people will be convinced they heard the voice of the Supreme Goddess and while it will be a very creative period for all of us, taking down all versions of the story being told and arguing out which one is the true one, it's not something I care to do today. You do realise I'm in my real size at home, don't you? Gawd...' Loretta yelled, then demonstratively straightened her skirts and checked her wings for damage.

Of course, she had known this was exactly what would happen and had tucked her wings in safely before Gabriel had even arrived, but she had to make a point.

'Sorry,' Gabriel whispered and this time, only Loretta's black-green hair flickered in the gust.

'Better. Now, to what do I owe the displeasure of seeing you on my precious day off, pray tell?' Loretta stepped onto Gabriel's outstretched palm as a means of getting to the ground.

'I need to talk to you and Daisy somewhere where I can speak normally. The issue is sensitive, I might forget to whisper while I'm explaining and I don't want to destroy your home.'

He might forget to whisper? A guardian angel getting emotional? Really! That was bound to be a juicy piece of gossip.

Loretta tried to hide her glee behind lazy annoyance, 'Daisy? But fairies live in a different flower colony...it's days from here...'

Gabriel humphed so that from her porch, Loretta flew into her living room table, 'Ouch. Watch it, you brute!'

'Sorry. It would take you days to fly there, I'm sure I could get us there in a few minutes. I've got these, remember?' Gabriel said as he spread his wings.

The eclipse over the giant sunflower was so sudden a few pixies ran out of their homes lamenting the end of the world. One of them just stood there, gaping at Gabriel's wingspan and started turning green.

Perfect.

Loretta huffed, 'Stop scaring the natives. And nevermind Trixy, she's always wanted a pair of wings like yours. Now slowly and gently, why don't we?' She did a folding motion with her hands.

Gabriel carefully retracted his wings and restored sunlight to the colony. The scared pixie was still gaping, still turning teal, so he whispered, 'Why is she turning green?'

Loretta stared at him, 'Ever wondered where the expression 'Turning green with envy' comes from, sugar?'

Gabriel nodded carefully. Slow, small gestures from now on.

'Well, now you know where from,' the pixie shrugged.

Slowly, Gabriel offered Loretta his palm again and carefully motioned with his head for take-off.

Great. Seeing Daisy was not how Loretta had planned to spend her day off. Bye-bye learning how to cook with poison.

Bye-bye books on practical jokes. Hello annoying world of goody-two-shoes fairies. Yuk!

Stepping onto Gabriel's paw, she muttered horrible pixie curses (*pixus cursus horrificus*) and purposefully dug in her pointy heels out of spite even though she knew the angel would probably only feel a prick, if even that. 'You so owe me, you know.'

Gabriel looked the pixie in her green eye, thought that if she was to fault for something, the 'owing' would be cancelled out by the punishment, but nodded nevertheless and offered, 'Shoulder or pocket.'

Loretta sighed, 'If I have to, I would prefer to sit somewhere in comfort, like in your ear, but since you're a boy, I don't know which dimension you just materialised from and whether you've had time to wash your ears today, I guess I have to settle for your pocket. But don't squash me!' she finished sternly, nudging her horn-rimmed glasses back up her nose as she climbed in.

Gabriel nodded. He wouldn't dare squash her. She was his means of finding out the truth about whoever was orchestrating the attacks on Grace.

He noticed Loretta tuck away a book about practical jokes before she left the house, and remembered how the bullies and the flower pot did not fit the profile of an assassination.

Could his hunch about the Watchers just having fun really be right?

It wasn't quite out of the question. After all, at the screens the pixie was perfectly positioned to orchestrate phantom attacks. The attacks on Grace could very well be a practical, a very evil, but simply a practical joke.

In fact, he would be relieved if this was the reason behind the attacks. If it really were the Watchers behind these attempts on Grace, it would be very easy to shame them to stop.

Gabriel started walking to get to a safe distance. If this turned out to be mean pixie connivery, as relieved as it would make him, he might have to reconsider his promise of not squashing a certain someone on the way back.

***

Once he was far enough from the flower, Gabriel stretched his wings and took to the air. From up on high, all the flower colonies they passed in the Thumbelinas' dimension emulated the zillion colours of the rainbow, each colony their own hue and their own species of flower. There were Caribbean blue daffodils and orange callas, peach forget-me-nots and lilies of the valley so purple they seemed positively black.

It was up to the thumbelinas to make the rainbows in every dimension that had rain, which also explained why one didn't appear everywhere after every rainfall. Fairies and pixies were fickle. To them, it was probably a bit of fun, making beings wish and hope for a rainbow after the rain and then deciding whether they were going to oblige or not, depending on whether such an act of creation fit into their daily frolicking and festive fun. Gods forbid they would ever consider this work or else all rainbows in all dimensions would cease forever.

He felt a tug at his shirt pocket. Descending onto the edge of the nearest meadow of yellow daisies, he tried to avoid the branches of oaks and pines. For a minute, he just stood amidst the thousand-year-old forest, inhaling the scents of honey-suckle meshed with pine and dew, taking in the sunlight streaking through the trees until he felt another impatient tug near his heart.

This almost felt like home. Almost.

'I thought someone,' Loretta made a face, 'was in a hurry. Now let me out.'

Finding Daisy wasn't as complicated as Gabriel had envisaged. Loretta had visited Daisy more often than she cared to admit and knew where to find her flower. In order not to scare the natives again, Gabriel folded his wings and picked up Daisy, then walked to a nice meadow where they wouldn't disturb anyone.

Once they were all sitting pretty, Gabriel looked at both of the Watchers sternly, 'Only four beings knew about saving Grace and I'm looking at two of them.' Ignoring Daisy's 'but...

but' protests, Gabriel continued, 'I need your whereabouts for the following dates and times,' he handed open-mouthed Daisy a sheet of paper listing all five of Grace's assassination attempts with methods, addresses and times, down to the second.

Loretta crossed her arms, 'Well now. If I had only known that you had an interrogation in mind...'

Daisy didn't let her finish, 'Well of course we'll provide you with our alibis for whenever you need so that you can eliminate us as suspects. We had nothing to do with it, I promise.'

Loretta still huffed, 'Well I never...this is how you repay me doing a kind deed on my day off?' Mumbling something about how she could be having fun with poisons right now, she grabbed the sheet from Daisy. 'Just these five times across the last six Earth days?'

Gabriel nodded. He prepared for a long wait. Matching Earth time to Agency or any other dimension time to provide alibis might take a while. It was probably going to be as complicated as conjuring up ten horoscopes, triangulating juxtapositions and some such.

'Easy. I was manning the screens on four out of those five instances,' Loretta relented, 'yesterday,' she pointed at the day the apartment was bombed, 'Daisy and I were both called in since the Boss was away. You can ask the Boss for the Agency tapes of the Watchers' station to verify.'

So not as complicated as horoscopes then.

He could check the tapes of the screening room to make sure the Watchers hadn't frozen time to slip away and arrange a little assassination on the side.

Daisy carefully took the list and started with the one instance Loretta didn't pinpoint, 'On this day,' Daisy pointed at the flower pot incident day, 'I think we were both off. I was visiting a godchild and Loretta...'

'Ask Missus Klaus. It's a private thing. I'm giving her lessons,' Loretta haughtily turned away, considering the matter closed.

Gabriel briefly wondered 'lessons in what', but decided to let it go. He could and would ask Missus Klaus.

'Well yes. About the other dates for me...' Daisy pondered,

'I was at the screens on the first day, for the shooting. As for the bullies getting her, I think Loretta and I were both on duty. That leaves the bomb in the veg cellar day – Loretta was manning the screens, do you think she would have let me have all the fun by myself?' Daisy said.

Gabriel's eyes widened at the 'fun' part.

He was right. This was all a pixie prank. The fairy had almost admitted to it.

If he wasn't so angry he would be relieved. No one was actually after Grace.

'Fun? You did this for fun? Well, well, well, the cat's out of the bag, isn't it. I knew you occasionally meddle, but why here, why with this girl?' he said.

Loretta raised her eyebrows in indignation at 'fun' as Daisy mouthed 'meddle?' looking hurt.

'Yes meddle. Which one of you meddled with Cinderella in the Magic Kingdom? She could have been happy, marrying the boy next door and the Prince would have married the Princess next door and ended the war between those two city states. But no, you had to meddle,' Gabriel looked at Loretta.

'Me? Do you really think this,' the pixie motioned at her studded, colourful, combat-boot laden, different eye-coloured self 'passes for a fairy godmother that would meddle? You've got to be joking.'

'Yes, meddle. Like you did with a certain X-ray, remember?' Gabriel retorted.[68]

Loretta bit her tongue. They were getting into an argument that was leading nowhere fast. She and Daisy should know better than to crack jokes at a distressed guardian angel.

Loretta turned to Daisy, 'Honeypuff, don't use words like 'fun' in the context of assassination attempts. He clearly misunderstood you.' Turning to Gabriel, Loretta added for clarity, 'The 'fun' Daisy mentioned was just me and her being a good team, which we are. She wasn't trying to say we consider assassination attempts fun. Have you ever heard Daisy make sarcastic remarks like that? Me maybe, but her, she's just not capable of hurtful language. Fairy, remember?'

Turning back to Daisy who was nodding, Loretta concluded, 'Daisy, Gabriel is not too keen on humour at the moment. Just tell him where you went.'

That's not actually all he wanted. More than anything, he wanted to find the culprit.

Daisy nodded and whispered, 'Well, actually, I did go see Ella that day...fairy godmother and all...'

Well, wasn't that convenient.

Gabriel made a note to check with Cinderella and Missus Klaus, but he was sure now that the Watchers would alibi out. As much as he wanted a quick fix, by the looks of it, these two were not his villains. 'You really had nothing to do with it?'

Both Watchers shook their heads in earnest, the insult at being suspected forgotten.

'This wasn't a prank for fun?' Gabriel asked Loretta just to be sure.

'Honey, please! Fun is fun and attempting to kill someone is actually dangerous not to mention it could cost us our job,' Loretta said patiently, like she would explain to one of her neighbour's thumbelings.

Oh.

He hadn't thought of it that way.

'Have you talked to the Boss lately about...anything?' he decided to check one last time.

'About what? How we have been doing a stellar job and what to do with our staffing problem?'

'Well, about how and whom we could recruit...for guardians or about succession planning...' Gabriel omitted whose succession planning he meant. He decided not to alarm the Watchers, just in case the Boss hadn't talked to them about wanting to quit.

'Succession planning...Daisy?' Loretta turned to the fairy.

Daisy stopped picking at a blue daisy and shook her head, 'Nope, doesn't ring a bell. We still recruit those who stand out the way we do - by sending recruiters like you. But now that you mention it, we should probably do something differently, if we ever want to get to all the saves in all dimensions that don't necessarily blip on our 16 priority screens.'

Loretta's eyes lit up, 'Yes, we should cast a wider net and do more preliminary work, including finding potential good recruits!' Loretta turned to Gabriel, 'About that, say, in your assessment, do you think Grace would make a good guardian angel?'

There it was. Just as he had suspected all along. 'Tell me honestly, did you two try to recruit her?'

The silence that fell over the forest was as sudden as the wrath of the Watchers.

'You stupid idiot! We're understaffed, yes, but not to the point of murder to recruit! Why would you EVER think we would go against regulations and recruit someone BEFORE their time? Before they are ready? They just wouldn't serve! Would you have been happy to have been plucked from your employ in the Crusades before you were done with your mission for your king? I know I wouldn't have been happy to be enlisted before I was good and ready! We all know what happens with reluctant recruits. They FAIL! This is the thanks I get for working overtime?!? AND I have to hear it on the only day off I've taken in six Agency months!' That was Loretta.

Daisy just turned puce and looked like she was having a heart attack, 'I would never...' was all Gabriel heard from her.

'Thank you for that. Now I'm sure you didn't have anything to do with the attacks on Grace and you've just saved me time double-checking your alibis with Cinderella and Missus Klaus.' Gabriel tried appeasing emotion with logic.

Logic seemed to have worked with Loretta. 'Fine! Now that that's settled, what's your plan?'

Daisy crossed her arms and turned away from both of them, waiting for a better apology.

Gabriel decided he would deal with extending an apology properly after he had completed saving Grace. He knew Daisy well enough to trust that she would do her job even when she was upset to the point of not speaking to him.

Gabriel sighed, 'I honestly don't know. I'm running out of ideas. You trying to recruit Grace was my second hope after the prank theory.'

'It looks serious then?' Loretta asked.

Gabriel looked so miserable that Daisy came up and gave him a hug, forgetting she was mad at him.

'Now what do we do?' Gabriel said out loud.

Daisy tapped her nose, 'Darling, I think you're forgetting something or someone, to be precise.'

'Who?'

Daisy patted him on the arm, 'As much as I don't want this to seem like we're trying to find...what is it that the humans call it...alternate culprit...? ...reasonable doubt? Anyhow, besides us, you're forgetting someone else who obviously knew about Grace.'

'Who?'

Not wanting to believe who timid Daisy was pointing at, but unable to argue with her logic and unable to resist showing Gabriel his place, Loretta smacked him in the back of his head, 'Switch your brain on, boyo.'

Oh.

'Are you going to interrogate her as well now?' Loretta huffed.

Annoyed that the matriarchal Watchers kept referring to any authority and their authority in particular as female, Gabriel made the automatic correction, 'Him, as I have been telling you for nearly a thousand years already, and to answer your question – I don't know. Maybe.'

Gabriel heard the collective gasp and decided to elaborate, 'I'm sorry, I am, well we all are running out of ideas on who is behind this. I still need to check out the possibility that Victor has been hanging out too much around you two and has picked up on your silly ways of having fun...'

It was Daisy's turn to huff.

'...and while I doubt our Boss would do something like this - I mean why would he...?'

'She,' Loretta and Daisy said in unison.

Gabriel didn't let himself be distracted, '...he was the only other person who even knew about this mission. So, either the Agency's communication devices are being tapped by whoever is after Grace - which means it's an inside job - or one of the four of us has a really big mouth.'

Loretta eyed him and tapped the side of her head, 'You're an idiot. Even if someone did say something to someone they shouldn't have - and I'm not saying anyone did - we found out why she was important for Earth and across dimensions only yesterday while the attacks on Grace started a lot earlier.'

'What are you saying?' Gabriel wanted the pixie to finish her train of thought.

Loretta pushed her glasses up her nose and said sternly, 'Use your logic. There are at least three viable scenarios.' She started crooking her fingers, 'A. Whoever it is either knew why she was important long before we did and that is why they are trying to kill her.

B. They are trying to kill her for an entirely different reason.

Or C. The attacks are not related at all and there might be multiple killers out there, some sort of a contract out on her, which is effectively again B.'

Gabriel nodded, 'I have been racking my brain about the first two options and coming up empty. The only one I haven't thought about is option C but from where I stand, there are too many similarities between the attacks for them to all be randomly orchestrated by different beings, so it must be either option A or B.'

'Similarities?' Daisy asked.

'Two of the attacks - the shooting and the last bombing - were remotely operated. Also, it appears that the bombs could have been dropped into the Earth dimension...from elsewhere.' Gabriel said.

That caught Loretta's attention, 'You mean whoever is after her is NOT from Earth?'

Gabriel nodded.

'From another dimension?' Daisy gasped.

Gabriel shrugged.

'From the Agency?' Loretta zeroed in on Gabriel's worst suspicions.

'I don't know. To be honest, I was almost wishing it was you two doing this for fun or to recruit her, then I could have told you to stop and that would have been that.'

Both Watchers nodded.

Daisy piped up, 'You said something about needing to check on Victor...'

'Grace and Victor have history, that's all. I was planning to speak to him next,' Gabriel said.

'Valhalla, you'll find him in Valhalla,' Loretta quickly volunteered, glad the interrogation was over. 'That's where I left him to soak his troubles a few Agency hours ago.'

'Did he happen to mention what his troubles were?' Gabriel asked.

Loretta shrugged, 'What else makes a guy want to drink himself into the oblivion. Women.'

The trio fell silent.

'Maybe this is good news? Maybe this is option B and Grace's troubles will end after you have a few choice words with Victor?' Loretta patted Gabriel on the arm.

Gabriel nodded. *Perhaps. If indeed, Victor's troubles had anything to do with his inability to kill a certain girl.*

47. Homeless

Grace

When Grace tottered out of Gabriel's bedroom the morning after the bombing of her apartment with her hair standing sideways, she was greeted by a girl who looked her age and quite human.

'Hi, I'm Lanie, Gabriel asked me to look after you while he's away,' Gabriel's stand-in said and offered Grace a hot mug of steaming coffee.

Grace gratefully took the mug, 'Hi, I'm Grace and not very human before my first cup of coffee, so thank you!' *Coffee first, brushing teeth later.* 'Aren't you going to have any?' she asked Lanie.

The girl laughed a tinkling laugh and shook her head, 'Coffee would be lovely, if only I wanted it. I just don't want it, that's all. Otherwise I would have poured some for myself already. The kitchen seems to be pretty well stocked.'

'My fault. Being human, I needed food, so Gabriel provided.'

'He cooked?' Lanie asked.

Grace shook her head, allowing the delicious latte to gradually wake her up. 'He paid.'

'Take-away?'

Grace nodded.

'Any good?'

'Pretty decent,' Grace said.

Both giggled.

Grace eyed Lanie's heart-shaped kind face and weird green-blue eyes and decided to ask about the things she hadn't dared to ask Gabriel yesterday. 'Are everyone's wings the same colour?'

Lanie looked surprised, 'He showed you his wings? I've been an angel only a short while, but I thought it was forbidden. Angels go to great lengths to hide their identities. Our wings and our transformation cocoons are like a signature, they are not the same.'

'I guess I didn't give him a choice, I noticed their shadow on the pavement when he was saving me,' Grace said.

'You saw them?' Lanie wondered, 'That's not supposed to happen either. Tell me, do you often notice magic around you?'

Grace shook her head, 'Gods no! I don't believe in magic, it's much too Harry Potter for my taste. I do notice things that don't fit, though. Like mistakes they make in the movies.'

Lanie looked at her and tilted her head, 'You don't believe in magic, but you take it as normal that guardian angels exist? Is that because of your religious upbringing?'

Grace shrugged, 'It's not a question of magic or faith. I guess, for me, it's a question of different realities. Just like it's ridiculous to think the human race is the only intelligent race on the supposedly only inhabited planet in the gazillion of universes, it's unreasonable to think there is only one reality. Even as humans, your reality was probably different from mine.'

'How very interesting, I haven't thought about it like that,' Lanie nodded. 'What if I told you there are magical dimensions? That Santa was a real person and that all the fairy-tale characters are real? What if there was magic on Earth?'

Grace shrugged again, 'That may very well exist in some dimensions. I'm not saying I deny there are unexplained phenomena on Earth. I, personally, cannot understand or explain weather. Maybe some people like shamans who are in touch with other realities can really conjure rain. In any case, all things like that need to be handled responsibly, isn't that the whole point?'

'You are probably the most level-headed person I have ever met,' Lanie summarised.

Grace decided to ask about something she definitely couldn't have asked Gabriel. 'Can I ask you something? It's not just coffee that you don't want, is it? It is everything?' Grace asked.

'Gabriel told you about 'no desires'?' Lanie smiled.

Grace nodded. 'How does it work, exactly?'

Lanie closed her eyes, 'When we are at the Agency, we feel... constant peace. I feel happy all the time, stable and serene. There is no need for food, there are no needs, urges, no desires. You see other beings for who they truly are, without judgement. You accept everything and regret nothing because you know that whatever choice you make is the best one in any point in time.' *Whenever she didn't see Peter or Alice or what those two were up to.*

Seeing the light go out of Lanie's eyes for a second, Grace decided to ask, 'But not all the time? Gabriel said angels can sometimes revert to their old selves, right? Why?'

'I don't know how about other species, but with humans, or former humans,' Lanie pointed at herself, 'it's the emotions that get us. Familiar triggers, familiar places and faces. Which is why we are usually sent to not our own, but other dimensions on saving missions. Me guarding you is an exception, Gabriel wanted someone who had joined the Agency after the attacks on you began,' the angel grew serious.

Grace was curious, 'So, if Gabriel was sent to Earth and he was from Earth, wouldn't that be...'

'More tricky for him?' Lanie finished for her, 'Why yes, except with Gabriel's hundreds of years of experience...'

Hundreds?!? How many hundreds?

'...and the Earth having changed so much during his time of service as an angel, there is little chance that he would revert back to being human. If he had died here yesterday, was recruited and put back into the exact circumstances before his demise, then seeing the faces of his loved ones and familiar surroundings would trigger an emotional response and make him want to be human again much quicker. Even something as simple as having your favourite cup of coffee could erode the angelic state.'

'Hence, no coffee for you,' Grace nodded.

'Yep, no coffee for me,' said Lanie and smiled.

Despite Lanie's protests, Grace insisted on going into work. After all, she hadn't told her uncle what had happened, so he full well expected her to show up. Lanie offered to keep Grace company until Gabriel came back.

Grace nodded her thanks at this girl who she couldn't help but instantly trust and glanced nervously at her watch. She was really late and while her journey from home to work was perfected down to a minute, she had no idea how long it would take her to reach the City from here. She remembered the tube stop and checked the TFL journey planner on her mobile to see how long it would take her to get to the City. Shoot, 50 minutes. She spotted the bike in the corner of the hallway, lock, helmet and all.

Probably Gabriel's.

That would do.

Lanie followed Grace to the hallway, nodded and turned into an angel pendant.

Grace attached her guardian to the necklace she was wearing and off she went.

Riding through the morning honks of London was exhilarating. Grace hadn't felt so alive in ages. She almost died yesterday. And the day before. And the day before and so on. Yesterday seemed thousands of years ago. Knowing that any minute could be her last, Grace was truly enjoying darting around London traffic.

As she disembarked and looked around for somewhere to fasten the bike, she noticed the stocks in front of the pub next door. Grateful for this surprising find, Grace mused that the reason she had never noticed them before was probably because the City people who came here rarely biked in. A few drinks down the line and the teetering mess in a suit might never make it home at night at all. There was simply no reason for the stocks to be there, so no reason to notice them either and yet, there they were.

'Finally,' was what her uncle crossly said when she opened the door. 'Having piss-ups with your friends does not entitle you to turn up late for work the next morning,' uncle Tom looked at her sternly. 'Explain yourself.'

'I had a bit of a scare last night. Someone bombed my place, literally. There isn't much left,' Grace said and put on her apron.

Della waived at Grace from Gabriel's corner booth and stuck her nose back into her silvery laptop.

'Did you have to go house hunting this very morning?' Her uncle reprimanded her.

Hoping he was making light of the situation to keep her

spirits up, Grace looked gratefully at her uncle.

No such luck. Humour had hid far far away from uncle Tom's face, finding the rare occasional visit painful enough.

Grace sighed, 'I didn't, but I will probably have to find a place, temporarily, at least while my place is being renovated.' Where she would get the money to renovate was beyond her. She knew her uncle wouldn't offer to help, just like he hadn't offered for her to stay with him and his family.

'I doubt you stayed under a bridge last night, so I'm assuming you will not have a problem finding temporary lodgings,' uncle Tom said, smirking, 'enough talk, get to work.'

Della waved a 20-pound note from the corner booth at uncle Tom and motioned for Grace and more coffee.

'I heard you are homeless,' Della said as Grace sat down, ready to listen to what Della had in store for her today.

'It's nice to see you again!' Grace smiled. The red-head had no patience whatsoever.

'Yes, yes, hello and all that. How would you like to be my house mate, honey?'

'You offer a complete stranger to come and stay with you, just like that?' Grace asked. *A lot of people around her seemed to be doing that lately. First Gabriel, now Della.*

'Just like that,' Della said, 'Don't tell me you need convincing. See here,' she turned her silvery laptop around and showed Grace an unfinished advertisement on Gumtree, titled 'RedHead11 seeking super neat house mate', 'I really am looking for a house mate and I like you, so don't argue.'

'It would just be temporary, until my apartment gets renovated,' Grace remembered Gabriel's promises of a miracle worker of a builder, but her own experience with the builders was far from miraculous. She was doubtful guardian angels were also builders, plumbers and decorators and could produce stuff for free out of thin air. He could help if she could pay for stuff. She would need temporary lodgings. Temporary cheap lodgings at that, since she needed to scrounge for money for the renovations.

As safe as it was, sleeping at angel central was not her first choice. Too close to Gabriel and she didn't want to be tempted. Falling for someone she couldn't have was not very savvy.

Besides, angel central as a venue could be compromised. Gabriel had explained that the assassin had to be within a line of sight to detonate the bomb at her apartment yesterday. They could have followed them to Gabriel's apartment, although he did swear he had tried all the evasive techniques that he knew.

'Oh good, you're not arguing, excellent. Since you are in a pickle, why don't you move in tonight, after your shift is over, ok?' Della pressed on.

If she made sure no one followed her when she left for Della's tonight, she might be safer in a place the assassin knew nothing about. Grace smiled, 'Ok, as long as you write the address down on paper, no emails or texts, don't ask, I'll explain later.'

Della ripped out a page from her chequered A4 ring binder, jotted something down and handed it over to Grace, 'There. We can discuss how much rent you can afford when you pop over with your stuff tonight. If you want, I can help you move? If you cannot afford any rent, the least that I can do is put you up for a couple of nights for free.'

Grace looked at her curiously, 'Tell me, do you do such kindnesses often?'

Della threw back her head and just laughed, 'You know what? I liked you on the spot. And I think we're going to be great house mates.'

'Temporary house mates,' Grace corrected her.

'Temporary things sometimes turn out to be quite permanent,' Della said. 'Now that that's settled, do tell, what happened yesterday?'

Grace told her about the shock of seeing her home obliterated, carefully leaving out being saved by Gabriel and finding out he was no longer human.

'You're not telling me everything,' Della concluded, pouring some more honey into her tea and throwing in a lemon. Tapping her nose, Della smirked at Grace's attempts to keep a poker face, 'Who did you stay with last night? I bet it's a guy. I bet that's why you didn't want to tell your uncle,' the red-head glanced over at where uncle Tom was trying to take the orders of three old ladies who kept changing their minds. 'Your uncle doesn't seem like the type who would approve if you did ask guys for help, not that he offered any himself.'

Grace smiled sadly. Della was very perceptive. She had certainly pegged her uncle right, already the first time they met, which was - unbelievably - just yesterday.

With her laptop forgotten, Della leaned in, eyes glistening, 'So, who'd you stay with last night? Was it a boy? Is he nice? Are you in love?' Della on a fact-finding mission was like a dog with a bone.

Grace blushed. She had had a crush on Gabriel before she knew what he was. And that knowledge had changed exactly nothing.

On the radio, someone was singing how they only had one life and they're gonna live it right.[69]

48. Mirror, Mirror
Boss

Although his trips to Dialysis X and Eerie were very satisfactory in terms of racking up personal saves, they didn't help.

The Boss had long started to wonder whether all those that they saved deserved saving. If someone had not saved Hitler from drowning when he had been a little boy, then the Earth dimension could have seen much less of evil in the 20th century.

Day in and day out, the calls came in. They answered the calls. They sent the angels. The angels saved all sorts of creatures imaginable in all sorts of imaginable dimensions.

Why?

What would happen if some of those creatures were not saved?

Chaos? A new world order in a couple of dimensions?

The tally of good and evil next to his revolving mirror - was that even real? He hadn't put it there. He had inherited it together with this office and this set-up from the being that had come before him. He didn't even know which dimension his predecessor had originated from. This office had the property of adapting the Boss' image to look like a being from the dimension of any visitor. Humans saw him as human. Yetis saw him as yeti. Pixies and fairies saw him as the Mother Goddess they worshipped in their flower colonies.

He had been presenting the world a multiverse illusion for thousands of years. Everyone saw whatever or whoever they wanted to see. A greater power, God, Goddess, King, mother, father, brother. To some he was gender-neutral or the closest thing to an equal or subservient or superior being from their own dimension whatever they needed to see to believe. He was all things to all beings.

On the outside, everyone saw the tally as mostly even. It projected an image of balance as well as provided feedback that the Agency was doing its job well, keeping it level. On the inside of his office, it reacted to momentary danger, with seconds' worth of precision. Only Gabriel and the Watchers knew – they frequented his office enough to notice.

That's why he had so much silver in his hair. He worried too much.

He looked at the white and black tally at either side of his revolving mirror. Why was good always white and evil always black? White was a funeral colour in Asia, Earth dimension while in the same dimension it was the colour associated also with weddings. Pitch-black heart was a bad thing and dark of the night was ambivalent, depending on the connotation. Jet black and raven black hair was considered beautiful. Go figure. Why not gold and silver or red and black? Colour aside, he was truly starting failing to see the difference anymore.

He had often suspected he was depressed. When he consulted the psychologists and therapists in the Earth dimension, one of two things tended to happen and only on one occasion was he pleasantly surprised. After he revealed even part of his daily concerns, the 'shrinks' as the natives called them invariably sent him to see a psychiatrist about his delusions then booked themselves quickly into a house with soft padded cells. Only on one occasion did the psychologist ask if she could see the Agency, to get a full picture of the multitude of his worries. He showed her. She was so enthused that she refused to go back to Earth and opted to stay as a guardian angel instead. It was seldom that people with a calling to help others chose to do so for eternity.

Lately, he was not so sure what was right and what was wrong anymore.

If he hadn't taken pity on Grace and pulled her from the smoldering car where both her parents and sister had burnt to a crisp, she would probably never have become such a do-gooder who longed to be rescued. With a normal father figure, she would never have mistaken Victor's bullying for strength and would have stayed away from him.

If Victor had not been such a reckless hothead and driven himself into a tree, then Gabriel would not have offered him the job to enable him to atone for his horrible deeds. Victor had the promise of becoming a good guardian angel, so a lot of good came out of the bad.

If Lanie had not been such a bleeding heart, she would have run away from the beggar and not ended up dead by accident. The bad was the result of the good. Of course, she would not have ended up dead had he not fiddled with the life of that beggar. He had only done that for the greater good. Lanie was showing promise - she could become as good as Gabriel and Victor, so good was definitely going to come out of the bad, whether the bad had been orchestrated or not.

If Gabriel had not chosen to be a guardian angel, who knows, maybe they would have won that battle and the face of religion on Earth would now be different[70]. Different good or different bad, he didn't know.

Not knowing and not caring were fast brothers. Perhaps it really was time for someone else to take over, someone who knew what was right and what was wrong. Someone who was willing to keep the balance and not let things run their course, which was tempting in the extreme.

Mirror, mirror on the wall, who's the fairest of them all.

Exactly, he needed someone fair, someone selfless, someone worthy to take his place when he retired. When, not if.

Now Lanie, Lanie was turning out better than expected. Perhaps she was even better than Victor. Certainly more creative – scooping Santa up with a syringe had been a hoot to observe.

If he had to pick the pecking order this very minute, it would come down to Gabriel, then Victor with Lanie coming in a strong third.

On the surround system, Kelly Clarkson was asking not to give up on her, to love her even with her dark side since everybody has one.[71]

Did any of it matter? Anything they did? Anyone they rescued?

Or would the world be different, but much the same even if the Agency ceased to exist altogether?

If something somewhere went horribly wrong, wouldn't that dimension rearrange itself to the new conditions and find a new balance?

The man shook his head trying to swat his recurring thoughts away.

If to do something good was as easy as not to do good, then why do anything at all?

The Boss rose. He looked at the heavy white oak door. All this light that was even now brimming from the sides of the door was making him tired. He stopped the revolving mirror with a swipe of his hand. Time slowed down. The other side looked pitch black, the opposite image of everything this side of the mirror.

His speaker sprang to life and suggested that he'd listen to his mother and that he'd learn[72].

The Boss massaged his temples. If he hadn't in thousands of years, the likelihood of learning how to see meaning behind it all now was probably low. He was tired.

Slowly, the Boss mumbled his spells and started his shuffle down the staircase, its black marble glowing invitingly. On the other side of the door, no one at the Agency paid any attention to the white oak door atop of the gleaming white staircase briefly opening and closing.

A few sunny hours in the ever enchanting Exhilaration dimension would do him good. He would go and save a bad guy for a change. Like with Victor, one never knew what good would come of it. So refreshing. He would leave the Watchers a note that he was going undercover as the dimension was due for a sleeper inspection. They would believe him, sure thing. They always believed him.

He was tired of being trusted.

49. Valhalla
Gabriel

Gabriel shoved the heavy wooden carved door like it was cardboard and entered Valhalla. The bar greeted him with familiar smells of stale beer and debauchery. In the dim candlelight, smacks of thrown punches occasionally punctured the noise of murmured laughter.

Ah, Valhalla. His second favourite dimension. Always there. Always fun.

Which is exactly what it said on the coat of arms that hung above the bar.

The jukebox started playing the Earth version of Valhalla's hymn by Blind Guardian[73].

A Kikuju warrior got up, bowed and offered his bar stool to Gabriel. Contrary to popular beliefs, correction, contrary to some popular but erroneous Earth beliefs, Valhalla was not a heaven meant only for fallen Nordic warriors. Gabriel bowed in return and took the proffered seat. No others were available.

Vikings dominated the scene, of course, but Gabriel spotted a group of Sikhs playing cards with upstanding Leuftwaffe Officers and what looked like a cohort of Centaurs at the table furthest from the bar. Celts were playing darts with Mayans, Mongols were playing drinking games with male pixies from the Flower Colonies. Bug-eyed reptiloids from Dialysis X and Chinese warriors were trying to compete with pirates in levitation.

It was a full house. Like on any other night in this dimension.

'Tristan,' Gabriel nodded at a boyish oxen-built Celtic warrior sitting next to him. 'Waiting for Isolde?' he enquired. It was a safe bet. Tristan was always waiting for Isolde.

Tristan nodded once and rose to meet a goddess of a woman clad in brown leather with a braid of auburn hair that ended between her shoulder blades. Contrary to popular but erroneous Earth beliefs, Valhalla was not a heaven meant for only male warriors either. Valkyries were also welcome. Very welcome. Any time.

18. 'Valhalla. Semper praesens. Semper ludicrum.

As the two lovers moved away, a familiar mop of dark hair lying on the bar appeared from behind Tristan's mighty form. 'Fancy atoning yourself, kind sir?' Gabriel said to the bowed head as he glanced at the clock.

He had to be quick here, if he didn't want to lose days, weeks or even years.

'I know that voice...' the head rolled over on its forehead and turned to look. Victor tried to focus his eyes that were stubbornly edging in different directions. Two of Gabriel swam into view. 'Ah, it's you...'

'Yep, so how do you want to play it – I clean you up or you

do it yourself?' There was little sense talking to Victor when he was so inebriated.

Victor considered the proposition. Last time he had let Gabriel 'clean him up' he vividly remembered the contents and smell of the bucket the bar keep had taken from him after Gabriel had lightly tapped him on the head to clear it. He shuddered and tried to hold back the impending vomiting. If any cleansing were to take place, it better be voluntary, 'Bar keep...give me Hell and Damnation.'

'Just one?' the bar keep enquired, humorlessly.

'How long has he been here?' asked Gabriel pointing at Victor.

'One hour,' was all he got as the owner of the bar reached for the bottle of murky liquid on the top shelf.

That meant 24 hours in Earth time. Time flowed differently in Valhalla than at the Agency or anywhere else. Twenty-four hours on Earth was 48 hours at the Agency and only one hour at Valhalla. All the guardians had watches that they could adjust to show the various times of the five dimensions they frequented. Most guardians hung out here this long only on their days off. Knowing how quickly they could pass their time here, most knew only to stop by for a drink or maximum for two. If Victor had been here an hour in between assignments and had gotten this plastered, then whatever it was, it was bad. *Perhaps this was regret over trying to kill a sweet innocent girl?*

'One will do, thank you,' Gabriel said to the bar keep. 'What happened, Vic?' Gabriel asked sternly.

Victor looked at the tiny shot of the murky liquid that had appeared in front of him.

So did the newcomers at the bar who were hoping for a show. The regulars did not even turn to look.

Hell and Damnation was a very individual drink, only for the brave or the stupid. Or both. Individual effects ranged from teleportation to various interesting dimensions to turning you into your worst nightmare, with passing out for weeks being the most boring of its effects.

With guardian angels it was the only drink that would sober

them up in seconds. The alternative, which Gabriel had offered to Victor was a quick purification of the system from toxins by upchuck.

Victor exhaled, 'Women' and down the hatch it went.

He grabbed the bar for comfort and shook his head to clear the fog.

One of Gabriel swam into view. Victor checked his upchuck reflex and felt it was gone. He was now stone cold sober. The mother of all headaches would come, but it would arrive tomorrow.

'Meaning?' Gabriel asked, noting the plural and hoping he was wrong about Vic's involvement in Grace's assassination attempts.

'Can't live with them, can't shoot them,' said Victor. Before Gabriel could even ask, Victor explained, 'One of my charges is a bitch on wheels and it is taking me aeons to convince this Princess to be charming - in the guise of a frog, mind you. There's a real hazard she might bungle up a date with the love of her life and I out of all people need to see that she doesn't. Again, in the guise of a frog. Like anyone would take advice from a frog seriously.' Victor shook his head, 'Plus, I've just had to unglue my other charge from around my neck. You would only hope she was trying to strangle me, but oh no, she was in the process of seducing me in a non-existing nightie. Christ, she's like a sister to me...except for all this wholesome goodness...'

Gabriel kept an eye on the time. What he really wanted to do was jump in and ask if Victor was done lamenting his job. Two minutes in Valhalla came and went, taking one Earthly hour and two Agency hours with them.

Meanwhile, Victor continued, 'Parallel saves in Earth-like dimensions where I turn back into a human quicker than you can sneeze are exhausting, man. I need sleep, I need to re-balance and I still need to save these two fools!' Victor showed Gabriel snapshots on his smart phone of a surly curvy brunette and an athletic blond. 'I think the Watchers are deliberately trying to punish me for something. Maybe it was something I said?' Victor lifted his brown eyes to Gabriel and met a stony face. 'Hey, what's up with you?'

'Have you or have you not been to Earth during the last six days?' Gabriel asked.

'Haven't you heard a word I've said?' Victor rolled his eyes, 'For the past Earth week, which by the way equates to six weeks in Gaia, not that it gives me more time, quite the contrary - I've had my hands full. Gaia is not called the second Earth for nothing - well, if it weren't for the purple sky, two moons, orange vegetation and the twin towers still standing, it'd be an exact replica. So, yes, sir, I've been to Earth, Texas to be precise. And now Florence, Italy. I've been to Earth dimension episodically, because that's where one of my two charges is. The bitch on wheels is in Gaia. I'm going back and forth between dimensions. To save them. Both of them. From themselves! At the same time! Which leaves no time for yours truly. Even to sleep!'

Gabriel considered whether to ask Victor out right about Grace and decided there were other avenues to find out whether someone was lying. First, they needed to stop wasting time. 'Upsie-daisy, you're coming with me,' he said and lifted Victor up by the scruff.

'Why?' was the most logical question Victor could ask, since 'where' was rather irrelevant.

'I need your help,' Gabriel said. *Well, technically it was true. He needed to interrogate Victor. Who would hopefully prove to be helpful.*

The silvery cocoon of iridescent light dissolved around the two of them at the Watchers' station. Loretta saw Vic, gave Gabriel an imperceptible nod, harrumphed at them and went back to manning the screens.

Gabriel turned Vic's back to the screens one of which was showing Grace talking to Della at the coffee shop. Gabriel then proceeded to fill Victor in on everything about the attempts on Grace's life without mentioning the name of his Charge, looking out for tell-tale facial micro-expressions to give him away.

Victor listened carefully to all the intel Gabriel had managed to amass so far, occasionally asking clarifying questions.

Meanwhile, Gabriel had observed no uncomfortable fidgeting, no smirking and no slips of the tongue. Vic's interest in the details was genuine. He was leaning forward and had not once asked about the identity of the charge.

Victor summarised the problem, 'What you're saying is that someone, probably not from her own dimension and possibly from our own Agency is after this girl, basically around the clock, you have no idea who and have not been able to find out yourself or with the help of the Watchers, whom you have ruled out as suspects. The only thing you do know is that the girl is somehow the keeper of Magic in the Earth dimension and that she has been saved at least once before, 12 years ago?'

Gabriel nodded.

'I need to ask - have you also ruled out everyone in her own dimension who could possibly want her dead?' Victor asked.

'Everyone alive - yes, which is why I'm talking to you,' Gabriel said, watching out for any signs of recognition dawning.

'Me? Why me?' Victor looked genuinely surprised.

'You used to date her, live with her actually,' Gabriel corrected himself, as unpleasant as that correction was, it was the truth.

'Is it Lydia? Nancy? Virginia?' Victor was going through his list of cohabitants chronologically. 'I could give you names of people they didn't get along with...'

'It's Grace,' Gabriel said.

Victor looked him in the eye, 'My Grace?'

For some reason, that didn't sit well with Gabriel, 'Not yours, but yes, you used to be together and you're atoning for what you did to her.'

Victor narrowed his eyes. It wasn't like Gabriel to be overprotective of his charges. He was always objective. 'Stayed too long on Earth, lately, mate? You're turning back into a human.'

Gabriel wasn't sure that was actually an insult. 'I'm going to ignore what you just said because you're obviously still a little drunk and we're in a hurry to figure this out,' he said, telegraphing annoyance bordering on anger. *Well, he was in a hurry.*

In all the time they had known each other, Victor had never

known Gabriel to be anything but affable. He could be wiping blood off his sword, but he would recount the save with his usual level-headed, calm demeanour. There was only one reason a man was truly angry at another where women were involved. 'You like her,' Victor thought he would start carefully by stating the obvious.

'Yes,' Gabriel said simply. He had grown to care for Grace in spite or perhaps because of her proneness of sliding to the floor whenever something surprising happened, her infuriating distrust of kindly helpful men and her good heart the size of a planet.

By the looks of Gabriel's smile, this was more than 'like'. Victor couldn't really blame anyone, much less Gabriel, for falling for the girl he had once known and loved. Grace was sweet and happy, quite his opposite, which is why he had held on too tight. 'Right,' if that's how it was between his mentor and his ex, that's just how it was. *Never ask questions you don't know the answer to.*

The speakers of the Watchers' station hiccoughed that like fallen soldiers, they will learn that love will be the death of them[74], then switched to Amy lamenting she didn't want to go to rehab[75].

Loretta cursed at the glitching speakers and they fell silent, having emitted enough warnings no one wanted to take seriously. Why bother when no one is listening?

For Gabriel, the conversation was getting irksome. 'I'm going to ask you once again - have you been to Earth lately to pester Grace?' Gabriel asked, his voice almost menacing.

'Are you insane? As much as I moan about my assignments, I actually like my job. I like being not dead and indestructible. Why would I jeopardise all this over a blast from my past? She was right to kick me out and walk away, I was not good for her. She deserves better and from what you've told me killing her would just mean she would be recruited as a guardian. Would you want to work side by side with one of your exes? I would rather take poison, thank you very much! Most of my exes hate me. They wouldn't be able to see past that, angelic form or not.' Victor finished in one breath.

To Gabriel, none of this sounded rehearsed. Jumping from accusation to conclusion, Gabriel sighed, sat on the edge of the Watchers' desk and asked, 'If it isn't you, then who?'

'Let's go back to the very beginning. What exactly did the Boss say about her being important across dimensions?' Victor asked.

Gabriel tried to remember. 'I think he said 'Her death will permanently change the face of her dimension and perhaps even this Agency. Or something along those lines,' Gabriel said. Then he remembered something Grace had muttered before falling asleep after they had watched the Terminator movie. 'Wait a minute, Grace had a feeling that the universe might be conspiring against her somehow, that it was out of balance, that the good was not winning anymore, no matter what she did... Maybe somehow she is the one upsetting the balance and something or someone is trying to right it?'

Victor scratched his jaw. What little he remembered of Grace was good, 'Grace is a good person. Does that mean that there isn't meant to be magic on Earth at all and to balance it off someone like her needs to be taken out? Is that what you're saying?'

Gabriel blinked. 'Loretta said that Grace was a guardian of all magic on Earth and by proxy in all the other dimensions as well...'

'If she's a guardian of all magic, I need to introduce her to one of my present charges, stuff she draws keeps coming to life and it ain't all pretty...'

Gabriel raised his hand, 'Later.'

Loretta said from behind Victor, 'If one guardian of magic disappears in one dimension it would destabilise that dimension and weaken the others as well. I've never seen anything like that ever happening, but there is always a first time,' she said.

'If that ever happened, what would happen to the Agency?' Victor asked.

'For one thing, we would all be much much busier,' Loretta said through gritted teeth.

Gabriel had to say it out loud, 'What if it's not about Grace or the Earth dimension at all? What if it's about the Agency?'

'The Agency?' Victor repeated.

'The Agency. Remember the tally of good and evil at the revolving mirror in the Boss' quarters?' Gabriel pointed upwards.

Victor looked blank, 'Not that well, no. I've only been there a couple of times...'

'Ok, well then. There is a tally of good and evil across all dimensions in the Boss' office and the last I saw of it – just before I leapt in to save Grace for the very first time – the black tally - for Evil - was way too high. And, apparently, when Grace met up with one of the newbie Goddesses, a meeting that the assassin was trying to prevent, the tally evened out or so you said,' Gabriel looked at Loretta who nodded.

'What are you saying? That without Grace, across all dimensions the bad guys would be winning? What are we, then, chopped liver?' Victor voiced his displeasure.

Gabriel considered that for a moment, 'No, but maybe whatever we're doing is simply not enough and whoever is playing for the other side might be winning at the moment.'

'How does Grace make a difference then?' Victor huffed.

'I suppose that one of the reasons why someone unknown would want her dead would be because perhaps she would make a difference across the board, across all dimensions, now or in the future...like maybe if besides being the guardian of magic on Earth, she was also destined to become a very powerful guardian angel or even our new Boss?' Gabriel suggested.

Victor knew Grace not to be vindictive, but having her as his Boss was not an appealing thought. His expression soured, 'You mean he was serious a few Agency weeks ago when he asked our help in finding him a worthy replacement?' Victor asked as Loretta gasped.

Gabriel noted that at least this Watcher had not been aware of the Boss' retirement and succession plans. That cemented his belief the Watchers were not in on it, at least not on the 'finding the new Boss' tack. Out loud he asked Vic, 'Did you think his request was just idle chit-chat?'

'No, but why would he choose to recruit someone as inexperienced as Grace when you are the obvious choice?' Victor wondered.

'I told him I don't want the job,' Gabriel said as Loretta gasped again.

Victor looked surprised, 'Whyever the hell not?'

Gabriel smiled, not surprised he had to explain himself. 'I like what I do now, helping beings across all dimensions, saving various universes a bit at a time. I don't want to sit there,' he pointed up, 'and pick who gets saved and know that someone doesn't. I prefer to know that whoever I save, gets saved. Holding the balance across all known dimensions and making hard decisions is not for me. I've never wanted that kind of responsibility.' He had learnt it the hard way, sending his men into battle and seeing only a few return. 'Deciding who lives and who dies - I don't have the heart for it.'

Victor nodded, 'And there is no way the Boss can persuade you otherwise?'

'None,' Gabriel was resolute.

Victor and Loretta looked at each other. Gabriel's refusal was unexpected. Everyone at the Agency had taken for granted that Gabriel was the most logical choice to step in.

'I wish you two would come to your senses about the Boss. Don't you think this would be a bit of a coincidence? An unknown assassin is after this girl and the Boss takes advantage to recruit her - an inexperienced newbie - as her successor? Do you really think she would stand idly by or worse, help the assassin do their job?' Loretta finally piped up.

'No, that would just be too much of a coincidence,' Victor said as Gabriel shook his head.

'So, we're back to the theory that someone's out to get Grace before she can right all the wrongs with magic on Earth and balance out evil across dimensions?' Loretta asked.

Gabriel nodded, 'Either that or someone is just trying to

undermine the Agency and create more work for all of us,' he concluded.

'I'm sure we'll be able to handle it. We'll just recruit more angels and train more recruiters. That will actually make the Agency more necessary,' Loretta noted.

'Like raise our profile? Who could be interested that that does NOT happen?' Victor asked, following the logic.

Loretta fluttered her wings, 'I might be mistaken, but I've heard rumours...that we are not the only balancing power out there. Apparently, there is also a Get Even Agency[76] that does much the same we do, except their means are more sinister. They let beings from all dimensions sink to their lowest point and then offer them a way out in exchange for something valuable.'

Victor and Gabriel furrowed their brows in unison.

Gabriel had never heard of such a thing, in all his 900 years of service, 'You mean, we have the diamond trade and gadgets where we make the money to keep us going and they collect 'contributions' from those they save?'

Loretta nodded. 'You object to their means, but they essentially do what we do.'

'So they are partly a rival agency and partly our natural collaborator?' Gabriel asked.

Victor raised his hand, 'Let me just stop you before you lose yourself in this garbage theory. Whoever told you about this anti-Agency was simply pulling your leg. The 'they' you keep talking about don't exist.'

'How do you know?' Loretta asked and crossed her arms.

'Because if they did, then considering my gently vengeful predisposition they would have recruited me instead of you, don't you think?' Victor parried.

'Maybe you're here on secondment?' Loretta stuck out her tongue at Victor.

'Isn't that nice. Good to know what you think of me. Not helpful, though. A stupid question, but are we sure the tally is correct?' Victor asked.

Loretta tilted her head and scratched behind her slightly longer left ear, 'Well, the Boss does say that pinpointing what makes Evil crank up a notch on any given day is near impossible...'

'So we don't know whether the tally is showing us the right stuff?' Victor pressed.

Gabriel shook his head, 'The tally is not to be disputed.'

'Why ever not?' Victor and Loretta stared at Gabriel. 'I mean, how do we know for sure HOW it measures what we think it measures? Do we even know for sure that white measures Good and black measures Evil or are we going on a lot of faith here?' Victor kept digging. Met with stony silence, Victor said, 'It seems we have a lot of questions and are none the wiser. I think now would be a good time to go and ask the Boss for help.'

'Now would be a good time for Gabriel to go save Grace,' Loretta said, pointing at the screen where the driver of a double decker bus was struggling with the breaks while the bus was gunning at full speed at a lonely female biker.

'You,' Loretta pointed at Gabriel, 'jump in and you,' she pointed at Vic, 'go consult the Boss.'

'Page Lanie,' Gabriel yelled as he jumped into the screen, hoping he would be on time.

50. Rehab
Grace

Grace was pedalling to Della's, her backpack laden with the few items she managed to salvage from her ruined flat. She mused whether it was too late to bake Emma's magical cinnamon apple pie as a thank you tonight and whether Della's kitchen would have all the ingredients.

Grace adjusted her earphones as Ella was singing about someone she was longing to see[77]. She thought about Gabriel, sighed and cast a cursory glance at the thinning traffic. The streets were nearly empty, which was normal close to midnight on a Tuesday.

Since last night's revelations, she had had a whole day to get used to the fact that she had a crush on an angel. A very effective angel as well. Gabriel had saved her countless times and by the looks of it, her saviour also delivered on his promises. When she had gone home to fetch her things, afraid her lovely flat would be looted of anything valuable despite the 'POLICE LINE DO NOT CROSS' tape, there was already a temporary door up and a text arrived on her mobile notifying her that the key was under the flower pot. Someone had bothered to clean the debris out as well.

Via a text message Gabriel had insisted that she keep the bike she had found in his apartment and gifted her a helmet, to boot. After the police had briefly stopped by to ask her questions about the bombing of her apartment, a fruit basket had arrived at the coffee shop. The messenger deposited a pink helmet next to it. It it weren't for the cellophane gift wrap, Grace would have run after him, thinking he had accidentally left it behind. The helmet had elicited a bigger wave of nosiness from the customers than the police. Even uncle Tom had enquired whether she had an admirer.

Pink was not Grace's favourite colour, but she wasn't going to look a gift helmet in the mouth. Just like she was going to gingerly accept Gabriel's help in renovating her apartment.

Because Gabriel had been doing such a great job of keeping

her out of trouble, she had expected him to help her move or at least escort her to Della's tonight. Instead, she was stuck with Lanie-the-pendant who was tucked away safely inside her fleece.

Turning left from London Bridge, Grace stopped pedalling downhill.

A double decker bus swerved after her and picked up speed.

Feeling the breeze ruffle the stubborn curls sticking out from under her brand new pink helmet, Grace inhaled the summer air. This July in London was graced with both of the two hot weeks of English weather in the summer. She wondered how living with Della might turn out. *Temporarily.* She missed her apartment already, she missed Cat and most of all, she missed Gabriel.

She told herself he was investigating, not staying away on purpose.

Probably.

Close to the London Dungeon, at a crossing near the London Bridge tube station, the pedestrian lights were mutely blinking yellow. Through Ella's magical voice, Grace heard honking.

She looked right and left and then behind her.

A double-decker bus was gunning right at her, at full speed. The driver was waving and shouting, the sounds muted by the window shield between them. His panicked expression came through all right.

Grace clutched her pixie pendant while inertia made her glide on as the distance between her bike and the bus evaporated.

A split second before the bus touched her back wheel, there was a white flash as someone stepped into the path of the renegade bus.

White magnificent wings spread out and the world slowed down. A myriad of glittering pieces of glass exploded in the air, quietly racing against torn white feathers and tiny drops of something red as Ella kept coaxing someone to watch over her.

Strong arms closed around her waist, making her skin tingle with warmth. In the bright light that enveloped her, Grace searched for those familiar blue eyes. 'Gabriel.'

Gabriel's hold on her tightened, which made Grace

ridiculously happy. 'Oh, Gabriel, I'm so happy to see you!' His eyes were so close she dissolved in their warmth.

'Grace.' His voice was throaty, sending shivers down her spine.

With panicky thoughts like 'is my breath alright' and 'oh my god, this really is happening' Grace closed her eyes, leaning in for her first kiss with an angel.

Gabriel silently took a faltering step forward, leaning into her even more, missing her mouth by a mile.

'Gabriel?' Sagging under his weight, Grace grabbed for him as he started to slide towards the pavement. The back of his shirt was slick with something wet and warm.

'Gabriel!!' Panic unwittingly crept into her voice as she cradled him in her arms.

Gabriel's eyes closed as he smiled, glad he had made it in time.

Ignoring Fray crooning about saving a life in her earphones[78], Grace knelt over Gabriel's unconscious body, feeling completely helpless. His lovely blond hair was matted with blood, the back of his head an indistinct mush, his T-shirt a speck of scary white in the pool of red forming on the pavement under them. He looked human and vulnerable and dead. He had to be dead, judging by the amount of blood seeping from him.

Lanie materialised next to her in a flash. 'Gosh, I'd better call this in,' was all she said, calm as a cucumber.

'Is that all you can say?' Grace demanded. 'MY guardian angel is DEAD and all you say is GOSH?!? Was Gabriel THAT expendable to you?' She was on the verge of hysteria. Tears were already streaming down her face and taking her mascara with them.

How could he be dead? He had sheltered her against the blast of a bomb from less than 10 feet away without a mark on him. How could he get hurt now?

Lanie smiled her zen smile, 'We can put him back together again. Like Humpty-Dumpty.'

'No one could put Humpty Dumpty back together again,' Grace wailed.

'Well, certainly not in this dimension,' Lanie said, took Gabriel's hand and started forming a pink cocoon around them. 'I'm taking him to the Agency where he will recover in just a few Agency hours,' she said, slowly fading.

'Oh, no you don't!' Grace grabbed Gabriel's other hand and with a loud pop materialised alongside Lanie and Gabriel's unconscious body somewhere very white.

A very angry Gothic Tinkerbell stared at Grace, 'Why did you bring her here?' she asked Lanie and Grace was a little glad the hostility was directed at someone else but her. The tiny Tinkerbell with combat boots, purple wings and black Kohl around her eyes reminded Grace of a very scary panda and looked like she could make grown men weep.

'I didn't say she could come along, she just hitched a ride,' Lanie said apologetically. 'Want me to fill in for you at the station while you deal with Gabriel?' Lanie asked.

This blatant peace offering worked as Tinkerbell harrumphed and zeroed in on Grace. 'So, we have a stowaway...'

Grace looked at Gabriel and then at the Gothic Tinkerbell, 'I'm here already, now are you going to waste time on arguing with me or are you going to try and undo this?' Grace gestured at Gabriel's unconscious body.

Loretta decided the girl had a point. *The sooner she started repairing Gabriel, the sooner everyone, including herself, would be happier.* 'He isn't all dead, just mostly dead,' Loretta reassured as the girl gasped. The pixie removed the angel's sword and set it aside. At the Agency, the sword would repair itself. *But bits of it were probably lodged in Gabriel's spine, so she had to extract them before any repairs.* Loretta would have sworn if there was time. 'Luckily Lanie managed to get him here before he was ALL dead. So as long as we resurrect him within 72 Agency hours, he'll be as good as new.' *With some bits firmly replaced, judging by the state of the back of his head.*

Grace was still reeling from the shock admission that Gabriel was 'mostly' dead.

The pixie eyed her appreciatively, 'Seeing how you're already all gooey and gory, fancy helping me get him on the bed?'

Grace nodded and helped the pixie heave Gabriel's body onto a bunk. The pixie quickly stuck some tubes onto Gabriel before she closed the transparent casket. Grace briefly wondered whether this was where the story of Snow White being buried in a crystal casket originated from.

Apparently, they were in angel rehab which looked nothing like the hospital wing in Harry Potter. The medical personnel was also nothing like the kind and elderly Madam Pomfrey.

Seeing the blood still pool under Grace's feet, Loretta shooed her in the general direction of the door, 'Go clean up. Second door on the left. I'll be a couple of hours. Go entertain yourself, now that you're here. Shoo!'

As much as Grace wanted to stay by Gabriel's side to make sure he was ok, she suspected there was nothing she could do but sit and watch the crystal casket. All she could do was clean up and stay out of trouble for a couple of hours.

How hard could it be, if she was at the Agency?

When Grace exited into the main hall, she was almost instantly mauled over by what seemed like a Yeti. Grace felt a little like hyperventilating. The Yeti begged her pardon and stormed on.

Grace found the showers. Standing under a refreshing waterfall in full gear, socks and all Grace half forgot to clean herself up, spying on the myriad of beings scraping themselves free of goo of various colours, only some of it their own. Angels back from messy saves. Some even nodded at her, mistaking her for a new recruit. The water pouring on top of her head had interesting qualities - it didn't smell of bleach, but took out the blood just the same. Grace wondered what it would do to her jet black hair. When she finally decided she was clean and disinfected enough, she stepped into the cubicle marked 'Instant dry'. It was a good thing she had held her breath in addition to closing her eyes as the notice taped to the other side of the Plexiglas suggested. The blast of hot wind made her hold on to the sides of the cubicle for balance.

Great, now she would look like she had curly fries growing

out of her head and god knows what colour, if the water did
have bleaching agents in it. Oh well.

On the upside, now she could explore to her heart's content!

Carefully avoiding centaurs, Yetis, fairies and angrier fairies, Grace was navigating her way back when a dragon's tail knocked her backwards into a room filled with monitors. There was a loud bark and someone said, 'Excuse you.'

Lanie steadied the chair Grace had dislodged. The Dachshund in the chair Grace had almost sat on stared at her accusingly. 'Oh good, finally something familiar, hello doggy! Is he yours?' she asked Lanie.

'Hello, I'm Jack,' said the dog, turned and hopped off the chair.

'Oh, beg your pardon,' Grace mumbled. She was still getting used to the fact that any kinds of beings could serve as guardian angels.

'Apology accepted,' the dog said, turning back to the monitors.

Grace skulked around the edges of the room, observing the goings-on of the 16 screens until a blond, kinder-looking version of the Gothic fairy spotted her. 'Oi, you, what are you doing here?'

Grace pointed at the general direction of the angelic sick bay and said, 'Gabriel's being resurrected. I tagged along and the scary-looking Gothic Tinkerbell told me to stay out of trouble for a couple of hours.'

The blond fairy fluttered her light blue wings as she laughed a tinkling laugh, 'You must mean Loretta. She's a pixie, though, not a fairy and whatever you do, don't call her Tinkerbell, they have fallen out. I'm Daisy, by the way. And I'm a fairy.' Daisy extended her delicate fingers and shook Grace's hand lightly. 'I believe you've already met Lanie and this is Jack, our Watcher-in-training.' The Dachshund nodded, ears flopping, 'We've been acquainted.'

Grace felt like apologising that she almost sat on him and mistook him for a pet, so she did. The dog wagged its tail once and without taking his eyes off the screens said, 'Bygones.'

On cue, the angry Gothic Tinkerbell materialised in the

doorway, 'You, Gabriel's charge, why don't you make yourself useful and go get me a hot chocolate. Resurrecting angels is tough work, you know.'

Seeing the light of hope in Grace's eyes aimed at the sick bay behind her, Loretta shook her head, 'He's fine. Still sedated, so no point of rushing over there yet. Let the man wake when he's good and ready. Meanwhile, I need hot chocolate! Now!'

Grace could swear she heard the pixie mentally add 'wench' to that command. She didn't care. This grumpy pixie had just single-handedly brought Gabriel back to life. The least she could do was go make her a hot chocolate and ignore the grumpiness.

Grace looked around for a coffee station or a kitchen. Instead she saw a waterfall of brown liquid that smelled like Earl Grey tea.

'On a second thought, it's past midnight somewhere and it's my day off, so bring me a lime margarita instead,' Loretta said even more crossly, which Grace didn't think was possible, but apparently it was.

The liquid in the waterfall turned yellowish green.

Marvellous! Thought control.

Now that she knew how to operate the drinks fountain, Grace was comfortable handing them out to anyone who wanted one.

***

The dust on the cogs of Big Ben billowed and gathered itself up into the form of the owner of the office.

What was she doing here?

The girl he had sent Gabe to protect was at the Agency.

Victor and Loretta had both tried to come and speak to him, so the Boss had made himself scarce. He had been avoiding most of his staff lately. The pixie had sensed he was near, but not seeing anyone, she had left with a shrug.

What was Grace doing at the Agency? Any mortals who had come this way usually never left.

He had no choice now.

51. Factory Settings

Grace

When Gabriel walked out of the sick bay two Agency hours after being resurrected, he saw Grace in deep conversation with a ghost over the meaning of Halloween. Yetis, dragons and angels alike seemed to know and acknowledge her, asking for repeat drinks without specifying what those were.

'Get me a hot chocolate, will ya?' Loretta called out to Grace from the Watchers' station.

'Not a lime margarita this time?'

Loretta harrumphed as Grace laughed.

'You seem to have made friends fast,' Gabriel said.

Grace jumped up and hugged him fiercely, 'And you seem to have forgotten to tell me I'm supposed to be the keeper of all magic on Earth, although I have a few questions about that. I mean I'm pretty much convinced magic should only be used for good, but what about necessary evil? Can evil even be necessary? I mean, it should, well, at least sometimes, for the sake of balance, right? Now if I don't believe or support magic used for evil, does that make me a bad keeper?' Grace rattled down.

Gabriel carefully disentangled himself and held her by her shoulders at arm's length.

To Grace, he looked like he was about to pat her on the shoulder. When she looked into his eyes, instead of the warmth she remembered seeing a few hours ago, she now only saw a look of polite interest.

That was all she got from the guy who had stepped in front of a bus for her?!?

'Are you alright?' Grace asked, wondering what had changed in the last two hours. *Well, besides Gabriel getting deaded and then resurrected.*

'Perfectly fine. I'm glad that you are alright.' Gabriel stood up straight to his full towering height. Still looking at Grace he extended his hand towards Loretta, 'Weapon, please.'

Loretta took a sword propped up against the Watcher's table and handed it to him, 'There! Happy?'

Gabriel nodded, 'Thank you!' and fastened the weapon in between his shoulder blades, folding his wings inward. 'We should get you to Della's after I enquire what Victor was able to find out from the Boss,' Gabriel said and turned to Loretta with questions in his eyes.

It felt like a dismissal. Like they were back to being strangers. Like the last week never happened.

'Thank you for saving me. Again. I'll say my goodbyes and then we go,' was all Grace was able to squeeze out. *After all, it was the polite thing to do.*

Gabriel nodded, already in deep conversation with the pixie.

Daisy observed Grace's good mood evaporating and thought someone should explain to the girl how the Agency affected the angels. She signalled Grace to come join her at the drink fountain. 'You shouldn't judge Gabriel harshly for...well...being who he is,' the fairy added.

'He doesn't look like himself after...after the resurrection. Don't get me wrong, I am glad he's alive, but something has changed. Like the factory settings were restored or something,' Grace said. She really was glad. *Different or not, at least he was alive.*

'Factory settings, yes,' Daisy laughed her tinkling laugh. 'That's actually the closest to the truth. The way he is now, that's who he truly is when he's at the Agency. When he's in his true form...when he's balanced. Everyone always finds their balance here. It's how this space influences us, the longer we stay here,' Daisy said.

Grace blinked, 'You mean when he was on Earth, getting friendly and flirty, that wasn't his normal state?'

Daisy sighed at the 'flirty' comment, 'No, that was his normal state too, just his normal state before he became an angel. On Earth, he was turning gradually back into the person he used to be. He was becoming more and more human. It didn't help that he hadn't re-balanced in a while, although I've never seen him go native in just less than two days...' Daisy said thoughtfully.

'You mean to say that yesterday Gabriel came to the Agency to get 're-balanced' as you put it?' Grace asked. *That would explain why he had been so distant and silent the day he had walked her home when her apartment went 'kaboom!'*

Daisy nodded, 'The weird bit is...it wore off too quickly and it shouldn't have.'

'Meaning?'

'Meaning it usually takes weeks for an angel to get used to familiar surroundings of his former dimension. Enough for his previous thought patterns and former behaviours to emerge. In Gabriel's case, the more time he spends on Earth, the more human he becomes. Still, it should have taken him at least a week to get in touch with his human side, emotions and all. When angels do that, inescapably their invincibility or angelic protection against death and maiming erodes. For some strange reason, within a space of just two days after his re-balancing Gabriel had nearly turned human again, which is why he mostly died during the last save...' Daisy did not like where her thoughts were leading.

Perhaps Gabriel was right. Could it be that whoever was after Grace was now targeting Gabriel to get him out of the way so whoever-it-was could get to Grace? Or worse, destabilise the Agency.

A part of Grace rejoiced that Gabriel was able to turn back into a human. Another part of her realised that he would never have mostly died today if he hadn't spent so much time constantly looking after her. She was willing to forgive his angelic level-headedness, even if it made her sad.

Just to be clear, Grace deigned to ask, 'So, if he stays on Earth too long, he will become human?'

Daisy nodded.

'And if he stays here too long, he will be less human?'

Another nod.

'And in between saves angels need to come back to the Agency to 'get their shots', so-to-speak,' Grace said rather than asked.

When Daisy raised an eyebrow, Grace commented, 'Veterinary humour, sorry.'

Gabriel waved at her from the awning of the Watchers' station, 'Stay here, I'll pop to see the Boss myself. You should be safe here with the Watchers.'

***

Gabriel was climbing the stairs to the Boss' office. According to Loretta, Victor had not found him and had gone back to saving one of his charges from bungling up an important date. Loretta had checked in on the Boss every hour on the hour without any luck either.

Their Boss was simply nowhere to be found.

Perhaps he was working the trenches himself while both, Gabriel and Victor, were on long-playing saves?

Suddenly, his hunch that someone might be after destabilising the Agency didn't seem like an incredibly stupid idea.

Continuing his climb, Gabriel hoped he would have better luck this time.

He opened the door to an empty office.

The Boss was nowhere to be found.

Gabriel hoped he had a reason for being AWOL.

A good one.

52. Cursus Pixus
Lanie

Loretta greeted Lanie's pink cocoon materialising at her desk with a grunt, 'Lucky I had just finished my hot chocolate, otherwise I might have inhaled it. You really shouldn't sneak up on pixies. I could turn you into something, you know...'

'I know, I know, hello Grumpy,' Lanie hugged the pixie who was only feigning moodiness. Few dared.

'Careful with the wings! Stop smothering me and go get yourself some tea, wench,' Loretta theatrically adjusted her purple wings more for show than anything else.

Lanie nodded her hellos to Daisy and Jack, who were glued to the screens. She found Grace at the wall fountain.

'I wondered if you'd still be here,' said Lanie to Grace, 'How's Gabriel?'

'Alive,' said Grace and smiled.

'Sorry that I didn't react quickly enough back there,' Lanie apologised to Grace under the encouraging eye of the Watchers. Everyone in the room understood that while the Agency would resurrect an angel any time, they would not have resurrected Grace, had she died in the bus mauling. Had Gabriel been a second too late.

'It's ok, Gabriel saved me,' Grace shrugged, thinking whether they would have recruited her as a guardian had she died and whether fraternising on the job was permissible for guardians.

There was an awkward silence.

Daisy patted Lanie's arm, 'You're still learning, honey. Quick wit takes time to develop, you know.'

Lanie nodded, looking sheepish.

Grace decided that a change of subject would take Lanie's mind off her guilt of not being fast enough on a rescue, 'Loretta, you've explained to me about the 16 priority screens across all dimensions, but could you zoom in on anyone you want, for instance?' Grace didn't even know why she asked.

'Sure, let me show you,' with an evil glint in her purple eye, Loretta pushed a button to pause reality, tapped her keyboard and one of the screens zoomed in on London and a particular address in Belsize Park. Grace could only assume this was Earth. Temporarily relieved from screening duty, Daisy dared a trip to the drinks fountain.

A girl was dancing around a bathroom in her pyjamas. The sun streaking in through the orange tinted windows filled the tiny flat with warmth and new hope. Unaware that anyone was watching, the girl raised her hands in a victory stance.

Lanie recognised the paramedic, Alice, the one who was dating Peter. She was holding something in her right hand. As Loretta zoomed in, a box on the sink whirled past that made Lanie's insides go limp.

No. It couldn't be.

She almost didn't want to see, but Loretta kindly zoomed in on Alice's right fist anyway.

A tiny blue cross was staring at her accusingly, vacuuming all the air out of her lungs.

Lanie's legs gave way and she almost missed a chair sitting down.

Maybe it wasn't Peter's? After all, it had been an Earth week since she had seen them smooch away on the steps of his house. Maybe they had had a one night stand and Alice had since found someone else, anyone else but Lanie's Peter to be happy with?

'Peter, darling, we have to talk...' Lanie heard Alice yell.

Not wanting to see Peter in his rumpled bed, Lanie closed her eyes shut, trying to fight the tears.

Alice hadn't found anyone else.

She was pregnant.

It was Peter's.

Loretta's particularly delicious but deadly to the uninitiated pixie curses (*cursus pixus*) carried all the way to the drinks fountain.

Daisy asked, 'What happened?'

They all saw Lanie disappear in a pink swirl of light, looking like someone up for voluntary martyrdom.

Daisy hadn't seen eyes like that since the Witch Trials in the Earth Middle Ages. This was what losing all hope looked like in human form.

'What did you do?' Daisy turned on Loretta.

The pixie had the decency to look ashamed.

'I thought we had agreed that it was never a good idea to show them how the lives of those they loved and left behind unfold after they are gone!' Daisy said, rolling her eyes.

Loretta hunhed and crossed her arms, 'I didn't know she was going to see THAT...'.

Daisy sighed, 'You are of no use,' as Loretta muttered something about being bothered on her precious day off. Daisy pointed at Loretta, 'Serves you right that you're going to take my shift now. I'm going to go find Lanie and talk some sense into her. I hope she delves head first into work or has some quality downtime to alleviate the pain.' She had seen lesser things derail good angels before.

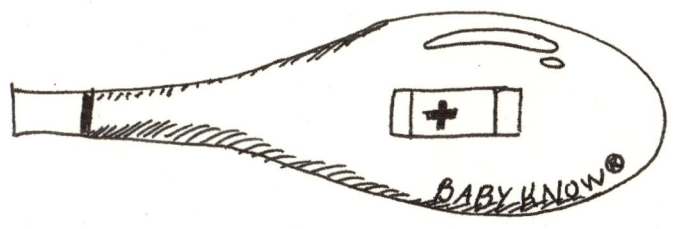

19. She had seen lesser things derail good angels before.

***

Lanie let the sand escape her fingers. She gathered another handful and let it aimlessly sieve through again as she listened to the deep green sea sing her swishing lullabies.

It was her day off and she could cry if she wanted to. In the dimension that she wanted to.

She realised now that she had waited too long. She should have done something when she had first seen the paramedic, Alice, kissing Peter as he was leaving his apartment one Earth week ago.

Except she didn't know what she should or could have done. She was an angel, she had no part in human lives except protecting them. She had diligently thrown herself into work and saving beings in various dimensions so that they could have a happy life. She had tried conning herself into believing that this was all she needed - to be good, to help others - in order to be happy.

And now it was too late.

Lanie squeezed her eyes shut. It hurt to remember.

The horror of seeing the paramedic's ecstatic face at the tiny blue cross on a white pregnancy stick came flooding back.

Peter and Alice were going to have a child.

Lanie remembered, how she had felt a hot poker of regret and pain twist somewhere in her solar plexus that had nearly made her double over.

She had never had a chance with Peter and it broke her heart.

Surprisingly, even after one Earth week in her new job with all the re-balancing and angelic calm on tap, she still had a heart that could be broken.

At the Watchers' station, Lanie had prayed there would be a distress call. About anything. Anywhere.

Instead, reality had proceeded like it didn't care.

Her hands had formed fists. She wanted to throw something, anything at the offending screen.

Instead, she had warped while thinking of somewhere calming and nice.

Now, here she was.

A speck on an abandoned tropical beach. Lanie wiped her tears away. All the saves in all the universes were of no help. The loss of someone she had never had but had cared about deeply twisted the dull blade of regret in her heart.

She was the one who had saved him.

For someone else. Peter was alive, but in love with somebody else. And he had a family now. With that somebody else.

That's all that mattered.

So why did she feel like this? Like someone had ripped a hole in her chest and her soul was being sucked out every time she thought about having to be without him. For all eternity, as it happened. Literally.

Had she met him before she died, maybe things would have worked out different.

'Honey, you would still have died. You would not have been more careful when doing a good deed because of meeting him or being with him.' Daisy fluttered her blue wings before she folded them and plopped down on the sand next to Lanie.

Lanie wiped her eyes quickly, 'I didn't know fairies could read minds.'

'Oh, honey, we can do a lot more than we let on,' Daisy sighed, as she dragged off her ballet flats and wriggled her pink-tipped toes in the sand, 'but in this instance, I didn't need to read your mind. Your deeds and face speak volumes.'

Lanie shrugged, 'So I'm transparent. Since I have signed up until forever, then I'm somehow guessing forever is not how long I will feel this bad. If you've come to tell me that I will forget and heal and all those other clichés they say about broken hearts, then save it. I already know. And I'm dealing with it in my own way.'

Daisy took a good look at Lanie. She hadn't seen her looking this drawn and this down...well...ever. She had seen angels cry, of course, mostly over lost charges. It happened.

She guessed that this here - angels feeling emotional about their former life - was why the Agency didn't have a lot of female angels. Well, former females who retained their form. Angels were angels. Females tended to be more prone to keep watching over their former family and loved ones, keeping them safe. Daisy understood perfectly why the Boss preferred to recruit orphans without attachments across dimensions.

It was time for the truth to help, 'Honey, you will not be able to forget, if you keep watching him, you know. And in the years to come, as you will see him grow old and frail, you will realise you cannot save him from dying and it will increase your pain of loss, not make it smaller. You will start begging the Boss to offer him the guardian angel deal and he will say no. Because very, very rarely does it happen that two of the same kin or two lovers are both guardian material.' *Sometimes, the pain of loss made very good guardian angels.* 'You have to admit that a continued romance on the job would be very distracting. It never leads to anything good. If we had got both Romeo and Juliet, it would not have ended well for anyone. Again.'

Lanie wiped her face again, her eyes gleaming red. She noticed that the back of her hand was getting shiny. Must be the peculiarities of this dimension. 'So, what are you suggesting? To go cold turkey? Leave it be permanently? Never see him again?' Lanie sniffed.

'It would be better that way,' Daisy hugged the weeping angel.

For a while they sat in silence.

Daisy was pleased.

Grieving angel - located.

Some sense - talked into.

Concepts - grasped. Hopefully soon also implemented.

Not bad for an hour's worth of work.

The fairy stretched her foot to touch the sapphire water, 'So, Heaven? Nice choice for an impromptu zen vacation spot.'

Lanie sniffed again, 'Is there no other way?'

Oh, Great Goddess! She was going to have to explain a lot more... 'Well, of course there are other ways,' Daisy said with a sigh, 'but you're not going to like them.'

A brief flicker of hope died in Lanie's eyes and her face fell again, 'Tell me anyway.'

So the fairy did. About how originally, the Boss had erased the memories of angels but they had started remembering anyway in their sleep and thought they were going crazy. By the time they dared ask questions the lifespan of their loved ones and family had passed in whatever dimension they had been from and some then really did go crazy from grief because they never could say goodbye and had to be decommissioned. Some had died from grief or started acting like they had a death-wish. Angel mortality rates had spiked mostly because they had become careless and were not found in time to be resurrected.

She told Lanie how the Agency had then tried to do the exact opposite - to let those who wanted to watch over their friends and family do so and how some angels had wasted away, trying to protect their families from every kind of danger. As a result they had been too distracted and had failed to save someone pretty important without whom the future of that someone's dimension could have been somewhat different. Good different.

By the time Daisy reached the prohibition part of her tale – how it came to be that for a time, angels were prohibited from returning to their former dimension and the result of that experiment, she was glad to see Lanie had stopped crying. *Yep, elaborating on the other horrible options usually put everything into perspective and helped convince that no contact was the best way.*

Daisy didn't feel the need to point out the ultimate alternative - Lanie becoming human again and fighting for her love. An orphan herself, this girl would never split up a family.

Lanie didn't know which was worse, knowing and remembering that she had met and fallen in love with Peter while never being able to go back to Earth or having the memories of him and all of her previous life erased. The other options Loretta had told her about seemed even crueler than the freedom of choice that she had now.

Some choice.

The Watcher had made it abundantly clear.

No more watching over Peter.

Ever.

If they thought this was going to make her forget, they thought wrong.

Eternity with a broken heart was going to be insufferable.

She could and doubtlessly would go head over heels into work again. Taking more trying cases in harsher dimensions than her current track record to the Magic Kingdom, the Enchanted dimension, Earth and other soft spots. She had even picked Heaven for a vacation.

No more. She needed to toughen up. That was the only way.

She needed to be somewhere that would be a complete opposite to...well...here, for starters. The sooner the better. In fact, the rest of her day off would be better spent forgetting and engaging in heroic antics. *Anything was better than pitying herself on a beach in Heaven.*

Daisy looked up and saw a bright red cocoon forming around Lanie. *Oh no, no, no, no. Pink-pager-Lanie with her pink cocoon was no more. Red meant only one thing. Where was this desperate soul off to?*

As the cocoon locked her in, Lanie told it the destination.

'Straight to Hel.' She had just lived her worst fear - falling in love and being rejected by someone who never even knew she existed. She had nothing left to fear.

The fairy scrambled to her feet. *This was not good. Lanie had never been properly prepped for travel in that dimension!*

In Hel, all your worst fears and nightmares came true. Worse, you became what you feared or loathed. No one dared attempt regular rescues there. Hence, all the horror stories about there being no redemption and no way back, especially in Earth religions and mythology, although even religion and mythology paled in comparison with the real thing. Inexperienced angels were not allowed there unaccompanied. The few that went usually never came back. That's why they had a Helreginne on a permanent post.

Correction - had a Helreginne. There was currently a vacancy.

Daisy was close to swearing.

Perturbed, the waves of the Heavenly ocean turned magenta.

Lanie was so not ready for where she had just gone. Out of all the hell dimensions, she had to pick Hel, the Norse mythological underworld!

The fairy needed back up to extract her.

Time to bring in the big guns. She parallel-paged both Gabriel and Victor with an S.O.S. Her next duty was to inform the Boss.

***

In the silence of the Boss' empty office a smart phone clearly pinged.

'Damnation,' said the office. Dust settled on the glass surface of the desk.

An S.O.S. from Daisy flashed crimson across it.

What now?

'Lanie. Gone to Hel over Peter.'

Double damnation. It looked like Peter had meant more to Lanie than any of them could have predicted.

Hel was one heck of a sticky situation to extract her from. Possibly a mission impossible. The quicker they found and saved Lanie, the better.

The Boss decided to send in reinforcements, himself included.

53. Breathe

Charlotte

On the hotel radio, Taylor Swift was complaining how she cannot breathe without someone but she has to.[79] Feeling slightly lost, Charlotte understood exactly how Taylor felt. After the stunt she had pulled on arrival, Victor had just disappeared on her as if he had never existed and it hurt.

Feeling tears starting to burn, Charlotte was very much aware of how foolish she'd been.

Since he had refused to tell her what he had said to her back on the farm, in the friendly banter of them checking into the hotel - *adjoining, but separate rooms, thank you!* - she had tried to get the hotel owner to translate the bits she had remembered. It turned out that 'Tuoi occhi sono come le stelle' meant 'Your eyes are like the stars'. She didn't remember the rest, but this was plenty. Charlotte had blushed when the lady who owned the hotel had told her what Victor had meant. *Her ruggedy biker fancied her and had from the very beginning!*

She had been so certain...and yet never had she been so misled.

On the evening of their arrival, Charlotte had excused herself and disappeared into the bathroom they shared, locking the door behind her like any proper Southern belle would. When she had appeared in Victor's bedroom in her nightgown - *not like any proper Souther belle* - she had propped up the door-jamb for courage and thought *Ravish me, ravish me now, before I lose my nerve.* Victor had taken one look and said 'If you're planning to go out in that dress, may I suggest a shawl, the nights are cold here.'

Charlotte's cheeks had burnt in shame. *Her one and only attempt at seducing a guy and he didn't even notice.*

He couldn't have NOT noticed. The nightie had been pink with lace and barely covered her privates. Unless this was how girls here went out to party?!?! Nooo...

It had to be the worst case scenario. He had noticed and had turned her down. Cold.

Why had he turned her down? Was her bad case of hero worship so unattractive?

Being a hot do-good biker he had probably rescued a few silly girls. He had certainly rescued her and for that she would be forever grateful. Without Victor egging her on, she would still be a farmhand, doing two people's worth of work and not pursuing her dreams in Florence.

Had she led him on too long and he had simply grown tired of waiting for her to reciprocate?

Had she said anything wrong? Done anything wrong?

Why had he evaporated?

When she had come out of the bathroom, mortified, dressed in jeans and a t-shirt, he and his stuff were gone. Simply gone. No note, no nothing.

That had been two days ago.

Charlotte remembered the times Victor had vanished as if into thin air at Aunt Mae's. He would turn a corner and when she had gone to fetch him seconds later he was nowhere to be seen. Fifteen minutes later he would be sitting on the porch, cleaning his helmet as if he'd always been there. She had wandered about those disappearances and briefly also about her sanity, but since he had always come back, she hadn't worried much about either.

Two days was much, much, much longer than 15 minutes.

Initially, she had thought he had just cleared off to find himself a different hotel and to give her and her embarrassment some space.

Hotels were on every corner here. It didn't take two days to find another one.

Even after factoring in some drinking time to ease the memory of a girl throwing herself at him.

The next morning, he was still nowhere to be seen. Feeling foolish, Charlotte had given him a day to come around. Especially since his precious bike was still parked outside her hotel.

When she had enquired with the hotel owner, the lady didn't remember him at all. *They had arrived together the previous day, how could she not have noticed!*

Now it had been two days and Victor was nowhere to be

found. The bike's presence in the street down below was no longer comforting.

Maybe something had happened to him?

At first, the bike had given her hope he would come back. Now she was worried. He would never have travelled anywhere without it. He had even brought it to Italy with him.

If the bike was still here but he was not and something had happened to him, then she needed to start making calls.

Hospitals. Police stations. The morgue.

Charlotte shuddered. *God, please let him not be dead. Maimed, injured, in Italian jail, but please not dead. She couldn't handle dead.*

Not him.

Picking up the ancient black analogue phone receiver, she started dialling the local police and stopped.

Charlotte realised she didn't know Victor's last name. She had never seen his passport.

He had never given her his last name and she had never bothered to ask. How selfish of her.

Now what?

There wasn't much she could do except wait.

Wait and hope.

What if he had simply done what he had promised - got her to Italy and after her mortifying display of affection had simply elected to leave? She was no one to him. A girl he had rescued once.

What if he never came back? Then she had a choice to make: try to get by in the city of her dreams or go back to the States with her tail between her legs.

On the air, Taylor was still having difficulties breathing. So was Charlotte.

54. *When Harry Really Met Sally*[80]
Sally

Sally deposited herself onto a chair by the bar and promptly started shredding a napkin.

'Do you know how embarrassing it is for a girl to go out by herself in New York on a Friday night?' she hissed at her bag.

'Then order yourself a drink and keep looking at the door. It's not like you have to pretend you're waiting for someone, you dumb-ass, you are actually waiting for someone,' the bag hissed back.

Ignoring the dumb-ass comment, after all, she couldn't get mad at a frog calling her names, could she, Sally ordered a club soda from the bar-tender who smiled warmly and winked at someone behind her but rushed to fill her order nevertheless.

Sally glanced over her shoulder. There was nobody there.

The bar-tender had smiled and winked at her?

Something strange was going on. First the fawning in the pizzeria, then the whistles from the construction workers on the way here, now the flirting barkeep.

'Sally, is that you?' Harry stared at her with his mouth open as the bar-tender gingerly put Sally's drink before her and retreated from competition.

Sally raised her eyebrows. *They had known each other since childhood and the dude had the audacity not to recognise her? What was the world coming to?*

'You're so...you're so....thin,' Harry blurted out as he sat down.

Sally sat up and smiled widely, 'Really?'

Harry leaned into the bar next to her and motioned at the bar-tender, 'Teddy, the usual and whatever the lady's having next is on me.'

'White wine, please,' Sally chirped. It was time to celebrate and one glass would give her plenty of buzz after abstaining from alcohol as per the frog's orders for two weeks.

Harry looked at her. Really looked at her. 'I almost didn't recognise you. Come on, give us a twirl.'

Lucy Hale was assuring everyone she would run this town on the radio[81].

Sally huffed, 'No. I'm not a tutu-wearing bimbette.'

'Aw, come on, Sally, you know you want to,' Harry's eyes glinted mischievously behind his horn-rimmed spectacles.

The bar-tender put Harry's beer before him and retreated to serve the other customers. The bar was filling up.

Sally let out a snort, but hopped off her chair. Harry took her hand and twirled her.

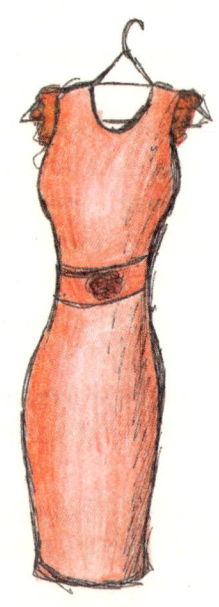

20. 'IF YOU DON'T LIKE WHAT YOU'RE SEEING, LOOK ELSEWHERE'

She was so surprised at his touch she would have keeled over if he hadn't steadied her. His hand felt awfully hot through the thin fabric of her dress.

'Easy, there,' he gently helped her sit back down. Harry let go of her hand and reached for his beer. 'Damn, woman, where are all your voluptuous curves? You almost look like one of them stick insects that look starved and go crazy from it.' He took a sip and nudged her wine closer at her, 'Here, have some calories, before you disappear altogether.'

On the radio, Katy Perry was singing how in another life she would be his girl and how all this money couldn't buy her a time machine.[82]

The magic of Harry's initial appreciation shattered, Sally felt her good mood disappear. 'Well, if you don't like what you see, you can find someone else to talk to,' she shot back and turned her back to him for good measure.

In her purse, Victor was shaking his head between his paws. *All that effort and here she goes with that mouth, again.*

'Sally, all I meant was you look different...less curvy, and I hope you did this for you, not because of what some dumb-ass guy said.' There had been plenty of those in school and it plagued him that he had been a puny weakling back then, sprouting up only in military service, and had not been able to defend her. Hell, he hadn't even tried defending her. She had grown up with constant mockery about her size. And now he was doing it too, except in reverse.

She turned back, looking half angry and half surprised, 'Why would you ever think I would do any of this,' she motioned at herself, 'for a guy?!?'

Harry looked uncertain, 'Well, girls usually do, don't they? I'm not saying it's right, I'm just saying it happens.'

Harry did have a point. When she'd been tortured in her teens by the kids at school, hell, by kids and sometimes even grownups anywhere, even getting fatso comments from lowly construction workers, she had always secretly thought she'd show them. All of them.

'Well, I didn't do this for a guy. I did this for me.' Because of a goading frog, who was admittedly a guy, but she was the one who had done all the heavy lifting - she was the one who had exercised, shopped 'til she dropped and had learnt how to eat healthily.

Sally put her right hand on her hip, trying to steady herself with toes that barely reached the floor, gave up and hopped off the stool instead, 'I did this because of me, so that I,' she jabbed her finger at Harry's chest, 'could have a better quality of life, look better,' another jab found a muscle, so she jabbed elsewhere,

'Feel better,' another jab found another rock-hard muscle, which fascinated Sally,

'And let' - jab,

'Me' - jab,

'Tell'- jab

'You'- since the last jab also found rock-hard muscle, Sally was briefly distracted by how well built Harry was under all that floppy flannel, so she finished with 'this feels pretty awesome.'

Sally was a little breathless from all that jabbing and all of a sudden too close to Harry's baby blue eyes. For the first time since she knew him she noticed how his black rimmed glasses made him look a little bit like Clark Kent. She sat back too quickly, making her chair teeter, 'Uh, I mean I look and feel awesome.'

Harry steadied her chair with his hand, brushing Sally's hip, which made her blush, 'Yes, yes you do,' he said quietly.

On the radio, someone was belting out something about how she didn't want to mess this thing up and how giving it a little time would bring them closer to the love they want to find.[83] The frog was mentally doing a happy dance since one of his legs was stuck behind a lip gloss tube and he was trying to disentangle the other one from Sally's keys. *Did she have to bring the tiniest bag imaginable?*

In the dimension where the hardest kind of criminal in New York was a thug from Jersey, a trio of wannabe Sopranos ambled into the bar.

Thugs from Jersey.

The point-man shoved a cigar into the pit of ginger scruff under his gold-rimmed sunglasses and told the bar-tender to turn that goddamn hick music off.

The bar-tender looked at Harry and the other regulars, 'Any of you object to my choice of easy listening music?' The regulars glared at the trio. 'If you don't like the music, I doubt you're going to like the service, so I suggest you go find yourself a sports bar down the street,' the bar-tender kindly offered.

The trio shut up and scanned the bar in search of an easy target.

'Lookie, what we have here, a princess and a frog,' the eldest of the goaders, with stubble and a golden tooth turned to Harry, then scanned Sally from head to toe, harrumphed appreciatively and offered, 'Princess, why don't you stop hanging around with losers and join us for a drink.'

Sally didn't mind getting attention from people she liked. This kind of attention she was not comfortable with. To avoid an unpleasant situation, she decided to be polite, 'No, thanks.'

The baldest of the trio didn't get the hint, 'Come on, honey, you're way too pretty to be drinking with him.'

Harry, who had stayed out of the conversation so far, turned his back on Sally, sheltering her from the trio, 'Gentlemen, I believe, the lady said no.'

The point-man who was also the shortest of the three sauntered over to Harry, coming up to a little higher than Harry's navel and smiled evilly, 'Got a problem, four-eyes?'

Sally saw the situation turning ugly in seconds. From the corner of her eye she saw the bar-tender picking up his phone and the other regulars clearing the scene for a potential bar brawl.

Harry took off his glasses and casually handed them to the bar-tender who slipped them in his cash drawer. Harry lowered himself to shorty, shielding his throat and enunciated, 'I'm repeating, in case you didn't hear from way down there, the lady doesn't want a drink, so I suggest you do as the kind bar-tender suggested and find yourself another bar.'

'Oh yeah? Well, why,' the shorty jabbed his finger into Harry's chest, 'don't'- jab, 'you' - weaker jab, 'make me....?' the shorty finished tentatively. Jabbing Harry's chest had not given him confidence his friends would be able to take this one down as easily as they originally thought. Floppy flannel was hiding a toned body. With the four-eyes' readiness to brawl shorty wouldn't put it past this one to win a bar fight if it came to it. He wouldn't put it past him to be trained in martial arts.

The frog in the purse was praying for the fight to break out so Harry, who was ex-military and had a black belt, would defend Sally and she could appreciate it and they would all live happily ever after.

Sally went scarlet with anger. She hopped off her chair and towered over the shorty, 'Listen, shorty, I'm not some damsel in distress who needs someone else to fight her fights. Not interested,' she told the shorty, 'not interested' she told the dude with the golden tooth, 'and hell no, not interested,' she told the balding dude. 'So, please, buzz off, why don't you, so we can all enjoy the rest of the night.'

Victor shook his head. *He knew it, but did it have to be the other way around?* Princess Charming defending her boy. Well, he guessed she couldn't help herself. Now there was no helping the brawl as the trio would not let a woman stepping in go unpunished, so Harry would have to fight for her. Who cares how they got to Harry defending Sally, as long as they got there. The frog rubbed its paws together in delight.

A swarm of 20 college kids flooded the bar and laughing merrily, pushed through to the till engulfing the trio and Sally, ignorant of the tension. The trio considered this a good time to retreat from public humiliation and exited before the door closed.

Sally sat back down and took a big gulp of her wine.

'Sally,' at her name, she faced Harry, ready to royally accept the due gratitude, only to be met by Harry so red he was near apoplectic, 'don't you EVER do something as STUPID as that ever again. EVER. You hear me?' Harry took her by her shoulders.

Taken aback by an assault instead of gratitude, Sally squeaked, 'Let go of me, you brute!'

Harry realised she was shaking like a leaf and he was the one doing the shaking. He let go and barely caught her as she stumbled on her stilettos. 'I'm sorry, you just scared me half to death. Don't you know you should not argue with guys that are packing?'

Sally was about to give him a few choice words about his behaviour, when she registered what he had said, 'Packing? You mean they had guns?'

Harry sighed and sat back down, making sure she was perched steadily on her chair, 'Yes, you idiot girl, they had guns, so you picking a fight with them was a dumb move.'

'You just called me dumb twice, thank you very much,' she huffed, picking up her purse and squeezing the frog mercilessly and on purpose in the process. *If she couldn't take it out on Harry or the trio, she could pass some pain along to the reason for her being here in the first place.* 'Well, I certainly hope you enjoy the rest of the night, I'm leaving!' And to think she was about to forgive him for acting like a Neanderthal because he had been scared for her. Because he cared what could have happened to her. *As if. He just thought she was stupid. Stupid and reckless and to the hell with him.*

Sally ignored Harry's pleading looks, pointedly detached his hand from her person as if it was a nasty insect and stormed out, as quickly as her high heels allowed it.

Harry signalled for the bar-tender to get his specs, threw some money on the bar for both their drinks and followed her.

'Going out was a stupid idea, a moronic one, actually, and because of you I made a complete and utter fool of myself,' Sally hissed into her purse, ignoring the passers-by.

Victor looked at her with reproach, not the least for squashing him, but more at her idiocy, 'He stood up for you. The guys had guns. He was afraid you would get shot. What part of this is insulting to you?'

Sally stopped, 'The part where he called me an idiot - twice!'

The frog sighed, 'For the sake of accuracy he called you idiot once, dumb after that, and before he called your actions stupid. But do tell, what do you call a girl who shows no gratitude for being rescued and doesn't even let the guy explain or apologise for things said not in anger, not to insult her, but when the guy is afraid she could have died?'

Sally sat on the empty bench at the bus stop. At this hour, no one was waiting for a bus. From afar she saw Harry exiting the bar and looking around. Probably for her.

The frog peeked over the edge of the purse, 'See, he's coming to find you, to tell you he's sorry he called you names. Sally, he's a good guy. You know he's a good guy!' Victor felt he was talking to a five-year old. *Sometimes the smartest people were the dumbest when it came to seeing things clearly.*

'I know,' Sally said, the fight having gone out of her completely as she saw the trio with guns creeping after Harry from the shadows. By the looks of it they hadn't gotten far and were looking for revenge.

'Sally, I think it's time to call the police,' Victor the frog suggested.

55. SOS
Gabriel

Unable to detect the whereabouts of the Boss, Gabriel was walking back down the white marble staircase to the Watchers' station. He had to take Grace back to Della's.

As she waved at him, smiling, all of their smart phones started beeping.

Daisy had paged all of them with an SOS emergency.

That was a first.

Never in his nearly 900 years had Gabriel had an SOS from any Watcher.

One of their own was in trouble.

This trumped anything else he had going on. Gabriel's jaw tightened.

He needed to get to wherever Daisy was as soon as possible to get instructions. There weren't a lot of guardians to go around, so whenever one of them was in over their head, the others had to help out. He knew the others would do the same for him anytime.

'You,' Gabriel pointed at Grace, 'stay here, and you' he pointed at Jack, 'man the screens.'

The dog barked. Grace felt like doing the same, but thought her quirky humour might not be appreciated, judging by the tight line Gabriel's lips were forming.

Gabriel didn't want to leave Grace unattended. Out of all those present, he had to trust the pixie, 'Loretta...'

'What did I do? It wasn't my fault...' the pixie whinged.

Silencing her with his hand, Gabriel ignored her lament, '... do whatever you need to do to make sure Grace is safe.'

The pixie swore her curses, unhappy to be left out of the save.

Gabriel opened a portal to Daisy's location.

Heaven.

That peaceful dimension should not warrant an SOS.

He had a bad feeling about this.

***

Lanie appeared somewhere hot and humid and instantly smelled the sulphuric acid.

There were screams. There was thick smoke. There was a whiff of burnt flesh that she didn't think came from a barbecue.

It was becoming increasingly difficult to breathe.

She was still suspended above ground but felt her head being hunched low between her shoulders. Around, she only saw hairy stripey yellow-black trees.

Lanie tried flexing her fingers and the two trees in front of her swayed violently. Her vision was getting foggy and everything looked smudged. Probably from all the crying she had done before.

She tried swaying on her feet and the two trees behind her swayed back and forth, propelling her whole body with them. Trying to dodge the other trees that had encircled her, Lanie thought she saw things happening behind her that she couldn't possibly have seen.

Great, she had eyes at the back of her head now.

Lanie tried shouting 'Hello' in this mock miniature waspish wood-grove, but somehow, her tongue felt weird and she only heard clacking and hissing.

She tried lifting her hands to her face. The two trees in front of her lifted off and hurtled towards her. She squinted to avoid being poked in the eye by the tree roots.

That's when she realised what she was looking at.

Not roots. Pincers.

She wriggled her fingers again. The pincers that seemed to have some shiny gunk all over them, rotated.

The trees were not trees. They were legs.

Her legs. All eight of them.

In her childhood, she had been deathly afraid of spiders. It was a hell of a joke, her turning into a giant tarantula in Hel.

She didn't like it, she didn't like it one bit.

Lanie tried thinking herself back to the Agency.

It wasn't working. The cocoon refused to form.

Lanie tried to look for her wrist watch to send an S.O.S. to the Watchers.

No wrists. No watch.

Tarantulas have no watches.

Adjusting to her new body, Lanie tried looking around her zillion legs, to see if the watch had somehow fallen down on the ground.

Below, she saw only black lava and ashes. No pink pager as Loretta still called the gizmo.

Oh boy.

Her only hope was that someone would come looking for her. The problem was, how were they ever going to recognise her?

21. Tarantulas have no watches.

***

Gabriel materialised by Daisy's side on the shore of Heaven in three seconds flat. Victor and a few more guardians popped up next. All Daisy had to say was, 'Lanie's on a bender, she just went to Hel. Without ANY instructions.'

This elicited a collective groan.

'Out of all the dimensions she had to pick Hel.' Victor swore. 'Am I assuming correctly that we didn't have time to assess her fears, hates and pet peeves properly during the few weeks she's been employed?'

Daisy nodded.

Victor cursed. 'So, she doesn't even know that she might never come back?'

Daisy nodded again.

More curses followed, interrupted by the fairy's cut-throat gesture.

'We don't have a lot of time to find her. Well, technically we do since time snakes in Hel three times slower than at the Agency - it's part of the punishment - but you know what I mean. Without knowing what she's doing, Lanie could perish there in a matter of minutes,' Daisy reminded them. 'Although I so hope she holds on until we find her,' she chimed.

Fairies. Optimistic in the face of evidence to the contrary.

'So, has everyone checked their worst fears at the door as per agreed protocol?' Gabriel enquired gravely, adjusting the back strap of his sword.

Gabriel knew his worst fear. Ever since the mercy kill of that Saracen boy in 1147 Gabriel's worst fear was to senselessly lose a life, to lose a charge when he could do everything possible to save them. That was why he had to be the best, facing his fear one day at a time, one charge at a time. In Hel, his fear would be tested in more ways than one. For them all to survive long enough to find Lanie, he had to look out for each and every one of the rescue team, just like they would look out for him. Knowing his fear, he had had 900 years to find ways to counter it and not freeze and die even when sorely tempted.

Victor's mouth twitched as he clenched his jaw. He had never been to Hel. Every other imaginable dimension of avarice - sure. The one where he would have had to deal with his principal fear - nope. His worst fear was that he didn't deserve to be a guardian. In Hel, he could hallucinate that he was driving himself and Grace into that tree. The Boss had explained to him that as long as he didn't do that on purpose, they would have offered him the atoning job. He would still have been recruited as a guardian angel, even if he had destroyed someone's life besides his own. Daisy had told him that the best way to keep his fear at bay was to simply BE the best version of a guardian angel he could think of. Victor briefly thought whether that would be the goody-two-shoes version Gabriel projected and everyone had come to expect as a standard or whether he could be the slayer he had enjoyed being in all the dangerous dimensions. Hel and time would tell.

The nods and twitches from all those assembled was a good enough check for Gabriel, 'We split up. I'll take the Northern corner, Daisy, you take the East, Victor the South, the rest of you take the Western corner.'

'The Boss said she'd take the Western corner,' Daisy said.

'He,' Gabriel and Victor said in unison and got waved off.

'How will we recognise Lanie down there?' Victor asked.

'Easy, you can spot her by her tears. The tears of angels shine like mother-of-pearl in all the Heavens and Hells. Good luck, boys,' Daisy said, hoping they wouldn't need to call on the Goddess of Luck. She wasn't equipped for Hel either. Nobody really was.

With that parting shot they all went to Hel to hopefully bring back an angel.

56. Babysitting Duty
Grace

After Gabriel disappeared from the Watchers' station to save Lanie, Loretta scratched behind her left ear. Jack and Grace were looking at her with the exact same faithful and trusting expression.

Babysitting duty.

Since in the Boss' absence Gabriel was in charge, she had no choice but to obey. 'Whatever you need to do' meant anything, right? As much as she liked the girl, Loretta had qualms about Grace's humanity being left intact after staying at the Agency much longer. She might not want to leave somewhere there was no hunger, no pain, no emotions, just peace. Grace had befriended more beings in two hours than Loretta had had in a year.

It was her first day off in six Agency months and she was stuck at work, babysitting!

Loretta uttered a few pixie curses, trying not to make them culprit-specific, lest she have to un-grow a nose or an extra body part later.

Where could she stick a living breathing human being where time passed quicker? Hel was not an option. Gaia, the second Earth would just be too confusing.

Time always passed quicker when one was having fun...

The only suitable 'whatever' option was Valhalla. Mortals were always welcome, protected and even occasionally let out. Depending on what sorts of fun Grace happened to witness there, they could always opt to erase her memories later.

Loretta rubbed her hands together. If she couldn't have fun mixing poisons, spending a few hours at Valhalla was the next best thing on her day off. 'Master Jack, you have the controls,' Loretta said, grabbed Grace unceremoniously by the arm and transported them for some fun and frolicking, texting Gabriel on the go.

When entering Valhalla, Loretta spotted the former owner of now Lanie's pink pager, still bravely drinking Oblivion after Oblivion. No one bothered this Knight in Shining Armour since everyone assumed it was a rescue gone bad. Loretta knew better. The rescue had gone perfectly. So perfectly in fact that the Knight had fallen head over heels in love with a girl who didn't return his feelings because she was already betrothed to someone else. If anyone had looked properly, they would have noticed the Knight casting envious glances at any couple cuddling up.

Pity. He had been their last Knight in Shining Armour.

At the bar, Grace eyed the Valkyries and stage whispered, 'Do I have to wear what they are wearing to fit in here? Because I totally would.'

Loretta smiled. *Well, the day wasn't a total loss. This one was a keeper.* She understood why Gabriel went out of his way to guard her. Grace didn't need props to fit in. In less than half an hour, she knew all the regulars, having half-dragged Loretta around from party to party, making the pixie introduce her.

'Don't drink anything on that menu,' Loretta pointed at the ancient manuscript taken down in red, 'But it's fairly safe to have the top three on that one,' she pointed at an A4 printout with ten names on it. 'You can start a tab and pay it whenever it suits you in the future. Or make a wager with the bar keep and if you win, he'll waive the payment altogether.'

'Has anyone ever bested him?' Grace asked.

'Some,' Loretta said cryptically and signalled to the bar keep for her usual drink.

Sipping on Dragon's Milk, Valhalla's version of a White Russian, Grace wasn't sure the milk in the drink had come from a cow. Grace decided to take advantage of the pixie's good mood and braved a question she had been dying to ask. 'Loretta...'

'Hunh?' the pixie was chewing on a celery from what looked like a Bloody Mary.

'Are guardian angels allowed to date?' Grace asked, taking another sip.

'Each other or cross-species?' the pixie specified.

Cross-species? That was news to Grace. 'Both,' she said. *More information couldn't hurt.*

'Well, I've partaken in a few cross-species entanglements myself... Some species are more compatible than others,' Loretta pursed her lips, looking at one of her former admirers. *Now that had been fun. Short-lived, but fun.* 'Gnomes and pixies are completely incompatible species on the account of similar foul characters. Epic fights.' *Hers most certainly had been.* Loretta didn't much care for regular escapes from an axe-aficionado with legendary fits of jealousy. 'The Agency even has guidance notes on which species play well together and which ones don't, it reads a little bit like one of your Star sign horoscope thingies, but it's roughly accurate.'

'Do you mean angels are allowed to date each other, same species or different?'

'If they find the time!' Loretta laughed.

'Well, you did...' Grace said slyly.

'Two dates in one Agency year does not a relationship make. Come to think of it, the rarity of spending time together had been the essence of our epic fights,' Loretta said.

Grace giggled. She took another sip for courage and a deep breath and only then asked, 'Is Gabriel seeing anyone?'

'Oh, so you have the hots for Gabriel?' Loretta concluded.

Grace blushed, 'Well...I doubt it would work out if one is human and the other an immortal angel...' she said.

'True, true, but he used to be human, so you have two options, really. One, you become a guardian or two, he becomes human again,' Loretta said, casting a wandering eye over the crowd.

'Is that even possible? Becoming human again?'

Loretta shrugged, 'Can't see why not. Humans can become angelic. Who says angels can't choose to be human again. No rule against that.'

Except they would stop serving as guardian angels. 'Has any angel ever given up his calling for...love?' Grace asked.

Loretta sighed. *Babysitting duty was worse than a trip to Hel. How did they end up from good, clean fun to discussing feelings and love and mushy emotions?!? And in Valhalla, out of all places.* 'Listen, sometimes they can. Very, very rarely. Gabriel, in all the hundreds of years that I've known him, has not fallen for anyone, has not had relations with fellow guardians, humans or cross-species and is generally ultra-dedicated to the cause he has promised to serve.'

Grace nodded. *Considering how quickly he transitioned back from friendly to distant stranger, all her tries at... anything...would probably be doomed to fail. She had to live with the knowledge that Gabriel was not interested in her. He was very good at what he did. Dedication had to count for something. The fact that Gabriel had not had 'relations' as Loretta had put it with anyone for a very long time was a small consolation.* Grace knew she was selfish to even think about derailing a guardian angel.

From the girl's silence Loretta gathered that the 'having relations with Gabriel' issue was now moot for good and took pity on her, 'Here, down this,' she put half of her remaining drink in front of Grace and then we can go play games.'

'Games?' Grace said, coughing. Whatever Loretta was having was definitely NOT a Bloody Mary. It smelled like passion fruit and tasted like kerosene.

'We can start with darts...' the pixie said, pointing at the far corner of the room where kilted warriors were keeping score while beings of all shapes, sizes and colours were lining up to try their hand at precision after a few drinks.

Grace giggled. 'Is this Valhalla's version of a breathalyser?'

The pixie snorted. *Good point.*

A few minutes later, Loretta's watch pinged and she realised she was going to have to leave Grace unattended.

Apparently, the Boss had decided She needed all the experienced guardians to help save Lanie. That also meant the Watchers. Both of them. An emergency topped babysitting duty any time. Also, the Boss' instruction trumped Gabriel's. Besides, the only danger Grace faced in Valhalla was facing the wrath of some alien warriors who she was beating at darts and Loretta was pretty sure that if push came to shove, most of the bar would step in to protect the girl. In Valhalla, for Grace hours would fly by like minutes.

Loretta waved at the girl and pointed in the direction of the bathroom. Once in there, the pixie evaporated.

Tristan was leaning on the bar in his usual seat, waiting for Isolde. His brothers in arms often joked that he always seemed to be waiting for Isolde. Tristan didn't mind their jabs. He loved Isolde, she had things to do, people to care for and as a warrior he was used to not being able to reach for his woman every minute he wanted to.

Waiting for her was his favourite part of the day. Because in the end, what mattered most was how Isolde's eyes sparkled when she arrived, when she asked him about his day and she told him about hers. She was definitely worth waiting for. Besides, it left him with enough time to get to know his warriors and all the other regulars better.

At the moment he was observing the new girl Loretta had brought along.

Grace.

Tristan was fascinated by the ease with which the girl had taken to this hardened and glorified resting place of the dead and the dying. Like a duck to water. There she was, throwing darts while standing on one leg, leaning onto one of the unfamiliar extra-terrestrials for support, carefully avoiding the thorns. One-legged darts. Tristan smirked. He hoped some of the regulars didn't trick her into strip poker next.

The door to the bar blew open and a gust of wind swept through the place, ruffling kilts, clinking armour and knocking a few dwarfs on their backsides. Icy Northerlies wanted to play. Probably looking for their long-lost mistress again.

The girl lost her balance and a cheer erupted from the group.

She had lost the game.

Tristan couldn't wait to see what her penance was. He saw her hugging all of the players, who humbly stood, waiting their turn. As she hugged the last contestant, the wind almost knocked her backwards.

As the warriors started to prep the board for the next round, the girl went straight for the door, trying to close it shut. Next, Tristan saw her stop pushing at the door, smile and exit the bar.

As the door closed behind Grace, Tristan thought he saw her talking to an Indian-looking man under Glasir.[84] The golden leaves of the majestic tree stood utterly and completely still in the centre of a raging inferno of ice funnelling toward the skies.

57. Kill the Prince[85]
Lanie

In Hel, Lanie had watched the Little Mermaid murder her prince over and over again in his sleep. She wanted to scream at the daft girl to do it right, for once.

With horror, Lanie was realising that in arachnid form she was turning into someone she never thought she could be. A cruel and possibly vindictive know-it-all. Pretty much the antithesis of what she had been in real life. Seeing how easy it was for people to be cruel to the less fortunate whom she used to help at the soup kitchen, she had always feared that somehow, somewhere deep down inside, cruelty was also part of her.

Hang on, maybe the arachnid form had nothing to do with how malevolent she was feeling.

In life, she had been afraid of turning cruel.

Spiders had been her worst fear.

Lanie seemed to remember Loretta mentioning Hel in passing. What was it she had said? That the Hel dimension had no voluntary permanent residents and no permanent guardian because no one wanted to stay too long somewhere where all your worst fears came to life? The last ruler of Hel, their Helreginne had perished saving someone from their worst fear several Agency years ago.

Maybe Ariel's worst fear was killing her prince?

Lanie searched for possible truths in what was left of her logical brain that, as it were, was filling up with annoying single-minded thoughts of juicy appetising bugs. If she was turning into a tarantula for real, her freaky-legged body was probably getting hungry by now. If she was ever getting out of here, she had to use the wits she still had for the time left before she lost her humanity completely.

Ariel. She had to concentrate on the mermaid.

From what Lanie could remember, in Andersen's fairy-tale, on the ship which sailed the newlyweds to their honeymoon, the mermaid had come very close to killing her prince in his sleep. She had drawn the dagger that her sisters had procured from the sea witch. She just couldn't go through with it, jumped into the sea and became the wisp of the waves.

Maybe Ariel's worst fear was to give in to her wants and kill the prince?

Maybe she was regretting the decision she had made? Maybe deep down, she wished she had saved herself, not the prince?

She had drawn the dagger, after all. Which means there was a part of her that had wished to kill him so everything would return back to normal and she could forget she had ever met him. To be a mermaid again, to live free and be blissfully happy even if a bit more curious than usual for her kind.

Maybe her worst fear was to be given the chance again and to decide differently and that's why she was returning to that one split second where she had drawn the dagger over the unconscious body of her beloved?

If the mermaid's worst fear was to have given in to her wants and killed her love, then that was exactly what she was reliving now, with all the dire consequences. Over and over again.

Lanie thought how she could help. If she could help the mermaid, maybe she could also help herself?

Forgiveness.

The mermaid had to forgive herself for that awful, unforgivable split second when she had wanted to kill the man she loved.

This was the dimension of everyone's worst fears. All she had to do to escape was to test her theory and then deal with her own fear.

It never occurred to Lanie not to try help Ariel. A nagging thought did surface that she might be postponing dealing with her own fears, possibly until the point of no return. If she were no longer human, she wouldn't remember Peter. Thoughts of juicy bugs would fill her days. Lanie shook off the thought that turning into a spider could be one solution of getting over Peter.

The earth shattered around her stripy legs.

Right. She'd better move on.

Praying that telepathy by pictures worked outside of the Magic Kingdom as well, Lanie closed her dozen eyes and prepared to transmit the visual image of the solution into Ariel's tortured mind.

58. Love and Mortal Danger
Gabriel

Without Helreginne, who would have known her realm, it had taken them a full Hel week to find Lanie smack in the middle of it - in the Southern lava swamp bordering on the watery East.

Who knew that this city girl was deathly afraid of tarantulas?

The only thing that had kept Gabriel from getting distracted was the knowledge that Grace was safe in Valhalla with Loretta. Time would pass quickly for her there – an hour in Valhalla was 24 hours on Earth and a week in Hel. He would be back in no time to continue his investigation.

Trying to avoid the tarantula's flailing legs - Lanie was doing a happy dance - Victor, Gabriel and Daisy huddled to discuss how to get Lanie out of her predicament.

'Ok, so she's afraid of tarantulas. How do you cure THAT?' Victor asked, pulling at his shirt collar and wincing as the material caked with congealed blood took some skin with it. His was lucky to still have half of his ear.

'Petting the spider to show Lanie all creatures are lovely and accepted will do her no good,' Daisy said.

'Let me guess, picturing the tarantula as something ridiculous would not help either?' Victor asked, remembering Professor Moody's teachings from Harry Potter.

Gabriel shook his head, 'No, not in this case.'

Daisy and Gabriel looked at each other. 'Love?' Gabriel asked, wiping the sweat from his eyes. Daisy nodded.

There was a swish of wings behind them and Gabriel heard a familiar voice. 'Looks like you have everything under control,' the Boss said landing on a spit of lava.

'Boss,' Gabriel nodded.

'What do you mean 'love'?' Victor asked, curious about the technique of exorcising someone's fears with love.

'She has to fight it from the inside. Substitute a survival instinct with an even better survival instinct or see her fear as something inconsequential or forgive herself for whatever episode she had with a tarantula that made her fearful or love herself even if she continues fearing tarantulas. It's always individual and might take time to figure out,' the Boss said.

Daisy held on to her head, 'Wait, Lanie is pictagramming me, I think she can still access telepathy, even in distress! Amazing! It will be so much easier to communicate with her!' Daisy beamed.

'Seems like the save is near-complete, I'd better go,' the Boss said and evaporated before Gabriel could ask him anything.

An out of breath Loretta arrived a few seconds later, 'Boy, were your lot difficult to find! I'm looking for the Boss, where is she?'

'He,' Victor and Gabriel said in unison.

'SHE sent me on an errand ... in this climate...ugh...'

'You missed her by seconds,' Daisy hugged the pixie and for once, Loretta didn't resist. Flying in sulphuric surroundings had made this Gothic princess go soft. 'But you can help me find out how to undo this,' Daisy waved at the forest of legs and lump of eyes that was Lanie.

Before the Watchers started to instruct Lanie on how to love tarantulas and harness the creepy-crawly feelings of her subconscious, Gabriel asked the essential question, 'Loretta, when did you get here and where is Grace?'

'What do you mean when did I get here? I've been here all along, half a week on an undercover mission. As for Grace, she's enjoying Valhalla, she's made fast friends and I'm sure she's being looked after for the half hour that has passed there since I left,' Loretta summed up, turning to doctor the tarantula.

'And you couldn't tell me or text me?' Gabriel asked.

'Couldn't. Undercover mission,' Loretta shrugged.

I'm wasting precious time arguing. 'You,' Gabriel pointed at Victor, 'watch out for them, just in case, while I go and find Grace,' Gabriel said and stepped straight into Valhalla, not bothering to wash off the soot and the blood.

Valhalla greeted him with its usual joyous turmoil. Gabriel unholstered his sword and handed it to the bark-keep as was the custom while he scanned the room for Grace.

He couldn't spot her.

Maybe Grace had gone to refresh herself the very moment he arrived?

Gabriel felt annoyed but hopeful lurking around the ladies' room. When five minutes had passed, he saw Isolde going in and asked if she could check if the tiny raven-haired girl was still in there.

Isolde just shook her head when she returned.

Starting to fear the worst, Gabriel turned his sights back on the room, hoping he had just missed Grace amongst the tall backs of the warriors and that she was too engaged in conversation to have noticed him.

No Grace.

Maybe she had gone out?

Gabriel took a turn around Valhalla, looking for tracks in the snow.

Nothing.

Shaking off the blizzard he re-entered Valhalla and scanned the room one more time.

No Grace.

Gabriel's shoulders dropped as did his insides. A dull pain started somewhere deep down.

Maybe she had gone home?

He shook his head at his own stupidity. She couldn't have. Only a being from the Agency could have taken her back to Earth. No one besides Loretta and Gabriel knew Grace was here.

Correction – had been here.

Grace was nowhere to be seen.

He didn't need Hel to make his worst fear come to life.

He hadn't been able to protect Grace. Even if Lanie going off the bend had not been a planned diversion, he felt that he had been duped into leaving Grace's side so that whoever was after her could finish the job.

She was gone and he had no idea where to find her or if she was still alive.

Somehow, what her disappearance would do to magic across all dimensions didn't worry him. What truly worried him was that he was never going to see her kind face again. Watch her crinkle her nose at unacceptably rude behaviour. Talk to her as the cat. Enjoy watching her as she went about the coffee shop. Sleep nose to nose with her. He would never hear her laugh again.

He had failed his mission. He had failed Grace. He had promised her nothing bad would happen to her and now she was gone. He didn't want her to die. She didn't deserve to die. Grace was the kindest, nicest person he knew. He wanted to see her live a long, happy life.

Images of time spent with her flooded his mind. Him walking her home, saving her from the drunks, falling asleep next to her, enjoying her touch whether he was a cat or a man. It wasn't much of a stretch of his imagination to see a life he could have shared with Grace – her hand in his during their walks in the park, her falling asleep in his arms in the house they shared, the kids they could raise, some their own and some adopted. He would have settled for just watching over her if she wouldn't have him.

All of that was gone now. She was gone. He had no clue where to start looking.

Gabriel felt deflated, all the fight kicked out of him.

His gut lurched as if he was on a roller coaster. Naming the dull feeling at the pit of his stomach was of no help. He couldn't possibly miss her. He hardly knew her, having followed her around for only one Earth week.

Yet he had given his life for her, stepping in front of that bus. At the time he had kept telling himself it was the right thing to do, that any guardian angel would have done the same.

You only miss those you truly care for.

Gabriel's breathing was shallow and fast. His head felt hot. His shirt felt too tight, so he undid the top two buttons, nearly ripping them off. Leaning on a table with both his fists, Gabriel fought for control.

It was all his fault. If he hadn't left Grace with the trigger-happy Loretta, she would still be safe.

Punching the table helped a little. Massaging his right hand, Gabriel felt rational thought returning together with the pain.

The bar radio mocked him that now that he can't have her, he wanted her and they love to see him breaking[86]. The barkeep switched channels. James Brown told everyone how he paid the cost to be the boss.[87]

Gabriel was thinking. Loretta had left her post not by her own volition. What had she said? *Undercover mission?* Conveniently from the only person who had the power to override Gabriel's instructions. The extent of the treachery beggared belief.

Seeing Gabriel crumple, Isolde took him by the arm and walked him to the bar.

'A stiff drink is what you need,' she motioned to the barkeep.

Gabriel shook his head, steadying himself against the bar. 'A drink won't solve this. I need my wits about me.'

Isolde took the drink the barman had poured and downed it herself. The drink wasn't at fault that someone didn't want it.

'Everything alright?' Tristan asked both of them. Isolde made an imperceptible nod and the warrior took up the bar stool next to Gabriel. 'Tell me. Whatever it is, that a drink cannot solve, tell me.'

So Gabriel did, without wasting any words.

Tristan nodded, 'So, you're looking for that tiny, friendly girl Loretta brought along an hour or so ago?'

Gabriel nodded. A week in Hel had been only an hour in Valhalla. His hope was retuning. Perhaps Tristan had noticed something. *Anything.* 'Did you see where she went?'

Tristan remembered the image of the funnel of infernal snow under the Golden tree outside and told Gabriel about the man he had seen talking to the girl.

Gabriel clenched his jaw. He knew that man very well. In fact, he had seen that man half an hour earlier in Hel and that man had not cared to mention that he had taken charge of Grace.

He had to find out why. Someone had some explaining to do.

Paling, he propelled himself to his feet. Slowly, Gabriel took his sword from the bar-keep and holstered it between his shoulder blades. Focusing solely on the interrogation he now had to perform, he opened a portal to the most secure room at the Agency and left without saying a word. Only archangels and the chiefest of them all had been granted teleportation access to this room, everyone else's attempts were rerouted to the Watchers' station.

As the white light enveloped Gabriel's fierce battle stance and the grim whiff of darkness, an innocent bystander might have mistaken his winged form for the angel that had fallen from grace a long time ago.

'Must be something rather important for him to leave without so much as a 'thank you'. Must be love.' Isolde said as Gabriel's cocoon disappeared.

Tristan pulled Isolde close, looked deep into her eyes and after careful consideration nodded, 'Not just love. Love and mortal danger.'

59. Lost and Found
Peter

The morning Alice's doctor confirmed her false positive test result, Peter decided to walk to work. He had been doing that a lot lately and it had nothing to do with him hating the morning rush hour on the tube.

For the past week he had been spotting Lanie everywhere on his route to work. He thought he had seen her near the church where her memorial service had been held. Peter had been on a bus and zoomed past.

At another time, he had been at a restaurant with Alice and thought he had spotted Lanie's Caribbean green eyes in a face of a stranger whose eyes had turned steely grey the moment he turned to look properly.

Every mane of lovely long dark hair on any petite girl disappearing around the corner made him race and go see if it was her.

It never was.

Some days he thought he was losing his mind, seeing glimpses of her everywhere. On other days he would give anything to see her again.

Alice was a lovely girl and accustomed to dealing with grief, but her never laudable patience had worn thin with him these last few days while they had waited for the results of the blood test. They had been having rows, lots of rows from the start. Even on the night after Lanie's memorial service when he and Alice had hooked up, it was after a heated disagreement over the appropriateness of grieving for someone Peter hardly knew. He hadn't told her about seeing Lanie everywhere he went, but she could sense his heart was not in their budding relationship. Alice insisted on calling it a relationship. She had tried to keep it all together, in her own way, but her misguided attempt of trap him with the pregnancy had been the last straw.

Peter knew he had to get over Lanie and be with someone equally good. Alice just wasn't the right choice. After the doctor had announced the results of the test on her phone's loudspeaker, Alice had packed up and left as quickly as she had moved in. Their whirlwind romance had only lasted two weeks. Now he had time on his hands to wander the streets and hope for the impossible.

Peter found himself in front of the hospital again. He glanced at the watch. There was still time. He might as well go in and say hello. All the candy stripers knew him by now. He had talked to them after Lanie's death and asked about her. No one but the night matron seemed to remember her. Apparently, Lanie had first appeared at the hospital on the same night he was brought into the ICU.

As he approached the matron's station, he saw a corner of a pinstripe skirt and his heart gave an involuntary lurch.

It couldn't be her. It always turned out to be some other candy striper. Always.

When the expecting mother that was obstructing his view was finally wheeled away from the matron's station, Peter saw Lanie standing there, in her candy striper's uniform.

He had now reached the point of hallucinating early in the mornings.

Peter blinked, but the apparition refused to budge. She was still there. Her face had not turned into the face of one of the familiar candy stripers, as usual. The girl still looked very much like Lanie.

With his heart in his throat, Peter started walking towards her. The air around him seemed to have turned to glue.

He held eye contact, afraid she would disappear if he blinked or even looked away from those green pools of light.

When he was six feet away, the apparition smiled.

It really was her.

Peter reached for Lanie, scooped her up into his arms and just held her close. 'It is you, oh god, it really is you.'

He looked at her. She was still smiling with tears streaking down her cheeks. He gathered her up again, more tenderly this time. 'I thought I had lost you. I kept seeing you everywhere.... you came back...'

60. A Change Of Guard
Gabriel

'What have you done to her?' Gabriel said without any preludes as he materialised in the Boss' office, finally finding the head of the Agency at his desk.

The chair swivelled round and the Indian-looking man resembling King Arthur eyed him warily but with delight that his best pupil had finally connected the dots, 'How did you know?'

For the first time in 900 years, Gabriel took a seat without being offered, 'I didn't. You just told me.'

Pink attempted to cut in with a 'who knew'[88], but both men waved her off.

'Is she alive?' Gabriel asked, hoping against hope.

'That depends,' the Boss said.

That meant yes.

Gabriel exhaled in relief. 'So she IS a bargaining chip?' he specified, reaching the only viable conclusion. 'Don't you think driving such bargains to secure a successor is treading dangerously on the dark side?' he asked pointedly.

'Perhaps,' the Boss said. 'But beggars cannot be choosers. I need a replacement. I've chosen you. You said no. I had to do something to make it easy for you to say 'yes'.' The Boss mistook Gabriel's silence for argument, 'Tell me, if you laid down your powers as guardian and returned to human form today, would you really spend the rest of your very short life trying to protect her?'

'Yes,' Gabriel didn't even have to think about it, 'Yes, I would. My turn. Would you be so vindictive and still continue with the assassination attempts just because I dared say 'no' to your job offer?'

The Boss just shrugged.

Gabriel took a long hard look at the man everyone trusted to run the Agency and keep the balance across all known dimensions and a couple of unknown ones as well. He could now see why a change of guard was warranted, 'You're not fit to keep the balance any longer.'

Another shrug.

'Why rescue her 12 years ago then?' Gabriel asked, hoping that the Boss would remember that he had sworn to protect human lives, not just keeping the balance.

'She was good angel material, but much more useful as a future adult. We had plenty of child guardians at that time. When the right time came, I sent you to harvest her. Instead you brought us Victor,' the Boss looked at the minute hand of the Big Ben move in slow motion.

'You sent me to recruit...'

'AN angel. You simply brought back the wrong one. Not that I'm unhappy with Victor... In fact, he is proving to be quite what we need...' the man mused. 'You know what, we need more guardians like Victor,' he said, 'because he knows the evil he is capable of and is therefore better suited to guard against it. If you had thought like the assassin, you wouldn't have wasted so much time figuring out who was after Grace. You would have solved the puzzle earlier. I am disappointed.'

'That's all she is to you, a puzzle?' Gabriel felt like reaching for his sword, all reverie forgotten. 'Why then did you send me off to protect her? For the fun of watching me fail?' Gabriel asked.

'Across the ages, I've learnt that having loved ones as a bargaining chip is so much more efficient in making someone accept propositions that were previously rejected,' the Boss said.

Loved one?

Gabriel was about to deny he felt that way about Grace when the Boss started listing: 'I know you are tenacious in saving your charges since you are loathe to lose them, but jumping in front of a bus when being near-human, Gabriel? You had exhausted most of your immortality when saving her from the bomb the day before and chasing after clues across Flower colonies and Valhalla left you no time to recharge... Also, charging in here to pick a fight over a girl...' the Boss tsk-tsked. 'Tell me, if I let the reformed Victor go back to Earth and he should romance Grace back into his arms...'

'She wouldn't...' Gabriel interjected.

'...How would that make you feel...?' the Boss asked, looking like the cat that got the cream.

Gabriel felt an iron fist clutch his right side as his pulse picked up. This was only slightly less worse than the one that had twisted his gut when he had realised he had lost Grace.

'Can I sense anger, resentment, perchance a touch of jealousy?' the Boss asked, pointing at where Gabriel's liver was. 'Your Anger centre. I can sense it heating up.'

A stony silence settled in as the clock's minute hand swam on.

'Grace was a test. Your test. And you failed. The one whom I had chosen for my successor failed. Now it could take another thousand years before I find an equally capable one to train up,' the Boss sighed. 'I would very much prefer that you do that instead. You should want to, since you no longer see me fit to keep the balance anyway,' he said with a sad smile.

The Boss wasn't going to let Grace go without getting the answer he wanted. For a brief moment Gabriel considered searching all dimensions. Unfortunately, he didn't know whether the Boss had stashed her away in a sufficiently safe one. *'Safe' being a relative term, considering what would have happened to Klaus in the Enchanted dimension, had Lanie not saved him.* Searching for her might take too long. *Grace could be any thing or any one, anywhere.*

This was blackmail. Pure and simple.

'No amount of talking is going to make a difference, is it?' Gabriel asked, knowing the answer.

The man slowly shook his head.

'You're leaving me no choice here,' Gabriel said, rising.

The greying kind-looking man finally smiled, 'Gabriel, you always have a choice. Always. Make the right one.'

Optimists, please go to Epilogue 1.

Pessimists, please go to Epilogue 2.

EPILOGUE 1 – Happily Ever After

Lanie

Lanie looked up at Peter, her lovely face so close that he wanted to take it in his hands and kiss her senseless. 'I came back. For you.' That was all she said.

People were milling about their usual lives, ignoring the hugging couple in the middle of the hospital reception - a man in an expensive suit and a barefoot tiny girl in a candy striper's outfit.

For them, the rest of the world simply did not exist.

Peter stroked her face, her hair, not wanting to break physical contact for even a second, afraid that she might disappear. 'I don't know how or why you came back...' Peter carefully omitted the 'from the dead' part so as not to push his luck, 'I doubt you know it either, I'm just glad that you did.'

Lanie nodded and wiped her tears. She laughed when she noticed that her tears were no longer glistening like mother-of-pearl.

It was official.

She was human again.

Early retirement, the Boss had called it.

After flying off the handle at seeing that tiny cross sign on Alice's pregnancy test, after a week that had seemed like years spent in Hel and her miraculous rescue, after surrendering her wings and her job at the Agency, she was human again.

Her fight to regain her human form had taught her oodles about love. In order to stop being the thing she feared most, she had to love herself, in whatever form - legs and all. She had had to forgive herself for unkind thoughts about the way she looked - legs and all - and for thinking someone else deserved love more than she did. To stop being a tarantula, she had to find a way to love her weakness of not fighting for her love. She had learnt to embrace her fear of being capable of cruelty. She had decided that to live her life until the very end - fears, mistakes and all - was as important as any other life they saved.

And here she was.

Human again.

When hearing her request, the Boss had told her that she could ask for one more thing before returning back to Earth dimension and it couldn't be immortality. She had chosen to remember being a guardian angel.

Loretta had snorted and muttered something about 'blowing them all out of the water', while Daisy had asked her if perhaps wishing for means of sustenance would be more sensible. Lanie had just smiled and shaken her head. If she had Peter, she had everything she needed. She didn't need a flat, clothes or money. She could find a job and get all those unimportant things later.

'Let's go home,' Peter said.

'Yes. Let's.'

They named their kids Gabriel and Daisy. Peter had protested a little about naming their daughter after a greedy calculating airhead from 'The Great Gatsby'. Lanie assured him that the Gabriel and the Daisy she knew were both good souls with huge hearts and a penchant for helping everyone.

Sally

Victor sighed. Some Princess Charming Sally turned out to be.

Right. He would have to do everything himself.

Victor flicked out the mini magic wand he had borrowed from the Enchanted dimension and sent a waste bin flying.

The waste bin promptly took out Harry's assailants as well as Harry.

'What the hell did you do that for? Was that a...a...?'

'Magic wand, yes. A mini one. And I did that because I had to because you failed to get the attention of that police man like I told you to and because otherwise Harry would be a goner.'

Sally looked at him crossly, 'He could be a goner now, seeing that he's buried under those guys, under all that trash and under that awful heavy bin.'

The sly frog offered, 'Why don't you go check on him?'

It would be the humane thing to do. After all, Harry had

defended her at the bar. Still, she had her suspicions about that frog. 'Why don't you check on him, why do I have to do it?'

This one wasn't too bright. 'Because, Sally, you would have to go and take credit for rescuing him.'

Sally looked appalled, 'Girls don't rescue guys!! You've got it the wrong way around.'

If only she knew! 'For your information, it's a myth. Women rescue guys all the time. Guys just don't talk about it all over the place. Heck, some of them don't even know about it even though it happens left, right and centre.'

'Oh yeah?' Sally looked like she was ready to pick a bar fight herself.

Victor spread his arms wide and tried to poise them in the general vicinity of his frog hips. 'Yeah.'

With her nose up in the air, Sally shook her head, 'I don't think so. I am not going to demean a guy and make him feel like a damsel in distress. What would that make me?'

Princess Charming.

'Princess Charming, that's who! You do realise it's a very perverted fairy-tale you are advocating here?'

He nodded in the direction of the heap of humans and garbage, 'Sally, you will have to take the credit for this.'

'Don't tell me what to do. Why would I take credit? I could never... I would never have been able to do anything like this!'

'Do you know how ridiculous 'the frog did it' is going to sound?' The frog eyed her warily.

Any minute now.

Silence.

'So, what am I supposed to say, I don't know how I did it, I had an adrenalin rush, people do weird and impossible things when they get adrenalin rushes?'

The frog shrugged, 'It worked for that vampire dude in that movie when he saved the girl from being squashed by the car... Well...almost worked. The girl clocked it. What other explanation would you offer, Spiderman did it?'

Sally eyed him warily, 'Fine, but why is it again that I have to do it?'

The frog narrowed his eyes at her, 'Don't you like the idea of people being happy to be alive and thanking you for it?'

'No, since I didn't do anything! Someone else did. You did. So, that's called impersonating...'

'A frog,' the frog finished for her, 'Don't be ridiculous, now go over there and save him! Frog march!'

Sally harrumphed but started moving, muttering under her breath, 'Goddamn pest, let's go out, he said, let's got to this bar, he said, let's get humiliated, why don't we...why did I ever listen to him anyway...' Still, she had to admit that his advice so far had not been all bad. He had gotten her to exercise and lose a few pounds. To her surprise she had discovered she even liked jogging. He had helped her pick a new wardrobe. So all her clothes now fit and looked good. And while she would never admit it out loud, vegetables and meats were a rather good alternative to constant lazy pizza.

All of a sudden she was out of road, standing in front of the fallen guy of her dreams who was opening his eyes and shuffling around for something.

His hand found her boot. Harry opened his eyes wide and looked up, 'It's you!'

'Yep,' she held out her hand to help him get up.

In mild surprise he took it.

Sally proceeded to de-lint him of papers and sausage skins and other garbage that had stuck to his clothes from his fleeting roll-around on the ground.

'Thh....thank you. What happened?' Harry stammered. He looked at his would-be muggers who were slowly starting to come around as well. 'I think we better leave before they wake,' he suggested.

Sally nodded, 'I'll tell you all about it later. You look like you're in shock. Can you walk? Want some coffee?'

From the shadows, Victor smirked. *Smooth.*

Harry nodded and let himself be led away, 'Unless you have something stronger...?'

The frog watched the limping figure and the girl fade into the distance. On the corner of the street, under the light, he saw Sally sigh, lift Harry's arm to her shoulders so he could lean onto her and speed up their limping escape. He knew her sturdy legs were good for something.

Victor's blue phone blinked an SOS. *Thank goodness he had managed to pry her away from unveiling all her mirrors or they would have been late for her date and then god knows what could have happened.*

As it happened, his job here was done. She couldn't possibly botch it up now. Not even this reluctant Princess Charming.

With one of his missions accomplished, he could accommodate a little search and rescue.

A week later, as Sally watched Harry sleeping next to her, she thought she could kiss that frog right now, if he was here. She felt a little annoyed that he had completely disappeared on her ever since that night when he had rescued Harry.

Sally wondered what would have happened if she had kissed the frog. Would he have actually turned into a guy?

Maybe he had been a figment of her imagination after all. The story of how she had rescued him that Harry kept telling everyone certainly sounded more and more believable the more he told it. She could have had an adrenalin rush and thrown that bin with amazing precision. Maybe there had been no magic frog after all. Still, she missed talking to it. Although, now she had Harry to talk to, so everything was all right.

Charlotte

Charlotte discovered herself in the middle of a huge white room with various mythical creatures buzzing about. Now she finally believed Victor about the Agency he had told her about.

He had come back a week after his disappearance. She had launched herself at him, fists first and sobbed into his jacket for leaving her. The composed stranger in front of her had quietly disentangled himself and apologised if he had seemed to lead her on. That his mission – *she had been simply a mission!* – had been to get her to safety, to Italy so she could realise her full potential.

When Victor had said he was her guardian angel, at first she hadn't believed him. Not at all. It had all seemed too incredible. She had forced him to tell her more.

That summer, in Florence, her hurt and fury over her one-sided love inspired her to paint like she had never painted before. The cold red anger glowed scarlet and punctured her canvases, her sense of loss simmered vile green under the surface. Her despair was molten black criss-crossing everything in sight.

He had occasionally popped by and kept her company, telling her about distant alternative worlds of pixie flower colonies, various religious hells, Valhalla and the enchanted and magic-stricken dimensions.

She realised Victor had told her stories to calm her down in order to prevent her drawing violent things, not just told her amusing things about his life – *was it even life if he was, to put it bluntly, the undead?* When she had shown him her versions of the dimensions he had told her about, Victor had corrected, where necessary and encouraged her to draw more, steering her clear of horrific beings that begged to come to life on her canvas.

His stories also served the purpose of her burying all hope of them ending up together.

She had finished art school and gone back to Tempest where she had accidentally caused Andy's death by pitchfork. He had minded a lot that she had upped and left, sticking him with all the farm duties. An unfortunate fall after words spoken in anger and she had one less next of kin left on this Earth.

To avoid everyone, Charlotte had simply called out to Victor and here she was.

His way of trying to keep her from toppling into depression was to prove that what he had been telling her about the Agency was all true.

So, now, here she was.

At the Agency that Victor had told her about so many times.

Next to her, Victor looked cold and distant. Not the warm, cursing, sleepy-head she had gotten used to on Aunt Mae's porch.

It was true then.

Angels abandoned human emotions when they were on the neutral territory of the Agency, just like Victor had said.

Victor pointed at one of the 16 screens in front of them where Andy's body was lying in the corner of the barn.

'He will atone for his sins,' Victor said with his voice in neutral gear.

'How?' Charlotte dared ask. *Ok, Andy had accidentally killed himself when he was trying to show her her place, but he was kin. She didn't want bad things happening to him in the afterlife.*

'As an atoning angel, we will assign him the anti-rape and anti-drug rescue missions.'

Charlotte looked at him. She could see a completely different face, a masque as cold and as hard as marble pulled over Victor's all too familiar features.

So, this was who Victor really was.

On Earth, he told her he was becoming more and more human, the longer he stayed. His older self. His bad self. Who he no longer was. Who he no longer wanted to be.

He was a guardian angel. Neutral, just and senseless.

This is what she could also become.

When she died, she had a slim chance of serving alongside Victor. She wasn't sure she qualified.

'You want to become a guardian angel? To live like this, with all the consequences?' For a brief moment, Charlotte thought she saw the long-lost old Vic, her Victor peek through in the concerned tone of this magnificent but alien creature.

He truly could read minds, then.

The old Victor was dead, had always been dead from the moment he had become a guardian. What she had seen during that fateful week in Texas was a glimmer of a temporary memory resurfacing. Like a hologram flicker. It hadn't been real. What was real was the angel standing in front of her.

Fine. They would be combatants in arms. She hoped they would remain friends.

'Yes. Yes, I would,' Charlotte said, accepting her fate and feeling a little of her pain let go.

'Someday. Not today.' Victor said. 'Meanwhile, we have to teach you how to draw happy, lest the horrors you can imagine come to life and make more work for us.'

Gabriel

'Then I choose to be mortal again. Find yourself another substitute and release Grace,' Gabriel said to the greying man in kingly robes.

The dark tally by the revolving mirror shot up a notch.

The Boss motioned to the tally, 'You see, Gabriel, you always have a choice, but every choice has consequences. This choice has bad ones. You do realise that while you may continue protecting her, you will not be invincible, she will not be assigned another guardian angel to protect her, she might still die and if we recruit her, you, too will return here,' the Boss smiled and added, 'to be with me.'

Gabriel nodded, 'I'm just counting on you doing the right thing,' he said at the tally and the white one shot up, 'and continue doing the right things until you've trained either Victor or Lanie as your successor,' Gabriel said, hoping against hope that he could get Grace out of her predicament, if he found a new replacement candidate for his Boss.

'Lanie went back to Earth. She's human. Opted for early retirement and after Hel I can't blame her. Victor is off in some violent dimension because he cannot handle both of his Charges getting their 'gooey marshmallow endings' as he put it, so he's not ready for the job either.' The Boss was thoughtfully inspecting a labradorite pebble in his palm.

The Boss closed his palm and tried his last gambit, 'You do realise I could just prevent your happily ever after on Earth and ask you both to stay guardian angels from this day forward? It's not like you know where she is to go save her.'

That was true. 'I can only assume you have her stashed somewhere close. You wouldn't just end her life because I refuse to do your job. You're not that dark or twisted,' Gabriel said, reassuring himself more than anyone.

'So, you still refuse?' the Boss enquired.

'Are you that dark and twisted?' Gabriel asked and added 'Sir' out of habit after a pregnant pause.

The Boss smiled widely.

'Very well, I'll comply. I'll take over if you'll let her live. All

I'm asking for is a small reprieve.' Gabriel bowed. 'Considering it is not a lot to ask, then you have to agree that a reprieve is reasonable.' Imagining the prospect of being stuck at a table for hundreds of years if not thousands, Gabriel suddenly understood why the Boss had itchy feet and why he had been frequenting the daredevil dimensions.

Acknowledging Gabriel's decision as well as his reasoning, the Boss smiled again. *What was another couple of decades of boredom, if he could balance it out by gallivanting around? The important bit was, he now had a successor.*

With a slight of hand, the man made the pebble he had been holding evaporate.

Gabriel could only assume that that had been Grace and that the Boss had had the decency to send her back to Della's.

As many decades as the Boss would allow them to spend together on Earth followed by thousands of years of serving the Agency.

Together.

It wasn't such a bad deal.

One thing he knew, he would talk to Victor before he left for Earth to ensure the Agency got better at succession planning even before Gabriel took the helm.

'Meanwhile, may I issue a suggestion, Sir? It would do you a lot of good to go travel the dimensions…maybe even restore your faith in fighting the right fight. Why don't you leave Victor and the Watchers in charge for a while? Temporarily, of course, as a test to see if any of them have it in them to take over?' Gabriel offered, hoping against hope the Boss would take him up on this suggestion. Perhaps the Boss would even change his mind and decide on a different successor. *One could hope.* 'For the past week, you have been absent a lot and so far, things have worked out, haven't they?' he finished persuading.

'Perhaps,' the Boss said pensively. 'I will wait for you, though. For another 50 years or so,' the Boss nodded and rose. The tally hovered at a precarious even keel.

'Sixty,' Gabriel said, shook the already outstretched hand of his now former Boss and went to lay down his wings to woo a girl.

EPILOGUE 2 – Happily Never After

The Boss

The Boss had half hoped that after Lanie's rescue from Hel, she would blurt out 'to turn back into a human again' when he had asked her what she wanted to do next. He would have granted her early retirement, if only she had asked for it.

She hadn't. Instead, she had asked him for the post of Helreginne and to see Peter one last time before they wiped her memory of the Earth dimension completely.

Who was he to dissuade her?

The Boss didn't regret a single thing. Good angels were hard to come by and Lanie was proving to be every bit as good as Gabriel and Victor. All was fair in, well, war.

Gabriel

'I'll take over if you'll leave her be,' Gabriel said to the greying man in kingly robes.

The white tally by the revolving mirror shot up a notch.

Victor walked in, 'Need any help?' he said to no one in particular.

Ignoring Victor, the Boss motioned to the tally, 'You see, Gabriel, you always have a choice, but every choice has consequences. This choice has good ones. You'll still be able to watch over her from here,' the regal man motioned at the room in general, 'And maybe one day, you can make her the offer I made you?'

Gabriel nodded, 'Not for decades yet and I'm counting on you doing the right thing and leaving her be for now,' he said at the tally and the black one shot up. 'You need to call off the attacks on Grace. Right now,' he said at the tally and the white one shot up.

'Already done,' said the Boss, thoughtfully inspecting a labradorite pebble in his palm, confirming he had single-handedly been behind every single attack.

Pink attempted to cut in with a 'who knew'[89], but both men waved her off.

'I also need you to continue doing the right things until we have trained either Lanie or Victor as your successor,' Gabriel said, hoping against hope that he could get Grace out of her predicament, if he found a new replacement candidate for his Boss.

Victor, annoyed that he had not been his mentor's first suggestion, made a face behind Gabriel's back.

'Lanie? Maybe in time. For now, she has chosen to take up the post of Helreginne. Apparently, once she learnt how to communicate in that dimension, she decided she wanted to try and manage it. Her worst fears - abandonment by a lover, being cruel, pointless dying - have already come to life, so she's an ideal candidate for the job. If she is successful at her new permanent post, we will get a hell of a guardian someday, but for now she is a supervisor of one dimension only. She wouldn't have the time to rule both, Hel and the Agency.'

The Boss turned to Victor, 'You didn't protest... so we might have another candidate for my job...curious...' the greying man said. 'Perhaps what is required is a healthy dose of vindictive justice bordering on complete impartiality - to good as well as to evil...' The Boss put the pebble down, 'Maybe in due time, but I don't think Victor's ready yet and you are still my number one choice, Gabriel.'

Deep down, Gabriel agreed that letting Victor take the reigns before all the stupid was beat out of him by centuries of experience could have unpredictable consequences. *Still, it was better to have a volunteer rather than a reluctant slave.* 'He learns quickly, he could learn from you on the job,' Gabriel vouched, hoping the Boss could be persuaded.

'I'm tired. I'd rather he learnt from you,' the Boss said.

'So I train Victor up and let him take over,' Gabriel conceded.

Victor just stood there, head bowed, listening to two men arguing over his fate. *Anything that got him off damsels in distress duty was good.* Judging that the Boss had still managed a few trips to Dialysis X, Victor didn't think he could lose out here.

The older man shrugged, 'When you consider him ready - as you wish, but we both agree he's not ready now. First he has to cure himself of the gleeful thoughts that neither of you got the girl.'

Gabriel nodded.

Victor blushed. *Dammit, he'd forgotten how quickly the telepathy function was restored when they were all at the Agency.*

'You always were and still are my number one choice, Gabriel,' the Boss said.

'As long as we are bargaining here - a small reprieve is out of the question?' Gabriel asked.

'Gabriel, I am truly tired,' the greying king sighed, looking his age. 'I had my eye on a couple of you. Grace was your test, Peter turned out to be Lanie's. Charlotte turned out to be Victor's. It was never my intention. It just happened. My best guardian angels - one falling hopelessly in love and the other being too cocky to even think he can do what I do after only two years of service. How nonsensical.'

At the 'falling in love' comment, Gabriel closed his eyes. The Boss had known before Gabriel himself had and still he had made his offer, 'You knew all along I would fall for her. Just like you hoped Victor would fall for his charge and why is it exactly that Lanie has taken up one of the insanest postings ever when she could have easily chosen to go back and live a long, happy life? Did you even tell her that it was an option for services rendered so far?'

Ignoring the accusations, the Boss shrugged, 'I thought your experience, Lanie's level-headedness and Victor's disdain for damsels would shield you against emotions, in addition to the re-balancing. Who knew you would all not measure up. Out of all of you, you are the only one who has the experience to actually be able to do it,' he said.

'So, you admit that you orchestrated all of it,' Gabriel asked.

The Boss spread his arms in an apologetic gesture, 'Guilty as charged.'

'When you hunt monsters, make sure you don't turn into

one yourself?' Gabriel asked.

The greying man nodded, 'You'll be wise to remember that as well,' he told Victor. Not having heard a definitive 'yes' from his trusted second-in-command, the Boss decided to make his last gambit, 'You do realise I could just off her now and offer her to become a guardian angel? Or you could once you take up the job? Then you could...' After all, that's how he had recruited Lanie.

'Yes, we could, but you and I are not going to end her life when it has not yet even begun,' Gabriel was resolute. Grace still had a good fifty years left, if not more and thousands of years spent serving the Agency would have to be a choice, not a chore just because the Boss wanted to retire. 'I'll serve if you let her live out her natural life on Earth however she chooses with whomever she chooses for however many years that might take,' he said.

Imagining the prospect of being stuck at a table for hundreds of years if not thousands, Gabriel suddenly understood why the Boss had itchy feet and why he had been frequenting the daredevil dimensions. When he took charge, as a first order of business, Gabriel decided to ensure the Agency was much better at succession planning.

The Boss smiled widely, acknowledging Gabriel's decision. With a slight of hand, the man made the pebble he had been holding evaporate.

Gabriel could only assume that that had been Grace and that the Boss had had the decency to send her back to Della's.

'There! All sorted. That wasn't hard, was it?'

Gabriel bowed his head. *He wasn't going to be taunted further.*

'We both know that when the time comes, in 50 years or so, you will be very tempted to offer her a job here. By then, staying in the safety of the Agency, you'll certainly have managed to cure yourself of emotions. Perhaps staying in more will even erode the importance of letting her live her life until its natural end with the mate of her choosing...and you might think about recruiting her earlier,' the Boss stood, concluding their discussion.

Gabriel considered it. He might be tempted, but time would tell. And he would make sure Grace had all the time she wanted to live a dignified life, even if it took 80 years.

'As of this moment, you are now officially retired. Go in peace. Do as you please. I hope you choose to go travel the dimensions...maybe this will restore your faith in fighting the right fight?' Gabriel offered, hoping against hope the Boss would take him up on this suggestion. Maybe he wasn't completely disillusioned. Maybe, unlike his predecessors, one day they would have him back on active duty. The Boss did love personal saves, especially in the insane and dangerous dimensions.

'I guess I could start with inspecting all the existing dimensions, one by one, to see where I feel most at home,' the Boss nodded dreamily and rose. The tally hovered at a precarious even keel. 'You can tag along as well,' he motioned to Victor, 'it's the closest thing to an apprenticeship I'll ever offer.'

Victor nodded.

'A wise choice,' Gabriel said to both of them and shook the already outstretched hand of his now former Boss.

Lanie

Lanie looked up at Peter, her lovely face so close that he wanted to take it in his hands and kiss her senseless. 'I came back. To say goodbye.' That was all she said.

People were milling about their usual lives, ignoring the couple in the middle of the hospital reception for whom the rest of the world did not exist - a man in an expensive suit and a barefoot tiny girl in a candy striper's outfit.

Peter stroked her face, her hair, not wanting to break physical contact for even a second, afraid that she might disappear, 'But I can't lose you again...'

Lanie nodded and wiped her tears. A few fell on Peter's expensive cashmere suit and glistened like pearls.

Peter looked into her eyes, searching for an explanation.

Lanie's disappearance, her watching over him when she was dead, her strange reappearance and her inhuman tears of pearls. It all made sense now. 'Are you an angel?' Peter asked quietly, still stroking her hair.

Lanie just nodded and smiled.

Peter kept stroking her hair. Alice and her false pregnancy scare, the weeks he had longed to have this girl in his arms – it all faded away.

She was here.

And she was not his to keep.

Lanie kept telling herself that she was a guardian angel now, that she had given up being human to help others. She couldn't go back to Earth. She had flown completely off the handle when she spied the paramedic doing a happy dance over a positive pregnancy test. If Gabriel and Victor hadn't found and saved her, she would still be trapped in her nightmare in Hel. There should be a way to keep everyone safe from their worst nightmares. No one should be driven to insanity like that. No one.

She wasn't going to surrender her wings and her job at the Agency just because she had met this nice man just as she had been leaving Earth.

She knew she wouldn't be able to give up watching over Peter. She had made her decisions and had asked for one last favour. The Boss promised to grant it, if it was within reason. Lanie had wanted to say goodbye in person.

Loretta had snorted and muttered something about 'being human again', while Daisy had asked her if perhaps this would hurt too much.

Lanie had just smiled sadly and shaken her head. If she could see Peter one last time, she would endure eternity without complaint. Besides, the Agency had means to help her forget.

'I have to go,' Lanie tore herself away from Peter, feeling physical pain. It wouldn't matter soon, once all of her memories connected with Earth were erased. Including this one.

'Will I ever see you again?' Peter asked, looking hopeful.

Lanie shook her head 'no'. She would never come back to this dimension. Peter saw her take a few backward steps and let go of her hand, making room for people trying to get to the reception desk.

When the crowd that had parted them dissolved, she was gone.

Peter blinked. She couldn't just be gone.

Yet she was.

'Peter?' Alice had materialised out of nowhere, 'You're here! Oh, you've forgiven me, thank goodness!' She clutched onto him for dear life.

He held on for comfort, confused.

'Let's go home,' Alice whispered to him.

'No, this, us,' he gently pushed her away, 'this is impossible, I'm sorry.' Even if Alice was still here and still real, Lanie was lost to him. He didn't love Alice. If he couldn't have Lanie, he deserved to be with someone as nice as Lanie, someone whom he could love, cherish and worship and who would adore him just the same. He patted Alice's arm and left the hospital without a word. Someone not as good as Lanie was not an option.

Charlotte

Charlotte discovered herself in the middle of a huge white room with various mythical creatures buzzing about. Now she finally believed Victor about the Agency he had told her about.

He had come back a week after his disappearance. She had launched herself at him, fists first and sobbed into his jacket for leaving her. The composed stranger in front of her had quietly disentangled himself and apologised if he had seemed to lead her on. That his mission – *she had been simply a mission!* – had been to get her to safety, to Italy so she could realise her full potential.

When Victor had said he was her guardian angel, at first she hadn't believed him. Not at all. It had all seemed too incredible. She had forced him to tell her more.

That summer, in Florence, her hurt and fury over her one-sided love inspired her to paint like she had never painted before. The cold red anger glowed scarlet and punctured her canvases, her sense of loss simmered vile green under the surface. Her despair was molten black criss-crossing everything in sight.

He had occasionally popped by and kept her company, telling her about distant alternative worlds of pixie flower colonies, various religious hells, Valhalla and the enchanted and magic-stricken dimensions.

She realised Victor had told her stories to calm her down in order to prevent her drawing violent things, not just told her amusing things about his life – *was it even life if he was, to put it bluntly, the undead?* When she had shown him her versions of the dimensions he had told her about, Victor had corrected, where necessary and encouraged her to draw more, steering her clear of horrific beings that begged to come to life on her canvas.

His stories also served the purpose of her burying all hope of them ending up together.

She had finished art school and gone back to Tempest where she had promptly got death by pitchfork from Andy the morning after she had arrived. He had minded a lot that she had upped and left, sticking him with all the farm duties. An unfortunate fall after words spoken in anger and her family had one less mouth to feed.

Charlotte didn't know what she had done to get Victor as a guardian angel. She did know why he didn't appear this second time she had been in trouble. Andy had been a bit too forceful expressing his anger. When Andy was angry, he jabbed and shoved. Her fall onto the pitchfork from the rafters had been pure accident.

If she was completely honest with herself, she hadn't really wanted to be rescued. She wasn't entirely sure she hadn't known that this could happen when she had volunteered to go help Andy at the barn this morning.

Dying, she had a slim chance of serving alongside Victor. She wasn't sure unwitting aided suicide qualified her for guardianship and feared that they might throw her out if they even suspected, but here she was.

At the Agency that Victor had told her about so many times.

Victor appeared at the top of the stairs and nodded for her to approach.

He looked cold and distant. Not the warm, cursing, sleepy-head she had gotten used to on Aunt Mae's porch. It was true then. Angels abandoned human emotions when they were on the neutral territory of the Agency, just like Victor had said.

Inside the white office, Victor pointed at the screen on top of the table where someone was filming Andy going about his daily business, ignoring Charlotte's body in the corner of the barn where he had left her.

'We will collect him, in due time. He will atone for his sins,' Victor said with his voice in neutral gear. She expected that he would at least be angry that in the end, his rescue had only been temporary. She expected him to be angry with her for not being more careful. At least the Victor she knew on Earth would have been. It all seemed a lifetime ago.

'How?' Charlotte dared ask. *Ok, Andy had accidentally killed himself when he was trying to show her her place, but he was kin. She didn't want bad things happening to him. Her uncle wouldn't survive any more tragedy. Burying her would be hard enough. Burying his only son, she couldn't even imagine.*

'As an atoning angel, we will assign him the anti-rape and anti-drug rescue missions.' Victor chose to take her question to mean how Andy would be atoning, not how he would die.

Charlotte looked at him. She could see a completely different face, a masque as cold and as hard as marble pulled over Victor's all too familiar features.

So, this was who Victor really was.

On Earth, he told her he was becoming more and more human, the longer he stayed. His older self. His bad self. Who he no longer was. Who he no longer wanted to be.

He was a guardian angel. Neutral, just and senseless.

This is what she would also become.

Soon.

'Would you consider becoming a guardian angel? Do you want to live like this, with all the consequences?' For a brief moment, Charlotte thought she saw the long-lost old Victor, her Victor peek through in the concerned tone of this magnificent but alien creature.

The old Victor was dead, had always been dead from the

moment he had become a guardian. What she had seen during that fateful week in Texas was a glimmer of a temporary memory resurfacing. Like a hologram flicker. It hadn't been real. What was real was the angel standing in front of her.

Fine. They would be combatants in arms. She hoped they would remain friends.

'Yes. Yes, I would,' Charlotte said, accepting her fate and feeling a little of her pain lessen. The knowledge that she would see her drawings come to life was also a small consolation, even if she was initially restricted to drawing things consigned to the Magic Kingdom and the Enchanted dimensions.

Sally

Sally was sitting at Harry's bedside at the hospital. It was a week after that fateful night at the bar. The thugs had beaten Harry so hard that he had ended up in a coma. What was worse, the minute she had needed that damned magic frog, he was gone. After he had suggested she call the police, he had evaporated, mumbling something about an SOS situation and how HE would have time to help if SHE hadn't unwrapped all her mirrors and been late for her date. They had both assumed the police would help prevent the worst.

They hadn't been able to.

The doctors had told her and Harry's mom that one of the blows had tapped Harry on his temple, right above his ear, in the soft area where the bones met. A one in a million swing shot had broken off a bone fragment that had punctured his brain. Harry was braindead.

Sally had been there all week, missing all her lectures, praying to her god, to Jesus, to the frog, to anyone out there to please send her a miracle.

The world was all out of miracles. Today was going to be the day that his mom was going to disconnect Harry from life support. An organ-donor, he was going to help others live a little bit longer. Sally stroked his hand one last time. There were no tears. She was all out.

No more movie nights or bickering with Vittorio over which of his pizzas was the best. No more picking on each other. No more Harry.

Numb, Sally walked out of the hospital. She didn't want to see this. She wanted to remember Harry, her Harry, alive and smiling and pushing his specs up his nose and making her laugh.

She blamed the frog at first. If he hadn't goaded her into going, this never would have happened. They had caught the bastards who had done this, and she was going to make sure they got what they deserved. But it wouldn't bring Harry back. Nothing would. And it was all her fault.

* * *

An elderly kind-looking man was waiting for Harry when he emerged from his body, looking around like a curious child.

They all wondered what the afterlife brought.

Recruitment duty. It had come to this.

The Boss sighed. He missed Gabriel.

He even missed Victor who was off in some violent dimension because as much as he hated losing Charges, he hated being hated more.

The greying man took a good look at Harry. Being ex-military was a bonus. He could be recruiting them a new Gabriel. 'Fancy serving as a guardian angel, captain?'

When Harry nodded without hesitation, the Boss smiled. He had a feeling something good was going to come out of this tragedy. Some day.

Grace

'Cute couple,' said someone behind Gabriel.

Gabriel turned and almost didn't recognise Lanie. A statue of Osiris from Ancient Egypt paled compared to how regal she looked. At five feet three inches, Lanie stood impossibly tall with ballerina-like poise and a newfound look of kind disinterest.

'I'm off to take up my new post in Hel,' a brief nod and a

cautious smile later she was gone in a puff of a rainbow-coloured light.

Gabriel wasn't surprised Lanie's aura had changed after her apocalyptic adventure nor that she had accepted the post of a guardian angel assigned to Hel on a permanent basis. He knew far too well that it had nothing to do with Lanie being a sucker for punishment and beating herself up about lost chances with Peter. She hadn't even recognised Peter as one half of the 'cute couple' on the screen. She couldn't.

After she was saved from becoming her worst nightmare in Hel, they had offered Lanie the option of erasing her horrible memories. She had thought about it and said yes on the condition of saying goodbye to Peter one last time. After she returned, Lanie had requested erasure of all of her memories from Earth – from before she had become a guardian as well as any encounters with Peter. From now on, every time she went to Earth, she would have to orient herself and learn the earthling ways like any other angel not born of that dimension. With the permanent post in Hel, the chances of her having to do that ever again were close to zero. Gabriel had administered the procedure himself, making sure her memories of being a guardian were retained.

After all, this was now part of his new duties.

The first thing Lanie had asked when she woke up was what she needed to do to be permanently posted to Hel. She said she could do a lot of good preventing real horrors in a place where everyone conscious or unconscious became their worst nightmare. She understood that she had to be there and live there and do the job around the clock in order to ensure that everyone who ended up in Hel, whenever and whyever their mind locked them there, could safely find their way back to sanity or an awake state.

'May your reign be long and safe, Helreginne,' Gabriel uttered the customary farewell greeting at the last ray of disappearing rainbow light. He had given the same farewell to the Helreginne before Lanie who had perished stepping, unshielded, between a father killing his son in his dream.

Gabriel took one last look at the screen where Peter and Grace were chatting away, Grace occasionally touching Peter's arm. She liked him. The way he was talking to her meant he liked her as well.

Gabriel was glad that after Lanie's goodbye, he had led Peter to find Grace, closing doors in his face and having gusts of wind blow litter at him so that eventually and inevitably he would stumble into Grace's coffee shop. Grace will have a good life with him. Gabriel had fast forwarded her life to see that there was a probability that if Peter and Grace ended up together, they would name their daughter Lanie. The 50-year wait was nothing. Even if he had to wait 80 years, Gabriel was sure Grace would accept when he offered her an option to be a guardian. Once Grace was by his side, Time would tell.

Dear reader,

Thank you for buying my book! I hope you enjoy reading it as much as I enjoyed writing it. ☺

The next one, **King of Time**, is a possible prequel to one possible Camelot.
At five to midnight on a New Year's Eve, Lila is in the throes of her writer's block when a hot dude appears in her apartment and claims to be Time incarnate and there to help. Next, she is mistaken for a princess, has to name the kingdom and tour it to solve its problems. All this while on her quest to find Imogen, her long-lost imagination, and finish the book she hasn't even begun. As Lila is trying to wrap things up, Time (who prefers to be called Adam) discovers emotions...

Intrigued? Good. Keep reading.

Love, Sky

Playlist*

1. P!nk. Who Knew. (I'm Not Dead, 2006).
2. Seal. A Prayer For the Dying (Seal aka Seal II, 1994).
3. The Red Jumpsuit Apparatus. Your Guardian Angel. (Don't You Fake It, 2006).
4. Taylor Swift. I Knew You Were Trouble (Red, 2012).
5. Alanis Morrissette. Uninvited (The City of Angels: Music From the Motion Picture, 1998).
6. Frank Sinatra. Witchcraft (Single, 1957).
7. Lady Antebellum. Just a Kiss. (Own the Night, 2011).
8. Robbie Williams. Angels. Single, 1997.
9. ABBA. Honey Honey (Waterloo, 1974)
10. Sarah McLachlan. Angel. (City of Angels: Music from the Motion Picture, 1998).
11. Kelly Clarkson. Because of You. (Breakaway, 2004).
12. Florence and The Machine. Seven Devils. (Ceremonials, 2011).
13. Jump5, Walking on Sunshine (Ella Enchanted: original soundtrack,2004).
14. Lady Antebellum. Hello World (Need You Now, 2010).
15. Avicii. Waiting for Love (Digital download, 2015).
16. Saosin. You're Not Alone (Saosin, 2006).
17. James Morrison. One Life (The Awakening, 2011).
18. Vanessa Carlton. Even Angels Fall.
19. Lily Kershaw. As It Seems (Single, 2012).
20. Katy Perry. E.T. (Teenage Dream, 2010.)
21. Dishwalla, Angels or Devils (Opaline, 2002).
22. Train, Calling All Angels, (My Private Nation, 2003).
23. Israel Kamakawiwo'ole. Somewhere Over the Rainbow/ What A Wonderful World. (Facing Future, 1993).
24. The Fray. How To Save A Life. (How To Save A Life, 2005).
25. ABBA. Angeleyes (Single, 1979).
26. Three Days Grace. Gone Forever (One-X, second album, 2008).

27. Ronan Keating. When You Say Nothing At All (Notting Hill soundtrack, 1999).
28. Beyonce . Halo (Single, 2009).
29. Depeche Mode. Angel of Love (Single, 2013).
30. U2. If God Will Send His Angels (Single, 1997).
31. The Penguins. Earth Angel (Will You Be Mine, Single, 1954).
32. Ella Fitzgerald. Someone to Watch Over Me (Ella Sings Gershwin, Vinyl album, 1950).
33. Kelly Clarkson. Dark Side (Stronger, 2011).
34. Takida. You Learn (The Burning Heart, 2011).
35. Blind Guardian. Valhalla. (Follow the Blind, 1989).
36. Savage Garden. Tears of Pearls (Savage Garden, 1997).
37. Amy Winehouse. Rehab (Back to Black, 2006).
38. Taylor Swift. Breathe (Fearless, 2008).
39. Lucy Hale, Run This Town (Another Cinderella Story: Once Upon a Song soundtrack, 2011).
40. Katy Perry. The One That Got Away (Teenage Dream, 2010).
41. One Direction. Taken (Up All Night, 2011).
42. James Brown. The Boss (Black Caesar, 1973).

Look out for Someone To Watch Over Me (the book) playlists on Spotify and YouTube.

Author's note

I have Lana Maklakova to thank for the idea of the book having alternative endings. It all started with a comment she made after reading the first draft of another book of mine: 'I, personally, imagined quite a different ending, something a bit darker, if you will.' The comment made me take stock of my friends and potential readers and realise that some of them are definitely pessimists and others are definitely optimists. Thus the various endings were born and now – thanks to Lana - all my books have different endings for the optimists and for the pessimists out there. Not because I played around with multiple endings and was lazy to pick one. Although, it is very tempting to postpone the choice for the director to make, should the book ever become a movie. Even then, movies have alternative endings with a life of their own on Youtube – the alternative ending of 'Mr. and Mrs. Smith' is a prime example.

Since I am a believer in the ying/yang approach, the optimistic endings were originally supposed to have at least one darker story among them– to keep things real - and *vice versa,* the pessimistic endings were envisaged to have one optimistic story in their midst – to keep hope alive. At the very last minute, I switched Sally's endings around as per the insistence of my editor, Shreeya Nanda, who protested against a drop of tar amongst the otherwise optimistic pot. So, if you are a realistic optimist or a hopeful pessimist, you'll just have to mix'n'match the stories yourself. Even better, if you manage to come up with yet another possible ending, tell me about it (Sky Sommers on Facebook).

As for Sally's adventures, look out for my next book, The King of Time.

Hugs-a-bunch, Sky

About the author

Sky Sommers is a pen-name. The author has published academic books under her real name, so it was necessary to distinguish fact from fiction. (Although law books being about dry facts is a matter of opinion.)

Why Sky? Because blue is her favourite colour. Why Sommers? Because she loves the Mummy movies and has seen the director's name - Stephen Sommers – on the screen more times than she cares to admit even to herself.

Sky used to live in Cambridge and in London, the UK, and now lives in Tallinn, Estonia, with her partner Marek and two sons with occasionally three more children of various ages sweeping through the house. It's a wonder she gets any writing done. If it wasn't for the support of her partner, she'd never have finished this one.

Probably.

Possibly.

Maybe.

Nagh, it would just have taken a bit longer than five years.

NOTES

1   P!nk. Who Knew. (I'm Not Dead, 2006).
2   For the adventures of the goddesses after the bet, please see S.Sommers. Goddesses: Hubble, bubble, Toil and Trouble. 2012. Kindle e-book.
3   Seal. A Prayer for the Dying (Seal aka Seal II, 1994).
4   The Red Jumpsuit Apparatus. Your Guardian Angel. (Don't You Fake It. 2006).
5   Taylor Swift. I Knew You Were Trouble (Red, 2012).
6   Your eyes are like twinkling stars reflected in the sea. – in Italian.
7   Alanis Morissette. Uninvited (City of Angels movie soundtrack, 1998).
8   Tuchis = ass in Yiddish.
9   Frank Sinatra. Witchcraft (Single, 1957).
10   Morgan Freeman has played God in Bruce Almighty as well as in Wanted.
11   The story of a girl being transported to New York from the Enchanted dimension was made into a prominent movie in 2007 called Enchanted, starring Amy Adams, Patrick Dempsey and Susan Sarandon.
12   Lady Antebellum. Just a Kiss (Own The Night, 2011).
13   Robbie Williams. Angels. Single, 1997.
14   E.g. Narak - Hindu hell, Bardo – Tibetan hell, Chinvat – Zoroastrian hell, Hades – Greek hell, Hel – Viking hell.
15   If you want to get better acquainted, some day please read S.Sommers. King of Time - working title, yet unpublished.
16   Momzer – rat bastard in Yiddish.
17   Nudnik – A pest, an annoying person in Yiddish.
18   ABBA. Honey Honey (Waterloo, 1974).
19   Sarah McLachlan. Angel. (City of Angels: Music from the Motion Picture, 1998).
20   Kelly Clarkson. Because of You. (Breakaway, 2004).
21   Florence and The Machine. Seven Devils (Ceremonials, 2011).

22   Jump5, Walking on Sunshine (Ella Enchanted: original soundtrack, 2004).
23   Lady Antebellum. Hello World (Need You Now, 2010).
24   Avicii. Waiting for Love (Digital download, 2015).
25   Saosin. You're Not Alone (Saosin, 2006).
26   James Morrison. One Life (The Awakening, 2011).
27   Vanessa Carlton. Even Angels Fall.
28   Lily Kershaw. As It Seems (Single, 2012).
29   Katy Perry. E.T. (Teenage Dream, 2010.)
30   Runaway Bride, 1999.
31   Dishwalla. Angels or Devils (Opaline, 2002).
32   Train. Calling All Angels (My Private Nation, 2003).
33   Israel Kamakawiwo'ole. Somewhere Over the Rainbow/ What A Wonderful World (Facing Future, 1993).
34   The Fray. How To Save A Life. (How To Save A Life, 2005).
35   S.Sommers. King of Time - working title, yet unpublished.
36   Ver dergarget! – Drop dead! In Yiddish
37   Oy vey! – Oh, how terrible things are! In Yiddish.
38   About the adventures of the goddesses, see S.Sommers. Goddesses: Hubble, Bubble, Toil and Trouble. Kindle E-book, published in 2012.
39   ABBA. Angeleyes (Single, 1979).
40   Three Days Grace. Gone Forever (One-X, second album, 2008).
41   Ronan Keating. When You Say Nothing At All (Notting Hill soundtrack, 1999).
42   Shadken – a professional matchmaker in Yiddish.
43   S.Sommers. Breathe With Me - working title, yet unpublished.
44   Ronan Keating, see note 42 above.
45   The Red Jumpsuit Apparatus, see note 4 above.
46   Beyonce . Halo (Single, 2009).
47   The Red Jumpsuit Apparatus, see note 4 above.
48   Depeche Mode. Angel of Love (Single, 2013).
49   Alanis Morissette, see note 7 above.

50 Sarah McLchlan, see note 19 above.

51 U2. If God Will Send His Angels (Single, 1997).

52 Robbie Williams, see note 13 above.

53 The Penguins. Earth Angel (Will You Be Mine, Single, 1954).

54 Ella Fitzgerald. Someone to Watch Over Me (Ella Sings Gershwin, Vinyl album, 1950).

55 E.g. Heaven is Heaven for most Earth religions, except Moksha – Hindu heaven - and Nirvana – Buddhist heaven. Eden or paradise is a separate dimension.

56 We know the story today thanks to the Brothers Grimm, who wrote it down in 1812 as part of their Children's and Household Tales, but the story itself is probably an adaptation of a French fairy-tale *Persinette* published in 1698 or *Petrosinella*, the Neapolitan fairy-tale dating back to 1634. It also mimics the 10th century Persian tale of *Rudaba* from the epic poem *Shahnameh*.

57 Guinevere (*Gwenhwyfar* in Welsh; *Findabair* in Irish and *Gwynnever* in Middle-Cornish - can be translated as White Enchantress. In modern English the name is spelled Jennifer - was the legendary consort of King Arthur who is rumoured to have had an affair with Sir Lancelot, the King's first night of the Round Table, which allegedly caused the downfall of the Kingdom of Camelot. The story long resonated in Cornish and Irish folklore, e.g. Tristan & Isolde (or *Tristram* and *Iseult* or *Drustan* and *Eselt* in Cornish with *Ousilla* being the Latinised form of Eselt), a 12th century Celtic (Cornish-Irish) legend also mimics this 5-6th century Arturian legend. There is, however, a chicken-and-egg type of dispute as to which tale predates the other.

58 Snow White (*Sneewittchen* in German) is a tale written down by the Brothers Grimm in 1812 in their collection Grimms' Fairy Tales. There are many variations of this story, e.g. in the Albanian tale from the middle ages

the maiden lives with 40 dragons and in an Italian tale
Bella Venezia, the girl lives with 12 robbers (a cross
with the Ali-Baba fairy-tale). In some Russian versions
of the tale the Princess lives with seven knights, not
dwarves. In the Indian epic poem *Padmavat* (1540
A.D.) the Queen questions her talking parrot, not
the magic mirror and in the Scottish fairy-tale Gold-
Tree and Silver-Tree, the Queen mother questions the
trout. (Gold-tree has elements of the Blue-Beard tale
as well as the Sleeping Beauty tale and charming
elements of polygamy and matricide.) As a result of
the modern fairy-tales the last but not the least of
which is Horowitz' and Kitsis' 'Once Upon A Time', we
have now permanently linked Prince Charming or
'Charming' with Snow White, but the character is
actually a stereotype heroic character that   permeated
though a lot of fairy-tales, even versions of Snow White,
Sleeping Beauty as well as Cinderella.

59   Beauty and The Beast (*La Belle et la Bête*) was first
published in France in 1740. There are many variations
on this tale as well. E.g. in Russian folklore there is
The Vermillion Flower (*Alenkii Tsvetochek*). While
we know the archetypal Beaumont version, the earlier,
1740 Villeneuve version gives a different background to
both Beast and Beauty – e.g. the prince was enchanted
by his guardian, an evil fairy who tried to seduce the
prince when he became an adult and enchanted him for
his refusal while Belle was actually a good fairy and
royalty, who was hiding out in the stead of the
merchant's dead daughter for protection against the
wiles of another evil fairy.

60   The Sleeping Beauty (*La Belle Au Bois Dormant*) was
first put to paper by Charles Perrault in 1697 in his
Histoires ou Contes de Temps Passé. The Brothers
Grimm retold it as Briar Rose. The tale was originally in
two parts, the second part telling of the attempts of

the Prince's ogress mother to eat the two children (Dawn and Day) who are born to the royal couple after the rescue of the princess. The cannibalistic part was later incorporated into Hansel and Gretel. Folklorists believe this fairy-tale represents an allegory of the seasons – the Princess is Nature, the 13th Wicked Fairy represents the 13th lunar month and Winter, whose curse puts the court to sleep until the Prince, i.e Spring awakens all.

61 H.C.Andersen. The Little Mermaid (*Den lille havfrue*, literally: the little sea lady), first published in 1837 and later adapted in theatre and animated films.

62 In very few and very modern fairy-tales, such as How to Train Your Dragon and Eragon, dragons know human-speak, can communicate telepathically and even let their riders see with the dragon's own eyes. Until present day, quite obviously, dragons have taken great care to keep themselves out of the sticky business of being seen as good. This is the best recourse against being overladen with help requests. A monster tag in most fairy-tales serves as a beautiful warning.

63 For the dragon's story in the Magic Kingdom, look out for S.Sommers. The King of Time - working title, yet unpublished.

64 The Penguins, see note 53 above.

65 The domed cathedral of the city, Santa Maria del Fiore, built by Brunelleschi.

66 Kvetching – to be annoying, to complain in Yiddish.

67 Farpitzs – all dressed up in Yiddish.

68 For the X-ray switch story, look out for S.Sommers. Breathe With Me - working title, yet unpblished.

69 James Morrison, see note 26 above.

70 If the battle of Hattin near present-day Tiberias in Israel on July 4, 1187 had ended favourably for the Christian, Jerusalem would not have fallen to the Muslims and this could have reportedly ended the

Second Crusade. As a result, neither the Third Crusade led by Richard Lionheart nor the rest of the nine crusades would have taken place. Reportedly, the fall of the Kingdom of Jerusalem could have been but was not a turning point in the history of the Crusades.

71 Kelly Clarkson. Dark Side (Stronger, 2011).

72 Takida. You Learn (The Burning Heart, 2011).

73 Blind Guardian. Valhalla. (Follow the Blind, 1989).

74 Savage Garden. Tears of Pearls (Savage Garden, 1997).

75 Amy Winehouse. Rehab (Back to Black, 2006).

76 There is actually a book by Janice Lynn called Revenge for Hire (The Get Even Agency Book 1). Dreamweaver Publishing, 2012 - but this is about payback for human playboys.

77 Ella Fitzgerald, see note 54 above.

78 Fray, see note 34 above.

79 Taylor Swift. Breathe (Fearless, 2008).

80 In honour of the Meg Ryan and Billy Crystal movie called 'When Harry Met Sally' (1989).

81 Lucy Hale, Run This Town (Another Cinderella Story: Once Upon a Song soundtrack, 2011).

82 Katy Perry. The One That Got Away (Teenage Dream, 2010).

83 Lady Antebellum, see note 12 above.

84 In Norse mythology, Glasir is a tree, bearing golden leaves located in the realm of Asgard, outside the doors of Valhalla, described as 'the most beautiful among gods and men'.

85 I have always misheard Muse's lyrics in Resistance (from their 2009 album The Resistance) as 'kill your prince for love and peace' - the real lyrics are 'kill your prayers for love and peace'.

86 One Direction. Taken (Up All Night, 2011).

87 James Brown. The Boss (Black Caesar, 1973).

88 P!nk, see note 1 above.

89 P!nk, see note 1 above.